Since securing the top prize in a widely-publicised UK writing con.... A....ka **Knight** has become .... tion with her debut novel, SINCE YOU'VE BEEN GONE, hitting both The Bookseller and Heatseekers bestseller lists and securing praise from the likes of Jackie Collins and Jenny Colgan. A former bakery owner, she has gone on to wide acclaim in her native England and now writes full-time. Anouska lives in Staffordshire close to the countryside where she grew up, with husband Jamie, her childhood sweetheart, their two growing boys and new baby son. When she's not writing or wrestling small children, she's still often found baking and will whip up a cake at the drop of a hat if asked nicely.

letting you go

Anouska Knight

HARLEQUIN® MIRA®

Harlequin MIRA is a registered trademark of Harlequin Enterprises Limited, used under licence.

Published in Great Britain 2015

by Harlequin MIRA, an imprint of Harlequin (UK) Limited,
Eton House, 18-24 Paradise Road,
Richmond, Surrey, TW9 1SR

ISBN: 978-1-848-45426-2

58-0915

Harlequin (UK) Limited's policy is to use papers that are natural, renewable and recyclable products and made from wood grown in sustainable forests. The logging and manufacturing processes conform to the legal environmental regulations of the country of origin.

Printed and bound by
CPI Group (UK) Ltd, Croydon, CR0

For Jim, who I love.
Always the same. Never changes.

12th September 2004

Alex burst from the break in the trees frantically enough that, had she left the woodland a little way further up the roadside, she might have missed him altogether. Any other time it would've been odd, him just sitting there in his cab, pulled over awkwardly on the track running up towards the house. But not today. It was as if he were waiting for her, his unmistakable battered blue tow truck a beacon of hope where it sat in the dusty layby. Her burning lungs had gasped at this meagre stroke of luck, if luck had any part to play here. His being there had saved vital minutes. Precious time reclaimed by not having to make it all the way back up the lane to the house.

Ted Foster's hands were already braced on the steering wheel, as if by some sixth sense he knew what was coming to find him moments before his daughter slammed herself, wild and startled, against his truck bonnet. Alexandra had looked crazed, *unrecognisable* when she'd sprung in front of his windscreen, the vein in her neck jumping with the emergency pulsing through her lean frame. Her eyes had been too white, as white as Ted's knuckles had been while he'd sat there, solemnly regarding the truths he couldn't take home.

Ted had made the call as they'd started through the small copse of trees and across the farmland beyond, calmly relaying to the operator the information Alexandra had managed to unscramble as her voice had cracked and her legs momentarily buckled.

Help is coming! The thought screamed through Alex's head. *Dad's coming, Dill, Dad's coming.*

Her pumps were no longer squelching against the dusty earth. Alexandra Foster had been the fastest runner in her year group ever since St Cuthbert's sports days, but she couldn't swim like she could run, and Finn knew it. People didn't run at all in college, she'd found. They ambled. Everywhere. To the cafeteria, the art block – allowing the effortlessly honed muscles of youth to slacken. Alex hadn't run anywhere since leaving high school last year, but dormant muscles had responded to her demands and she was flying. Ted was flying too. His own burst of adrenalin allowing a man of over fifty to keep pace with his seventeen-year-old child as they rushed in panicked determination to where she had left them.

Alex could hear Rodolfo's heavy barks guiding them back to the water's edge, rudely echoing above the peaceful gushing of the river. *The Old Girl,* the locals called it, *Mind the Old Girl and her changing moods.* They'd all had it drummed into them as kids. Dill too. He knew, he *knew*! Alex felt her throat tighten again, her heart twisting as they burst through the long grasses back into the clearing by the alder trees.

Finn had nearly reached Dillon further downstream when he'd turned and screamed at Alex across the water, screamed at her not to come in any deeper but to *run! Run for help!* So she had, back to the house, instead of floundering on uselessly against her own panic. She thought they'd still be in the water now, but they were back in the clearing, Finn kneeling in the dirt crouched over two wet gangly legs, dripping indifferently where they poked out from under him. Dill looked tiny beneath Finn's teenage frame, as if the water had shrunk him. A mischievous little boy, playing possum.

Ted skidded in beside them on the floor, Finn moving instinctively from where he had been desperately pressing a rhythm into Dill's sodden chest. Alex watched her father, useless again as Rodolfo's barking turned to whimpers and Ted took over the task of thudding urgent hands into his boy's chest.

'You spit it out, son, you hear me? You spit it all up right now!' he commanded.

Finn was standing over them both, his hands locked at the back of his head, motionless as he watched. The water hadn't soothed the nettle stings angrily covering Finn's legs where his long shorts hadn't protected them just half an hour ago. Half an hour, when stingers and the end of the summer were their only cares in the world.

'Son, you start breathing, son. *Right now*!' Ted pleaded.

Alex watched her father punctuating his need with every downward lunge against her brother's skinny body. But Dill wasn't doing what he was told.

Ted breathed into Dill's bluing lips. Still, Dill's legs didn't move from where they peeped beneath his father's body. One of Dill's shoes was gone. Alex's thoughts started to fire off like the cracker-bombs their mum had confiscated from Dill that morning. The world seemed to fall away then, numb beyond the mystery of that one missing red pump. Dill couldn't walk home with only one shoe! Where was it? He had been wearing them both when Alex had followed Finn into the undergrowth, away and out of sight for just a few silly minutes. They needed to find that shoe, right now, right—

Alex heard her father's voice falter. 'Dillon Edward Foster. You cough it up, son… or your mother is going to be awful upset.'

I only left him for a minute… But Alex wasn't as sure now. She'd been distracted.

'Dillon Foster, *BREATHE*!'

Alex watched in silence as her dad tried to breathe life into his child, his huge hands grappling at Dill's expressionless face for better purchase. Alex felt the agitation lurch inside her chest. Her father wasn't being gentle any more, he shouldn't be so rough with him! Didn't he realise? He was going to hurt him.

Something warm spilled down both of Alex's cheeks.

'BREATHE, GOD DAMN IT, *BREATHE!*' Ted shook

Dill as if trying to rouse him from a stubborn sleep. He sank his mouth over his son's again and, *at last*! Alex thought she saw Dill shift beneath their father's solid frame. She held her breath… Yes! She could definitely hear it, a new sound! A breathy, jarring sound! Struggling to make its way clear of where it originated.

Something gave in the pit of her stomach. *Oh, Dill! Thank—*

Ted turned his head from the little boy's face, strain etched in his eyes. Alex watched her father's chest convulsing in short, sudden jerks beneath his shirt. She'd never seen her father cry, not for anything. Alex looked to those two legs again, the shoed and the shoeless. Nothing. Dill's body was limp again with the loss of their father's movements to animate him.

Finn began pushing his hands up through the sides of his wet hair. He turned away to face the alder tree hanging mournfully over the passing waters, a cork archery target hanging forgotten from its trunk. Alex watched as Finn slowly crouched down to the earth again, his broad teenage shoulders closing in on him like a pair of redundant wings.

No… *No!* This was wrong! They'd only left him for a minute.

A broken gravelled voice cut through Alex's fragmented thoughts.

'Where were you?'

It didn't sound like her dad. It didn't look like him either. Ted's features were contorted in a way that made his face almost foreign; laughter lines suddenly gnarled and hostile. Alex opened her mouth to speak, but there was nothing.

'Where the hell *were* you?' her father demanded, taking in the state of Alex's nettle-stung arms and legs. Alex watched him look accusingly at Finn's lower body, Finn's matching affliction where the stingers had got him too. Finn's shirt was inside out. Ted was piecing it together, Alex could see the furious disbelief growing in her father's eyes and waited uselessly for him to turn that look on her. When he did, it came like a hot iron through her chest, his voice broken and deformed.

'YOU WERE SUPPOSED TO BE WATCHING MY SON!'

CHAPTER 1

Not everything can be damned-well helped! Sometimes, all you can hope for is time and if you're goddamned lucky... distance.

Alex was buttering her way through another loaf of bread with enough vigour that the bulbous handle of the butter knife had indented her fingers. She stopped herself before tearing through another slice of extra value wholemeal and shook the words from her head. There had been other words too, following her down the years like a long shadow. But these were the only words she could do anything with – all she had to offer her family as pitiful recompense for the damage that could never be undone. *Time* and *distance*.

Alex pushed her father from her thoughts and reacquainted herself with the view through the kitchen hatch. The twins were still eating their lunch, too busy devouring their own meals to notice their dad, stealthily enveloping his jacket potato inside one of the flimsy serviettes. Alex bulk bought them from the wholesaler's every other Wednesday along with the rest of the food bank's sundries. The 2-ply napkins weren't really built for doggy-bagging, enshrouding food like a precious treasure to be hidden in the earth for safekeeping, but the father quietly sitting across the dining room wasn't deterred, already slipping the wrapped jacket potato into the rucksack at his feet. Alex felt something inside her ache for him the way it had ached for Bob Cratchit when her dad had taken her and Jem to see *A Christmas Carol* at the Tower House Theatre. It had been a treat for being such good big sisters to their new baby brother, but Alex hadn't been able to eat her ice-cream at the interval, she'd been so worried for poor Mr Cratchit. Alex remembered how her dad had gently patted her back through every scene, his broad hand ready with fatherly reassurance. Back when he could still look at her.

'Three more soups please, Alex my love,' Dan smiled, blustering into the community centre's kitchen so quickly that his flop of black hair looked windswept. He began promptly dispensing a flurry of fresh cups of tea from the urn while Alex's attention returned to the family out in the dining room. There was something voyeuristic about watching a grown adult hiding food for his children. Something akin to slowing down for a better look at a car accident. But then this was what it was all about, wasn't it? This life she'd chosen. To play her small part, do good – as if a person could even up the tally of all the right and wrong they'd been party to somehow. One of the twin boys glanced up and caught Alex staring. She looked away too suddenly and immediately felt as if she'd short-changed the kid a smile.

Alex hated starers. She remembered the staring as they'd all been sat in St Cuthbert's chapel saying their goodbyes to Dill in front of all of those people. All those eyes. Tragedy and rubber-necking were old friends, her father had said with the arrival of weeping relatives to the church. *Wailing like banshees*, despite having never sent Dill so much as a birthday card when he was alive. Alex tried to recall their faces now, those obscure weeping relatives who'd come to support the four of them with their lingering embraces and heavy knowing looks, but her memory had clung to very little of that day beyond the desolation in her mother's features and the stiffness in her father's back.

'Bugger me, Alex! How many sarnies are you making? What are you going for… edible Jenga?'

Another slice of bread gave under the rigours of clumsy buttering. Alex took stock of the bread mountain and grimaced. 'Sorry. I was just…'

'Away with the fairies?' Dan's eyes narrowed. 'Are you OK today? You look tired. A bit spun-out.'

Alex had told Dan, once. The very brief version. Peppered with a few hazy justifications for not visiting her hometown much any more. Busy lives. Long car journeys. A troublesome allergy to her mum's beloved dogs. 'No, I'm good, thanks. I didn't sleep much last night. Bloody car alarm outside the flats,' she groaned.

'Yeah, I really hate that.' Dan looked justly sceptical, but of course he wouldn't realise what today meant. Few people would, not even the banshees. Would they be thinking of Dill today? Would they remember to imagine him turning nineteen, handsome and strong, towering over his mother and sisters? It was official. As of today, there had been more birthdays spent lighting a candle for Dill than watching him blow one out. Nine years with; ten years without. His short life seemed to get shorter each year.

'Sure you didn't just have a hedonistic weekend, Foster? Been out larging it with Mr Right, maybe? About time he turned up.'

Alex smiled. Her weekend had consisted largely of a thousand variations of Dill's imagined adult life. Drinking in The Cavern with their dad. Globetrotting with a girl-friend. Teaching his kids to ride their bikes. The fantasies were endless, but they always ended the same way – a warm summer's evening back in Eilidh Falls, a family gathered again, laughter, children with Dill's quirky dimple or other features of his, running around the same gardens they'd all played in as children.

'You wouldn't tell me anyway, would you?'

'Hmm?'

'Mr Right? If he'd turned up and rocked your world?'

Alex took a deep breath and centred herself. 'Sorry. I guess a lady never tells.'

'Blimey, *twins*.' Dan exclaimed pushing his glasses up his nose. 'Can't be easy. How old are they, seven? Eight maybe?'

The children out in the dining area were finishing the last of their bangers and mash almost simultaneously. They were at that threshold between little boys and young lads; a few adult teeth peeping from lips unapologetically slathered in gravy. The age of mischief, her mum had called it. Dill had taught them all a lot about mischief.

Alex watched those two boys and swallowed against an unexpected snag in her throat. 'They're seven. Dad's first time. He's just squirrelled.'

'Ah,' Dan acknowledged, his head furrowing beneath his flop of hair. 'Well no wonder I couldn't tempt him with the soup. He wasn't gonna slip that into his backpack for later. Spud was it?'

'I probably should've made the situation clearer,' Alex replied. But she hated it. Walking bemused newcomers through the procedure, hitting them with the spiel on support workers and benefits entitlement before they could sit down and enjoy a meal in peace. The twins' father had wandered in to the Trust's lunchtime session more wide-eyed and bewildered than the kids; that familiar mixed heavy look of desperation and gratitude nearly always held together by a debilitating undercurrent of *this is not my life!* Alex got it. This wasn't really her life either, at least not the one she'd once envisaged.

Dan sighed, retrieving a replacement jacket potato from one of the ovens 'Well, he's going to need all his strength while the kids are still off for the summer hols. Is Mum here too?'

Alex regarded the two young boys, wondering when their last opportunity to get into mischief had been. 'I think Mum's left. After Dad was made redundant.'

Dan finished bothering with the potato and shook his head. 'Blimey. Tough break for the kids. But who are we to judge, right?'

It had been part of the training when Alex had first started here after ditching uni. Listen, yes. Encourage, yes. Second-guess the mechanics of a family's downfall? Who was ever really qualified to do that?

'Put the butter straight on it this time, Dan, don't give him the little tubs.' It was a small deterrent to squirrellers, but a deterrent nonetheless.

'You know, it always stuns me when the mum jumps ship,' Dan's said quietly. 'We bang on about equality and all that, but it's still a shocker when it's the dad left picking up the pieces. Know what I mean?'

Alex shrugged, but she knew exactly. Mothers pressed on, held everyone else together while their own hearts broke quietly. Hers had. Blythe would be pressing on right now, right this minute, two hundred miles away.

'You sure you're OK today?' Dan was watching Alex readying the soup bowls with the same look he reserved for the elderly visitors to the food bank he worried needed more help than the trust could offer. 'I thought it might be love but on second thoughts, you seem a bit...'

Alex's smile was automatic. 'Manic Mondays, Dan!' she lied. Dan was a good guy. He'd be quick to offer his sympathies but it always felt like borrowing clothes she liked the look of, knowing they'd never fit right. 'Now hurry up and get those soups out, they're going cold!'

'OK, OK... I'm going, I'm going.' Dan loaded the last teas onto his tray and jostled back out through the kitchen doors. Alex's thoughts meandered straight back to Eilidh Falls. She would call them all later, before they sat down to dinner together. Six o'clock, same time every year, no variations, no surprises. Alex dreaded it. She dreaded the thanks her mother would lavish on her for sending flowers and she dreaded hearing the consolatory lilt in Jem's voice planted there by Alex's perpetual absence. But most of all, Alex dreaded the complete normality of the conversation she would have with her dad. The shooting of the breeze. She had to wonder what they would have done for conversation all these years had it not been for oil changes and tyre pressure.

'Oi.' Dan's face popped through from the other side of the hatch and startled her. 'You don't fool me, Alex. I might be a speccy kitchen hand with a flair for jazzy garnishes,' Dan waved the tray of food and drinks flamboyantly past the servery hatch for Alex's appraisal, 'but I'm tuned in to the ways of women, you know. I know what's eating you.' He looked over his shoulder towards the twins playing air hockey with the condiments on the table. 'You're really worrying about them, aren't you?' Alex's thoughts shifted from one broken family to another. She sent a small request into the universe that a little time and distance might help them too.

'They'll be OK, Alex,' Dan reassured. 'Look at them.' One of the twins began giggling at something his father had just done with the pepper pot. 'They might be going through the wringer but they're still a family. A family can get through anything if they just stick together. Am I right?'

Alex could already feel the return of that automatic smile.

CHAPTER 2

'Crappy *neon*, Alex. Neon! It's a florist's not a bloody tattoo parlour! You should see it all lit up at night. One big, craptastic eyesore.'

'Jem, please stop saying *craptastic*, darling. You sound like a teenage boy.' Alex heard their mother sigh in the background and allowed herself a little one of her own so the other two Foster women couldn't hear it. The call was on loudspeaker. It was Blythe's way of pulling Alex as best she could back into the heart of the family home while she prepared the meal Alex never came back to eat.

Jem exhaled irritably again. 'Carrie always did have a flair for cheapening her environment.'

'Jaime Foster, you catty girl.' Alex heard their mother tease.

'Better a cat than a total bitch, Mum.'

'Oh, Jem.' Their mum didn't like bad language of any sort. Never had, although Blythe would turn a deaf ear if Ted or the girls used an obscenity so long as there was a legitimate reason. Like stubbing a toe, or winning the lottery. Not that anyone had ever won the lottery.

'Alex knows what I mean, mum,' Jem called back to Blythe. 'You know what I mean, right Al?'

Alex was decompressing, gradually leaving the carnage of Dill's birthday the way those crazy scuba divers she sometimes watched on Discovery would gradually leave a doomed shipwreck in the murky depths, steadily and cautiously in case they got 'the bends'. Returning to the surface of Foster family life felt a lot like that sometimes. Something to take steady before the change in pressure did something catastrophic to Alex's system. Thankfully, although Jem's evergreen hang-ups with Carrie Logan – arch-frenemy since their days at Eilidh High – had never made much sense to Alex, they were good enough to change the subject from Blythe and Jem's visit down to the churchyard earlier. (It had been one of those trivial fallings out between teenage girls, Jem had claimed, the kind that burn on ferociously like the light from a dead star, years after the main event.)

Alex could feel the tension leaving her shoulders as Jem vented about Carrie. It felt good. Normal. This must be what it felt like for those mental free-divers, Alex always thought, when they found oxygen again after plumbing the depths on just one devoted lungful of air.

Alex had taken a reassuring breath of her own just before dialling her parents' number. It hadn't been half as uncomfortable as she always prepared herself for. It never was. She shouldn't be so hypersensitive; she had no right. They all deserved so much more from her and what did she do? Drag her heels all day as if phoning her family was the worst thing in the world. *You will remember this next year, Alex. You will remember that* you *make it worse, not them.* But guilt was a lot like love, doing funny things to the mind.

Jem had railroaded the conversation beautifully as ever. Jem was an excellent railroader, a seasoned expert at smoothing the awkward away with a nice thick layer of normality, as if they were all just enjoying a regular everyday catch-up with each other. Blythe too, as unwaveringly warm as she was thoughtful, had gushed about the flowers Alex had sent home, lest Alex's woefully inadequate annual gesture ever go un-championed. 'Oh, Alex… sunflowers and thistles!' Blithe had delighted, 'Such a simple posy but, just so beautiful, darling. Really, the perfect choice. Ted? Come tell Alex how beautiful those sunflowers are,' her mum had encouraged. 'Your dad commented on them, darling, and you know how oblivious Foster men are. Did you know, your father wanted sunflowers at our wedding? Your grandma Rosalind said they weren't a traditional choice though, so that was that.'

Alex did know that. She also knew how fond her dad was of the colour the thistles gave to the hillside behind the farmhouse, but she wouldn't allow herself to question who it was exactly she always sent the flowers for. Ted hadn't gotten round to mentioning the sunflowers when he'd finally come on the line anyway. He'd had to dash off on a callout, thinning out their already skinny chat about the price Alex was paying for diesel down south.

Alex felt another pang of guilt. As soon as she'd heard the front door closing after her dad at the other end of the line, that tightness in her chest had begun to release. She was resurfacing.

'Boring you, am I?' Jem asked.

'You're boring me a little bit, darling,' Blythe echoed. Alex could tell her mother had her head in the Aga. Blythe was exceptional at keeping her kids and cooking in check at the same time.

'No… Sorry, Jem.' Alex smiled.

'You know what I mean, though, don't you?'

Alex rallied herself. 'About what?'

'The *neon*!' Jem asserted.

'Sure. Neon… for a florist's.' Alex agreed. 'I mean, if Carrie's making *crazy* decisions like that, what else is she getting up to in there, huh?' She was teasing, but Jem missed it, her high-school nemesis was still ram-raiding her thoughts. Alex thought she heard her mother laugh but it was difficult to be sure over the clanking of the table being set.

'*Exactly*,' Jem huffed, 'that cow is not to be trusted.'

'Jem!' Blythe implored. 'Change the record.'

Dill's birthday had become sacred, more sacred than Christmas even and Christmas wasn't a day for *crap* or *bitch* or *cow* either.

'You can't tell me off, Mum. I'm twenty-four.' Jem let out a sudden yelp. 'And you can't whack me with a wooden spoon, Mum!'

'Want to bet, young lady?'

Alex smiled into the phone. It was impossible not to feel steadied by her mother. Throughout everything, Blythe had held the balance.

'I'm sure there are more riveting topics you and Alex can talk about besides Carrie Logan, Jem, surely? Can't you gossip about men, or diets or something… like normal sisters?'

It had occurred to Alex years ago that she and Jem were not *normal sisters*, not if swapping juicy titbits about boyfriends and diets was the standard. Alex still wasn't wholly sure whether she should feel more or less sad about that. It wasn't love or affection she and Jem were missing, but years. Those intense teenage years where experiences and emotions were heightened and giddy and sisters confided and shared. Alex had left for uni and overnight it was as if something seismic had shifted leaving Alex on one side of a gaping chasm and Jem on the other. Not just their age gap. Alex could feel something else there stuck between them, something more than five big teenage years. Whatever it was, Alex had never poked at it, in case it turned out she was responsible for that too.

The phone had fallen silent. Something furtive seemed to be going on at the other end. 'OK, OK,' Jem whispered. She feigned an over-excited tone. 'So guess who we saw? At the church?'

Alex ran through the usual suspects. Blythe had already told her how Susannah and Helen had each left flowers for

Dill this morning, but other than Blythe's old choir-buddies and the Reverend no-one else sprang to mind. 'I give up. Who did you see?'

Jem laughed then. An odd, pre-cursory chortle. 'Guess.' But Alex didn't have time to guess, Jem couldn't hold it in. 'Only *Finn.*'

Alex felt her thoughts slow down, sinking to the bottom of her brain like globules of wax in a lava lamp – heavy, vivid, helpless colour.

Finn. She'd been pressing that name to the back of her mind all day and Jem had just let it loose. Thoughts of Dill nearly always came piggy-backed by thoughts of Finn. Bound together by time and circumstance.

Jem was riding out the pause. All of a sudden, she could wait all day. Alex made a grab for something coherent. 'Finn? But…' she managed.

'I know, right?'

'Finn's back in the Falls? But… I thought…'

'I *know*. The rover's returned and, by the looks of things, he's all done with the intrepid explorer bit.'

Alex could feel a warm uncomfortable sensation brewing over the back of her neck. Jem would test her this way, now and again. She'd poke Alex like a bruise just to gauge if she was still tender, and all Alex could do was do her best not to flinch. It was like being ambushed. Stupid really, that she would be ambushed by this of all news. Eilidh Falls was his home, after all, of course he wasn't going to stay away *forever.*

Alex held the phone, waiting to hear the next nuggets of Jem's reconnaissance back home to filter down the line. Surprise began to twist into resignation. Finn had gone back to settle down, with a wife probably. And a family. *Children*. Beautiful children, sharing his glorious scruffy hair and playful eyes. He could've met a thousand women as he'd backpacked and odd-jobbed his way around the planet, exotic and captivating like the places he'd daubed on his bedroom wall. His 'Great Adventure List!' *Their* list.

Alex waited for news of the impossibly beautiful wife and their impossibly beautiful offspring to sock her one through the earpiece. Blythe had gone quiet in the background. She'd have been pleased for sure to bump into him, Alex knew it. Her mum's fondness for Finn had never waned. Blythe had never blamed Finn.

'Mum turned into a bashful teenager when she saw him, didn't you, Ma? She thinks he's even more handsome with a bit of colour on him.'

'I was not bashful, Jem. I just think it's a shame that boy hasn't been snapped up. He should be bouncing a small child around on those lovely broad shoulders of his by now. "Too busy for love"? How can anyone ever be *too busy for love*?'

No wife. No impossibly beautiful children. Something briefly floated inside Alex before she could stop it, like a hot air balloon momentarily lifting a few inches from the earth before bobbing back down again with a thud. Finn was single then. Fab. Just as it was fab whenever George Clooney came back onto the market. Fab and uplifting and irrelevant all at once.

'I wonder,' Blythe lilted, 'perhaps he's *gay* now. He has been broadening his horizons for the last two years. I'll bet he's tried all sorts of new things. Food and… well, *whatnot.*'

Alex startled. Gay? *Gay?* Finn was not gay! No way. You couldn't be *that* close to a person and not know something like that, Alex decided with ultimate certainty.

At the other end of the phone Jem was being uncharacteristically quiet, waiting for Alex to bite. Alex shrugged as if her sister could see it. 'Susannah must be happy. To have him back safe and sound,' she bumbled.

Finn had spent the last two years somewhere the ogher side of the planet. Had he been walking it all out of his system the way he used to, only instead of rambling around the countryside he'd gone rambling around the globe? Two years as far away as he could …

'I guess. He was painting the railings on St Cuthbert's wall, you know. Finn's the new maintenance guy about town. He's got the contract for the church. He's re-opened Torben's hardware shop too. On the high street.' Jem's voice dropped to a whisper. 'And in case you were wondering, throwing tools around hasn't done him any harm either, Al. He's like… *buff* now. No more noodle arms,' Jem chirped.

Alex's lava lamp brain was heating up. Torben's? Right across the street from the garage? Alex imagined her father's mood each time he looked out across the high street.

They would be virtually face to face, every single day. Alex swallowed. Her dad would have an ulcer by New Year.

'He asked after you, Al.'

Blythe had moved back into motion in the background but the clinking of tableware had become more delicate while the conversation played out between her daughters.

Alex's thoughts were swirling faster and faster now. 'Erm… That's nice.' *That's nice?* And the rest. Alex expected Jem to laugh again but Jem was waiting it out instead. Well what did Jem expect her to say? *Did he, Jem? DID HE? What did he ask after me, exactly? Did he ask if I'm sorry I cut him loose like a ground rope? Whether I'm sorry for what I said? Did he ask if it still hurts when I think about him?*

There was a light thrumming in Alex's ears and she forgot briefly about what Jem was or was not saying at the other end of the line for a moment, suddenly taken aback by just how many of those statements she could answer with a resounding *yes*.

'He asked if you might be around for the Viking Festival. He couldn't believe the hype now either but he said it would be good to see it all in full swing. He also said it would be good to see you.'

Something cold danced down Alex's spine. It was always mind-boggling that Finn had ever wanted to set eyes on any of them ever again. Alex closed her eyes and pictured her dad in his Christmas pudding jumper standing over Finn in their front yard, wild and enraged as Finn's blood had mingled with the whipped cream on his best shirt. The resistance in Finn's expression, the horror in Susannah's as she and Blythe had shielded Finn where he sat awkwardly amongst the shattered crystal on the path.

Alex's heart was gently pattering, just at the recollection. They shouldn't be having this conversation. Her dad could walk back into the house at any moment and hear them all, chatting away, saying *that name* in his kitchen.

'Yes, darling, why don't you come on up here for the Viking Festival? It's only the weekend, you wouldn't need to miss any work.' Alex took a few extra breaths. They were both in on it, Mum and Jem. Finn was home, get Alex back there too and hey, presto! Lightning might strike. Didn't they ever learn? 'It really would be lovely to see you, Alexandra.' There was a tinge of pleading in her mother's voice. It hurt just to hear it.

'I don't think I can make it, Mum. We're so short-staffed, weekends are for catch-up,' she lied, 'next year, for definite.' To her mind it was a simple equation. Stay away from the Falls and nothing ugly like that would ever happen again.

Alex heard the front door of her parents' home rattle open in the background. 'Forgot my damned phone,' Ted groaned, his heavy boots trouncing across the hallway into the kitchen. All three Foster women fell silent.

'You girls *still* gassing?' Alex heard her father ask. 'Who's the big subject now then?'

The thrumming in Alex's ears had suddenly elevated to a thud inside her skull. She wanted to reach down the phone line and gather up all the particles of the name they'd all just been so carelessly bandying around between them.

Jem and Blythe both offered an answer to Ted's question at the same time.

'Flowers.'

'Vikings.'

Alex just held her breath.

CHAPTER 3

Free-diving. Now there was a paradox if Alex had ever heard one. How could depriving yourself of vital breathing apparatus ever be pedalled as liberation? There was nothing free about it, Alex decided, cautiously navigating a path through the cool water of the swimming pool, repeating with each tentative stroke the mantra her mother had taught her.

In through the nose, out through the mouth... nice and steady, you're doing it. This was at least rung number three on her 'fear ladder'. You had to build a fear ladder to climb, metaphorically, if you wanted to face your fears; she'd seen it on *Dr Phil*. Lolloping in the Jacuzzis or having a blast in the hydro-spa over by the shallow end would've been respectable first steps, Alex really should've started with those on that first, ill-fated, visit to the gym pool. Only she hadn't realised at the time that a person could actually faint underwater. Lucky for Alex an eager teenage lifeguard with the very strong pincer grasp had fished her out and attempted unnecessarily to administer mouth-to-mouth.

'Oh bless her, she still has her tag in,' one staff member

had astutely observed of Alex's brand-new-for-the-occasion swimming cozzie.

'Nice suit though, it's one of the second-skin range we sell in the in the gym shop,' Alex had heard another reply.

'Which colour is that?'

'Looks like the Torpedo.'

'She doesn't swim like a Torpedo. She should've bought the Pebble.'

Alex cringed. Just the memory of her foray into the deep end was enough to jellify her legs again. She felt her rhythm beginning to slip and locked eyes on the pool edge ahead of her.

In through the nose, Al... Better. Much better.

She'd get there. Back to that point she was at once upon a time, before she started letting the anxiety win. When she could still enjoy a nice, invigorating dip.

Her breathing was steady. There was definitely something in her mum's advice. It was far easier controlling her breathing with a rambling inner monologue. Blythe's mantra wasn't as jazzy as the *Ain't no thing!* version Alex had heard on Oprah's self-help special, but it was still coming in handy in the wake of Alex's new found bravery with the wet stuff.

Alex heard a splash too close on her right and tried not to falter again. Her concentration was rubbish tonight. Jem and her mum had taken something from her without realising it earlier this evening. The tension was supposed to ease after calling home, that's how Dill's birthday always worked. Only now she felt weighted down by something new, something she hadn't anticipated. It had been niggling at her since she'd put down the phone to them. Finn setting up shop, right across the street from Foster's Auto's.

Why can't you ever just take the easier route, Finn? It was a thought that had whispered through her head so many times before. And as ever, it came shadowed by another. *Why did you always expect him to, Alex?*

Yes. Why did she? She was selling him short, again and again and again, slipping straight back into the same old habit as if it were a favourite sweater. Had she forgotten? All sweaters had been returned. Lines had been drawn, ties cut, mix-tapes given back.

Another splash to the right and Alex's coordination left her.

Don't panic... don't panic... but somebody else's leg brushed against hers under the water then and it was all over. It was too late, she was already rearing up like a woman demented. One of the senior swimmers was blinking curiously at Alex through her goggles.

Brilliant, Alex! That had nearly been two widths in a row. *You wimp. You big fat bloody wimp.*

Alex made it to the edge of the pool and heard a giggle as she clambered out beside the Monday night couple. They came every week and spent most of the session huddled cosily in the Jacuzzi, although the guy had ventured into the main pool a few times. He'd done his Daniel Craig in Speedos impression past Alex last week. She'd stopped and pretended to fix the locker key strapped to her wrist while he'd thrashed past and Alex had discreetly hyperventilated.

Alex squelched her way beneath the poolside clock and through to the changing rooms. Nearly eight-thirty. Good. Enough was enough for one day. Just a couple more hours and Dill's birthday could be put to rest for another year and she wouldn't have to think about awkward exchanges with her dad for a while.

Alex opened her locker and made a grab for her shampoo and towel. She nudged her jeans accidentally and her phone slipped from her pocket. She whipped her hand out, somehow catching it before it hit the floor.

'Whoops. Butter-fingers. Nearly lost it that time.' Alex looked along the lockers to one of the old chaps who came swimming every week too. White-haired and friendly-faced, Alex always felt a bit guilty for curtailing their conversations, but the old lad didn't seem to realise the perils of wearing white swimming trunks and Alex always found herself glancing down like a wide-eyed child to check if they were any less see-through.

'Oh, yes,' she agreed. 'Nearly, that time.'

Alex's eyes dipped without warning. It was like being told not to look at the sun as a kid. *Don't look, don't look!*

'You should try dropping a cigar in your lap, young lady. I was driving my golf cart last weekend, burned straight through my trousers it did. Just look at the blister it's left me with,' he said, pointing to his hairy upper thighs.

Alex glanced sheepishly towards him. 'Oh yes, would

you look at that.' Penis. That's all Alex had just seen. Old man penis. Actually it was worse than looking at the sun. Far, far worse. She wanted to take her eyeballs out and wash them in the pool.

Alex's phone bleeped. She seized her chance at a diversion. 'Sorry, I really have to take this,' she fibbed. 'Would you excuse me?' Alex flashed him a smile and slipped into one of the changing stalls. Jem's name blinked demandingly on the caller display, puncturing the stillness of the cubicle. *Thank you, sis.* She couldn't chance another look at those trunks, she wouldn't sleep tonight.

Alex unlocked her phone. She just needed to kill enough time for the old lad to finish in his locker. *Twenty-three missed calls, Jem?* Tickly tracks of water were streaking down Alex's back and shoulders where her wet hair clung. She rubbed them away and frowned at the urgency on her phone. That was a lot of calls from Jem. Carrie Logan must have death-stared her or something.

Alex hit the button on her phone and listened to the most recent of Jem's voicemails. Jem's words reached up over Alex's collarbone, conquering the silence of the cubicle, pressing in on her with the same cold claustrophobia as the swimming pool.

Mum's sick… suspected stroke… need to come home.

Squeeze. Squeeze. Squeeze.

Alex held her breath as if she were still in the pool and hit redial. She waited – Mum's sick… Mum's sick… with each impatient second.

'Alex?'

'Jem! What happened? Is she OK?'

Everything around Alex had faded into oblivion. Jem was talking in whispers. 'I'm not supposed to have my phone on. We don't really know yet for sure. Malcolm Sinclair found her. At St Cuthbert's. In the churchyard. Alex, I... I can't...'

'Slow down, Jem! Where is she now? Where's Dad?'

'Kerring General. We're here now.'

Jem wasn't a crier, even when she was a kid. When Robbie Rushton stuck a drumstick through her spokes and Jem had flown straight over her handlebars she hadn't cried, she'd pinned Robbie to the ground instead and given him a dead arm. A whole week had gone by before anyone had realised Jem had fractured that wrist, the same one she'd used to punch Robbie with. But Jem's voice was wavering now. This alone made Alex want to cry immediately. She clamped a hand over her mouth in case.

'They're all over her, Alex. They said time was the most critical thing but Malcolm got her here really quickly. We're so lucky he was in the churchyard, Al.'

Suspected stroke. The words swirled in Alex's ears like trapped water. Blythe didn't like a fuss. To be bundled into Malcolm Sinclair's police car and rushed anywhere would have been beyond mortifying for her. 'She's going to be OK, isn't she, Jem?'

There was a flurry of activity in Jem's background, Alex strained to make any of it out.

'You know Mum… tough as Dad's old boots.' But Jem had hesitated.

Alex looked at the scant belongings she had with her. The urge was there – keys, coat, get home to Mum – and then the inevitable thought.

Dad.

Alex forced herself not to think about what she would say if she went back up there. She could already hear the first whispers in her head… *This was always going to happen, Alex, eventually. You knew that.* Because every one of Dill's birthdays without him had been one too many, and there was only so much quiet heartbreak the human body could take, even her mum's.

No. She couldn't go up there. It would be better for everyone if she didn't. One less thing for them all.

'Alex, are you still there?'

Alex took in a deep breath, just to remind her lungs that they still could. 'I'm here.'

Jem sniffed. 'Alex?'

'Yeah?'

'You need to come home.'

2nd November 2006

'You need to come home.'

Alex inhaled, deep and steady, filling her lungs with as much of his delicious scent as possible.

'I don't want to hide behind a phone, Foster. I want to do this properly. Show him how serious we are, about doing things right.'

Anyone would think Finn was going to ask for her hand in marriage. They were a cool billion light years from that. Well, maybe they could just make it out of their teens first, at least.

Alex watched the candlelight dancing over the far wall, laying soft shadows over the edge of Finn's face. They'd synchronised, his naked torso rising with breath as hers gave its own away. Rise and fall, the movement subtle like a gentle tide, so slight and easy it felt as if she might not need oxygen at all any more. He was enough.

Finn had a look of curious wonder in his eyes, a need finally met. Perhaps it was just the play of the light over his face, but Alex felt that way too, as if she'd made it to where she was always supposed to have been. She thought she'd be embarrassed, but it felt like the most natural thing in the world, to lie here beside him now, skin cool and sticky from their first adventure of each other. She never wanted to move again, her body wasn't finished nuzzling in the glorious afterglow of what they'd finally just done. What she already needed to do again.

'I missed you, Foster.'

Alex held back the goofy grin trying to make its way over her face, as if too sudden a moment might make it all disappear again like an illusion. 'I missed you too, Finn.'

His face was close enough to her that she could see tiny flecks of hazel in the green of his irises, the contours where laughter had left its footprint in the lines beside his eyes. Finn ran his fingertips from Alex's hip along her naked spine and began trailing delicate circular shapes over her shoulders. Alex felt her goose-pimples rise to greet him. Finn had found her again. He'd come all this way and he'd found her.

Alex reached her fingers to tease a lock of hair behind his ear. She'd been so buried in her coursework she hadn't noticed the sudden arrival of winter in the city, not until she'd watched it walk in on the ends of his hair. She'd opened the secured door of her student halls and there he was, waiting under a tree, pearls of new snow clinging to the same long layers he'd worn through college. Nearly two hundred miles and he'd been standing there as if the end of the earth wouldn't be too far.

'Your mum told me how to find you,' he'd said. And that was it, the snowflake that tipped the avalanche.

It was a perfect crisp November night and they'd spent it, some of it, talking through the year they'd spent adrift while the Old Girl had carried on flowing and the world had carried on turning. And now here they were, naked and blissfully fatigued in a single bed in a pokey little bedroom in a student house a million miles away from Eilidh Falls. And it was perfect.

Blythe had given Finn the address. Alex sent a quiet *thank you* out into the snowy darkness and hoped her mum would somehow feel it and think of Alex and Finn right then. Blythe was a sucker for a good love story; she'd probably compared theirs to the kind of love all of Blythe's favourite operas were made from. Of adversity and triumph and explosions of something precious happening between two people. *Luminous and powerful, darling!* She would say. *Love as beautiful and terrifying as a bolt of lightning!*

Finn propped himself up on an elbow. 'What are you thinking about?'

Alex's hand naturally migrated to the hardness of his stomach. The grin got the better of her as soon as she opened her mouth. 'Lightning.'

Finn's mouth gave in to a smile too. He was still beautiful; the tiny scar Ted's wedding band had left over the bridge of his nose hadn't changed him. A monster had risen in Alex's dad that night. Thankfully, none of them had ever seen it since.

Alex didn't see Finn's head furrow. 'OK, so what are you thinking about *now*?'

She didn't want to let any more thoughts of her dad in. 'Nothing,' Alex replied but she already knew it was too late. She stroked Finn's side. A futile gesture, as if she was trying to tame a piece of her coursework before the clay hardened and left her with something incomplete, misshapen.

'Let me tell him, Alex.'

'No. Not yet.'

'Alex, he can punch me all he likes if it makes him feel better. It won't change anything.'

'I know. I just… don't want you to say anything that…'

'But I *want* to. I want to say it to him. I love you, Foster.'

'I love you too.' She really did. It was the only certainty. But Finn's expression had already changed.

He cut her a smile and nodded softly to himself. 'I know you do, Foster. You just don't want anyone to know it.'

CHAPTER 4

The sky was like a lingering bruise on the outskirts of town. Alex pulled off the main road and cruised alongside the Old Girl into Eilidh Falls, the light still steeped in the eeriness of a new day. Just over two hours without a dip into a service station was a new personal best, made possible only by non-existent traffic and two eyelid-expanding double espressos before leaving the flat.

Alex pinched between her eyes, trying to stave off her tiredness. Her dad would go mad if he knew how little sleep she'd had. She shifted in the driver's seat, ignoring the growing ache in her back. This close to home it was pointless trying to push Dill away. He was all around her here; Dill belonged to Eilidh Falls. The tiny pocket of the world that had claimed him forever. Was it the same for Jem, she wondered, when she came home too? Jem played her cards so close to her chest you never could tell.

Another sign counting down the miles back to the Falls whizzed by the truck window. Time and distance, that's all her dad had wanted, and she'd delivered. Now she could feel it all being undone, one mile at a time. It was always this way on the drive back to the Falls. Dill always found his way into her thoughts, transporting her back there again, setting her down perpetually on the banks of the Old Girl with him, their weeping father, and Finn in his mournful silence, as if those few cataclysmic moments had soldered them all together forevermore.

Finn had tried so hard, but Ted was never going to see it.

Alex shuddered at the recollection of that Christmas. That first Christmas after. *He didn't know what he was doing, it was the drink, not your father,* Blythe had tried to say evenly as she'd gathered up sticky shards of Granny Ros's Tutbury crystal bowl from the garden path. That was the last time Alex had seen Finn or Susannah anywhere near the house. It was also the last Christmas Alex had seen her dad anywhere near a drink, and the start of all that prickly quiet between them. Thick grey silences wedged between all the safe things they still managed to talk about, like ice forming between rocks, threatening to shatter them both.

A heavy grogginess was starting to filter in behind Alex's eyes. She tried to keep them focused on the road ahead. Dad would never say it, that this new catastrophe was most likely a consequence of Blythe having to wish Dill a happy birthday down at St Cuthbert's, but it would be there, in one of those silences where the rest of Alex's failings resided.

A flash of black came up on Alex's right side. Some sleek four-by-four sped aggressively around her. She let them pass like one of the more able swimmers back at the leisure centre, as if she had any choice. Alex checked her rear view for any more surprises. She was nearly home. *Get it together, Alex. Mum needs you on the ball.*

Nope, she would not think about Finn's return any more. It wasn't even her place. Mum was all that mattered. She would get there and find out her part to play. She would get her mum's things together, help her wash and dress if needs be, grocery shop, cook for them, tidy the house. She'd only be back, what, a day or two? There were a hundred ways to pass a couple of days. All she had to do was help Blythe get back on her feet, and keep as best she could out from under her father's. Simple. Everything was going to be fine, Alex smiled. It wasn't like her Mum ever even got ill. Give it a week max and Blythe would show them all, this was just a blip in an otherwise blemish-free record of health. A momentary stumble. Wasn't she due one after all these years? All these birthdays? Alex gripped the steering wheel a little more assuredly. Her mum would soon be back on her feet, and then Jem could get back to London and Dad would be back busting a gut keeping the garage going and Alex could just get back out of everyone's way and they could all breathe again.

A particularly plucky yawn suddenly took hold and Alex gave in to it wholeheartedly. She sat up a little higher in her seat and began watching the familiar landscape of her youth tumble past the windows of her battered old Nissan.

Welcome to Eilidh Falls!

The sign had changed; for the benefit of the tourists, no doubt. Beneath the salutation, an image carved into the wood of a Viking longship under a hail of arrows fired from the banks of the Old Girl. As soon as Alex rolled past that image, the illusion that any amount of time or distance could ever really make a difference to her dad quickly evaporated.

CHAPTER 5

It hadn't been a nightmare exactly, Jem decided. More of a troubled sleep kind of thing, like in her teens. A sort of half-hearted insomnia. But definitely not a nightmare. Nightmares featured monsters and fear and peril, not the constant dull weight of words left unsaid.

Jem fidgeted in her old bed trying to get comfortable. She never slept well in her parents' house any more, she realised. Not since those hideous years in high school when the late-night anxieties had first kicked in. It wasn't easy sleeping on a lie every night, notching up the days she was keeping them all in the dark. Maybe her mum was right, the therapy might've helped Jem if she'd stuck with it, but it had seemed so OTT at the time.

'Jem! It's *3am!*' she remembered her mum rasping from the kitchen doorway, eyes blinking and vacant after catching Jem fixing a peanut butter sandwich for the third night in a row. 'Is it nightmares, sweetheart? Or is there something else that's bothering you? You haven't been yourself lately, Jem. If you're having nightmares it might help if you talk about them.'

'I'm OK, Mum.' Jem had reassured. 'I only have night-mares in the run up to maths tests, honest.' She hadn't mentioned those long school trips stuck with Carrie Logan and the other bimbos. Or the eve of Eilidh High's end of year discos when Jackson Cox was always expecting a slow dance with Jem and, rumour had it, a proper good snog.

Jem lay awake in bed remembering how she had tried to play it all down to her mother. To allay the worry she had seen in the tiny furrows on Blythe's faintly freckled forehead.

'It's not healthy for a fifteen year old girl to be sneaking around in the dark every night.'

'I'm doing peanut butter, Mum, not cocaine,' Jem had tried, but it didn't matter. Blythe wouldn't have it. Alex had buggered off to uni and that had left Jem alone under the spotlight. By the time she'd crawled out of bed the next morning her mum had already made the appointment.

'She says she doesn't want to see a *shrink*, Helen, but I'm not taking any chances. You can't be too careful with… bereavement,' Jem had overheard her mum confiding in Mrs Fairbanks.

'You can't be too careful with peanuts, either,' Helen Fairbanks had replied. Blythe had taken *careful* to a whole new level after that.

*

Jem stared into the nothingness above her childhood bed and inhaled deeply. Her old bedroom still felt like a bolthole

– a pocket of refuge in the middle of whatever mess their family was dealing with. She used to spend so much time in here, hiding out. Maybe that was why she'd been so rubbish at sneaking around downstairs back when her mum had kept on busting her in the kitchen – not enough practice.

Jem rolled over onto her side and looked across her bedroom bathed in twilight. Uh, now she couldn't stop thinking about peanut butter. Maybe she could she make it down to the kitchen without disturbing Dad across the hall? She was more gentle-footed now. Her legs twitched, ready to give it a shot but then she remembered the new pup down there. The thing got all excited as soon as anyone looked at her, Dad would wake up and it wasn't fair on him. He'd been awake half the night too, floorboards creaking under his restless pacing.

Jem's legs twitched again. She felt a sudden need to get out of the farmhouse and get to Kerring General, just as she had the last time tragedy had hit here. When they'd brought Alex home from the Old Girl, soaking and catatonic. Alex had looked like a little wet ghost, Dill's bow and arrows clamped in her taut hands. Just one more minute with Dill, it was all Jem had wanted, so she could take it all back, all those awful things she'd said to him that morning and tell him the truth instead. But they all just kept saying the same thing, over and over; *it's too late*.

Jem wriggled down into the bedding and let her thoughts

travel back to the hospital. *You have to wake up, Mum,* she thought anxiously. *You have to be OK and you have to wake up. So I can drop my bomb on you.*

Jem squeezed her eyes closed beneath the covers. In the long dark hours of the night, she'd made a vow. No more hiding, no more lies. They had a right to know. She'd tell Mum first, then Alex and Dad. Maybe it would be Dad who would try frogmarching Jem off to Dr Bullock PsychD's office this time.

Jem flinched at the recollection of her very brief spell in therapy. Pleading had been a complete waste of breath at the time, obviously. 'Of course you don't need to see a *shrink*, Jem,' her mum had carefully nudged, 'but it can't hurt just to get a few things off your chest, can it? Think of it like tidying your room.' But Jem didn't like a tidy room, thanks. She liked a bombsite nobody dared or desired to enter and wanted her jumbled little mind to be left just so too. Sleep was for wimps, anyway, she was fine as she was. Jem had been all set for hiding out behind one of the waterfalls up at Godric's Gorge and dodging the appointment altogether, but then her mum had given her that look. It had stilled Jem. Dill had gone. Then Alex. Jem had known instantly what that look had meant. *Please don't let me lose this kid too.* Anything was preferable to seeing her mum look that way again, even an hour with Dr Bullock.

'I feel that Jem is likely suffering from delayed anxiety. It's only just been a year since your son's death, Mrs Foster.

Grief can manifest itself months, sometime years, later in all sorts of ways.'

*

Jem shook her head against the pillow. *Nitwit.* Dr Bullock hadn't the faintest idea that he'd been Jem's unwitting accomplice.

'The sleep issues have coincided with your sister Alexandra's leaving for university, haven't they?' he'd asked. 'The start of the Autumn term? Detachment issues? Fear of another sibling leaving the family home? All very explicable.' All very perceptive of the doctor. Only he'd missed that the sleeplessness had also coincided with the Autumn term at Eilidh High too, and the return of two bus journeys a day with Carrie's crew.

It had been a lot like being stuck on the school bus, trundling sluggishly through her own psychoanalysis, sitting politely while Dr Bullock made all the necessary stops on the way to his grand resolution. The friend conversation, the boyfriend conversation, the drastic-new-hair conversation. Jem had felt an inexplicable sense of relief when they'd finally gotten around to the Dill conversation.

Spilling about her argument with Dill in the days before the accident had been easy. Even sharing how she'd never thought those jagged words she'd thrown at him would be the last ones Dill would ever hear her say. She hadn't meant to talk so much about that, but she had to give them something. And it had felt good almost, like loosening your fist and realising that your fingernails had been sticking into your palms all that time without you knowing. Her mum had nodded, as if it had all made perfect sense. This was something Blythe could work with; there was light at the end of the tunnel. Jem knew her mum had never suspected that Jem's opening up had been an exercise in frugality. Give a little here so that the bigger things could be held back.

Jem remembered her mum's locket pressing uncomfortably against her ear as Blythe had locked Jem in an embrace in the car park afterwards. She remembered feeling her mother's fingers deftly teasing strands of Jem's new hairstyle and she'd known that Blythe was mourning the loss of something more than her little girl's hair.

'Jem? I don't want there to be any more secrets between us, OK? Secrets can pull people apart. Even little ones,' Blythe had whispered.

Jem could have just said it. Right then. It had practically been a green light situation for sinking bad news. The words had been there, on the tip of her tongue. But then she'd felt the cold press of that tiny locket again, she'd pictured the little photographs it held inside of her conventional parents and their conventional marriage, and the truth had dissolved like sugar on her tongue.

'OK, Mum,' Jem had said. 'No more secrets.'

CHAPTER 6

Alex slowed for the approaching turnoff to Godric's Gorge and the run of waterfalls after which the town was named. She knew the road by heart, how many dusty laybys there were to allow the occasional passing car making its way to or from the falls, the cluster of properties that lined the dusty track there and each of the families who lived in them. In one of those properties, the large cream farmhouse with the spindly wisteria her mum couldn't get to grow right, Alex knew her dad would be awake already, drinking his morning coffee out on the front porch, smoking his first roll-up of the day. Alex let her hand hover over her indicator before settling it back onto the gear stick. She looked at the clock on the dashboard. The hospital ward wouldn't let her in at six-thirty and Jem would probably still be sleeping up at the house, which wasn't going to make conversation with her dad any easier.

Jem had accused her of being paranoid. Ted wasn't awkward around Alex, he was just usually preoccupied, that was all. Running a garage by himself took a lot of energy, didn't it? Easy for Jem to say, she always had something useful to contribute. Knew how to pull a conversation right out of him.

Alex automatically shifted up a gear and passed the turnoff for home. No point disturbing them this early. She followed the road down off the valley. Eilidh Falls high street was deserted, the only movement where great swathes of fabric in reds and golds fluttered lazily from the street lamps lining the road through the busiest part of town. *Wait, was that a...* 'Bloody hell! There's a huge dragon hanging off the Town Hall roof...' Alex blurted.

Jem hadn't been kidding. She'd told Alex about Mayor Sinclair's ramping up of the annual Eilidh Viking Festival a few times but it had never appealed, not that Alex had really grasped just how far the town had taken to gearing up for the festival, loosely based on the arrival of marauding Vikings to the area some 1200 years before.

'Viking Fest is gonna be a national treasure eventually, Al. Like the cheese rolling in Gloucester!'

Alex let her eyes follow an endless run of circular shields all along the old library gates as she drove past. 'Flipping heck... It looks like something off the history channel... on acid.'

Alex let her foot off the accelerator to take a slower look at the settlement of re-enactment tents down by the riverbank. Were they supposed to be the Anglo-Saxon presence then? A few of the tents looked more regal than the others, Alex was trying to get a better view and draw on her sketchy Viking knowledge from her St Cuthbert's Primary days when something black appeared like an ominous apparition at the front end of her truck.

'Shit!'

Alex reacted, stamping on the brake, probably harder than was necessary. She bounced in her seat while the truck jarred to a halt around her. The eyes glaring back through the windscreen at her looked amused. Alex felt herself swallow and ready an apology for the burly gentleman in the business suit who'd just stepped straight off the kerb and directly into the bloody road in front of her, but something about his smile made her hesitate. She'd only been travelling at a jogging pace and wasn't entirely convinced that his hands braced on her bonnet, cigarette still burning away where it was sandwiched between his knuckles, wasn't a touch overly dramatic.

Alex looked up at his face again and was reminded of a gorilla. Large and unpredictable. He definitely didn't look like a local, tourist probably, not that the suit made any sense. Alex had nearly gotten her *sorry* out when he grinned. He lifted his hands and brought two balled fists down hard on her bonnet. Alex flinched. He seemed to approve of her silly girlish movement. 'You stupid tart. Watch where you're going,' he delivered, his Hollywood smile sharpening the words as they left his mouth. Alex's mouth dropped open a little, a nervous thumping started in her chest as he pushed himself off her truck and casually strolled over to the black four-by-four parked across the street. Alex swallowed and found her voice again.

'Nice,' she muttered, once the ape was safely back inside his truck and *definitely* couldn't hear her. Alex had a rule about confrontation. She didn't do it. Jem was the sister for that. Jem wasn't backwards in going forwards like Alex, she was made of tougher stuff. Jem would've smiled sweetly just then and flipped the horrible git the Vs. Jem wouldn't have been intimidated, she'd singlehandedly confronted a group of teenagers once for calling Millie Fairbanks *Clubfoot*; the girl had no fear.

Alex began cruising again along the last of the high street. She drove steadily past her father's garage still with its heavy arched wooden doors in blue keeping her eyes well and truly off the hardware shop opposite as if merely glancing there would constitute an act of total betrayal. She drove towards the little primary school with its bright hanging baskets and sunflowers grown spindly through the summer holidays, on past the adjacent church – also St Cuthbert's – with its newly refurbished railings and worn stone path. Her mum had been round there last night, alone, slumped over in the churchyard before Mal Sinclair had found her. Alex's throat tightened. The hospital was only another two miles beyond the bridge, it was hard to resist pressing down a little harder on the accelerator but this was the stretch of road where Millie Fairbanks had lost two inches off her left leg after Finn's dad had signed their faulty car off.

Alex tried to take the incline of the old bridge in the wrong gear and the truck juddered around her in protest. She dropped it down to second. Ted reckoned you could always tell a local from an outsider on how slow they took the bridge. *Bloody tourists, careering in and out like they own the place.* Even over the ruckus in the pub on back-gammon nights, Alex's dad had said how they'd hear the screeching of tyres when some wazzock took the bridge too fast. Every time they heard the screech, Hamish would put a pound in the pot, ready for the next time he had to have his beer-garden wall rebuilt. 'Someone is going to get themselves killed at the bottom of that bridge someday,' Hamish liked to warn his patrons, 'as if the Fairbanks girl hadn't come close enough.'

Alex took the bridge cautiously. The Old Girl and the rest of Eilidh high street fell away in her rear view mirror, Alex's shoulders releasing a little the more the bridge shrank into the distance. A light twinkling of morning sun on water held Alex's attention on the disappearing view. It made her feel sorry to leave it back there without a proper look, it wasn't often she thought the Old Girl pretty. She had time for a little look.

Alex pulled over onto the side of the road in case she nearly killed anyone else before breakfast and shut the engine off. Her door cranked outwards like an arthritic hip. She sat there for a few moments with her feet on the cool earth outside the truck. It was so quiet here. Alex held her face to the sky. The air felt lighter up here in the Falls, lighter than it did back in the city anyway. Cleaner. Good for the soul. She'd taken it for granted as a child. She wanted to inflate herself with it now, purify herself with it. Alex clambered from her truck before even questioning herself and slammed the door shut behind her. The morning sun was spreading its greeting along the river catching like crystals on its changing surface. She'd spent so much energy distancing herself from this place, she'd almost forgotten its beauty.

Alex took in the view back towards the river where it cut past Hamih's pub. *You used to play Pooh sticks off that bridge with Jem, Dill Pickle.* Alex would invigilate while Mum and Dad watched from The Cavern's beer garden.

She missed him so much it ached. She missed Dill too.

None of the self-help articles ever said what to do about her dad. There wasn't a fear ladder for that, no psychological tool that would make her apology substantial enough to brave offering it again.

You're not here for that. You're here for Mum. And then you'll be gone again. Out of his way.

Alex shook off her inner monologue. She always became the same useless wimp when it came to Ted, that was a given, but Alex had decided on the drive up here that she would at least shuffle up a couple more rungs of her self-help strategy while she was here. She was going to pay a visit to an old adversary. The Old Girl looked welcoming now, winsome and pretty, just as she had been a thousand times before on still summer mornings such as this. Perfectly safe, if you chose the right spot.

Alex shuddered. That was a few rungs up yet. The Old Girl was right at the top, the end goal. She was going to wade into the Old Girl one day and she was going to do it without becoming a dithering wreck. Just like that. Tra-la-la. Alex quivered a little at the prospect. *One step at a time*, Dr Phil said. She could start up at the plunge pools, in the shallows. Alex found herself drifting away with her thoughts. Yes, before leaving the Falls again, she was going to achieve something. She was going to stand in the plunge pools up to her knees. That was the benchmark, *that* was something realistic she could aim for, a rung she could climb.

Ain't no thing but a chicken wing, she reassured herself.

She'd seen an allegedly phobic woman on *Oprah* say this, again and again like a magical spell of protection while someone had steadily placed a boa constrictor around the woman's sweaty neck. Alex had watched intently and the woman hadn't even blinked. The not blinking thing wasn't as impressive as having a snake near her windpipe though, in fairness.

Alex watched the sparkles on the water. 'Ain't no thing but a chicken wing,' she said aloud. It felt strange. Liberating. She'd read that in the *Climb your fear-ladder* article too. *Face your fears and assertively tell them, 'No! I will not be a slave to you any more!'*

She locked eyes on the riverbank. 'No', she said in a small voice, 'I will not—'

This was ridiculous. She was losing her mind. Alex let out a little laugh. Then she cleared her throat and tried it again. All this clean air was flushing something out of her, it felt kinda good. And weird. 'Ain't no thing but a chicken wing!'

she called, louder this time. The wall of evergreens called back with a small echo. There were only squirrels and, rumour had it, a headless ghost she might disturb back here. Sod it, call it coffee jitters but she was going to go for it. She'd see a car coming a mile off before anyone would hear.

She took another lungful. 'AIN'T NO THING BUT A CHICKEN WING ON A STRING—'

'From… *Burger King*?'

Alex snapped her head round to her right side. Her heart hurt, like it had a stitch. It might actually have just stopped.

The mud was the first thing. New toffee-coloured mud spattered across his jaw. She glanced up and down, scanning him for possibility.

Oh God. Oh my God.

Another pain in Alex's chest. She felt the beating in there fire up again on all cylinders. This was why kids pedalled stories of headless ghosts in the forest, the mulchy floor spongy enough that any person with a half-decent pair of trainers and a degree of athletic grace (that was Alex out then) could suddenly, soundlessly appear from the woods and scare the crap out of you.

Finn looked stunned too.

Alex didn't know where to look. The mud was a running theme. His trainers were caked in the stuff, so were the calf muscles glistening with tiny beads of sweat. He hadn't been a runner in his youth. He hadn't been so defined, either. She tried to take him all in. His chest was heaving beneath his t-shirt, fervently but steady, like a racehorse. A thin white wire trailed down from the headphones either side of his face giving the rise of his chest a glancing blow on its descent to one of the pockets of his jogging bottoms. Joggers cut off at the knees. He wasn't just a runner now, he was a *hardcore* runner.

Alex was dumfounded. 'You've... changed colour.' Her voice caught in her throat. Maybe he didn't notice. He'd appeared from the trees as fluently as he did in her sleep. Alex swallowed, her heart already migrating to her mouth. Finn gave a gentle yank and sent the earplugs tumbling towards his waist.

He looked down at himself. 'I guess that would be mostly the mud.'

It wasn't the mud, it was adventure seeking in the southern hemisphere while Alex had been making vats of chilli con carne at the food bank. He probably smelled of coconut oil and ylang ylang now, she usually smelled of fried onions and disinfectant. His hair had changed colour too, lighter at its edges than it was. It still sat long just over his ears but it looked more deliberate now, like he'd just fallen off a billboard advertising surfboards, or cranberry juice, or something full of antioxidants.

'You haven't changed colour.' He smiled. 'Still a striking red head.' Alex cringed at her own statement. 'Well, actually you look a little less red than the last time we spoke if I remember right.' He offered a half-hearted smile.

She was going to die. Right here on the spot. The last time they'd spoken had been in her student bedroom. Trying to be quick, efficient, like ripping off a plaster, hadn't worked. There had been nothing clean and clinical about it. Just lots of arguing and hurt. And red faces, obviously.

'Actually, you look a little pale, Foster. Are you OK?'

She hadn't heard her name on his lips since the last moments before watching him walk away through the snow. *Be kind to yourself, Foster*, he'd said. Because not having the balls to go home and tell her dad about them sure as hell wasn't being very kind to Finn.

Alex swallowed again. Finn's breath was levelling off but hers was becoming shallower. She felt a bit fuzzy, actually.

'I, er. Actually just, I erm… just tired, actually. Long drive.'

Finn's eyes narrowed. She didn't want his eyes to narrow, he was always working something out when he did that.

'Jem said you don't come back here. Don't they have fast food where you live now?' Nope, he'd lost her. '*Burger King*, wasn't it?' Alex cringed. The woman on *Oprah* hadn't sounded like such a muppet when she'd said it. 'Or have you come back for a run in one of the most beautiful spots in the world? It's some morning, isn't it?'

She felt a hand rub up the back of her neck and realised it was her own. *Stop that, you're not a child.*

'No, no… definitely not a runner. Or prolific burger eater.' She smiled feebly.

'But you do come back up here to the Falls though? Evidently.'

Oh God, this conversation felt like swimming. *In through the nose, out through the mouth…*

'Yeah, um, not really. It's difficult with work and stuff and…'

'Work?'

'Yep. I erm, work with disadvantaged people.' Disadvantaged people? *Nice one, Alex.* She wasn't exactly in the Peace Corps. *Don't try to impress him, you plonker. He's travelled the world!*

'Disadvantaged people? Must keep you busy.'

Alex laughed a laugh that didn't belong to her.

'I thought when you left your university degree, you'd find another course somewhere?'

'Ah, no.' Alex batted the notion away, a silly childhood whimsy. 'No I didn't, actually. I er, I left uni for good.'

'I know.' He said matter-of-factly. 'That's too bad. Your work, all through college, I mean… you have a gift, Foster.' He shrugged.

Alex swallowed again. Only her mother said that. *Have.* Not *had.* As if there was still discernible potential in her somewhere. Alex looked at her shoes, embarrassed if anything. Mum would've loved this, this meeting of theirs in the forest like two star-crossed nymphs, back when Blythe's heart would have been still up for the excitement. Reality thudded home. 'Actually, I have to go. I need to get to the hospital.'

The look on Finn's face switched immediately. 'Are you OK, Foster?'

'Oh, no… I didn't mean… it's Mum. She er, she had a stroke last night.' The words seemed to double back in her mouth and head straight back down her throat, clenching her heart in an angry fist. Suddenly there was a lump forming at the back of Alex's throat, she could feel it coming. *Don't cry! Shit! Alex, if you cry now he'll comfort you and then you'll be dripping snot into his muddy chest before you know it and it'll be all over.*

'I'm sorry, Foster. Is there anything I can do?' Finn's hand reached out for a second and grazed Alex's elbow. Their skin touched briefly and she very definitely felt it, the same as before, exactly as Blythe would always describe it.

It felt like lightning.

CHAPTER 7

Ted Foster had woken up an hour ago to the sound of muffled whimpers drifting in off the landing. For a few dazed seconds, he imagined he were still a young man, sitting bolt upright in bed ready to trudge wearily across the hall to check on each of his three children, see which one of them was having a restless dream. He stretched his back through and reached up to rub the greying bristles of his face, turning to see if Blythe had woken too. Her pillow was as neat and plumped as she'd left it yesterday morning after Jem had helped her change the beds. Blythe had been grumbling about engine oil finding its way onto the bedspread again. 'Well what can I do,' Ted had protested, 'if some evenings I rush my shower because I can't wait to climb into bed with a show-stoppin' redhead?' Jem had started grinning at her mother then but Blythe had turned that beautiful porcelain chin of hers away in mock disapproval.

God damn it, Blythe.

The dawn was finding its way along the top edge of the curtains, waiting respectfully to be invited in. Ted took his first deep breath of the day and set a hand on the piped edging of Blythe's pillow. She'd disapprove of all the fuss last night. All those strangers talking over her with their penlights and charts, as if she weren't there sleeping beneath them. They were just kids. What did they know about her? A woman whose laughter they'd never contracted, whose neck they'd never smelled, whose beautiful voice they'd never heard singing on a morning.

More impatient whimpering found its way through the gap under the bedroom door. Ted set two unwilling feet on the cool floorboards and went to find the source of all that disgruntlement. He quietly opened the door so as not to wake Jem down the hall. The door shushed open. Ted looked to his feet and the bundle of straw-coloured fur waiting expectantly there. The damned thing had sniffed him out and here it was, sitting there with its head cocked ready for breakfast no doubt.

'Made it up the stairs then?' This was their first Labrador, he'd heard they had more spring in them than most pups. Probably should've gotten something with less spring, not that he'd had any intention of having any more dogs, springy or not. The Cavern was an ale house, not a pet market. The damned thing had been what Blythe would call an impulse purchase, like half the stuff she'd bring home from the supermarket. Impulse purchase was about right. There it had been, all wide-eyed peeping out the top of Roger Muir's coat. The runt, Muir had said. Ted knew instantly that Blythe would love it. Her face had lit up like one of the kids' when she'd seen the pup, that smile she seemed to put her whole body into. A smile she didn't have to think about. At this time of year to bring that smile back into the house was nothing short of a blessing.

The pup cocked her head the other way.

'If you were smarter, dog, you'd have tried my daughter's room,' Ted sighed. The girls had always gone gaga for puppies, just like Blythe. Ted wasn't one to shout it from the rooftops but he'd always quietly beamed when somebody remarked how alike his girls were to their mother. Daughters should be like their mothers and Blythe and their girls were the most beautiful creatures in the Falls. He'd challenge anyone to say they weren't. Of course, the same folks had said on occasion how Dill got his looks from Ted, but it was easy to tell the difference between true observation and politeness. Besides his dirty blond hair Dill had looked very little like him, Ted knew that. No matter what the heart wanted to be true, there was no disputing what his eyes told him every time he'd walked passed the photographs of Dillon hanging in the hall downstairs.

Blythe had taken herself off into the frozen garden and cried for an hour straight when he'd taken down the *Son* from the garage sign. He shouldn't have climbed up there, yanking it away with his own hands, he realised that now. But he couldn't bear seeing it any longer. It would be a lie to have left it up there, calling out an untruth to everyone passing by. The Fosters' name would come to an end when the girls married, they all knew that. There were some people who'd known it before Ted had.

That same old hollowness began to yawn like a chasm inside him. The puppy squeaked for attention again but Ted was resolute. 'You'll have to wait, little one. I have something to do before breakfast.' The bastard was good and dead now. No more a part of the town, no longer a thorn in their sides. And when Ted made it to the churchyard, by God, he hoped he'd find that the old son of a bitch had finally taken the last of his poorly kept goddamn secrets with him.

2nd November 2006

Alex felt him tense, harden like her clay; Finn's whole body beside her suddenly off limits, no longer hers to touch.

'That's not it. It's not that I don't want anyone to know, Finn. I just *can't* upset him again, he's my dad. I've already put him through so much.' Finn took his hand back, slow enough that it wasn't like a punishment. Only it was. Alex stopped herself from grabbing it and bringing those fingers back to her again. 'Now's just… it's not good timing, Jem's getting into trouble at school and—'

'So how long, Alex? I'm ready to get my lights punched out to stand up for the way I feel about you, how long until you're ready to stand up for how you say you feel for me?'

Alex's palm was still lying against Finn's chest. Should she move it? Everything about him was starting to feel defensive. The way he was pushing his hair away from his face, the tension through his arms.

'I do feel that way, Finn. I love you.'

'Do you?'

She was losing him. She could already feel it. 'You know I do. You've always known.'

'So tell him. Tell him, Alex. Tell him we're young and in love and we'd do anything to change what happened. But we *can't*. All we can do is keep moving forwards and sometimes that means moving against the current.'

Something had shifted in the air between them. It was a similar feeling to watching one of her clay pots lose its shape when it had stood to be so beautiful before she'd cocked it up. Maybe if she was careful, deft enough, she could bring it back again, coax it all back into shape. 'He's my dad, Finn. I can't keep pushing him. I love you, and I love him too. I need him to have the chance to understand.'

'Understand what?'

'How sorry I am! It happened on *our* watch, Finn! I can't be sorry for that *and* ram you down his throat at the same time. You know what he thinks we were doing!'

It was all coming flooding back. She didn't want to go there right now. It would spoil everything, the candlelight, the snow outside. The taste of him still on her mouth. She was going to wear that taste away with these awful words.

Alex spoke quietly. 'I just think we should keep things private, just for a while.'

'Hide our relationship, you mean?' Finn was not speaking quietly.

'Not *hide*, just… take our time.'

Finn propped himself angrily against the headboard. 'You want me to love you in secret, Alex? Hide how I feel, like I had to when my dad skipped out on my mum and me?' Alex took her hand back. He couldn't feel her now anyway.

'That was no fun, Alex. Pretending I hated my own father because if I didn't I'd be reminded of all the reasons why I should. I knew he hadn't checked those brakes properly for your dad, I knew he'd rushed Mrs Fairbanks' service to get to a shitty *poker game*, but I *didn't* know how to tell anyone that I still loved him anyway because he was still my dad, or even how what he'd done to Millie Fairbanks and her mum wasn't enough to stop me *still* wanting him home with us again.'

'Finn…' Alex felt herself shrink away in her too-small bed. Suddenly she felt totally, shamefully naked.

'I know what my old man did, Alex. I know what he did to Millie, and your dad's business and to my mum and me. But I still loved him. Only I had to do it in secret. I had to hide it.' Finn shook his head. 'I'm not signing up for that again, Alex. You don't do that with love. You stand up for it and you take the blows and you bleed for it if you have to.'

'I'm responsible, Finn. Don't you get that? I lost Dill, *I lost him*! He was just a little boy, and I didn't protect him. I stopped watching and I lost my baby brother. Their only son! I can't just go home and—'

Finn's eyes were greener with anger. His arms flailed wildly. 'He died Alex! He didn't get lost, Dill died! I had him in my arms, I could feel the knot in his lace, how I could free him!' Finn's body rippled with angry heartache. 'But it was too tight. My fingers were too big and I couldn't pull him from the root in time and he died. And you're *right*. It *was* on our watch. But what can we possibly do that will *ever* make that better?'

Alex felt the hurt inside begin to twist into something resentful. 'Not ram our happy-ever-after down his throat, Finn!'

Finn was suddenly up on his feet next to Alex's books and their abandoned clothes, a naked ringmaster in the circus of Alex's life. His arms were aloft again. 'Fine! Well, what about all this? What are you going to do when you get a first with your degree, Alex? Because you will. You'll graduate with flying colours and get the job you've always dreamed of in a career you'll love. Then what?'

'Finn.'

'Let's see, what about when you want to get married? Or buy your first house, or have your first kid. Are those things off limits for Ted Foster's throat too? Or is it just *me* you can't ram down it?'

'You're being ridiculous.'

'No, *you're* being ridiculous, Alex!'

'No I'm not!' She heard the tears in her voice. They were coming, they were en route. 'Dill won't get to do any of those things because of me.'

Finn pinned his hands on his hips and shook his head.

'Don't shake your head! Dill won't ever bring a girlfriend home for my mum to cluck over, or help my dad out at the garage so he's not breaking his back working on his own all the time. He'll never grow up and have a laugh with Jem instead of only ever pissing her off! Dill won't graduate, he won't even flunk!' Alex's voice wobbled. It almost stopped her but the thought was too heavy to be left inside her head. 'My brother will never go home to the Falls and tell my mum and dad that he's met "the one"! The *one* person he can't imagine living his life without because he knows there'll never be anyone else who'll ever come close! So *how can I*?'

Alex felt the first tears escape the corner of her eyes. She saw Finn relent, the tension slipping with an almost indecipherable dip of his shoulders. Gentle, calm Finn was trying to come back. 'You're right, Alex. Dill won't get to do any of those things now. And I'd do anything to change it. To go back and stay right there on the riverbank, instead of messing around in the undergrowth where we couldn't see. But we can't change that now.'

Finn moved silently back to the bed but Alex looked away. He stopped short of reaching her.

'I need my dad to know that I haven't forgotten what I did, Finn. That I'll never forget. *Sorry* just isn't a big enough word,' she said quietly.

Finn shook his head gently. 'You're right, Foster, it's not. But you have a life to live. How are you going to do that if every achievement, every bit of happiness or fun you have, feels like an insult to Dill? Live half a life because he lost his? You can't hide from your own life, Alex.'

CHAPTER 8

Ted moved quietly between the headstones, taking in the riot of discarded colour across this quiet little corner of St Cuthbert's. Blythe would never have left Dillon's grave in such disarray, not unless she really was as ill as he feared. No-one had tidied the mess of abandoned flowers because no-one else had been party to Blythe's *episode*, as the docs kept calling it. No-one except for that damned Sinclair boy.

Ted bristled. The Sinclairs had a knack for lurking somewhere within the fallout zone of another family's heartache. Ted made his way over to the granite stone next to the yellow blooms left scattered across the ground and checked that he was as alone as he liked to be here. If Blythe had been home this morning, he'd have given her a kiss and told her how he needed to get an early start at the garage before slipping away to this yearly ritual of his. To visit his boy the morning after his birthday, when the rest of them had already been and gone, just to be sure he wouldn't be crossing paths with the wrong well-wisher. Year in year out, he'd given way to a person who had no goddamned right in this world to mourn his boy.

Ted regarded the abundance of flowers Blythe and Jem had arranged with care in the water pots. He tried not to examine Blythe's reasons for coming back down here alone yesterday evening, tried not to feel so inadequate because of them. Ted looked over his shoulder again at his peaceful surroundings. The churchyard was no place for a mother, it was sure as hell no place for child. He wanted to break the silence, speak out the way other people could. *Morning, son*, he always wanted to say, *sorry I don't come by as often as your mother...* But Ted wasn't like Blythe. Once he was here, in the middle of all this quiet, he could never get the words out.

Ted crouched beside Dill's headstone ignoring the immediate ache in his knee joints. It had been Jem's idea, to have an image of an arrow etched into the granite. He'd hated the thought, he didn't need reminding how Dill came to be reaching so far over the water, or that it was him who had given Dillon permission to keep that goddam bow set – him who was supposed to be showing Dill how to use it. But Jem had hardly spoken a word in the run up to the funeral and Blythe had forbidden him from saying anything to risk unsettling the girls any more than they already were.

'Do you think it will be any easier for Alexandra? To be reminded of her mistake?' Blythe had argued.

The Finn boy barged his way into Ted's thoughts twisting something inside him on the way. *Not now, Ted.* He pinched at the tension building between his eyes. There was every chance Alexandra was going to turn up here in the Falls, he knew she would. Alexandra loved her mother too much to think up one of her endless reasons to stay away. But now wasn't the time to pick at old wounds, not when Blythe's needs were greatest.

Over on the church path, movement stole Ted from his thoughts. He watched the elderly couple and their little dog stop and take in the temporary wooden cross where the mayor had been buried back in January. *That's it, pay your respects to the pretentious bastard.* Arrows or not, at least Dillon's memorial was modest, befitting of a Foster. Not like the monstrosity the town was awaiting to be erected in the mayor's honour once the earth had settled around his good-for-nothing carcass.

Ted reached into the pocket of his overalls and pulled out a clean rag, running it over the letters engraved before him. *Beloved son.* Blythe and Jem had already cleaned and tidied Dillon's plot yesterday morning of course, read and replaced the cards of the bouquets Helen Fairbanks and Susannah Finn still remembered to leave each year. Ted never read the cards, all that was between the women. They'd been good to Blythe over the years, long after she'd stopped singing with them and the rest of the choir girls, but only Helen Fairbanks had carried on coming up to the house. *But that was your choice, Susannah. I never said you couldn't come into our home, just not that boy of yours.*

Ted felt that seasoned nip of guilt towards Susannah Finn. He thought of the way Susannah had stood in front of Finn while Ted had fought his rage. Ted promptly laid another thought over the top of the previous one as if laying salve over a stubborn cut that wouldn't heal. *Her boy had it coming.*

Ted replaced the redundant cloth in his pocket and began gathering up the stems lying forgotten on the ground. He didn't know much about flowers but he knew these ones had arrived after the rest or Blythe would've already had them neatly arranged in the water pots she and Jem had finished with yesterday morning. No, these had arrived later in the day. Fancy, expensive types ordered from one of those overpriced florists. Ted looked about himself for one of the fussy little miniature envelopes with the cards inside to reunite with them, but there was nothing. He tried to jolly through it but he'd already felt his back go cold. Of course there wasn't a card. These were them, that one last anonymous bouquet that always turned up. Ted felt an instant rage burning up his neck. 'Even now, you've got your filthy hands on my family, you son of a bitch.' He'd been a fool to hope that this might be the year they finally stopped arriving.

Ted gathered up the last of the stems, a few at a time in big hands used to handling wrenches and jacks. *Never a card.* But then there were some who couldn't find the words weren't there? Could only ease their conscience by sending Dillon a hollow gesture before sodding back off to their own neat and tidy lives. Ted straightened up, trying to calm the resentment building in him but there was already a burning along his eyes. His voice was hoarse and metallic as the first tears tried to overcome him.

'God damn you and your goddamned flowers,' he growled under his breath.

Ted deftly eradicated the trail of moisture over his cheek with back of his wrist. The rage was instant. He knew he shouldn't do it. He knew it was wrong. Knew that if there was a God in heaven who by chance might be glancing down upon him right now, right at this minute, then he was damned for sure.

Good men don't do these things, he told himself, looking out across the churchyard to the plot of disturbed earth awaiting its monumental tribute to that charlatan. Mayor Sinclair, pillar of the community and all round nice guy. *A good man*, the *Eilidh Mail* had reported, *if only there were more like him*. Huh. The trouble with this town was that there were too many like him. People you thought you knew, *trusted*, right up until they nearly destroyed everything you held dear.

Ted's stomach churned, the blooms suddenly heavy in his hands. Flowers were for conveying sentiment, what sentiment did these convey? Regret? Shame? *Love?* The anger was already flaring in his stomach; an ember he knew would never completely die away. He should have felt shame for what he was about to do, here in the middle of St Cuthbert's churchyard at the grave of his boy. And maybe he did feel something like that, but it wasn't enough to stop Ted from taking the heads of those pretty, expensive, anonymous flowers and crushing them right there in his hands.

CHAPTER 9

The song on the radio. The birds outside. The sun warm through her windscreen. The tinny sound of the truck speakers. She was distantly aware of it all melting away, the tiredness pulling her under.

*

'Alex? Can we put an apple on Rodolfo's head? I can hit it, I promise!'

Alex turned her face towards Dill's voice. The sun felt warm on her skin. She wanted to hear it again, a voice she'd accidentally forgotten. Like the taste of flavour left behind in childhood.

'I'm a good shot, Al, honest.'

She glanced back over her shoulder and saw Finn's smile mirroring her own. Dill was beating a path to the riverbank, swishing at the grasses with his new bow. Mum had tried to confiscate it like his cracker-bombs, this unexpected early birthday present from the mayor, no less.

Finn reached out and ruffled Dill's scruffy straw-coloured hair. 'Let's check your aim first, Dill Pickle.'

Alex watched the dimple at Dill's cheek pucker and disappear as his mouth moved with each concentrated swish of his bow. His features were changing, maybe he would become more like their dad after all, the soft rounded edges of his little-boyhood just beginning their surrender to the harder lines of adolescence.

Dill looked at the dog then threw Alex an angelic look, eyes squinting over cheeks risen with mischief.

'Don't try that butter wouldn't melt thing on me, Dill,' Alex laughed, 'I saw you in action earlier. I'd stay out of Jem's way for a while if I were you.'

Finn laughed. 'What have you done at your sister now, buddy?' Finn had paint spatters all over his shirt. Or was that mud? No matter, he'd turned it inside out anyway. Rodolfo woofed and very sensibly fell back to trot beside Finn's legs, before Dill could do a William Tell on him.

'Nothin'.' Dill grinned.

'You big fibber, Dill Pickle,' Alex said. 'Y'know how I can always tell when you're fibbing?'

'His lips move?' Finn teased.

'*No.*' Alex bumped Finn with her shoulder. She looked back to Dill. 'Your dimple gives you away, little brother.'

Dill gave in immediately. 'I caught Jem snogging the bathroom mirror! The *actual* mirror!' His nose wrinkled. 'Ew, she's so gross, she looked like the fish me and Dad caught when we went fishing in the plunge pools.' Dill made a face, presumably of a fish gasping its last. 'I think she needs more practice. Yeeuck.'

'Jem is spending a lot of time in the bathroom, come to think of it.' Alex bit at the smile on her lips. Finn let his own smile run a merry riot all over his face. Something floated inside Alex when she saw him do that.

'Know much about *snogging* do you, bud? What are you, *nine*?'

Dill stopped swishing and jabbed his bow towards Alex. 'I know you like to snog my sister,' he grinned, 'and if my dad catches you guys on the porch again, he told Mum he's going to see how much you *really* like her, Finn, and tell you all the gross stuff Alex—'

Alex lunged. 'Dill! God, shut up!'

Dill bolted. Alex was going to throttle him. No wonder Mum had asked her to take Dill out while Jem cooled off. Jem had been set to murder him back at the house.

Alex made a grab for him. Incapacitating Dillon with relentless armpit-tickling was probably one of her favourite things to do, second only to snogging Finn's face off on the front porch.

'One sister trying to kill you not enough, huh, Dill?'

Dill squealed in that way smaller children do when they're being chased and The Fear has gotten a hold of them. She'd nearly got to him, but they were both giggling too much to effectively chase or flee from the other. Alex made a final lunge when something cumbersome, a black and tan furred lump of warmth scuttled beneath her knees sending her reeling into the grasses with a clumsy thud. Rodolfo whimpered. Dill looked on for about half a second before erupting into the same breathless laughter he was holding onto from his toddlerhood.

Rodolfo whimpered again. Alex whimpered too. 'Bad dog, Rodolfo.' She lifted an arm up to examine it and grimaced.

'Hold on, don't move!' Finn was beating back the thicket of nettles with Dill's bow. He looked kinda clumsy about it, Alex thought, but it felt sort of *romantic*. Totally worth the stings.

'Don't, Finn, you'll get stung too!' Like she meant that.

Finn slipped an arm beneath her back. Alex let him. Finn lifted her out of the nettle patch. Alex breathed in a hit of his warm skin and the body spray she didn't think suited him but said she liked just the same because he was Finn, marvellously gorgeous, artistic, Finn.

'You're not going to snog now, are you?' Dill drew one of his arrows from their sheath and held it out to them feathers first. 'Cos if you are, can one of you please shoot me first? Don't bother with the apple.'

*

Alex jolted awake to a short, sharp, unpleasant sound at her truck window. Dill disappeared from her mind leaving behind him only a dull echo of the stinging sensation Alex had felt creeping through her legs. More tapping at the passenger window pushed away those last wisps of Finn too.

Alex blinked. Kerring General loomed in the near distance. She pieced it together, remembered her mum, Jem's call, the journey home. Alex rubbed the tiredness from her head. *Finn.* On the roadside. That bit hadn't been a trippy dream. Alex shifted a little and felt an uncomfortable fuzziness sear through one of her calf muscles. Her legs were locked together awkwardly in the foot well, a tingling sensation raging all the way down into her feet.

Pins and needles, loony. Not nettle-rash. She tried to flex against it.

'I knew you wouldn't wait until morning.' The voice was dampened by glass. Alex checked for drool at the corner of her lips and tried to see around the hand softly rapping fingers adorned with pretty rings against her passenger window. Jem had been a sandy blonde last Christmas, sporting a victory roll if memory served. The girl standing the other side of the glass was all long layers and choppy fringe in a shade much closer to the deep red Blythe had passed on to both of them. Dill had taken more of their dad's features, their mum had said. More angular and fair. But mostly he hadn't reminded Alex of either of their parents in particular.

Alex smiled through the glass. It regularly caught her off-guard how attractive Jem had become since emerging from her tomboy chrysalis. Without Dill, Alex's theory couldn't be properly measured, but she'd long suspected theirs was one of those families where the children had become progressively more beautiful as they'd come along. This morning though, Jem looked even more the butterfly than usual, striking and fragile all at once.

Alex reached across the passenger seat and pulled on the door handle. 'Hey, stranger. What time is it?' The car park had filled up since Alex had pulled into one of the far bays and dozed off.

Jem crouched down in the truck doorway. 'Time you stopped sleeping with your mouth open? It's eight-thirty, how long have you been here? Or shouldn't I ask?' She reached lithely over the passenger seat and pulled Alex's head in for a kiss. The question was on Jem's face before she could ask it. 'Alex, have you been swimming?'

'Not exactly.' She wouldn't call it *swimming*. Alex gave in to another yawn. 'I haven't been here that long, I don't think. Couple of hours?'

'Hope not, Al. They're hot on the parking charges here, the thieving toads. Like anyone wants to be stuck at a hospital.' Alex pulled her pumps back and grabbed her rucksack from the passenger foot well while Jem slammed the passenger door shut. Alex skipped to keep pace with her, glancing across the hospital car park as they walked. There was no sign of him. Jem pulled an expensive looking phone from the breast pocket of her denim jacket and checked the screen. 'He went in already. I hung back to make a call, I didn't spot you until after he'd gone inside,' she said reassuringly. Jem returned her phone to her pocket, slipping her free arm around Alex's waist. 'Honest, Al, don't go off on one… he didn't know you were here or he'd have waited to say hi.'

'OK.' Alex smiled, trying not to leave such a tiny word hanging in the air all by itself. What had she been expecting anyway, a greeting party?

Something mildly panicky was rising through Alex's body the closer they got to the main hospital entrance. She wasn't ready. She didn't have the words, for her mum or her dad. How did you apologise for finally putting your own mother in hospital? For being the root cause of her broken heart?

Jem nudged Alex with her hip. 'So what's this? The beach bum look?'

Alex glanced down at the denim cut-offs and faded *Jaws* t-shirt she'd yanked on in the middle of the night as the espressos took effect. 'It wasn't exactly a deliberate outfit.'

'Just when you thought it was safe to go back into the water?' Jem read. 'Keeping the fear alive, are we?'

Alex let out one of those breathy laughs that wasn't worth the effort seeing as it wasn't going to fool anyone. That fear was well and truly alive and kicking, like a great white killer shark, if great white killer sharks had legs. 'Feels like ages since I last saw you, Al.' Jem's voice fell lower. 'How are you doing?' It wasn't a good sign when Jem was quiet. It was like her defence mechanism. As if not talking about a thing could make it disappear.

'I'm good.' Alex smiled. It wasn't Jem's job to check on her, Alex was the eldest. She missed her role. 'How are *you* doing, Jem?' she countered, pulling Jem in to her a little as they walked past A&E. It was always a strange sensation Alex felt when they got together, as if it was possible to miss a person even more when they were within reach.

'I'm OK. I'm just glad I was already up here and not

still in London when Mal called. It was a bit of a shock, Alex. She didn't look great last night. She didn't look… like Mum.' Alex's throat narrowed as they crossed the hospital lobby. She should've done more to stop this from happening, somehow, instead of hiding from them all.

Jem reached for the lift button then stopped suddenly, as if something had just short-circuited in her head. She placed her hand flatly against the wall and held herself there.

'She has to be OK, Alex,' Jem said quietly. 'I'm not ready for her not to be around yet.'

Alex hung back. She swallowed her own thoughts and tried for *upbeat*, being the big sister. 'You think Mum's gonna check out before she's seen one of us walk down the aisle, Jem? Unlikely.' Blythe had made endless references to the great altar race over the years. 'Course she'll be OK. Like you said, tough as Dad's old boots.' But Alex felt as if someone had just kicked her in the neck with one.

A cycle of what ifs began circuiting Alex's head. What if she'd have come home this weekend, just for once? What if she'd have been with Blythe in the churchyard? What if that could have made the difference?

Alex stopped herself. There was only one *what if* that could've ever made the difference and they all knew it.

What if I hadn't followed Finn into the bushes?

CHAPTER 10

The Acute Assessment Unit was quiet. No drama. No urgency. Jem announced herself at the intercom. The doors onto the AAU opened. Alex followed quietly as Jem gave the nurses stationed at the central desk a salutatory smile and headed for the second side room on the left. Their roles were already set – Jem, the daughter who knew her way around, what to do, where to go – and Alex, the bumbling visitor.

Alex rubbed at the back of her neck. It was impossible not to feel anxious at what lay on the other side of the door in front of them. This awful ominous build up smacked of one of the games she'd watched last night on Takeshi's Castle, the maze game with its skittish contestants where the only difference between salvation and some unknown horror was a couple of inches of plywood. *And what's behind door number two?* A scary Japanese monster? An emotionally estranged father? An unrecognisable mother.

Alex eyed the door as Jem reached to push on it and felt an unpleasant lightness in her stomach. She could have taken a running jump, like the nervy lunatics on Takeshi, but Jem was already a confident step ahead, silently slipping through the door.

The smell was subtle as it hit. Alex shuffled quietly across the threshold, the scent as familiar as a favourite winter coat. She readied herself. She always readied herself.

'Hello, Dad.'

Ted was standing, grey and monolithic, beside the only chair in the room. Alex lunged clumsily at him for their obligatory kiss. Ted turned from where he'd been watching her mum sleeping to receive Alex's kiss. They bumped jaws awkwardly. His skin felt rough, bristly with the greying beard that wasn't hanging onto the last of its blond quite as well as the rest of his hair. Alex gave him his personal space back and tried to remember the last time they'd made physical contact for anything other than this awkward hello–goodbye ritual of theirs. The last time she'd hung onto his arm or pecked him on the cheek for no particular reason.

'I spotted her in the car park. She still snores like you, Dad, mouth wide open and everything,' Jem chirped, filling the void with warmth before anything cooler could creep in there. Ted rewarded her with a lazy smile. Alex wished she could think of something to say of equal worth. Nothing came. She shuffled back to the bottom of her mum's bed, away from that distinctly subtle cocktail of her father's – coffee, morning tobacco, the last engine oil her mother's flowery detergent could never quite purge from his overalls.

'You shouldn't have driven through the night, Alexandra.

Folks fall asleep at the wheel all the time,' he said softly. He gave Alex a few more seconds' eye contact before his attention returned to her mum. Alex watched his huge gnarly hands move gently over her mum's hair. It looked redder against the stark white of the pillow. Jem was right. She didn't look like their mum. Not sick, at least, but older. Different. Fallible.

'Is she…?' Alex tried past the lump forming in her throat.

'Your mother's just sleeping. She'll be right as rain once she's had a good sleep, slowed down for five damned minutes.' He was rubbing his thumb and forefinger together, he did this when something was niggling at him and he couldn't light a cigarette.

Alex looked at the stranger in the bed. She'd never seen her sleeping like that, straight as an ironing board, sheets neatly tucked beneath her arms. It was all over if anything happened to her. Blythe was the thread holding their patchwork family together. It would all unravel without her.

'Did she like the sunflowers?' Alex heard her own voice.

Alex saw her dad's forefinger begin back and forth against his thumb again only with more intent though now, as if trying to eradicate a sharp little irritant that kept finding its way back under his skin. Alex wished she hadn't asked.

'I, er… I know purple is mum's favourite colour but the yellow…' *But the yellow was for you, Dad. Please don't clench your jaw.* He did it again. Jem saw it too and tried to pretend she hadn't, which only made it a hundred times worse. 'The yellow looked nicer against the thistles I thought…' Alex was already floundering. Ted winced and she knew then that she'd already said something wrong.

'Please, can we not talk about goddamn flowers? Just for five minutes? What the hell difference do flowers make anyway? Your mother wouldn't have even been down there if she wasn't having to cart the bloody things around.'

Alex felt herself recoil. Had her flowers arrived late? Was that why Blythe had gone back to the churchyard? Was it Alex's fault Blythe had gone back there alone?

'Sorry, Dad, I didn't mean…' She didn't know what she meant. Stupid girl.

Ted's hand opened out where he'd been rigidly holding it at his side. Alex wasn't sure if it was to placate her or to silently implore her to just. Shut. Up. Why didn't she ever have anything better to offer them?

Jem caught Alex's eye. 'We'll go and get the coffees, Dad. We don't want to overwhelm Mum when she wakes up, all cooped up in here together.'

Jem waited for the door to swing closed behind them before she spoke.

'He's tired, Alex. He didn't get much sleep last night.'

'It's fine, really,'

'Alex,' Jem's hand was already on Alex's forearm, 'the flowers, that wasn't a dig at you back in there. It was my fault, I was doing his head in on the ride here, I was going on about these evening flowers mum got so upset about. He'd already had his fill before we got here this morning.

Honestly, Al, it was just bad timing, that's all. Don't be so quick to take it to heart, OK? He's tired.'

Alex tried to relax her shoulders, let some of the tension slope away. 'What *evening flowers*?'

'Pass. That was what I was trying to work out with Dad in the car, until he bit my head off. Something Mum was talking about when Mal first got her into A&E. No-one could really understand what she was saying though.'

'Oh. I didn't know about that.' Alex tried not to feel out of the loop. 'Did Mal know what they are?'

Jem shrugged. 'I didn't think to ask Mal about it, actually. The nurse said it was all part of it, Mum being confused.' Jem rubbed her eyes as if she hadn't slept much last night either. 'Flowers that arrived in the evening, I guess.'

Evening flowers. No-one else had flowers delivered, it had to have been Alex's bouquet that had arrived late. Great. No wonder Ted was so pissed off with her already.

'What are you thinking?' Jem was studying her. Big tired blue eyes glancing out through the breaks in her fringe.

'Nothing.' Alex smiled, but it didn't reach her cheeks. She'd used one of the big flashy online department stores that offered astronomically priced 'botanical giftware'. Never again. What good were flowers that didn't arrive until the evening?

'Come on, Al. I need caffeine.'

Jem began to walk off but Alex could feel she was onto something. 'They were my flowers, weren't they? That Mum had to go back for.'

Jem looked puzzled. 'Yours the ones with no card?'

Alex nodded. She never sent a card.

'Sunflowers and thistles?' Alex nodded again. 'Then I'm sorry, sis, but as much as I know you like to be the bad guy and all, you can't take this one for the team. I signed for your bouquet after breakfast.' Jem squeezed Alex's arm. 'I don't know why Mum went back down there alone, Al, but whatever her reason was, it wasn't your flowers.' Jem turned on her heels. 'Come on, I'll show you around.'

'I don't want to go for coffee, Jem.' Alex called after her, 'I want to be here on the ward, when she wakes up.'

'Me too,' Jem reassured. 'There's a family room just through here. We won't be far.' Jem began to edge along the corridor again but Alex stayed glued to the spot. She hadn't come this far to hide out again. If her dad needed to sound off at someone then she could at least provide that for him.

Jem looked at her expectantly. Alex folded her arms and looked at her own feet like a stubborn child who didn't want to go to school. 'What *did* Malcolm Sinclair say, Jem? What happened in the churchyard? Has Mum been ill this weekend? I need to know what you and Dad know, Jem.' Alex was already picturing it again. Her mum collapsed in the cemetery overcome with the sadness of another birthday denied to Dillon. The utter needlessness of so many years without him, and not even the luxury of someone to hate for it.

Jem retraced her steps back to Alex and let out a long sigh. Jem was being patient. It was gift she rarely shared with anyone else. She leant against the wall beside Alex.

'Malcolm had to carry her in. He said Mum was agitated. She was mumbling about these bloody flowers,' Jem shrugged, '*The evening flowers! The evening flowers!* Something like that. She was still pretty worked up when me and Dad got here.'

'About *flowers*? Well, who normally sends flowers for Dill?'

'Nobody, really. Us, Helen Fairbanks always does. Susannah Finn too.' Finn's mum had never stopped being kind to them, even Alex. After everything Finn had put up with because of her.

Finn was there in her head again. 'Anyone else?' Alex pressed.

'Alex, hate to break it to you but I don't actually have all the answers.' Jem's patience was starting to wear off. 'There probably weren't any *evening flowers*, Mum was very confused. What does it matter?'

'It matters if it's enough to upset Dad like that. I've only been here five minutes and I've already annoyed him.'

Jem looked at Alex and sighed again. 'I've already told you, Al. He sounded off at me earlier too. I only asked if he thought we should go back to the church today in case anyone *had* dropped more flowers off for Dill and they needed tidying. He blew at that, too. He's worried, and probably shattered. I know he didn't sleep well, he went for a walk at 5.30 this morning for crying out loud. Probably chain-smoking.'

Alex nodded. That would be the next thing. Their dad was

going to get lung cancer off the back of all the worrying he'd had to do. Alex was going to wipe them all out eventually while she was bound to live a long and healthy life with bags of time to think about how she'd set this nasty little trail of dominoes up.

A familiar knot tightened in Alex's stomach. Her mum's grief must be unbearable. People didn't get over the loss of their children; it was a universal truth.

The question fell from Alex's mouth. 'What if it wasn't a stroke?'

'What do you mean?'

Surely it was their mum's heart that had finally had enough. 'Are they sure it wasn't her heart, Jem?'

'It was a stroke Alex. Not a heart attack.'

'But what did Mal see?'

Jem shook her head and huffed. 'Mal was… a bit sketchy actually. He said Mum looked unwell. I think he saw her in the churchyard and just went over to say hello, I guess.'

'Did she look upset? Did he think Mum had been crying?'

'What? No, I don't think so. Alex, you're as bad as Dad.'

'What do you mean?'

'With the random questions! Dad practically interrogated Mal last night, *What have you said to my wife? Are you responsible for this, Sinclair?*' Jem solemnly tucked her hair behind one ear and shook her head. 'You should've heard him. Dad was really horrible to Mal, actually.'

'Dad thought *Malcolm* had upset Mum?'

'Apparently. I tried to tell him. Mal Sinclair couldn't upset himself. Mal's just like his dad was.' Jem had been fond of Mal, once upon a time, and the mayor.

'Sorry, Jem. I should've been here.' Alex shrank back against the corridor wall.

'Dad wanted to know what they'd been talking about. Mal said they hadn't had a chance to talk about anything except the fluttering she was having and…'

'Fluttering? Again? Jem, why didn't you say that?' Alex knew it would be her heart. 'We need to tell the doctors, before it happens again!' It was a miracle they hadn't done her in before now, the fluttery palpitations her mum habitually played down since their sudden onset a decade ago.

One of the nurses at the desk was looking over at them. Jem blew her fringe from her eyes again. 'I'm going to need coffee if we're getting into all this, Al. It wasn't her heart, OK? Will you please listen to me? If the fluttering business had bothered her that much, she'd have seen somebody about it before now.'

'Do you really believe that, Jem?'

Blythe liked to make light of it. It was like a butterfly trapped in a jar that was all. You didn't trouble the doctor over a butterfly heart. A stampeding herd of wildebeest in there, fair enough, but not butterflies.

Jem smiled sweetly down the corridor towards the nurses' station. Alex slumped back against the wall next to her mother's room. Whatever it was that was in her mother's heart, wildebeest or butterflies, Alex knew why they were in there. Alex was staring at her shoes again when Jem gently kicked her own foot against Alex's.

'It was a stroke, Alex. Nothing anyone could've foreseen. Nothing anyone else is responsible for. Let it go.'

The door into Blythe's room swept open. He might've looked older, but Ted was still a mountain of a man, tall and broad and handsome, as fathers should be.

Alex stood a little straighter. Her dad came to stand in front of her and scratched softly at the flop of grey-blond hair over his eyes.

'I shouldn't have snapped at you just now, Alex. I'm just a, er, a little…' Alex watched him try to choose his words.

'It's OK, Dad.'

Ted managed a brief smile. Jem's eyes bounced back and forth as if she were spectating at Wimbledon.

'I didn't think you'd wait to drive up here to your mother, you should've come to the house,' he said. 'I waited for you on the porch.' He would've waited there longer for her too, had he not started thinking the same old thoughts, tying himself in knots until he'd found himself stalking angrily down to St Cuthbert's.

'It was early. I didn't know if you'd be awake…' But she knew it was a rubbish lie before she told it.

'You're my daughter. And it's never too early in the day to see your child arrive safely home, Alexandra.'

CHAPTER 11

'Jem? Are you hungry yet? I think we should wait until Dad gets home. Shall one of us call him?'

Alex's voice bounced up through the house as she sniffed the contents of the heavy casserole dish on the kitchen table. How Helen Fairbanks had managed to hoist all that cast iron and lamb hotpot up to the house and leave it on the porch deck without putting her back out was an enigma, but Mrs Fairbanks was one of those practical can-do women, cut from the same old-school cloth as Blythe and Susannah Finn. 'Jem?' Alex yelled again. Jem had regressed back to her early teens since they'd got back to the house. She'd been upstairs on the other side of a closed bedroom door while Alex had skulked around the kitchen in quiet contemplation. Someone had to keep the new puppy from chewing or piddling on anything else and Jem still seemed immune to all things cute and cuddly. Alex meandered back out from the hall. Their parents' kitchen was still homely and vast as any of the other farmhouse kitchens along the track, it still smelled of the dried lavender Blythe had tied to the beams and the ashes in the Aga, despite the new addition to the household peeing with excitement every time Alex walked into the room.

*

Alex's stomach growled. Helen Fairbanks' mercy meals were legendary. Over by the log basket a bundle of fur the colour of wheat fields heard the noises of Alex's gastric processes and began wagging herself to death again. The pup waddled excitedly towards Alex, a wet trail in her wake. 'Agh, not *again*!' Alex groaned. 'You're like a tap… *dog*.' The dog needed a name. Alex seemed to be the object of its unwavering affection and if they were going to have this intimate relationship of ankle-licking and wee-clearing every time the thing set eyes on her, the dog definitely needed a name.

Alex listened to the bump bump bump of Jem finally plodding down the wooden stairs. Jem bobbed lethargically back into the kitchen, her hair tied up now like the renegade ballerina she'd briefly been in her childhood. Alex had only just shook her own out, her scalp was still throbbing from having had its hair follicles pulled back too vigorously, too carelessly in the rush to make the drive up here.

'You cut your hair,' Jem observed, reaching for the auburn tendrils sitting against Alex's shoulders. Alex finished placing a knife and fork aside the last of the three placemats their mum had already set out for Jem's weekend stay.

'Yeah. Think I should've just hacked the lot off though.

I have to keep it tied back all the time at work, so…' Not to mention the swimming issue. It only took a few strands to break free and start floating around her face to freak her out completely.

'Looks nice, anyway. You look like Mum did, in that photo she used to have of her and Dad.' Alex frowned. 'At the mayor's annual dinner.'

Alex fished for the memory. 'Oh, yeah. The one with Mayor Sinclair letting Dad wear his gold BA Baracas chains. I haven't seen that picture for years.' She smiled. It was one of her dad's favourites. He used to tell everyone how he'd fallen in love with their mum all over again that night, she looked so beautiful. Like Grace Kelly. Grandma Ros had insisted that picture be kept in the hallway where visitors would definitely see it, having your photo taken with the mayor and his wife was a badge of honour too shiny to be left in a back room.

Jem moved lethargically over to her chair. Her mood seemed to have been on a steady decline since their debate on who should to call Mal for a proper chat about what had happened last night. Alex was probably just over-scrutinising again. Finn had accused her of that the night he'd showed up at her university digs, of looking for a problem until she found one.

An image of Finn, chest heaving with the rigours of his morning run poked Alex in her mind's eye again. This morning was a fluke, it didn't mean they would keep bumping into each other, not necessarily. Even if they did, a simple *hello* would suffice. Just a nice, polite hello, like old friends. They weren't kids any more, were they?

'Neither have I actually.'

'What?'

'Seen that photo of Mum and Dad and the Sinclairs. Can't say I miss not seeing Louisa's sour face every time I come into the house though,' Jem said. 'You know, she called me a thief once. Said I'd stolen one of the ornaments from Sinclair Heights. Like I'd want anything out of the mayoral mansion.'

Mal hadn't grown up in a mansion, but he'd been the most well kitted-out kid Alex and Jem had ever played with. Ted had said they were the perks of being an only child. Mal had told them over toasted marshmallows one night that his dad really wanted Mal to have a brother but Louisa said no because she detested being fat.

'Ornaments?'

'Yeah, that miniature Viking ship, of Dill's remember? I was showing it to Mal, he had one similar and was trying to tell me how valuable his was because it had these markings on the bottom.' Jem's face twisted as she recalled the tale. 'Then Louisa saw me showing Dill's ship to Mal and freaked. Said I was trying to steal it, that it belonged to a set of theirs *Malcolm's father keeps in his private study.*' Jem imitated Louisa's acerbic voice. 'She told me it was *about time I stopped acting like a little thug* and how coming from a family with no money was no excuse.'

Alex whistled. 'That'll do it.'

'Oh yeah, she also said I should start behaving like a "lady".' Jem held her fingers up to denote inverted commas. 'Starting with rectifying my *boy's haircut*.'

Alex bit at her lip. She felt for Jem, everyone knew Mal's mum was a tyrant. Alex had been lucky on the 'boy-friend's mothers' score, Susannah Finn had treated Alex like a daughter, virtually.

'To be fair, you were always a bit thuggish, Jem. But you never looked like a boy… not once your crew cut grew out a bit, anyway.' Alex smiled, trying for a little light relief at the expense of Jem's historic rash makeover choices. *I just wanted a change*, had been Jem's official line when the head had sent her home. Alex had made a few of her own dodgy fashion statements in her teens but only Jem had ever come home from school with a short back and sides.

Jem wasn't listening; she was too busy looking blankly at her mobile phone.

'So who won?' Alex asked, straightening the place set-tings. Her mum always laid the table so elegantly, an art form with its own choreography.

'Won what?'

'The battle of the Viking ship?'

Jem winked. 'There was no way she was keeping that lit-tle carved ship. It's in Dill's room now, go and have a look.'

Alex caught her smile before it dropped. She didn't go in there. Mum had kept it nice, unchanged. Everything in its place like her finely laid table settings. Alex didn't even want to risk moving the dust in Dill's room.

'I believe you, Jem. How'd you get it back off her?'

Jem grimaced at her phone and slapped it onto the table, slumping into one of the chunky wooden chairs. 'Louisa? I'd have prised it from her bony fingers if I'd have had to, Al. As it happened, Mal's dad came home. You should've seen Louisa's face when the mayor told her she'd made a mistake. Nearly killed her handing it back, you'd have thought she was handing me Mal's inheritance. Anyway…' Jem wriggled herself more upright in her seat, 'your room's all sorted, Mum and I already changed all the bedclothes yesterday.'

'Thanks, Jem.'

'No worries.' Jem lifted her phone again, twisting it in an attempt to find a gobbet of phone signal somewhere over the tablecloth. She huffed and stood up again. 'I could do with a drink. There must be a bottle of Pinot here somewhere.'

There wasn't, Ted was teetotal now. Blythe didn't keep a drop in the house any more, Jem knew that just as well as Alex.

'Are you OK, Jem? You seem preoccupied?'

'Hmm? Sorry. It's just work, being difficult.' Jem's phone had been bleeping all afternoon, until they'd driven back into dodgy mobile signal territory and the bleeping had died a death.

'Is that who you were on the phone to?' Alex asked. Jem had been up there for over an hour. 'You haven't given your work the house number have you, Jem? You've said it before, they don't exactly respect your work–life balance.'

'Ha! Nope, those lines have definitely been blurred.'

Alex felt a pang of territorialism. Jem was needed here, her swanky jewellery company could sod off.

'Can't they cope on their own for a while?' Dan would never bother Alex here. He'd already insisted she take all the time she needed from the food bank. Jem came back to the table, examining the base of her glass. She poured the water Alex had set out and hovered. 'George is under a lot of pressure, Alex. We have a huge opportunity coming up. There's a lot to get through.'

'Who's George? Your boss? Or just the bloke tasked with tracking you down to Mum's bedroom phone?' Alex felt her eyebrow rise like her dad's would whenever he used to catch them on his bedroom phone.

Jem looked guilty. She set the water jug back down and braced herself on the back of the chair. 'George can be… difficult. Thinks everything is always so simple… black and white,' she muttered, sliding back into her seat.

'How nice for George.'

Jem obviously didn't want to get into it. 'Did you call me before?'

'I wanted to know if you were ready to eat? Or do you think Dad might leave the hospital soon?' Alex pulled the lid away from Mrs Fairbanks' pot and beheld six fat juicy dumplings proudly peeping from a puddle of rich gravy. Saliva rushed into her mouth. She never ate like this any more. Casserole for one? Unlikely.

'That was Dad on the phone just then.'

'Still nothing?' Alex asked. It had only been an hour and a half since they'd left them at Kerring General, Ted still pacing, Blythe still sleeping. Soundly they all hoped.

'Nope. I told Dad to go and get a paper, have a smoke or something, not that I want to encourage his bad habits. I think the nurses are wearing him down though. They've promised to call him if there's any change, he was just mulling over leaving.'

'We'll wait then. He must be starving.' Alex clamped the lid back onto the pot, her stomach grumbled again in protest.

Jem nodded at Alex's tee. 'I don't think Jaws is willing to wait. Come on, dish up. I'll put Dad's in the oven.

Alex was still weighing it up when a ladleful of food fell onto the plate in front of her.

Alex bit into a tender piece of hot lamb and nearly slipped taste bud first into a state of euphoria. 'Bloody hell, Mal Sinclair got lucky marrying Millie! I wonder if she can cook like her mum.'

Jem smiled disinterestedly. 'Who knows? Probably. Millie's probably perfect wife material, she'd have to be to get the green light from Louisa Sinclair just to spend time with her little Malcy, let alone *marry* him.'

Alex detected a nip in the air. She wasn't completely convinced it didn't smell of sour grapes. Nothing drove a wedge like an old boyfriend. Jem had never admitted to it but their mum had seen her and Mal 'in a tryst' outside Frobisher's Tea Rooms in town once. Blythe had called Alex up at university specifically to tap her for inside knowledge.

'I thought you and Millie used to be good friends?'

'Years ago, maybe.'

'Oh.'

'Do you see her much?' Alex asked with a mouthful. 'When you're home? Don't tell me she's still gorgeous and slender, not with food like this firing out of her mum's kitchen?' Millie Fairbanks had always reminded Alex of Sandra Dee on *Grease*. Prim and lovely, and only a pair of black satin trousers away from total sex-goddessdom.

'Not really.'

'Not really what? Not really gorgeous or not really, you don't see her much?'

'I don't see Millie.'

Jem yanked a slice of bread in two. Alex silently chewed a piece of swede. 'That's too bad. I always liked Millie.'

'A few ballet classes doesn't make you besties, Alex. Anyway, she was pallier with Carrie in the end.'

Alex took another bite of food. It was probably best not to get into it. She'd eaten four melt-in-the-mouth potato morsels before Jem spoke again. 'Did you know they have a kid now?'

Alex backtracked her thoughts but couldn't find where they'd left off. 'Who?'

'Mal and Millie.' Jem laughed under her breath. 'They even sound like they should be a couple.'

'Oh, yeah. I think I heard something. A boy?'

'Alfie. He's four. Looks just like his dad did at his age, apparently.'

'Oh.'

'But I hear he has Millie's dark eyes, not blue like Mal's.'

'I see.'

Jem nodded wistfully. 'Helen spent nearly the whole time I was at the mayor's funeral walking me through all of her grandson's milestones. It was lucky she'd taken her funeral handbag and not her everyday handbag or I'd have been looking through albums of the things, I reckon.'

'You went to the mayor's funeral?'

'Sure. He was always nice to me when I hung out at Mal's house, unlike his serpentine wife. I really liked him. Didn't you?'

'I guess. I never really saw much of him after Mum finished helping him at the library.'

Jem shrugged. 'I liked him. He always asked me stuff about Dill, as if he thought it was important to keep talking about him or something. Anyway, someone had to go. The Fosters and Sinclairs go way back. Everyone knows…'

'The Fosters and Sinclairs have the longest bloodlines in these parts,' they both said in unison. Jem grinned. She had a brilliant grin. Infectious, Alex always caught it.

'Good old Mum. The genealogical guru of Eilidh Town Hall.' Everyone wanted to be of Viking descent in Eilidh Falls, the mayor had been no exception. 'So the mayor wasn't cast adrift on a burning pyre then?' Alex teased.

'No pyre.' Jem smiled.

'Why didn't Mum and Dad go?' Blythe and Ted had moved in the same social circles as the Sinclairs once, until

Helen and Millie Fairbanks' car had collided with a wagon at the bottom of the bridge on Eilidh high street, just after it had left a service at Foster & Son's Autos.

'Not sure, it was weird. They both had this mystery bug they didn't want to pass on. So I went on my own.'

Jem reached for more water. Something pretty caught Alex's eye. 'Jem! Your bracelet! Did your company make that?'

'Ah, just a little something I knocked up.' Jem said modestly.

'It's beautiful, Jem,' Alex admired, running a finger over the edge of the bracelet. 'I bet you've sold a few of these.' Pottery had been Alex's bag. She'd been all set to become the next Emma Bridgewater.

'I wish. I've only made two, they're such a bugger to make. I do love them though. They're my best pieces.'

'Have you seen *Wedding Wars*?'

'*Wedding Wars*?'

OK, so Alex probably needed to rein in the late night telly watching. 'Jem, I'm telling you, you should go into the bridal market. You'd make a fortune.'

'And deal with all those finicky bridezillas or, worse, their mums? No thanks. They're not all as chilled out as Blythe, you know. Just ask Mal.' Jem stabbed at a piece of carrot then thought better of eating it. 'I wonder when her next meal will be.'

Alex had stopped eating too. She pushed a slice of potato around her plate. She'd been hasty, hopeful this morning of her mum waking up and them bringing her home in no time. Then they'd come in to change Blythe's catheter and Alex realised. Blythe wasn't just sleeping, she was dependent. For now, at least.

Alex sat perfectly still, listening to the clinking of Jem's cutlery against her plate and a houseful of silence behind it. 'She needs to come home, Jem. It's too quiet.'

'She will. This place will be jumping again once she's home.' But they both knew that it probably wouldn't. It had been years since either of them had heard the sounds of their childhood. Years since Blythe's voice had effortlessly chased the rising and falling of dramatic melodies while *Madama Butterfly* or *La Traviata* played through the house. When Blythe did eventually come home it would just be more obvious. Dill had taken all the noise with him.

12th September 2004

'You're *lying*.' Ted's voice sounded thin against the cheery 20s jazz playing out in Frobisher's Tea Rooms.

Louisa's hand was trembling. Her glass lying upended on the table-top. She wiped at the lipstick smeared messily from her lips. Ted saw the tears pooling in her eyes and felt nothing. He might have worried that he'd hurt her, been too rough, if he could think straight.

Louisa's eyes darted about the tea rooms but the waitresses wouldn't see them sitting here. Louisa had chosen the booth, tucked away by the little side window.

She swallowed back angry tears. 'But you know that I'm not, don't you, Ted? I can see it in your face.'

He should never have come here. Then he wouldn't have had to listen to her spiteful proposition, wouldn't have had to push her away. Wouldn't have made her *want* to hurt him back so cruelly.

'Stop talking, Louisa. Just…'

He brought his sleeve over his own mouth, in case any of that red was left on his. His hands were shaking too. Ted rose slowly from his chair. Louisa's eyes grew wide.

'Where are you going? You can't just leave.'

He should never have come. 'Home, Louisa. To my family. I promised my son we'd play with his new arrows.' The bow and arrows. Ted pictured Malcolm bringing them over to the house for Dillon. He felt himself hunch over the table for a moment, his fingers grasp the edge of the table-top.

Louisa's chin wobbled. She held herself rigid and glared up at him. 'You go back to her then,' she spat. 'To that frumpy little wife of yours. But I hope you're good at pretending, Edward Foster.'

CHAPTER 12

'Every case is different, Mr Foster. It's still very early days and there's no saying how your wife's symptoms will continue to present. I'm afraid it can be something of a guessing game in the initial weeks.'

Alex could tell her dad was trying to decipher how old this man delivering the fate of their family could possibly be. For a moment she found herself playing along. Dr Okafor was handsome in that way all young, intelligent here-to-help-your-suffering-loved-one people were, with his rectangular-rimmed glasses and candy-pink shirt that was only ever going to be OK on an acute assessment unit because he was educated, and knowledgeable, and because it complemented his flawless black skin perfectly.

Alex glanced at Jem to see if she was evaluating Dr Okafor too. Jem's hand was resting comfortably through the crook of their dad's arm. 'You're saying she might be in hospital for *weeks*? Even though she's woken up and managed to drink and…'

Dr Okafor lifted his hands apologetically. 'We are very

encouraged by your mother's progress this morning, Miss Foster, but before you go in to see her you must be made aware that recovery can be unpredictable and sometimes erratic. As the swelling on Mrs Foster's brain reduces, we would hope to see further changes in the rate of her progress but it can be a very... *disorientating* experience for your mother.'

Alex found her voice. 'So what are you saying, Doctor?'

He looked softly at Alex, as if delivery was something they spent a whole semester's study on in med school. 'It is quite possible that your mother's symptoms could get worse before she starts to feel better, and that is something we should keep in mind. Did you know that your wife suffers from arrhythmia, Mr Foster?'

Bingo. Dr Okafor had just delivered a body blow. It didn't matter how much older and wiser Ted was, this guy, this kid, knew stuff. Important stuff that he didn't. About his Blythe. 'Arrhythmia?' Jem ventured.

'It's her heart, Jem.' Alex's voice snagged, unready to speak when she'd wanted it to.

Dr Okafor smiled and dipped his head. 'That's correct. Arrhythmia is essentially irregular beating of the heart, its rhythm. Sometimes this can be the cause of the stroke, sometimes the effect. Has your wife ever complained of problems in this area, Mr Foster? Any discomfort, breathlessness, palpitations... maybe no more than a fluttering sensation?'

Alex felt her neck burning up. *I did this to her.* She knew it. She'd known it since she put down the phone to Jem in the cubicle at the leisure centre.

Alex heard her dad clear his throat. He wasn't going to be caught out by a snagging voice, his age and experience at least gave him that much. 'My wife's a busy woman, Doctor. It takes a lot to slow her down. If Blythe has had any problems with her heart,' he cleared his throat again, 'she hasn't shared them with me.' Alex couldn't read her dad's expression. Her mum wouldn't have kept that from him, would she? Her parents didn't keep anything from each other, they didn't have secrets, they just weren't the sort.

Ted battled on. 'Would she have had these palpitations all the time, Doctor? Or could they be triggered by something?'

Jem looked just as surprised by Ted's obliviousness. Alex frowned. Why hadn't her mum shared this with him? She deserved his support, why forfeit that and hide a fluttering sodding time-bomb, waiting to go off in St Cuthbert's churchyard?

'The symptoms might have been present day to day, Mr Foster,' said Doctor Okafor, 'or just here and there for no particular reason. There can be triggers. Stress, for example, can be a factor. There are many aspects we should consider.'

The burning in Alex's neck was sweeping up through her head. *Stress can be a factor.* Stress. Define stress, Doctor. How about, say, the drowning of your only son? The years robbed of celebrating his birthdays like a normal family. The thought of him gasping his last desperate breaths while the daughter you'd entrusted him to was making goo-goo eyes at her boyfriend in the bushes. Would *that* be an aspect worth considering? Would *that* affect the rhythm of a mother's heart?

Jem was looking over. *In through the nose, out through the mouth...* Alex could feel her heart thudding in her chest. Was arrhythmia contagious? Like an infectious yawn, jumping from one person to the next? She hoped so. She deserved it, she bloody well deserved it.

A bleep began pulling Alex from the internal disaster gathering pace inside her ribcage.

'I'm terribly sorry. Would you excuse me? I'll come and find you all again as soon as I'm back on the ward,' Dr Okafor said apologetically.

Ted offered the doctor his hand, his acceptance of the younger man's competence – his gratitude for it. Somewhere on the periphery, Alex heard Jem utter her thanks to the doctor too, then Jem's voice grew louder beside Alex's ear. 'Come on, let's go and give her a kiss.'

They filed into Room 2. Alex went in last, Blythe's tired eyes dodging Ted and Jem, finding their way straight to her. Alex felt the muscles in her face ready themselves for a full on explosion of something unsightly. No. She wouldn't. She had no right to cry so she swallowed it all down and let her throat close around it like a drawstring.

'Hey, Mum,' Jem said softly. Alex watched Jem sweep the hair from their mother's face so it framed her equally on both sides of her pillow. Jem dove straight in for a kiss.

'Mum? Alex is here,' she declared, as if presenting their mother with the magic tincture that would save her.

'Hi, Mum,' Alex croaked. She needed to learn to swallow before she spoke, like her dad. Alex nudged herself forwards to the edge of her mother's bed. It felt like nudging herself towards the edge of the pool at the leisure centre, her breathing elevating with each tentative step forwards. Blythe's eyes slid shut as if she were drifting off to sleep again but Alex knew it was her invitation to nuzzle in all that paleness. Her mother's cheek was warm, Alex laid a kiss there and held her face over it for a few seconds, to be sure it stuck. 'Hi, Mum.' she whispered again, her voice steadier now. 'Didn't see about those butterflies then?' Alex pulled back to see her mother attempt a smile but one side of Blythe's mouth remained slackened, unwilling.

Blythe mumbled. Alex tried to make it out but it was like trying to pick out a familiar face on the other side of mottled glass, the outline of her mum's words there but the detail obscured. Alex took a steadying breath. That awful sound couldn't have just come from her mum, from the same place those beautiful arias used to reach from on Sunday mornings when Alex was still lazing in bed and her mum was trying to keep pace with her favourite sopranos.

'How are you feeling, Mum?' Something had happened to Jem's voice too. Ted's face was grave, his oil-stained hands hanging at his sides, both thumbs rubbing relentlessly against their neighbouring fingers. He was clearing his throat again, over and over, trying to ready his voice like an engine on one of his cars, it was turning over but not quite ready to fire up like it should.

Blythe murmured again, more decipherable this time, as if she were simply drunk or groggy from the dentist. 'Hell-lo. My darl—' Blythe stopped.

'Oh, Mum.' Jem whispered.

Ted still wasn't ready, his thumb still rubbing back and forth. Alex felt that drawstring in her throat tighten again. Her mum's eyes shone with effort. Somebody had to return her pitiful attempt; someone had to validate it. It came from nowhere, an eruption of fortitude.

'It's all right, Mum. Everything's going to be all right.' Alex smiled, forcing her facial muscles to do what her mother's couldn't and bluff through this new horror that had descended on them. 'We're going to help you get back on your feet, Mum. You're going to be OK.' Alex felt herself default to work mode, it was like an outer body experience. She knew this role, the gentle encouragement, the championing of small steps back to something more familiar, more bearable. For a few sweet seconds Alex was galvanised, and then she caught sight of the small glistening trace of saliva escaping from one side of her mum's mouth. Something began crumbling inside her. Blythe didn't need a square meal and a few shopping bags of emergency food. It wasn't Blythe's financial situation that was broken. It was her self.

CHAPTER 13

Susannah Finn had left a chicken chasseur on the front porch. Two mercy meals in two nights. First Helen Fairbanks, now Finn's mum. The chasseur had been repeating on Alex for the last hour. At first she'd thought it was the indigestion keeping her awake but she'd tried a glass of milk, two Rennies from the back of her mum's medicine shelf in the pantry and, finally, the last dregs of a bottle of Gaviscon that been out of date for four months. Three trips downstairs, three clean-up operations each time the puppy had bounded towards Alex's legs, peeing as she went.

Alex sat in her dad's chair, the puppy asleep in her lap. She looked out through the lounge window onto the darkness outside. The front path was lit pale by the moonlight. It must've looked the same to Susannah as it did the last time she'd brought a food parcel up to their house, the sherry trifle Susannah had made for them all the Christmas after Dill's accident.

It had started with a kindness. That was Helen and Susannah's role, to help Alex's mum, jolly Blythe's family as best they could through the festive season. Helen had knitted Ted a Christmas jumper with a giant pudding on the front and wanted Alex and Jem's reassurances that they'd make him wear it at least once. Susannah had made them all the trifle because she knew how the girls had enjoyed it the year before.

Alex stared into the darkness and remembered Susannah and Finn pulling up to the house. Alex had stationed herself there at the window on snow watch. It had been trying all day. Alex had watched through the glass as Finn had carried the large crystal bowl up the path. Her dad had been out there on the porch, freezing despite Helen Fairbanks' cheery jumper, his Christmas bottle of Jack Daniel's already opened and half gone. When he'd stood, Alex had first thought it was to greet them.

Alex squeezed her eyes closed and felt for Susannah all over again. Susannah hadn't known what she was walking into, what she was walking Finn into. She must've thought about it earlier this evening when leaving that chasseur on the porch. Ted must've thought about it too, he hadn't touched Susannah's dinner tonight.

'What do you think you're doing bringing *him* to my house?' Ted had slurred. Susannah hadn't read the situation, hadn't realised the danger. Why would she have? None of them had seen him that way, it wasn't the norm. Alex remembered how she'd wanted to intercept, but she'd froze instead.

Jem had heard Rodolfo bark and had gone outside to tell him off on the porch. Their dad's voice had twisted. He'd waved his glass of JD and slurred at Jem, spilling some on his shoes. 'Joy to the goddamned world! Mrs Finn has brought her little boy over. He probably wants to try his luck again with your sister. Perhaps you can go start a house fire, Jem? So he can watch us burn while he has another crack of the whip.'

Susannah's face had lapsed in horror.

Blythe rushed from the house. 'Ted, that's enough. You're upsetting the girls.' But it had been the tremor in Blythe's voice that had scared Alex the most. That was when Susannah and Finn had stopped walking, hovering halfway down the lawn like two rabbits spotted by a fox, as Ted stepped off the porch.

'Ah, look, Blythe. They've brought dessert! Now I'm not saying I don't like, what is that? Trifle? Now I'm not saying I don't like trifle, Susannah, but I don't think it's really a fair swap now is it? My son, for your trifle? Lose a child, gain a pudding… I mean, call me ungrateful…' They'd all watched in horror as he'd took another glug from his bottle.

Alex made it out through the hallway and onto the porch. 'Dad, don't,' she'd tried. They'd all tried. But he was like a juggernaut.

Susannah had tried to turn Finn back towards the car. Jem, fearless Jem, had tried to hold her own father back, all on her own. A thirteen-year-old girl with skinny arms trying to stand against the biggest man in their lives. Blythe hadn't thought twice, she'd taken no chances and had gone back in to call the police.

'Stay away from my son, Ted. You're upset, we all are.'

'Can't he talk for himself, Susannah? Fight his own battles?'

'He's eighteen years old.'

'S'posed to be a man then. But you're no man, are you?' Alex rubbed the puppy in her lap more vigorously while she pictured her dad jabbing a finger into Finn's chest. 'You're just like your father aren't you, boy? He hid behind your mother too. You're a coward, just like him.'

'Don't speak to my son like that. And don't you dare touch him again!'

'Take what you want from my family and then leave us to pick up the pieces. The consequences of your actions. Well you're not coming near my family again, *Finn*.'

'I'm warning you, Edward Foster.'

Blythe rushed back out of the house then. 'I've called the police, Susannah. I'm sorry. Please, take Finn home. Now.' But the juggernaut just kept going.

'I don't expect you to see it, Susannah. You're his mother. A mother can love anything. A mother's love goes beyond all, it doesn't matter what her son has done, or even what piece of shit fathered him.'

Blythe began sobbing. 'Ted, please.'

'And what have you got, Susie? For all your unconditional love? A selfish little bastard who only cares about himself, and getting his end away WITH MY DAUGHTER!'

That was when Finn had pushed his mother behind him, still managing somehow to hang on to the trifle.

'I'm sorry for what my dad did to your business, Mr Foster. And I'm sorry I couldn't get to Dillon quicker than I did. I tried. I promise you, I tried. But I don't only care about myself, you're wrong about that. I care about your daughter. A lot. Actually, Mr Foster… I'm pretty sure that… I love her.'

He hadn't meant to, but Finn had flipped the switch.

'What did you say to me?'

'Son, go wait in the car,' Susannah tried again. Finn didn't move.

'I'm not leaving you here, Mum.' Finn had straightened up; he'd looked older to Alex then. Not the lad she'd been wiling away free periods at college with, but a grown man, standing firm, a matter of feet from her father.

Ted staggered further across the grass, closing the distance between them. 'What did you just say about my daughter?'

Finn seemed to reconsider. And then, 'I said, I love her.'

Alex heard the crack. Finn's face exploded in a red riot. The blood was so much brighter than everything else, redder than Ted's Christmas jumper, redder than the strawberries that would pepper the path shortly afterwards.

Ted snarled like a wild animal. 'If you love my daughter, let me hear you say it again, boy!'

Alex looked at Finn, the blood was streaming over his mouth. She shook her head, imploring him not to. *Please, Finn… don't*, she mouthed. Alex saw something in his expression shift – step down. Finn looked beaten, in every sense.

Ted stood over him, nostrils flared like a wild animal. 'Didn't think so.'

CHAPTER 14

Ted's back was aching. Hunkering over car engines wasn't a job for the over sixties, not even for spritely and dashing senior citizens like him, Blythe had teased. 'A man with André Rieu's hairline and the jaw of Michael Douglas shouldn't always be caked in grease. Ted should allow himself more down time, he could learn to enjoy the garden with her, they could take trips away, go spend time with the girls. What Blythe had meant was that he couldn't keep on slugging it out alone in the garage as the arthritis slowly advanced.

Ted swirled the mug of coffee in his hand and repositioned himself against the flaking blue doorframe so the twinge in his muscles didn't bite too deeply. It felt good to get out of that godforsaken hospital. It had been Alexandra's idea. She'd turned into a mother hen yesterday, clucking around devising a plan of action they could all work with. It was good to hear her with a bit more life inside her. Not like her mother.

Ted cleared his throat. Alex was right, it did make sense for the girls to stay at the hospital in the daytime. He needed to keep the garage ticking over, keep the money coming in. *Keep out of everyone's way.* Then the girls could go back to the farmhouse and Ted could go to see Blythe then. The evenings would be just for the two of them.

And what about the long term? What if she needs help? Well he wasn't having a stranger to care for her. No chance in hell was that going to happen. Maybe it was time he started winding things down here. Stop putting it off and just accept it. It wasn't going to be like when his old man hung up his wrench and handed it all over, the responsibility and the good family name. There was no-one Ted could pass the baton to. All those generations of Foster men who'd lived and grafted here in the Falls and now they were at the end of the line.

Maybe Dillon wouldn't have wanted to be a grease monkey anyway; the world worked differently these days. Sons didn't always follow their fathers.

Ted looked at the backs of his hands, veined and battered from years of work in the cold, a sixty-three year old man not knowing what it had all been for. To sell to some snot-nosed developer who'd knock the place down and stick something else for the tourists on here. *Souvenirs of Ragnarok,* or some other nonsense. He'd spent his whole life here, he'd fought for this place, this family business. This was the yard he'd unwittingly sent a young mother and her child from in a death-trap. The same yard he'd held on to by his blackened fingernails one desperate job at a time after the papers had used words like *negligent* and *sloppy* and people had stopped coming. *Never again*. Never again would he hire help after what Susannah Finn's scumbag husband did. *Now I've got to watch your goddamn son coming and going across the street.*

Over the road, Torben's shop door swung open. Finn stepped out with another pot of paint and climbed the ladders back up to the new sign there. Finn had grown into a man, something Dillon would never do. Now here he was back again, strolling about the Falls without a care in the world while Dill lay perpetually sleeping in St Cuthbert's. And why? *Because that little bastard was pawing at my daughter in the nettles while her brother was fighting for his—* Ted stopped himself. He'd promised Jem he'd try to keep a handle on his blood pressure after losing his temper with Malcolm Sinclair in the hospital. He could already feel it rising like mercury in his veins.

Ted rubbed a rough hand over his bristles, annoyed at himself for inviting the mayor's boy back into his thoughts. He let his grievances with Finn slip away while the more pressing issue crashed back into his mind. Did Malcolm know? After all this time? Ted had lain awake nearly half the night thinking about it. *He knows all right, the whole sordid tale.* Ted had seen it in Malcolm's eyes at the hospital. He hadn't meant to be so hostile towards Malcolm but it was a knee-jerk reaction. The urge to protect his girls from this dirty little secret, instantly there again.

Ted rummaged through his pockets, but he'd promised her. He felt the packet of tobacco in his breast pocket but left it there. *We don't need any more secrets between us right now, Blythe.*

Over at the hardware store, Finn was painting out the lettering on Torben's old sign. Ted began bothering at the rough skin on his thumb. Three goddamn days he'd spent up that ladder with his little artsy brushes, flashing that grin on the women as they stopped to admire his work. How had Alexandra ever fallen for all that, with his little pencils and pads, acting like some virtuoso? Ted scratched the back of his head. *Stop winding yourself up, you old fool.* He pushed himself off the doorframe and lobbed the last dregs of his drink onto the yard floor before heading back inside and down into the refuge of the garage pit.

A familiar motor was pulling into the yard when Ted resurfaced for more coffee.

Holy shit and damnation. The sharks were already circling. Ted waited for the silver Aston to find its spot.

'Goddamn woman,' he muttered.

The petite elfin blonde pushed open her door and swung her knees out from the car as if she was Princess Stephanie of goddamn Monaco. Louisa Sinclair had smelled blood already. Ted looked away while she gathered her bag and gloves and sauntered through the blue doors careful not to brush her expensive clothes against anything that might soil her.

'Hello, Edward.'

Ted's blood ran cool over the back of his neck. The backgammon boys down at the Cavern were all wild for the

Mayor's widow. Ted had thought her beautiful once, stunning even, now all he saw was a woman aged with bitterness and venom. All the lipstick and pearls in the world weren't gonna save that.

Ted snuggled his hands up into his armpits. 'Louisa,' he replied tentatively.

'How are you, poor thing?' Louisa drawled. Louisa Sinclair formed her words as if they were each a perfect little package, like those fancy canapés she used to have served at her awful dinner parties.

'Something wrong with the Aston, Louisa?'

'Oh no,' she laughed, a small breathy sound, sharp and sickly like a puff of cheap perfume. Louisa wouldn't bring her car here anyway.

Ted sighed. 'Well shall we cut to it then? Some of us have to work for a living.'

'Oh don't be like that, Edward. I'm only calling in on you to say how sorry I am to hear of Blythe's ill health, poor thing. You must be worried sick.'

Ted clenched his teeth. So little officer Malcolm had saved the day then reported back to his mother. Now Ted had to stand here and listen to Blythe's name spoken in perfect, sickly sweet formation.

'Blythe is going to be just fine,' Ted replied mechanically, taking the rag from his pocket and wiping the oil from his hands, 'thank you for asking. Is there anything else I can help you with, Louisa?'

Louisa reached out to touch his hand but Ted drew it

away before she could make contact. 'Edward. I do believe you are being ungracious. I'm merely extending a courtesy to an old friend. Much in the same way I would expect you and Blythe to do. Which reminds me, we didn't see you at Alfred's funeral in January.'

'Sorry for your loss,' Ted remarked coolly, but they both knew Ted was glad Sinclair was good and dead. Louisa's eyes hardened. 'We were sick. Didn't want to spread it around, Louisa. No-one would have thanked us for it. Anyway, Jem went, in our place.' Blythe had said she felt sick, Ted had just played along.

'Yes. I saw her. I have to admit, Ted, I didn't recognise her at first glance. Jem looks quite the picture of femininity, now that she's started dressing… appropriately.'

Ted shifted. Dancing around with a snake wasn't going to stop it biting. 'Wind your goddamn neck in, Louisa.'

Louisa's lips narrowed. 'I was merely saying, Jem looks less the little tomboy now and—'

'I couldn't care less what you think, Louisa, of *any* of my children.'

'*Any* of them? How many is that again, Ted? Such an ambiguous number, the amount of offspring a person has. So hard to keep an accurate tally in some families, no? I suppose Blythe knows *exactly*—'

'Stop right there, you poisonous piece of work,' Ted growled, closing the distance between them. 'Just to be clear, Louisa, whatever you might think, Blythe is more the lady you've ever been. *My girls* are more the ladies you'll ever *be.*'

Louisa's face held but Ted knew he'd hit home. She smiled anyway, it was her last stand. 'Ah yes. It's so sad, isn't it? Tragic, really,' Louisa said lightly crossing her arms over her handbag. 'Am I ever going to stack up against a Foster woman? No apparently, by unanimous decision.' Ted had heard this lilt in Louisa's voice before, the thinly veiled anticipation before she delivered a sharp piercing wound with surgical precision.

'Leave us alone, Louisa. And keep your boy away from my wife and girls.'

'My *boy* probably saved your wife's bacon, Ted. None of this is Malcolm's fault.' It was the first time she'd sounded genuine. Louisa was right. It wasn't Malcolm's fault, it had never been Malcolm's fault – any of it. He was just another kid, *another one*, caught up in their mess. Ted felt sorry for Malcolm then, but that didn't change the fact that he couldn't have Malcolm shouting his mouth off around Blythe and his girls.

'Just keep him away, Louisa.'

'Malcolm's a police officer of this town. I can't tell him where he can and can't go!' Louisa mocked. 'I'm his mother! It's just my job to steer him, as best I can.'

Ted's heart was trying to thud its way free of his chest. He'd never hurt a woman, but the notion of knocking her into the concrete pit beneath the car behind him did a round in his mind. He stepped back from her. 'Then you steer him well away from anywhere he might go upsetting anyone, Louisa, or so help me…'

'Gladly,' she spat. 'But just so you know, Ted. Call it the curse of strong Viking genes but the characteristics of *certain* bloodlines in this town run strong. Have you seen my grandson lately?'

Ted knew Malcolm and Millie Fairbanks had a child now; Helen Fairbanks was forever coming up to the house with new photos of the boy for Blythe to admire. Helen had never stopped coming up to the house, she'd taken Millie up there too while she was still in her wheelchair so the town knew Bill and Helen didn't hold Ted responsible for her faulty brakes. 'No, Louisa. I haven't seen your grandson.'

'It's uncanny. Beautiful almond eyes; that flop of blond hair. You of all people should know that family secrets don't stay secret forever, Edward. Blythe and her genealogical talents for tracing back family trees should've told you that much.'

'I warned you before, if you open your mouth I'll make damned sure you go down too, Louisa.'

Louisa held her hands up but she wasn't the surrendering type. She wasn't the mayor's wife any longer, she was his widow. There were no more public engagements, no dinner parties up in that tacky house of theirs. Louisa didn't have as much face to lose as she had back then. When it had happened. Before Ted could stop it. Ted felt his back stiffen. He was a fool, a damned fool to have ever let it happen.

'I won't have you upsetting my wife, Louisa.' But Louisa didn't care for Blythe.

'Really, Ted, I have no desire being the talk of the town, but Malcolm's going to put two and two together eventually. And when he does ask me, I'm not going to lie to him like you have to yourself all these years. My son deserves to know the truth about his father.'

CHAPTER 15

The horrendous suited jaywalker who'd so warmly welcomed Alex back into town the other day was standing two places behind her now in the queue at Freya's Deli. Different suit, same showy four-by-four double parked right outside like he owned the place. There was a delicate hint of cigarettes fighting the smell of freshly baked croissants in the air around the countertop. Alex had only popped in to get her dad a nice sandwich for lunch, something on wholegrain with three food groups to keep his strength up. He wasn't eating properly. He needed to eat, he worked too hard, he worried too much. He needed to eat.

'Anything else?'

'Yep, can I get one of those vanilla bean shakes please?' Alex asked, trying to keep her face angled so that unpleasant man didn't spot her. Not that he would necessarily recognise her. She'd actually bothered to sort her hair out this morning, borrow a touch of Jem's makeup so she didn't look like an extra from *Night of the Living Dead* every day. Times had changed; it used to be Jem nicking Alex's stuff. Alex hoped Jem still loved vanilla shakes. *Guess we'll find out when I get to the hospital*. 'And, um, a bottle of the fresh-pressed apple, thanks.' A small commotion broke out in the queue as Alex fished for change in her back pocket. She kept facing forwards, she didn't want to look at that foul man again particularly.

'Sorry, do I know you? You look kind of familiar.' The young girl behind the counter couldn't have been older than sixteen.

A small child cried out from somewhere in the queue. 'Wasp!'

The girl behind the counter glanced over and swatted at something over the croissants.

'I don't think so. Sorry.' Alex smiled.

'It's Alexandra, right? I think you used to babysit for me.' She pointed both index fingers at herself but all Alex could see was several rows of stud earrings and lots and lots of eyeliner. 'It's Darcy. Hopkins.'

'Oh my goodness, Darcy? I didn't recognise you! I'm stunned you recognised me, actually.'

Darcy transformed from autonomous server into a bubbly teenager.

'No way, you were like, my favourite babysitter! I was bummed when you stopped coming over. Mum had Carrie Logan instead, do you know her? I think she was in your sister's year. She was *not* cool.'

Alex smiled. She'd babysat for Darcy for two lucrative years before Darcy's mum had called Alex and said that they were cutting back on nights out, that they'd call if circumstances changed. They never had. Carrie didn't need to be cool, she just needed to be trustworthy around children.

'I'm only working here for the summer holiday, I'm starting my A-levels in September. I'm going into performing arts, hopefully.'

'Mum, *WASP*!'

'It's not a wasp, it's a bee. It won't hurt you.' The woman waiting behind Alex was getting restless.

Alex nodded approvingly and handed over a tenner. Darcy must be about sixteen now. Alex had been the same at her age, full of confidence and all set for the world. Alex took her change and crossed her fingers for Darcy that nothing horrendous would happen in her life and mess it all up. 'Take care, Darcy. Good luck with everything.' Alex smiled and shuffled her way back outside past the hands flailing at an insect she couldn't see herself and several people chanting, 'If you don't bother it, it won't bother you.'

Alex took a left out of the deli and caught a brief shot at the hand-tied posies in buckets out front of Wallflowers. She stopped automatically to look them over, inside Carrie Logan was savagely deadheading something. The world had advanced its hair straightening technology since Alex had last seen Carrie, Carrie's corkscrew blonde curls all ironed out now and pulled back into a sleek ponytail running just past the collar of her gilet. Alex casually crouched for a better look at the flower display. Her mum loved flowers. Jem didn't have to know they were from here. More bees congregated over the lavender bushes either side of the shop door.

Ooh, her mum *loved* lavender, Alex could put some fresh in the kitchen for when Blythe came home.

Something dive-bombed Alex's ear. 'Shoo, bee.' One of the little blighters had got a whiff of Jem's shake. 'Shoo.' Alex took a sidestep. Then another. It wasn't easy deterring a plucky insect with hands full of takeout. Alex tried to do one of those casual *I'm-not-panicking-about-a-bug-in-my-face* strolls that people did when they started to panic about bugs in their faces.

'Shoo! *Shooo!*'

Alex scanned the road for a break between the cars where she could cross for the garage. *Where did all these cars come from?* Viking Fest wasn't starting until the bank holiday weekend. They weren't all here for a stroll up to the plunge pools, surely?

Something buzzed, right beside Alex's ear. No! It was going to go in her bloody ear! *Bugger off, bee!* She began shaking her head, a little at first so she didn't upset the food she had balanced precariously in her arms. The bee buzzed. She skipped a couple of paces along the kerb and cranked her head back in one motion. *Oh tits, Alex, you've angered it!*

Alex turned on her heel, whichever direction – she didn't care – and launched herself chest-first into a pedestrian. A cold explosion of vanilla bean milkshake compressed between her and a blue t-shirt.

'Sorry!' she yipped.

At first, she thought it might've been the man from the

deli too. The body she'd just thumped into had hardly moved under her clumsy force, like a padded wall. Alex got a glimpse of a set of ladders and a hammer, half covered in milkshake, embroidered into the breast of the blue t-shirt.

'I thought you said you weren't a runner?' he said. Alex heard the smile in his voice before she looked for it on his lips. No mud this time. This time Finn had Jem's shake spattered over him instead.

'Oh my goodness… I am, so, sorry. I wasn't looking where I was going. Really… I'm sorry.'

Vanilla flavoured milk tracked down one of Finn's arms, a large creamy area of t-shirt was already clinging to his stomach. Alex knew that stomach by heart, she'd committed it to memory after just one, single, perfect November night.

She was about to apologise again but she felt something tickle her scalp. Alex began shaking her head as if she was in her youth moshing to Nirvana again, something which incidentally she'd only ever done in Finn's room.

'Whoa, there, girl.' Finn laughed. 'It's only… *milkshake*?'

Alex slowly straightened up. She saw the yellow drip come into view from where it had tickled her and watched it run off the end of her hair.

'Oh, hang on. You have a stowaway.' Finn smiled. Alex froze. 'Hold still.' He came in closer, vanilla filling Alex's nose. She held her breath while he carefully parted her hair. 'Come on, little fella. Come get some shake.' Alex saw the edge of his smile, a broad run of lovely teeth uniform as the new railings he'd put in around St Cuthbert's.

'It was the bee's fault,' Alex said sourly. 'It wanted Jem's shake.'

Finn teased the insect from Alex's hair.

'Guess the bee won.'

'What happened to *don't bother them and they won't bother you*?' Fat chance. The world did not work that way.

Finn held his hand out. The small invader sat inconspicuously on his palm, behaving itself.

'See. He's not bothering anyone now.'

'Trust me, I didn't start it. I was trying my best to keep my distance, the thing just kept gravitating towards me anyway.'

On Finn's palm, the culprit appeared to be recovering from the calming effects of its new host. A small motion and it was on its way again. Alex watched it fly off. She realised Finn was still watching her. 'Maybe it couldn't help itself.'

Alex felt a flush rise in her cheeks. Someone in dainty heels skipped over the pavement behind them.

'Hi, Finn. I just saw! Do you need anything? I've brought you some paper towels. Oh my God, Alexandra Foster!' Carrie stood a little off side. 'Finn and Alex! Together again, in Eilidh Falls. I heard about your mum, Alex. Hope she's OK. Jem home too, I take it?'

Carrie looked Alex over, her eyes hovering on Alex's grubby Converse pumps. She smiled one of those smiles super-groomed women reserved for other, less-up-to-scratch women. GHDs weren't going to straighten that kink out of her. Alex followed her shadow from her battered pumps over the pavement. Her shadow was touching Finn's shadow. Did her shadow not know the rules? 'Hello, Carrie. Yep, Jem's home.'

Carrie watched Finn trying to get some of the excess off his front. He wasn't really achieving much.

'I think you're going to need to whip that off, Finn.' Carrie sighed. Alex rolled her eyes before she could stop herself, but Finn saw it. He gave her a smile before Carrie could see. *Time to go, Alex.* She decided to think up lines to politely get away, before Carrie insisted Finn whip off anything else.

'Jem come back alone has she? No husband, or… partner in tow? I look out for her from time to time on Facebook, but no sign. Any ideas?'

'Any ideas about?' Alex could taste vanilla. Finn was so covered, she was finding it hard to concentrate on what Carrie was saying.

'Why Jem isn't on Facebook. Everyone is on Facebook, it's where we all convince one another how perfectly our lives have all worked out.' Carrie laughed as if she only thought that was what everyone *else* did on Facebook.

'Er, I don't know. Maybe Jem's life isn't perfect enough yet.' She shrugged.

Finn had given up with the paper towels. Alex looked an apology at him. A car horn beeped twice across the road.

Alex turned, an Aston Martin was just pulling from her dad's yard. Alex saw him walking back into the garage and wished she'd timed her collision with Finn better.

'I'm really sorry about the mess I've made. I have to go.'

'Off already? Tell your mum and dad I said *hi*, Alex.' Carrie smiled. 'Jem too!'

'Bye.' Alex said.

She turned to cross the street before Finn spoke behind her. 'Thanks for the shake, Foster.'

*

Louisa hadn't noticed the small drama unfolding across the street behind her. She was too busy watching the colour drain from Ted's face. Ted looked absently out through the yard gates towards the florist's. He didn't recognise the girl at first, his eyes only picking Susannah's lad out. He looked like he'd an accident with some of his paint. Louisa turned to follow the direction Ted was staring off into. It made Ted pay more attention to what they were both looking at.

The girl turned and Ted recognised the same profile he used to look in on, soundly sleeping in her room, on his way to bed. The face he'd given a thousand goodnight kisses to before she'd gotten all grown up and he'd forgotten how to just plant one on her cheek without waiting for invitation.

Did he just touch her hair? Ted felt himself turn to stone.

'Well, well. He is nothing if not persistent, that one,' Louisa cooed. 'Some people, hey, Ted? No shame.'

Ted could feel his hands beginning to shake at his sides.

Alexandra had been back a matter of days and he was already bothering at her like a bee around a honey pot. *Son of a bitch.*

'It's like I said, Edward. They're all grown up. I can't control my Malcolm any more than you can control your little Alexandra. Do tell Blythe I said hello.'

CHAPTER 16

Dr Okafor had returned after lunch with a small splodge of something mayonnaise-like on another cheerily coloured shirt. Aside from the mayo stain, Dr Okafor had also returned with an endless stream of miserable information.

Alex and Jem had listened intently, thanking the doctor with all the warmth they could muster in case it could be traded in to buy their mum any more care than she was already receiving. After a brief spell loitering in the AAU corridor, Jem had disappeared to sort some pressing issue out with work leaving Alex to her watch post in Room 2.

A small clock ticked lethargically on the wall opposite. Jem had been gone ages. Probably hadn't gone to sort out work at all but gone to get her head together. This was always how she'd dealt with her challenges, find a door and disappear behind it. Alex had found Jem in her room this morning, looking out of her bedroom window with a cup of cold coffee held forgotten against her chest. It was like living in a houseful of yoyos; one person's mood picking up while another's dipped.

Alex heaved a satisfying sigh and watched the subtle changes in her mum's face as she slept. Alex had been hopeful yesterday, Ted had seemed to defrost some when she suggested they split the visiting hours between them. He'd even buried his hands into his overall pockets and rocked back on his boot heels, nodding approvingly like he used to do when Alex would rev the engines for him down at the garage. *But then he was like stone again this morning, Mum,* Alex wanted to say. *Tell me what to say to him when we're alone, Mum. Because I never know.*

Her dad had been off when she'd walked into the garage today. There was a strange atmosphere in there when Alex had taken in the baguette she'd managed to salvage from its dousing of sticky milkshake.

Alex shifted squeakily in her seat, the backs of her thighs sticking to the upholstery where the skirt Jem had lent her had come up shorter on Alex's frame. She'd found herself cemented to the squeaky green vinyl chair for most of the day, trying to make up some of the years she'd been missing in action with a bit of hard time here in Kerring General. Where every second stretched like a slurred word.

Alex looked at her phone, sitting mute on the arm of her chair. She wanted to text Jem, check she was OK, but Jem liked her privacy. If she needed some time to herself, Alex didn't want to be the one to cramp her. Alex's thoughts returned to what Dr Okafor had said out in the hall. Concerns he'd planted in her mind like booby traps she kept stumbling into.

Pneumonia, blood clots, bedsores.

Blythe had been drifting in and out of sleep much of the day. *Day 3*. Alex was supposed to be back to buttering loaves and wiping down plastic tablecloths by now. Day 3 and no packing up of bags to be seen anywhere, only the grim long-haul starting to take shape before them all. Malnutrition, falls. *Heart failure*. Alex began picking at the hem of Jem's cotton skirt and watched her mum sleeping. Blythe's recovery was starting to resemble a twisted game of luck.

Alex whispered as quietly as she could and still hear her own voice. 'I'm sorry, Mum. I'm so sorry… for everything.'

She was breaking her own rule. No crying while she was in the Falls. Alex lay her face against her mother's sleeve and felt the warmth still emanating from the arm they now knew had lost much of its movement. Like Dill's. Alex felt her facial muscles tense. She let it all come out, her body twitching with silent shudders to the gentle repetition of her mother's restful breathing.

When she moved her face away again there was a dark stain just beside Blythe's wrist, a small blackish smear where her mascara had rubbed from her face.

'Alex?'

Jem had perfected the art of slipping in and out of places unnoticed. Alex jumped up instinctively, Jem didn't need to know she'd been crying. Alex smiled as jovially as possible and felt a burn where her legs had peeled too quickly from the seat.

Jem squinted. 'Come on, big sis, you need a change of scene.'

CHAPTER 17

A piece of carrot cake the size of a child's head sat untouched on the bench between them where the sunlight was just about filtering through under the shadow of hospital. Jem had gotten two plastic forks so they could share but Jem had snapped the tines off hers and was now fiddling with four little shards of plastic in her lap. Alex sat counting the apples in the tree across the small leafy courtyard Jem had found in the hospital grounds, *Garden of Reflection* the small brass plaque on the wall read. They couldn't see it now though, a lady hooked up to a mobile oxygen system was standing in front of it having a cigarette.

Jem stopped watching her. 'Did Mum ever smoke, do you think? Like, before she had us?'

Alex lost count of the apples. 'Maybe. Smoking was one of their generational things I guess. Like teenage sweethearts and marrying for life.'

'I don't think Mum would've ever smoked. She's too much of a goody-goody,' Jem decided.

Alex smiled crookedly. 'Maybe she has a past we don't

know about.' Maybe their mother had two lives, maybe everyone did. Maybe Alex would get a second run at it too.

'Mum? A dark horse?' Jem grimaced. 'Nah. What you see is what you get with Mum,' Jem added wistfully. 'No nasty surprises.' Jem looked across the courtyard in bloom and collected her thoughts. 'Or maybe we all have something to hide. To a certain extent,' she added absently.

'Are you trying to tell me you used to smoke or something, Jem?'

Jem gave a tired laugh. 'I tried it once, round the back of the science block. Carrie Logan dared me to take a drag of one of her mum's she'd smuggled in. Kind of an initiation thing into her little gang.'

'Wow. Now who's the dark horse,' Alex teased. 'So did it help you fit in?'

'Nope. I was never going to fit in there.'

She nearly had. She'd pretended with the makeup and the fashion and the hair faff every morning before school, and it had been worth it for a while, just to belong. Then, like an idiot, she'd confided in Carrie.

The glass doors onto the small courtyard slid open and a pushchair wheeled out in front of a slight woman with long dark straggly hair. The gardens were suddenly alive with sound, inconsolable wails bouncing off the glazing on all sides around them.

'And that's why I won't be first to bring a grandchild home,' Jem groaned quietly.

'Grandchild, Jem? One of us has to bring an acceptable bloke home first.'

Alex tried to convey a polite smile to the young mother but the woman's eyes were darting around the raised flowerbeds, trying to keep up with the little girl who'd shot out from beside her legs to play hopscotch on the paving stones. The child looked like her mother, but with a softer, happier face. Alex watched the little girl run behind a cloud of big pink daisies, a flick of dark hair and she was gone.

Alex spotted two wide brown eyes peeping from over the planter bed opposite. The slice of carrot cake sitting between Alex and Jem had caught her attention. Alex smiled at her through the daisies. The little girl's eyes briefly looked back at the unwanted dessert before settling on Alex.

'Poppy! Come have a drink,' came a voice from the bench behind theirs.

'That's her,' Jem whispered. 'With the mucky feet the other day. Remember I said? I think her husband is on the ward opposite the AAU. She's been here every day we have.'

Alex found her eyes briefly gravitating towards the mother's feet. She was wearing flip-flops that looked like they'd seen more action than Alex's Converse. She made Alex think of some of the mums she'd seen at the food bank. Women at the mercy of bus timetables and clement weather. The flip-flops of people with cars didn't usually get the opportunity to become so thinly worn.

Alex watched the mother offer a drink to her daughter with one hand while cradling the baby at her breast with the other.

'I don't like water, Mummy.'

The mother swept a few wayward strands from her child's face. 'I know, baby.'

'Can I have some juice instead?' Alex heard the hope in her voice.

'No, baby.'

'But *why*, Mummy? I haven't drunked any juice for a long time now, Mummy. Please?'

'I know, I'm sorry, baby. When Daddy's better—'

'Now who's staring?' Jem murmured, disturbing Alex's earwigging. She settled back into listening to the breeze rustling the greenery around them. The Viking festival would be busy this year, if it stayed like this. The Falls were beautiful in the summer. Alex finished counting again. Twenty-three. Twenty-three rosy red apples. No, twenty-*four*. Shoot, had she counted that one already?

'Alex?' Jem said after a while.

'Hmm?'

'Do you remember what Mum used to say to us? About lightning… only striking once and all that.'

'I remember.' Had Jem met someone? Was she about to spill all? Alex stole a sideways glance. Jem was staring into space.

'Do you think she realised that lightning can also burn down what you know and care about too? Or do you think she thought that none of that matters. That everything else becomes kinda… *secondary*?'

Alex was stunned. Was Jem in love? 'Jem, have you met someone?'

Jem leant forwards a little onto her knees and looked at her feet. Alex assumed a similar position while she psyched herself up in the swimming pool changing rooms before going in. Jem turned to look at Alex then, glacial eyes like their dad's.

'It's not that straightforward, Alex.' Jem looked apologetic. For a fleeting second, Alex wondered if it could be Finn. *Don't be so ridiculous.* Like he was even hers to keep tabs on anyway.

Jem looked suddenly marooned, ashen with some big burden she was keeping all to herself. A married man, then? Her sister was fraternising with another woman's husband. Alex chastised herself again. No. No way, not Jem. They hadn't been brought up that way. Marriage was sacred.

'Wow. Well… I don't know, Jem. Lightning's lightning I guess. You'll have to ask her yourself.' Blythe was going to be ecstatic. It worried Alex, their mum's heart didn't need any more stress, even the good kind. 'Maybe wait until she's on her feet though, Jem. You know how excited she gets.' But Jem seemed anything but.

'Eugh!' came a rattled voice. 'Blast and damnation!'

Alex and Jem turned sharply to look back over the bench towards the hospital doors. The woman with the nose tube had slumped awkwardly out of her wheelchair.

'Hang on!' Alex yelped, leaping towards the doors. 'Oh my goodness, are you all right?'

Jem already had the woman's other elbow and was helping her back into the chair.

'Dropped my lighter, didn't I?' the woman croaked. Her nose tube had been knocked off centre. 'Thanks, girls. I should get myself one of those new-fangled vaporiser things you see everyone sucking on. I could stay up on the ward then instead of coming down here and bothering everyone.'

Jem arched her eyebrows.

'Are you sure you're OK? Can we take you anywhere? We're ready to head back in now anyway, aren't we, Jem?'

'Home?' the woman croaked hopefully. 'Go on, girls. I'm just going to have one last puff. Calm my nerves.'

Jem's eyes rounded before she turned for the doors. Alex gave a parting smile and followed Jem through the glass.

They walked slowly back towards the lifts. The two of them fell into a natural rhythm, walking the corridor with the same stride, the same heavy silence. They probably looked like twins from behind.

'Hang on,' Jem declared. 'We left our rubbish on the bench.' Alex watched silently while Jem ducked back out into the Garden of Reflection. A few seconds later and Jem trotted back up the corridor, auburn hair flowing back over her shoulders and an expression on her face that said the world was full of oddities and she was the last surviving normal one.

'All sorted?' Alex asked.

'Well I didn't get chance to chuck our stuff away, if that's what you mean? I didn't want to embarrass her!'

'Embarrass who?'

'Grotty Feet! She's just nicked our cake!'

CHAPTER 18

Dust like a psychopath. It's what their mother did. Everyone knew when to give Blythe breathing space. She'd either be gardening ferociously or dusting like an obsessive-compulsive menace. 'Just like your grandma Ros, your mother,' Ted used to whisper to Alex before throwing her a look of camaraderie. 'Work out your frustrations with a feather duster, instead of fists, like your sister,' he'd teased, because little idiosyncrasies like that ran in families too, it wasn't just the obvious stuff like receding hairlines and big awkward babies getting stuck like Dill had.

Alex shook out the wrinkles of her mum's lounge curtains and drenched the windowsill in the Mr Muscle she'd found under the kitchen sink.

You are getting worked up about a ham and chutney sandwich for crying out loud. Get. A. Grip.

He'd forgotten them. So what? She was being pathetic. How was her dad to know she'd gotten up at six to make fresh sandwiches? Had she asked him if he wanted fresh sandwiches for work? No. Had it been his idea to read Blythe's scrawled recipe notes on the fridge door – *Ted's healthier favourites* – and be suddenly inspired with gourmet sodding sandwich ideas? No. Had Alex even reminded him to pick them up on his way out of the house? Honestly? Alex's heart sank. She hadn't thought she'd need to.

And then there was yesterday. A *thank you*. That was all she'd been hoping for. Wouldn't Jem have gotten a *thanks*, a smile maybe, if she'd dropped his lunch in at the garage? Jem would've just grabbed him a heart-attack-in-a-bun from Brünnhilde's Baps on the high street but no, Alex had decided to push the boat out and queue for twenty minutes in a posher-looking deli for a posher-looking baguette instead. Offer him something his arteries, and her mum, might appreciate.

Alex finished buffing the windowsill. His voice had been sharp yesterday. 'You shouldn't have wasted your money paying tourist prices for yuppie food, Alexandra.'

*

The phone rang out in the hallway. 'Leave it! I'll get it!' Jem called down but Alex was already padding from the back lounge out into the hallway where the cordless was stationed.

Alex hovered over the console table. 'Hello? Alex speaking.' It was a habit, saying her name when she answered the phone. It was what she and Dan did at the food bank, to put callers at ease.

A couple of seconds' silence then the caller hung up. Again.

'Agh. That's *three* times, you rude bugger!' *Telesales gits.* 'Three bloody times!' Alex suddenly felt a disproportionate need to track the responsible individual down to their anonymous little booth in their anonymous little call centre, wrap their phone cord snuggly around their ignorant neck and scream, *My mother is sick in hospital, you knob, stop calling and hanging up on me!*

The phone rang again. Alex glared impotent fury. She was about to lunge for the receiver but it stopped ringing abruptly. Alex heard Jem shuffling across the landing, the wire dragging across the floorboards, Jem's bedroom door closing again behind her.

Alex pulled in a deep breath and released it again. Her elbow caught the can of polish she'd set down. It toppled, knocking the phone from its stump.

'Stop pressuring me, George! You can't expect me to work to your timeframe on this! This is a BIG deal for me,' came a distant voice from the earpiece.

Alex felt a flush of treachery and very gently replaced the cordless back on its post before she accidentally earwigged any more. George was starting to sound like a real plank. Not like Dan, he'd texted Alex everyday so far to tell her there was no rush to get back.

Alex returned to dusting the pictures of her family hanging along the hallway walls. She'd made her way through nearly half of the hanged frames before she slowed enough to take a look at the pictures inside them. All the Foster men had the same look about them, even back to her dad's great grandfather William Foster who, rumour had it, fathered a child with somebody other than great, great, granny Alice Foster.

'Alice raised that child after William brought him home. That was what women did for their husbands in those days, Alex,' her mum had told her and Jem.

Alex studied her father's great grandfather William and tried not to dislike him too much. He looked a lot like her dad, maybe a bit scrawnier. Alex moved along the wall. The same fair hair and serious eyes recurred again and again, tumbling all the way down the generations of Fosters to Dill, in this picture sitting full-grin on an inflatable dolphin wearing one of Jem's bikini tops. Alex laughed involuntarily. She re-ran through the last few photographs. Dill seemed to break the run, there was something softer about him than the rest of the Foster lot. It was that dimple. That one, odd little indentation on his left cheek that set him apart from the rest of them. It had given Alex the perfect target to lay slobbery kisses on.

Jem's feet pattered downstairs with purpose. 'Jesus, Alex. It's not even eight-thirty, you're as bad as Mum. Where's Dad?'

'Left already. About half an hour ago. *Without* his lunch.'

Jem astutely read between the lines. 'Well, maybe he forgot?' She began wriggling into a pair of sandals, shrugging an arm into her cardigan at the same time.

'I guess. Where are you going anyway, I thought we were heading into town this morning while Helen and Susannah see Mum?' Helen Fairbanks had collected her casserole dish first thing and had given explicit instructions for Alex and Jem to have a break from the hospital and go throw themselves into the Falls' increasing Viking festivities for a few hours instead.

Jem checked herself in the hallway mirror. 'Work. I need to avert a freaking disaster and I'd rather do it some place I can yell. Like on my mobile phone, in the car… somewhere there's some *sodding* signal. I won't be long.' Jem pulled a lip-gloss from her bag and began dabbing herself with it. She shook her fingers through her fringe.

'You look nice… for a phone call,' Alex said idly.

Jem flashed her a look in the mirror. 'Well, you never know who you might bump into, right? Take yesterday, how lucky was that? You borrowing my best MAC makeup before running into Finn. And Carrie, the vile creature. Poor you.'

Alex's stomach did a gentle roll. 'How do you know I saw Finn? And Carrie?' Alex added *Carrie* to imply Carrie and Finn were of equal significance, or insignificance, whichever way Jem might read it.

'How do you think, Al? Dad saw you.'

Alex felt another flip in her stomach. That explained his foul mood since yesterday then. Ted had hardly said a word over dinner last night. No wonder he'd left the sandwiches.

Jem stuck a kiss on Alex's head. 'Won't be long. And you might want to check the back door too, I saw the dog was out by Dad's workshop when I was upstairs.' Jem disappeared over the step calling, 'And she needs a name! Think of something Mum would like.' The door rattled shut behind her leaving Alex alone with the family gallery again.

Alex scanned the run of pictures hanging in the hallway. Jem looked so different now to her teenaged self. Alex's school photos were the worst, she'd happily admit, but *crikey, Jem, that haircut really was horrendous.* Alex studied her sister's solemn expression. She hadn't realised Jem's eczema had been quite so obvious back then, an angry patch of pink skin either side of Jem's mouth. It was stress-related, her mum had told her. But Alex had never seen for herself, she'd already left for uni by the time Jem had been having trouble at school.

Alex heard footsteps again on the path outside. Jem must've found the puppy. Oh, crap, not under her car wheels again. Alex jumped for the door as Ted bustled in through it, greying blond hair like a short thinning mane.

Alex stared vacantly at him. He'd left twenty minutes ago, he must've got nearly to the garage before doubling back. He was always forgetting the garage keys and always having to come all the way home for them. It drove Mum mad.

'Housework?' he asked. 'This early? I won't come in with my boots then.'

Alex felt startled, like she'd just been caught cleaning a neighbour's flat or something. 'Oh, OK. Do you need me to reach you something?' she asked.

'Please. In the kitchen, on the side. You've gone to all that effort and I nearly forgot my sandwiches.'

CHAPTER 19

Alex could feel a little spring in her step, dampened only by Jem's conspicuous quietness. The distance between her and her dad seemed to have shortened. All right, just by the length of a ham and chutney sandwich but it was a start. A very promising start. The pup was prancing on her lead in front, Helen and Susannah had called to say they were staying on at the hospital with Blythe and that they'd even had lunch together in her room. The day was looking up. For a change, it was only Jem letting the side down.

'How did the call to work go? Yell much?' Alex didn't really want to ask, Jem didn't share anything until she was good and ready anyway but Alex felt bound by the rules of big sisterhood. She had some time to make up to Jem in that arena.

'Do you ever feel backed into a corner, Alex?'

Alex remembered how Jem's voice had sounded while she'd sat in the changing room cubicle. *Alex, you need to come home.* 'Sometimes. Everything all right? Hey, stop pulling, dog… Crikey, she's strong.'

The pup seemed to know her way along the road into the

top end of town, yanking at the makeshift lead Alex had fashioned from a length of rope she'd found in Ted's workshop back at the farmhouse.

Alex looked down on the view opening out before them. The townsfolk had erected more flagpoles along the route into town, so much fluttering red and gold in fact that the entire high street looked as if it was in motion.

Jem sighed. 'There's this situation, and… I don't know how to handle it.'

Really? Jem knew how to handle every situation. Jem was cool under fire. Jem was efficient and to the point. 'Sounds important, Jem,' said Alex. Jem was not a ditherer.

'It is. There's like this important… unveiling thing I suppose you could call it and…'

'And?'

'And I don't want to rush what I'm doing, but there's kind of a timing issue.'

Jem wasn't known for being cryptic. Jem was bubbly or impassioned, or she was fiercely quiet, or standing up to little shits like Robbie Rushton. Those were Jem's gears. Alex wasn't used to hearing her ruffled.

'So, like a deadline?' asked Alex.

Jem pinched the bridge of her nose. 'Yeah, I suppose so. Well, no, I don't know there is definitely a… *deadline*, but… there might be. You see, there's this really important group of people who need to know… well, what I'm all about, I guess. But there's a possibility now that one of them might be… moving on. Sooner than I'd thought.'

Jem's voice sounded strained. 'And if she does move on, before I'm ready to…' Jem was nodding her head slowly, as if hoping she could tip the right words out of herself.

'*Unveil* this thing?' Alex helped.

Jem nodded again. 'Then I might not…' She trailed off.

'You might not get another chance?'

Jem smiled weakly. 'Something like that.'

Alex nearly tripped over the puppy then spotted a new attack of bunting stretching zigzags of colour all over the main road through town. She gave the town's festival decorations budget a fleeting thought and then got back to Jem's predicament. It all sounded like a lot of aggro for Jem's line of work, didn't it? Some sort of highly classified *unveiling*? Alex wondered if it was their Winter Collection that Jem was getting her knickers in a twist over. She loved checking in on Jem's company website, feasting her eyes on the season's new line of exquisite shiny things, the precious metals, diamonds and other twinkly items, knowing that Jem had a hand in them. But Alex had never realised Jem's job caused her so much stress.

'So I take it your boss is a bit keener than you are, to get a move on with the *big reveal*, I mean?'

'Exactly.'

'And he's giving you a hard time?'

'He?' Jem questioned.

'George, isn't it?'

Jem kept her eyes fixed on the dog bobbing in front. 'Yeah, George.'

Jem was maintaining a thick, foggy vagueness between them but Alex had the distinct impression she was breaking down barriers here, peeling back the layers of a personal matter Jem might actually be about to share with her big sister and – shock horror – maybe even seek her advice on. 'So let me see if I've got this right, this George is putting pressure on you—'

'Not pressure!' Jem said defensively, 'More of a... *firm nudge*.'

'OK, a firm nudge then. But you're not quite ready? To *unveil* what you need to before a deadline that... may or may not come? Is that right?' Jem really was being vague.

'Pretty much. And no. I don't think that I'm ready. I *really* don't. But I have a duty of care, morally.' Alex watched as Jem began rattily twisting the silver bangle around her wrist.

Morally? Alex's forehead crinkled. 'Are you going to tell me what you're on about exactly, Jem? I might be able to give better advice?'

Jem's bangle-twisting intensified. 'I can't.'

'You *can't*? You are still designing jewellery, right? You haven't shifted to MI5 since Christmas?' Jem threw Alex a half-hearted scowl. None of this made sense, the vagueness, the mithering... Jem was usually the brave one. 'Can't you just go for it, Jem? These people must have confidence in you. In what you're about. What's the worst they're going to say?'

Jem knew what the worst was. *No thanks. That kind of*

thing is not *for us. Therefore* you *are not for us. You're not the Jem Foster we thought you were, now get lost.*

Jem tensed up. 'They might reject what I come out with, Alex. It could be a really costly mistake. I'm talking irreparable damage to my relationship with them.'

Alex was still frowning. Maybe Jem was working for MI5. She'd be a brilliant female James Bond, Alex thought, secretive, resilient, excellent cheekbones. Still, Alex wanted to alleviate some of this awful pressure Jem had been under with work while worrying about their mum on top of it all. *Mum.* What would Mum say? She would be able to give Jem sterling advice.

'You know what, Jem, you obviously don't want to get into the details with me so I'll just say this. I think you just need to trust your own instincts. Have a bit of faith in yourself.' Blimey, that sounded a lot like Blythe. And did Jem's shoulders just relax a fraction? Alex gave channelling their mum another go. 'Presumably these people have worked with you before, right?' asked Alex. Jem nodded. 'And they value you, well they must do, you're great.' Jem shrugged, but Alex could see she was listening. Jem was actually listening to Alex's excellent big sisterly advice! 'Then everything will be fine, Jem. Even if they hate what you're going to propose, they'd be mad to lose you over it. Maybe you should have a bit of faith in them too?'

But Jem had misplaced her faith before. Thought it was a good idea to go out on a limb and allow that part of herself she was always holding back to finally peek out into the open. Jem felt a familiar tingle starting in the skin around her mouth. Great. Add a flare-up of a bloody skin condition to her worries. Alex was still smiling at her encouragingly, but Alex didn't know she was being duped. *Unveiling.* Well that was one word for it. Jem smiled back. Another deception. Alex looked so open, so willing to be supportive. Jem opened her mouth to say it, she wanted to just say it. But the thoughts raced in like a S.W.A.T team, shutting her down.

You tried to let it out once before, Jem. You thought your friends would support you. That mistake had only fast-tracked her to a child psychologist.

Autumn Term, 2007, Eilidh High School

'*H*air cut! Hair cut!' Two of the boys were chanting, the other standing watch.

Jem felt Carrie's unease changing shape. It had started out as a silly misunderstanding. Jem putting her foot in it, Carrie's catty response. Usual stuff. If the older boys hadn't smelled the cooling cakes and wandered in to Home Ec, if they hadn't started spectating, egging Carrie on…

'Go on, Carrie. If you're right, she doesn't *want* long hair, do you, er…? What's her name again?'

Jem tried to yank herself free but Sarah was sitting on her arm, Sarah's upper body sprawled over Jem's back, pinning her to the spot. It was all bluster at first, but Sarah had stopped giggling. She felt something coming too. Jem's heart began trying to thump free of her chest. Jem hadn't meant to offend her, she didn't mean for Carrie to feel small. Carrie's mum's car was a classic, she'd said. Not an *old banger*, Jem had never said that.

'Jem. Her name's Jem,' Carrie said vacantly. She sounded distant. Jem felt the atmosphere shift. She tried to reassure herself, this couldn't get worse, could it? Carrie had already told them the worst thing she could about her. Now they all knew. The whole school would know by home time.

'Jem?' one of the boys sniggered. 'Oh yeah, you're the cowboy mechanic's daughter, aren't ya? What kind of name's *Jem*, anyway?'

'Short for Jaime.'

'*Jaime*? Ha, she's even got a boy's name. Go on, Carrie. Give her a haircut that matches, dare ya.'

More sniggering. Jem felt her face flush with adrenalin. Hot, horrible, adrenalin. *She won't do it*, Jem told herself. They were messing around, Carrie wanted to be popular with the lads but she'd never go that far.

'*Hair cut, hair cut...*'

Carrie crouched against Jem and Sarah. She leant down towards Jem's face, still cheek down on the floor between the tables where they'd all baked Victoria sponges together last lesson. 'I'll just take a little bit off, Jem,' Carrie whispered. Her voice sounded strange, apologetic. Like Carrie wished the older boys hadn't come in either.

'Don't,' Jem managed. But her voice sounded small and feeble. Carrie hesitated, then her grasp on Jem's ponytail intensified. A few hairs pulled tight at the base of Jem's neck. 'Carrie, don't.'

Carrie stopped pulling. The sharp tugs at the base of Jem's neck ceased.

The chanting stopped.

'Oh my God, Carrie! Are you mental? I thought you were kidding!' Sarah skittered away as if it had only just dawned on her that she'd been sitting on Jem the whole time.

'Shit! She did it. That girl's just scalped her mate!' a boy's voice said. 'Carrie, you nutter!'

'If she grasses, we were *not* here. I'm not being done for it, I'm already on a warning,' somebody said.

'Carrie?' Sarah whimpered. 'Isn't this like, a *hate* crime or something? Won't we get *expelled*?'

Jem pushed herself up from the wiry classroom carpet. There was jam on her sleeve where Sarah had pushed her into some of the morning's mess. She put her hand to her head. Her hairband came away in her fingers.

Carrie looked pale. And then she managed a weak smile for her new friends.

'She won't grass,' one of the other boys said.

'How do you know?'

Jem ran her fingers over her crown, against the alien sensation of short, tufty hair.

'Because then she'll have to tell her old man why she looks like a bloke now. My mum used to take our car to his garage, reckons Foster's already disowned one of his daughters. *Jaime* here ain't going to tell him the truth, is she? And risk getting disowned too?'

CHAPTER 20

Susannah Finn's B&B peeped into view, still open for business, still welcoming with its permanently open doors and thoughts of Susannah's son immediately swamped Alex's head again. Jem had been lost in thought for the last ten minutes of their trundle into town leaving Alex's mind to roam too freely. *Maybe it couldn't help itself*, Finn had said. Alex had blushed like a total buffoon when Finn had dealt with the winged demon. She had to stop that. Acting like an idiot whenever Finn put himself between her and bees or nettles or anything else with the potential to sting.

Alex read the sign swinging over the doorway she and Finn had walked through a thousand times together. '*The Longhouse*? When did Finn's mum change the name of the B&B?'

Jem pushed her sunglasses onto her head so her fringe sat back from her face. 'The same time the rest of the Falls started going history nuts. Mum said it's the best thing Susannah ever did, she gets booked up now for most of the summer, not just Viking Fest weekend.'

'That many people come?'

Jem shrugged. 'Sure, Al. They hold traditional markets here now, living history weekends. Over there look, the terrace with the lights in the trees, that's where they put the winner's podium after the river race. The *Victorious Vikings* get to sit at the head table and have their photos taken with a big roast pig and the native maidens they've claimed from the riverbank, all kinds of stuff. The *Eilidh Mail* usually covers it.'

'Native maidens? Claimed?'

'Pillaging's frowned upon in modern society, Al, so some bright spark came up with banners. Any invader who manages to make it all the way downriver without capsizing earns the right to offer his banners to a maiden on the riverbank.'

'Politically correct pillaging?'

'You get the gist.'

A group of men had commandeered part of the terrace. Their voices bubbled up and the puppy pulled the rope tighter around Alex's hand. Alex felt another yank and then the lead loosen in her hand.

'Hey! Dog! Bugger, Jem, call her.'

'Call what? She needs a name, Alex!'

'She needs a proper collar and lead.' The puppy was skipping playfully around the group of men. 'Jem. Look, there's Mal, you could go have a word, find out what happened in the churchyard.'

Jem looked over. Officer Sinclair was leaning against someone's car. 'I think he's busy, Al. Oh look, they're building a raft for the boat race.'

Two of the men were binding old water bottles together with lengths of cord while Malcolm Sinclair and a bald chap sitting with his very wide back to the pavement watched. It had to be Hamish, 7th place runner up at the 1988 World's Strongest Man and landlord at The Cavern. Alex appraised the raft with interest. 'Huh, from back there you can't tell they're making it out of—'

'Crap.'

'Well, I wouldn't call it *crap*, Jem. It's recycling.'

Jem craned her neck towards the puppy squatting next to Mal Sinclair's driver's door. 'No, *crap*. Did you bring a baggy thingy?'

Alex groaned. 'That thing never stops pooping and piddling!' She rummaged in her back pocket. 'I could only find sandwich bags at the house.'

The puppy finished and made a break for Hamish's feet. No big surprise, really, Hamish smelled of pork scratchings and had done for the last twenty years. Mal saw Jem and Alex approach and stood bolt upright like a toy soldier.

'At ease, Mal.' Jem smiled brightly. Alex saw Jem's face change, she had been forlorn all the walk down here but something had just flickered through her features the way it had when she'd stumbled across a full jar of peanut butter in the cupboard yesterday.

'Hi, Mal. Long time no see,' Alex said warmly.

'Alex, it's been a while.' Mal gave Alex a stiff embrace then looked formal and fidgety again all at once. 'Jem... How are things, y'know, with your mum?'

'She's doing OK, thanks to you, Mal. Baby steps.'

'Yeah, thank you, Mal,' Alex said. 'We're so grateful you were there. We don't know what might have happened if you hadn't been.'

Jem nodded in agreement. 'We were saying to Dad the other night, how Mum was so lucky that you happened to be passing and saw that she wasn't feeling well.'

Mal scratched agitatedly at his beard. 'Please, don't thank me. Really… you don't need to do that.' He sounded apologetic to Alex.

'Are you all right, Mal? You look pale?' Jem asked.

'Little Alexandra and Jem Foster!' Hamish exploded in haughty exclamation. 'Ted told me how you both look like your mother, thank goodness, preferable to that grumpy old bugger, but he didn't say what a pair of beauties you've both turned into!'

'Hamish!' Jem teased. 'You saw me last Saturday when I brought Mum to The Cavern for lunch.'

'Not in that skirt I didn't.' Jem chortled while Mal pretended there was something behind him to look at. Hamish could be a little bit pervy but only ever with people who knew he was just being an old goat. 'And what about you then, young Alex? It's good to see you back in these parts, girl, if only they were under better circumstances, hey?'

'Thanks, Hamish. You're looking well.'

'I know,' he said, stoking his beard into a point. 'You make sure you give your mother a kiss from me when you see her.'

'I will, Hamish.' Alex smiled. It was nigh on impossible not to be fond of old Hamish, he was something of an institution, a local hero even. It had been Hamish who'd freed a five year old Millie Fairbanks from Helen's crumpled car when the construction wagon had taken the bridge too quickly. Hamish who'd brought Ted home, sober and lost, from the police station after Finn and Susannah said that they wouldn't press charges. If there was a crisis afoot, Hamish was a good man to have around.

'Well you're all coming home to roost. You know who else is back in town, don't you? That sweetheart of yours, young Alex. Susannah Finn's lad.'

Alex felt her face go warm. She wasn't supposed to be thinking about him any more. 'Oh?' Alex said aloofly.

Hamish winked at her and the warmth in her cheeks intensified. 'This little critter belong to you?' he asked, scooping the puppy up in his massive frame.

Alex watched the pup licking Hamish's face. She hadn't noticed in her peripheral vision that Mal had moved next to Jem. Alex turned and just caught Mal saying something into Jem's ear and some unknown concern for Blythe clenched inside her. Alex pretended not to see.

'Puppy! Mummy, look!'

A leggy blonde in a summer dress was crossing the terrace, a little boy pulling her by the hand. Millie Fairbanks had been Shirley-Temple-cute throughout her time at St Cuthbert's Primary, even in callipers. She'd been drop dead gorgeous throughout her five years at Eilidh High. But

Millie *Sinclair*, as she was now called, was full-blown Amazon beautiful.

A little boy with a mess of Millie's blonde hair was standing beside Alex, gazing up at the ball of fur in Hamish's huge hands. 'Please can I stroke the puppy, Hamish?' he asked.

'Of course you can, Alfie,' Mal said leaning down and laying a kiss on the little boy's head. Mal seemed to be in a different spot every time Alex looked at him. Mal turned and kissed his wife stiffly.

Millie giggled. 'I wish you'd shave that thing off, Mal. I'm starting to get sore. Hello, Alex... Hi, Jem.' Millie's voice was light and warm.

Mal rubbed a hand over his new beard. Jem put the face on she used to use for church and family gatherings. 'Hi, Millie. We meet the handsome little Alfred at last.'

'He's so soft!' giggled Alfie rubbing chubby fingers through the puppy's fur. He spun then to address Alex directly. 'What's his name?'

Alex took in Alfie's pretty round face half hidden by a mop of blond hair. His eyes were inquisitive and hopeful but not the shocking hue of blue she'd been expecting for some reason. There was something about him Alex found both beautiful and haunting.

'Actually, she hasn't got a name yet, Alfie.'

'You could call him Donatello. Or Raphael.'

'Ninja Turtle fan?' Alex asked. There had been a few come through the food bank. Alfie bounced his head.

'Hmm, Donatello. Good call.' Alex smiled. It didn't sound a million miles from the usual names Blythe went for. They'd had an Isolde, Rodolfo and Figaro so far. Jem said Blythe had been holding out for Mimi this time but their dad had vetoed it.

'I'm sorry to hear your mum's unwell,' Millie said to Jem. 'Is she on the mend?'

'Thanks, Millie. She's got a few hurdles ahead of her but, you know Mum. Not one for staying down long,' said Alex.

'Good. That's good to hear. Mum's gone with Susannah to see her this morning, she was taking the WI photo albums in.' Millie grimaced. 'I was hoping Blythe might help me actually, when she's better of course. After Mal's dad passed away, we had a sort through his things. He'd started a family tree at some point, was *convinced* he had Viking blood, wasn't he, Mal? I thought we might dig—'

'No!' Mal had been so quiet Alex jumped when he spoke. 'I don't think Blythe's going to be up to wading through all our rubbish just yet, Mils.'

Millie looks startled. 'Oh. All right. Well maybe I'll make a start. There are a few families that have been here in the Falls so long, it makes you wonder if, well if you go back far enough, were there ever any crossovers? We've probably all got the same grandfather.' Millie laughed.

'You can't put all your faith in birth certificates and paperwork anyway, Millie,' Malcolm said brusquely. Millie looked at him as if he'd grown a third eye. 'Sorry, honey, I just meant… how accurate are family records anyway?

They're only as good as the word of the person who had them filled in, aren't they?'

'I don't think you can trace back to Vikings anyway, Millie,' Alex offered. 'Mum said that records only go so far back, after that it's just names and characteristics anyway.'

Millie went to reply but something had just caught her eye. 'Sorry, would you excuse me? There's Emma Parsons, Mal. I'm just going to try and catch her.' Millie turned to Jem and Alex. 'Her daughter's in Alfie's preschool class, Poppy. Poor family, Mr Parsons had a horrific accident, he was working under a car and the jack gave. The man has a broken sternum and no money coming in. I'm really worried about them. Emma will be walking all the way to the hospital again, I'll bet. Of course, she can't drive, it was their car Mr Parsons was fixing when it fell on him.'

Alex and Jem looked out onto the road as Millie nipped off to intercept the brunette they'd seen in the hospital gardens, stridently pushing her pram along the road while her little girl tried to keep pace. It was a good walk to Kerring General, no wonder her flip-flops had been so worn.

'Grotty Feet,' Jem whispered. Alex jabbed her softly with an elbow. Jem pouted and went back to checking her phone. 'Come on, we have to go too, Al,' she said taking the puppy from Hamish's hands. 'I've just missed another call. From George.'

CHAPTER 21

Alex was moving up a rung on her fear ladder. The plunge pools at Godric's gorge weren't as intimidating as she thought they might be. The Falls weren't really waterfalls, not like the ones you'd see rainbows over or Superman rescuing foolhardy boys from. Actually, Alex realised, their local beauty spot was really just a very decent sized water feature cutting through the landscape. She'd even gotten her shoes and socks off, and she could've stood in the water if she'd wanted, only it looked a bit cold and she hadn't even brought a towel so, hey ho, she couldn't really and that was that.

Alex breathed satisfying breaths that smelled of moss and sunshine. Blythe had looked *great* this afternoon. Helen and Susannah had done what no hospital could and had put some of the colour back in her mum's cheeks.

Dad was at the garage, Jem had buggered off somewhere and Godric's gorge was basking in the late afternoon sun. Alex put her hands on her hips lifting her chin to the warmth of the sky. She took a deep lungful of fresh air and realised, for the first time since she could remember, it felt good to be here.

Alex kept breathing in that fresh air, listening to the gentle gushing around her.

'We really must stop meeting like this, Foster. People will start to talk.' Alex didn't startle. She hung an arm across her head and squinted up to the top of the first waterfall. Finn was picking his way across the top of the rocks. Alex spotted the large rectangular pad in his arms and the small backpack and realised immediately what they were. She pulled at one of the reeds next to her while Finn effortlessly made his way down the rocks jutting from the side of the first gorge.

Alex waved a reed at his belongings. 'I didn't know you were still an artist,' she said. It surprised her. It felt easy to talk to him, this person she'd banished to her past, imprisoned there.

'Old habits die hard.' He smiled. He was wearing a white tee under the blue shirt, the colours accentuated the skin tone his travels had given him. 'You know how it is when you let a thing get under your skin.' Alex thought she might blush again. *What a sap.*

'Still putting your shirts on inside out then?'

'You do remember my mother, right? She still goes spare if I get paint on my clothes.'

Alex grinned. 'So, can I have a look?'

'Maybe next time.' Finn pouted. 'I'm a bit rusty. Actually I just wanted to get a bit of landscape practice, while it's still quiet up here. So, are you going in?'

Alex looked at the water. 'In there? Oh, no. It's not warm enough and I haven't brought a towel or anything so…'

'Really? It's just that you looked like you were psyching yourself up.' Finn dropped his things to the grass and pushed the hair from his eyes. ''Course not, no one takes twenty five minutes to make an in-out decision.' He smiled.

Alex smiled back. Sod. Had he'd been up there the whole time? Did he see her scratch that bite on her backside? The midges up here were on steroids.

Finn began picking through the pebbles near the water's edge.

'So, Foster. You still a crack shot?'

This was too easy. It felt too easy falling back into their old stride. 'Still a better shot than you.' Something playful in her voice made her heart flutter in warning. *Don't do this, Alex. You are not seventeen any more.*

'Let's see it then.' Finn held his hand out for hers. His fingertips were blackened with graphite from his sketching. He dropped three pebbles into her hand and gently closed her fingers around them. The stones felt smooth and solid, the way his body had when she'd bounced into him yesterday. 'Pick your target, Foster.' Alex was pretty good at this. Alex *used* to be pretty good at this. She surveyed the water, gently flowing off from the plunge pool.

'The small black rock, with the moss on the right face.'

Finn nodded, his jaw tensed. Bugger. She hadn't done this for years. She wasn't even sure what was at stake but it felt as if there was definitely something. Alex focused on that small black rock with the water gently breaking over it.

She selected her first pebble, poised her arm and concentrated. She narrowed down on the target. She used to nail this, there was a time she'd have bet Finn a piggyback home on getting three straight hits. Alex released and came a good foot wide of target.

'Dammit.'

'Looks like I'm not the only one who's gotten rusty, Foster.'

'Shhh.'

This time, Alex, just a little curve…

'Ooh, close that time! I can't believe that missed,' Finn teased.

'Would you just shush for a second?'

'You always did get ratty when you missed.'

'Really? I can only ever remember *you* missing,' she said confidently.

Last pebble. He was looking at her, she could feel it. He'd been looking at the rock across the water before.

Alex calmed her thoughts and breathed.

In and out, nice and steady. You're doing it.

The pebble hit and ricocheted off at an awkward angle. Finn whistled beside her. 'Nice aim, Foster.'

Alex clasped her hands together in satisfaction. 'Your turn.'

Finn had already chosen his missiles. He sent the first one off with a respectable effort. But missed. Alex laughed under her breath, she could tell he was concentrating properly this time; his eyes had narrowed. She heard a light *splosh* in the background.

'I think that hit. It definitely scuffed,' she observed.

Finn ran his fingers through the hair that had come to fall in front of his eyes. Alex heard the last *splosh*! And realised she'd been watching him instead of the challenge.

Finn caught her looking. 'You win, Foster. Best of three?'

Maybe he was the challenge.

'I have to go, I'm cooking tonight.'

'That's too bad, Foster. I was hoping maybe we could give it another shot.'

The words hung between them.

He means the pebbles, Alex. He only means the pebbles. She tried to let some of the new tension in her shoulders ebb away. What would it hurt anyway? Why couldn't she stay and throw a few more rocks with him? Ted had already seen Alex with Finn and despite her initial concerns he'd been totally pleasant today. 'Thanks, love,' he'd said when Alex had passed him those sandwiches. '*Love*'!

Say it. Just pick up a few stones, now, and say 'on second thoughts, Finn, best of three!' Just say it, Alex.

Finn looked away briefly then gave her a small smile. 'You know, thinking about it, I should probably be getting back.'

Too late. 'Sure. Me too.' She smiled.

Finn collected his things up from the ground. 'I have to go – I've got this commission I need to get done.'

'You're painting for work, Finn? That's really great.' It was great, not that being a handyman wasn't a good trade, it was just that Finn had blown the competition out of the water at college. The art block had been an exposition of his talent. Walls covered with his still-lives and portrait studies, vibrant and gloomy, testaments to the breadth and depths Alex already knew Joseph Finn had.

'As I said, I'm a bit rusty. But I'm getting back into it. Brings a few quid in on the side and I get to keep a few skills up. How about you, Foster. Still throwing pots?'

'Oh, no.'

'No?'

'Nope. I haven't really done any art since I left uni. I don't even think I own a paintbrush any more.'

'That's too bad. You should stop by next time your passing my mum's place. I have a small studio space round the back. Actually, I'm hoping to get a few hours in there when I finish work tomorrow. You visit your mum every day I'm guessing?'

'Er, yep. Then my dad keeps her company at night.'

'Well, you know, if you were passing tomorrow, I don't know, on your way home maybe… you could stop by. Borrow my brushes, if you wanted.' Finn smiled playfully before a grin got the better of him. Was he being *bashful*? He rubbed the awkwardness from his mouth and left a grey smudge over his cheek from the graphite on his hands. Alex swallowed a smile. 'Seriously, Foster. My mum would love to see you.'

A very light thrumming started up in her chest. Something light and butterfly-like. It would only be a mooch around. And Susannah would be there and it would be so lovely to see her and, well, after how things ended with Finn at her university halls he was just being so… *cool*. It wouldn't be like they were parading around in public. Ted might not even be aware of it.

Alex breathed deeply. 'Sure. Sounds, nice.'

Finn bit on his bottom lip as if he was about to aim another pebble and was concentrating on his target. 'I wasn't sure about coming back to the Falls, Foster. But, I don't know, I'm starting to feel glad that I did.'

Alex felt a funny sensation, like driving over the bridge outside The Cavern too fast. A dangerous, reckless feeling. She was starting to feel glad she'd come back too.

CHAPTER 22

Alex yawned at her reflection in her truck's rear view. There were dark shadows under her eyes. *Yeah, thanks for that, Jem.* Yesterday had been a good day, rounded off with an ambitious attempt at baked cod and green beans last night (another one of her mother's fridge note recipes) pulled off to near perfection, much to Alex's astonishment. Alex had even enjoyed a solid half hour of conversation with her dad over that delicious dinner about Viking raid tactics and the common belief that most of them were high on mind-altering drugs at the time of their conquests. Alex had been all set for a decent night's sleep after that, and then Jem had decided to bumble around the kitchen cupboards at some ungodly hour, setting the puppy off again.

Alex tapped her steering wheel while the lights changed. *Migraine my backside, Jem.* The only migraine Jem had this morning was the kind of migraine she could buy at The Cavern for a fiver a glass. Alex wondered if that's where they'd ended up last night after Mal had called Jem out of the blue for their impromptu catch-up. Must have been a good'n, Jem wouldn't even open her bedroom door this morning, now Alex was going to have to wait to hear what Mal had seen happen to their mum in the churchyard.

It was still playing on Alex's mind, the details of what may or may not have caused her mum's stroke to hit while she was visiting Dill's grave. Jem would've come to the bedroom door and told her, wouldn't she? If Mal had said anything worrying. If Mum had been distressed or if anything obvious had triggered the stroke? Maybe it really had been just bad luck and nothing at all to do with the strain of Dill's birthday.

She has arrhythmia. Don't go letting yourself off the hook just yet, Alex reminded herself.

Alex chewed on her lip and pulled into Foster & Son's yard. *Baby steps.* That's the term Jem had used. It seemed a good approach in general, Alex had decided this morning while whipping up Blythe's egg and bacon breakfast muffins. Baby steps. *If you can make all this effort to get back home, Mum, then the least I can do is try too.*

Alex grabbed the Tupperware box from the passenger seat. 'Righto, Dad. Let's see what we can do with these muffins.'

Wonders could be worked by the tasty and wholesome, Alex had seen it first hand at the food bank. She would use her mother's food to keep the lines of communication open between her and Ted; he'd responded well to Alex's cooking so far, this would be her back door in – the way she would gently remind him that she could still do some things right. Alex let the idea form in her mind again. *You're getting way ahead of yourself*, she warned. But it wasn't completely far-fetched. It would be a *very* long road but eventually, her dad might start to remember that Finn could still do some things right too.

Alex took a last look in her rear view mirror at Finn's hardware shop. Finn was right yesterday. Old habits did die hard.

Alex left her truck in the sunshine and stepped into the gloom of the garage. It always smelled of coffee and cold metal. She could hear her dad had tuned in to the same classical radio station Blythe listened to at home. Alex pushed her keys into her jeans pocket and walked past the car stationed over the pit in the floor.

'Dad? Hellooo? I thought I'd drop some brunch in on my way to Mum.' Alex winced at her use of the word *brunch*. Was it a yuppie word? She stepped around the air compressor Ted used to very carefully pump their bike tyres up with when they were little and headed towards the office through the back.

He probably hadn't heard her. Some big-lunged lovely was belting out *One Beautiful Day* on the radio in the workshop. Alex knew Puccini a mile off. *Madama Butterfly* was second only to *Norma* in their house, thanks to Maria Callas killing it with 'Casta Diva'.

Alex was already humming along to the melody when she reached the office door. Ted was stood poker straight, one hand braced on the edge of his desk, the other clamped on the phone receiver. His shoulders were rising and falling in steady rolls.

'Dad? Is everything OK?'

He didn't turn. *The hospital, had they just rung?* Alex was about to ask.

'What time did your sister get home last night?' Alex felt a small rush of adrenalin, a whiff of a telling off. She'd broken a window on his shed once and that conversation had started with similarly cryptic questions.

'Ah, I'm not sure. I was asleep. Why?' Must've been pretty late. Maybe Jem had gone partying and then woke the neighbours on her way back in.

Ted's knuckles whitened over the phone 'You happen to know what she was doing out with another woman's husband all night?'

For a second, Alex hesitated. 'Oh, you mean Mal?' Alex relaxed then. 'We bumped into him yesterday. With Millie. Jem asked him if they could have a word, about him helping Mum. They probably just got chatting about old times. I've brought you some—'

'He's married!'

Alex looked up from her breakfast muffins, her secret weapons, just as Ted brought a fist down hard onto his desk. Alex jumped.

'You don't go around with married men when you goddamn feel like it! People talk!'

Alex felt the shock on her face. His voice, it wasn't rage, it was something else. He sounded distraught.

'Dad, I don't think… Jem wouldn't.'

Ted's eyes were enlarged. He glared coldly at Alex

and all that distance began to stretch out again between them.

'Why can't you girls just stay away from what's no good for you? Why can't you just let things lie? Instead of hanging around the sons of no good bastards hell-bent on destroying our family?'

CHAPTER 23

Jem felt as if she'd been slipped inside a velvet-lined purse, cushioned from the outside world and all its terrible mistakes. The entire farmhouse had fallen deadly silent once Alex had finished humming over whatever it was she'd been baking at first light.

Jem was sitting on her bed in a cold damp bath towel, her hands placed on her lap, face looking squarely out across the gardens to the tree where their old rope swing still hung. She missed those long summers, playing with Malcolm Sinclair and her brother before they'd started high school and Dill had just become her annoying little brother, something she'd outgrown like an ugly shoe.

A terrible knot tightened in Jem's stomach. A knot that hadn't been there before she'd met with Malcolm last night. He'd regretted it immediately; she'd seen it in his face. But it was too late then, it couldn't be undone.

Jem felt another bout of tears burning behind her eyes. She wanted to go back. To live yesterday again so she could politely decline Mal's request to meet, to keep things how they were, not what they'd now become. What had they become? What were they to each other now? Oh God, it was such a mess. *You stupid idiot.* How could she have not seen it coming? It was there all along, all the time they were growing up. A connection. A spark. And she hadn't realised what it had meant, not fully, and now it could never be the same again.

Jem wiped her eyes again. He'd asked afterwards if she would tell anyone. Would she tell Alex? But how could she? Alex and Dad, they couldn't know!

'We have to keep this to ourselves, Mal,' Jem had said catatonically. 'Private. No one else can ever find out.'

'Do you really think we can keep this secret, Jem? The game's changed now. Everything has changed,' Mal had responded.

'I can keep a secret Mal,' she'd told him.

Jem wiped her wrist rattily at her wet eyes. *Yes, because, you're excellent at lying to your family, aren't you, Jem? This should be a fucking breeze.*

But Mal, he hadn't been so confident. 'Millie will know something's up though. I know she will. I'm sorry, Jem, but I'm a terrible liar.'

CHAPTER 24

Alex used the cuff of her jacket to neaten up the mascara under her eyes. She wasn't completely convinced the tears had stopped yet. At least she'd managed to get out of the garage first. She'd left him there, doubled over in rage to the backdrop of a trembling soprano. He couldn't even bring himself to tell her who'd been on the phone tittle-tattling, he'd been so incensed.

Alex gave in to the tiny spasms the crying had brought to her breathing and watched an old chap fumbling with the parking meter by the ambulances. It was a silly misunderstanding. Whoever had felt the need to ring her dad had clearly got the wrong end of the stick about Jem and Mal, of course they had. And who even did that? And how could Ted be so quick to believe something like that of Jem anyway? Didn't he know her at all? Jem would never do anything to break up another person's marriage, it wasn't in her genetic makeup. She'd never be able to face their mum for a start.

Alex stared vacantly through the windscreen. *If his opin-*

ion is that low of you, Jem, there isn't much hope for the rest of us. And nothing for Finn.

Well, there was no confusion now at least. *The son of a no good bastard hell-bent on destroying their family.* Didn't exactly smack of a second chance.

Another juddering breath made its way out of Alex's chest. She was an idiot. A few nice run-ins with Finn and she'd been a naïve teenager again. *Stupid girl.* Did she honestly think that Finn would want this kind of hassle again? Just to be friends? If Jem and Mal Sinclair had the gossips flexing their muscles just think what seeing Finn and Alex around town would kick up again. The first time had been awful enough.

Have you seen them, carrying on as if they haven't done anything wrong? Youth of today. Brazen as you like.

*

You know what they were up to, don't you? While the poor boy was trying to hang on to the tree? Ted found them half-dressed, I heard. I said that girl's father would end up in a cell at some point.

*

They left him. A nine-year-old child with a disability. Gerry says it wasn't a disability, exactly, but Dillon never had full use of that one arm, I used to look after him at nursery. His nerves had gotten all stretched at birth, somehow. The poor child had no chance in those currents, even without that compromised arm of his. Can you believe they just left him? Gerry's looking for a new babysitter for Darcy. It's just not worth the risk.

*

Alex gripped the steering wheel and locked her arms out against it. Finn didn't need all that again. The finger-wagging. The reminders. She checked her face again in the truck mirror. Her nose looked red and puffy. Great. Just what her mum needed. She looked about the hospital car park for a bin, somewhere to lob her muffins. *Secret weapon.* It was laughable. *She* was laughable.

*

The buzzer onto the ward didn't appear to be working when Alex got up there. She'd been waiting for the puffiness to even out again before showing her face. Alex pressed on the intercom thingy again, suddenly remembering the conversation with Jem, in the Garden of Reflection. 'It's not that straightforward, Alex,' Jem had said. For a split second, a fleeting sniff of doubt clouded Alex's brain. Jem and Mal? No way, it wasn't even worth considering.

The door onto the AAU clicked open and a woman with an evenly greying bob and a pair of glasses hanging from her neck pattered through.

'Alexandra, my darling girl!' Helen Fairbanks' warm welcome hit Alex like a ball against the back of her head. The angst dissipated immediately.

'Hi, Helen. Back again already?' Alex smiled warmly.

'Just checking in on your mum. I thought her hands were looking a little dry yesterday so I've brought her some cocoa butter I wasn't using. She's looking much healthier I think this morning, darling. Better than you I'm afraid, Alex. Is there something the matter? Ooh, are those muffins?'

'Er, no. I mean yes. They are muffins.' She'd found a bin in the car park but the thought of throwing food away wasn't as easy as it used to be before she'd gone to work at the food bank. 'For the nurses.' Alex smiled.

Helen was already taking Alex by the elbow, leading her gently to the seats along the corridor wall so there was zero chance of Alex slipping through her grasp without a nice chat first. Some people invaded your personal space when they spoke to you, got right up close so you worried how your breath might be shaping up or whether they were looking at the imperfections in your complexion while you tried to talk unselfconsciously, without breathing all over them. But Helen Fairbanks was just familiar. Like a friendly aunt, who smelled of cocoa butter and Yorkshire puddings and would never dream of holding against a family that her five year old daughter had been terribly hurt because of the actions of one of their employees.

'Would you like one, Helen? They won't be as good as yours, I'm afraid.' Helen already had an arm through Alex's.

'Oh, lovely!' Helen said, taking a muffin. 'Now then, let's just pop those down for a minute. I wanted to check on you all, Alex. Properly. How are things? How's your father dealing with all this?'

Alex bit at the inside of her cheek. *Devastated. Frustrated. On the verge of exploding?* 'He's doing his best. I don't think I'm helping much.'

'Of course you are! Do you know, your mother said the very same thing to me about your dad once, after our little bump with the truck. I did *not* brake too late, by the way. It was the wretched snow and, well, we won't say too much about Martin Finn's workmanship. Anyway, your poor father was under so much pressure at the time, keeping the garage going, trying to make ends meet. If he's sounding off at you, my love, it's because he needs to lean on you. Like he did your mum back then.'

'I don't think he's very good at leaning on anyone, Helen.'

'Well I told your mother that too. The thing is with these men, Alexandra, you have to let them lean on you without them actually feeling that they're leaning on you. Your mother realised what a good friend I am and that I talk a lot of sense and so instead of worrying about your dad being so tired and grumpy, she went out herself and did a few little jobs to help the situation.'

Helen looked pleased with herself. Alex remembered her mum being thrilled when she'd been able to stop cleaning for the posh families in town and work in the family records department at the Town Hall instead. Alex hadn't remembered any signs that her parents' marriage might've wobbled though.

'Thanks, Helen. I know all this is hard for him. Mum's like, his world.' Alex felt a stab of pity for him then. She was dead right, her mum was his world. Of course he was emotionally charged.

'Oh I know that. I don't believe a man has ever loved a woman more than your father loves your mum, other than my Bob of course.' Helen gave Alex's arm a squeeze. 'Through thick and thin your parents have stuck together. Through things no family should have to endure.' Alex swallowed. Even from Helen it was hard to be reminded. 'I only hope Malcolm loves my Amelia that way. She's besotted with him, you know. Mind you he has got the mayor's good looks. Just not the mayor's silver tongue. Malcolm's been trying to talk his way out of something today, my antennae have been twitching. I think he's in trouble with Millie.'

'Oh?' Alex's antennae were starting to twitch too.

'Oh yes. Millie lost him last night. I had her ringing up after midnight asking if I'd seen his police car driving past, which I sometimes do if I'm watching the TV in the bedroom with the curtains open. I said, whatever you do, Amelia, don't phone his ruddy mother looking for him. Louisa will accuse you of something or other, being a bad wife for not knowing where your husband is at that hour.'

Alex replayed through her head her father's insinuations about Jem and Mal. She laughed uncomfortably. 'Ah yes, Louisa. Always so positive.'

Helen pulled a clump of muffin and popped it into her

mouth. 'She is not and I don't mind saying it. I love that boy, Alexandra, Malcolm is a super son-in-law, a wonderful husband to my Millie, and you should see how much he loves our little Alfie. He's a smashing father. But between you and me – ah, *lovely* muffin – between you and me, Malcolm didn't get his good points from his mother, I can tell you that. Louisa Sinclair is a bit of a...' Helen looked about them to be sure they were the only ones in the corridor. She dropped to a whisper and sounded it out. 'A bit of a *b-i-t-c-h.*'

'I kinda got that impression. Jem's not a fan. I don't think Louisa was very kind to her when she used to hang out with Mal.'

'Well she wouldn't be, would she? Louisa always had it in for your mother, Alex. She was always making little digs about Blythe at church, her hair, her dresses. I think Louisa needed to knock your mother down to make herself feel better, I don't know, about her own hair and dresses I suppose. Some women are insecure that way, and your mother, well she's just so meek and well liked in the Falls, I suppose that's what made her Louisa's target. As I said, a *b-i-you-know-the-rest.*' Helen took another pinch of muffin. 'Thank the lord my Millie isn't like that. Insecure, I mean. Malcolm should've called last night instead of worrying her, but it's not like he's one of *those* husbands... doing things he shouldn't. Oh! Hello, Mrs Parsons, how is your poor husband?'

The doors onto the ward opposite were trying to gobble

back up the woman trying to manoeuvre her pram through them.

Alex jumped to hold the doors while a wide-eyed little girl with her finger in her mouth stepped through beneath her. 'Let me get that for you.'

'Thank you.' The mother smiled. 'Hello again,' she said uncertainly to Helen.

Helen was already patting the little girl on the head. Alex saw her accidentally leave a crumb in the girl's hair. 'Have you been to see your daddy? Is he feeling better?'

The woman smiled self-consciously and began unbuckling the baby from the pushchair. 'Getting there, thank you.'

'Oh, wonderful! You won't have to keep doing this dreadfully long walk every day then, will you?'

'Sorry, I need to feed her. Poppy, stay by Mummy, please.' Alex found herself straining to hear, the woman's voice was so quiet. She looked like she hadn't slept for a week. Alex had noticed yesterday, when Millie had gone to catch her up, that Mrs Parsons was very slight for someone with such a young baby. They had lots of new mothers visit the food bank and the general consensus amongst them was how hard it was in the first year to get the baby weight off. The wonders of breastfeeding, then?

'Of course, we'll give you some privacy. Help yourself to a few of these marvellous muffins! Alex won't mind, will you? She'll only give them away, look how slender she is!' Helen said jovially, moving her and Alex towards the water dispenser further down the corridor.

'Poor woman,' Helen whispered as they walked. 'Millie knows her from the preschool. She lives in one of the terraced houses, up by Susannah's B&B.' Alex could see the little girl tucking into a muffin in the reflection of the water tank. 'Parsons, her name is. Emma or Emily, I forget. Malcolm thinks she's a battered wife. He's tried to check in on them but if she doesn't report it, well… They've been having a few *disturbances* at the house, things getting broken, that sort of thing.' Helen winked knowingly. 'Of course, she's never there now, at home. The horrible toad must demand she be here all day every day, as if she hasn't enough on with the children! If he was my husband, I'd take my frying pan to him.'

'That's terrible. Does she have any friends or family she can lean on?'

'Millie's been trying to arrange a play date with Alfie and the older girl, keep a bit of a friendly eye on them, but she says the mother's never home, it's like she doesn't want to be at the house while he's here. No wonder she looks so exhausted. Aren't some men horrors? Well I hope it was her that kicked the jack over, that's all I can say. It's a shame that car didn't finish the rotter off.'

Alex watched their reflection in the water butt. The little girl was offering her mum a bite of her muffin, but Mrs Parsons wasn't looking at her daughter, she was too busy tucking muffin after muffin into the back of her pram.

CHAPTER 25

It was an odd experience, watching a person's headstone being sited. Or in the case of the late Mayor Sinclair, his whopping archangel memorial piece. The air had gone cooler once the sun had dipped behind the church spire. The clock tower said nearly six o'clock, the memorial guys must've been at it all afternoon. Alex could see it was an archangel because in all the struggling most of the canvas tarpaulin had come loose and was sagging around the angel's base like a dropped bathrobe. Alex was trying to pretend it wasn't happening across St Cuthbert's churchyard, three men in high-viz jackets toing and froing with a series of ropes and pulleys, trying to look professional before disaster struck.

She was being a coward. Hiding out with Dill, knowing that at the north side of town, there was a chance Finn would be in one of Susannah's barns behind the Longhouse wondering if Alex was going to turn up.

Alex finished picking up the last of the yellow rose petals that had blown all over Dill's plot from somewhere. 'So no burning ship for the mayor, Dill? I heard he was a fan.

Maybe he's playing it safe hanging out at St Cuthbert's, just in case he wasn't descended from Vikings.'

Maybe she was playing it safe too, coming here to quietly ask that Blythe have another good day tomorrow. Coming to Dill with her tiny apologies. This seemed the only place she could make them, where she could say the words out loud and no-one would tell her how insubstantial they were.

St Cuthbert's bells began ringing for six pm. Alex followed the steeple all the way up to where it reached for the endless cerulean sky. She should probably come to church more often, not that she was completely sure what she thought about Heaven. She wasn't sure if her father had lost his faith when they lost Dill or whether he was just too angry with God to come to church any more, but Mum still came. Blythe had stopped singing in the choir, but she still came.

The memorial guys were battling on. Alex cast a cursory glance across the other, less ostentatious, headstones. Most of them were filled with more text than Dill's. *Beloved son and brother*. A dedication as short and sweet as his time had been.

'You're still beloved, Dill Pickle,' Alex said quietly.

Dill hadn't had a chance to become a beloved father, or uncle or grandfather like most of the others laid to rest here. They'd never know if Dill's kids would've inherited his summer freckles, or that daft dimple, or whether or not they'd have used those traits to deadly effect in the art of charming their mothers.

'Do you remember Mum's face, Dill? When you opened

the box from Mal and all those shiny sharp bits were inside? Mum's eyes were like saucers.' Dill's eyes had been like saucers too. Alex remembered, Dill had only been obsessed with learning how to shoot an arrow on target once Malcolm Sinclair had turned up at the house with that archery set. An early birthday present, something Mal's dad had found in the attic, going to waste.

'Mum was so upset about the mayor sending you a gift like that, Dill.' Granny Ros had gotten both barrels over the washing up. Blythe didn't care that it was only going to go in the bin back at the Sinclairs' house. It looked expensive, and dangerous. Blythe had been set to have Jem politely ask Mal to take it back. 'But you charmed her on that one too, Dill Pickle.'

Alex smiled but it was bittersweet. She remembered the afternoon so clearly. The last minute change of plan. Their dad nipping out in the pickup on an emergency callout, Jem and Dill driving Mum mad with the arguing.

Alex swallowed. 'Dad would've shown you how to shoot them properly, Dill. So your arm didn't get so tired.' She bit down hard on the inside of her lip. Her voice came out strained and wiry. 'I'm so sorry I left you, Dill.'

CHAPTER 26

Alex rubbed at the little dark splodge on her parents' bed-spread. Didn't Jem say they'd changed the beds last week-end?

'Jem?' she shouted across the landing. 'Has the dog been in here?' Could it jump this high yet? *Houdini* they should call her. She'd slipped her lead enough times this week. No answer from the direction of Jem's room. Alex followed the phone cable from the socket beside her mum's bedside table down onto the floor and under her parents' bedroom door. She picked up the last of the towels from the laundry basket on her mother's reading chair and arched her back to see out onto the landing.

Jem's door was still shut, she must have been holed up in there all day. Alex had come home with a tiny inkling of something being off and had checked for signs of Jem leaving the house for some reason. Jem's shoes and keys were all still where they'd been this morning. Alex felt another stab of guilt. Was she doubting Jem, too? Off the back of one nosey sod's assumption? Alex thought about her mum asking after Jem today and Alex's guilt melted into irritation again.

'Did you even make it into the shower today, Jem? Must've been a really good catch up with Mal seeing as you didn't make it to see Mum today,' Alex wanted to shout. *Or down for dinner, for that matter.* Maybe she really did have a migraine.

It was no big deal, Alex had told herself. Her dad hadn't called to say he wasn't coming home so he was clearly in about as much of a hurry to eat with his family as Jem was. Alex was used to eating alone anyway so, no big deal.

Alex might've thought about letting this upset her, but there was something about the Parsons woman and her two little girls at the hospital that had started occupying a grow-ing spot in the back of Alex's mind. The Parsons woman, squirrelling. Maybe her awful husband was blowing all her food money on gambling, like Finn's dad used to.

His name had come from nowhere. Alex felt a surge of guilt. She should've dropped in at Finn's place by now. But she couldn't do it. This morning at the garage, it had been a short sharp reminder how paper-thin her dad's toler-ance was. Arranging to meet Finn on purpose would be like sucker-punching a big hole straight through the middle of it.

Alex picked up the empty laundry basket and stepped over the phone cable into the hall. The puppy began wag-ging its tail, excitedly reversing as Alex stepped towards it. 'Stay off the beds, you naughty dog. Hey, no, wait! You can't go in there.'

Alex set the basket down and followed the puppy to the door at the end of the hall. Dill's door had never been closed.

'It's not a weird shrine, if that's what anyone is thinking,' Blythe had said lightly over dinner once. 'Boys' things never go out of trend, do they? And one of you girls might bring us a grandson home one day, and he can play in there with his uncle Dillon's things and we'll tell him what a hell-bat he was. It's not like we need another guest room anyway, we already rattle around this big old house.'

Jem thought it was their mum's way of making sure he didn't get forgotten. Letting everyone know that it was OK to look at Dill's things and remember him. Alex did not go in here.

'Hey. Dog. Come on! What's this? What's this in my pocket? Come on, let's go and get your ball.' The puppy was having none of it. She was already buried beneath Dill's bed, two corn-coloured back paws scrambling to get under there too. 'Hey, no, come on, dog. Out of there.'

The floor creaked behind her. Alex spun back nearly taking her own eye out.

'Dad… You scared me.'

Ted had his hands in his pockets. It made him look childlike. 'I'm sorry, for snapping at you this morning, Alexandra. It was bad timing. You caught me off-guard.'

Alex tried to get her bearings. 'That's OK. I should've let you know I was coming. You were, erm… in the middle of something.'

Ted nodded. 'Who's your sister on the phone to?'

'Work, I think. I think they're hounding her.'

'Good,' her dad said absently. 'That's good.'

Alex mentally punched herself for wandering in here. 'Can I fix you some dinner?' she asked hopefully.

'No, thank you. I ate at the hospital. I'm tired. I think I'm going to go take a shower.'

'Oh, OK. Well I've just put fresh towels in there.'

He rocked back on his heels. 'Thank you, Alex.'

'It's fine.' Alex smiled. He'd just apologised. For snapping. Something lightened inside Alex's stomach, a knot releasing just a fraction.

'I'm going to go then, take my shower.'

'OK.' Alex gave him a lopsided smile.

Here she was standing amongst Dillon's things, precious things, and he hadn't said anything that suggested it wasn't OK for her to do that. Hadn't made her feel like a stranger in their house when it would be so easy. *He's trying, Al*, she told herself confidently.

Ted turned to leave then held back stiffly in the doorway.

'When you're done in here, Alexandra… just make sure you leave things the way they were. It's just your mother, she doesn't like things upset. Probably best if no-one comes in here.'

CHAPTER 27

'Watch where you're goin! *Jesus!*' Alex started at Jem's sudden outburst; she almost deployed the emergency stop her father had made her practice again and again as a learner driver lest she become a notoriously late-braker like Mrs Fairbanks. 'Sorry. But honestly, these people. Getting to the souvenir shop for a crappy plastic battleaxe is not worth dying for.'

Alex felt her lungs easing again after the sudden excitement. 'Blimey, Jem. You're like the girl on that film… *Lock Stock and Two Smoking Barrels.*'

'What girl?'

'The girl who's comatose on the sofa when the bad guys come in for the drugs, then she springs up and—'

'Blows them all away with the big gun?' Jem said disinterestedly. Jem was like that girl, kind of. All or nothing, war or peace, funny or furious.

Alex stole a quick sideways glance at her sister. Most of Jem's face was hidden behind her Ray-Bans and fringe. Her mouth had a hard set to it this morning. Jem had sat in silence on the way into town. Alex had tried several conversation starters, what to have for tea, when was the last time they'd watched *Point Break* before last night, how pretty did Millie Sinclair look the other day in that dress, you'd never know she had one leg shorter than the other, would you? Jem wasn't biting anything though, bar her thumbnail.

St Cuthbert's spire peeped into view beyond the banners snaking over the high street inviting visitors to *Go Beserk!* Which didn't really make sense, Alex thought, because it was the visitors to the town who were supposed to help the Anglo Saxons fend off the invading Vikings who were, by definition, the true beserkers they'd all learned about in school.

Alex tapped on the steering wheel. 'They were putting up the mayor's headstone at St Bertie's yesterday, I wonder if Mal's seen it yet. An angel, it's huge, probably visible from space.'

'An *angel*?' Jem said coolly. She was still looking out of her window. 'Because the good old town Mayor was whiter than white?'

There was a spike in Jem's voice. Was she ill? Alex had dug out migraine pills last night but Jem hadn't taken them. She'd finally emerged from her room just in time to catch Alex rifling through their old DVDs. One short sharp reminder of the sanctity of Dill's bedroom and Alex had found herself suddenly in need of a couple of hours' escapism. Patrick Swayze in a wetsuit had seemed a reliable choice.

'He doesn't really do it for me.' Jem had said. 'All that macho stuff, I've never got it if I'm honest.'

Alex had carried on watching the movie and wondered if maybe Jem had a serious condition of the brain, not just the aftereffects of a migraine and/or hangover, but she wasn't going to argue with her, not after Jem had relayed the late-night conversation she'd had with Mal. Blythe had been happy and well in the churchyard, not stricken with grief as Alex had convinced herself. Alex had thought to casually ask what else they'd been chatting about all night, then decided not to push it. Why prod when you can quit while you're ahead?

Alex knocked her indicator on and pulled into one of the bays near Brünnhilde's Baps. A teenage boy was taking a selfie with his head positioned alarmingly close to the whopping Brünnhilde statue's best assets.

'What are we doing, I thought we were going straight to the hospital?'

Alex shut the engine off resolutely. 'We are, but I want to get Mum some flowers first. I saw Dill's and, well, they do the trick, don't they? Brighten a place.'

Jem looked through the windscreen at Wallflowers' shop front.

'From here? I'll wait in the truck, thanks.' Jem put her feet up on the dash and went back to her thumbnail.

'Seriously, Jem? So Carrie was an idiot at school. Weren't we all? Isn't it time to just be friendly and get on with it?' Alex had a thought. *You big hypocrite.* She was totally avoiding Finn. And not even because she didn't like him, but because she *did*. How school-yard was that?

'What do I need to go in for, Alex?' Jem snipped. 'She's not having any of my money.'

'Actually, Jem, I think I might have left my purse in the hall.' Jem groaned. 'Well I had to put it down to mop up the dog's piddle on the way out and you were too busy!' Jem had been attached to the phone, again, but saying so might trip off her mood.

'Fine.' Jem huffed again and got out of the truck. 'But I am not in the mood for Carrie sodding Logan.'

Alex followed Jem onto the pavement towards the new array of flowers Carrie had in tubs outside. Fewer bees today, thankfully. Alex scanned the buckets. Jem was already flipping through the icons of her phone. 'Four whole bars of signal. Hoo-*bloody*-ray.'

'These are pretty. Mum likes pink, right, Jem?'

Jem shrugged. 'I suppose.'

Alex looked at her. Jem looked washed out in the sunshine. She never left the house without killer makeup and Alex could see now, Jem hadn't even put base on this morning.

'What's that look for, Alex? Yes, I think she likes pink, but would I stake my life on it? Probably not. Maybe she prefers yellow? Who knows? And why am I supposed to know all the answers anyway? I don't know every little thing about Blythe Foster? Do you?'

Alex lowered her handful of flowers. 'What is wrong with

you this morning, Jem? And yesterday, actually? Have I done something?'

Jem looked away down the high street, then at her sandals. 'No. Look, just shout me when you're ready to pay.'

'Let's just get these then.' Alex huffed. 'We'll go with the pink and hope for the best. Before standing this close to Carrie's shop sends you completely over the edge.'

Alex pushed on the glass door and stepped into the cooler air of the florist's, the heady scent of hydrangeas and newly cut timber was immediate. Wallflowers was very minimalist inside, more like a side street gallery, all white walls and sporadic Perspex displays. An unpleasant banging sound was coming from somewhere out back. Carrie looked up from where she was strategically placing pheasant feathers into a bunch of something purple.

'Eugh, this noise! Sorry, oh *hi*, Alex! Oh… hello, Jem.'

Jem smiled flatly. The hammering banged on. Carrie shook her sleek ponytail over her shoulder. 'Sorry about all this racket, I'm having work done.'

'Not on your face, unfortunately,' Jem mumbled. Alex heard herself laugh nervously.

'I want to take the shop hard into the bridal market, so, more workspace!' Carrie hadn't heard Jem. Good.

'Sounds promising,' Alex replied. Alex saw Carrie give Jem a stealthy once-over while Jem wasn't looking. Jem looked ace, Alex thought, even without the makeup. Jem poked disdainfully at a tulip arrangement and puffed out her cheeks.

'I've got to be honest, this place was a *joke* when I took it over, but our Facebook page has gone *mental*.' Carrie thrust a business card into Alex's hands. 'You should follow us, Alex. Tell your friends. Especially the well-heeled ones who aren't married yet. What about you, Jem? Planning on walking down the aisle any time soon?'

Jem was still idly looking around, arms folded across her chest, clearly unimpressed. She seemed geared up for an awkward silence. Alex intercepted it. 'I was saying to Jem, about this wedding programme, *Wedding Warriors* or something. The things people buy, the money they spend is *unbelievable*. Jem makes jewellery now, *amazing* jewellery and I was telling her she should—'

'Jewellery? As in, like, pretty jewellery?' Carrie handled her words like they were made of salt. Her mouth was doing this funny thing around them.

'No, the ugly sort,' Jem answered sarcastically. Then she smiled it off.

Carrie smiled back. It was going to be sharp looks at dawn at this rate. 'No kidding. So do you, like, have a Facebook page or something, Jem?' Carrie asked brightly.

'Jem doesn't do Facebook. Do you, Jem?' Alex flashed Jem a look. Confrontation, of any proportions, made her toes curl.

Carrie twigged it wasn't worth waiting for an answer from Jem and turned to concentrate on Alex instead. 'Everybody's on Facebook. It's where we all go to pretend we're all happy fabulous people, isn't it, Alex? I always wonder when a person our age isn't on Facebook, if maybe they've got something to hide. What do you say, Jem?' Carrie asked innocently.

Alex was starting to see why Carrie rubbed Jem up the wrong way. Carrie was putting a filter on it for Alex's benefit, that much was obvious. But under the childishness Alex could feel an unpleasant charge in the air.

'I'm not on Facebook either, Carrie. Just these, thanks.' Alex set the pink flowers on Carrie's glass counter.

'Ah, peonies. For your mum?'

'We just thought we'd brighten up her hospital room, didn't we, Jem?'

'Well, I've had the whole gang in this week. You two today, Finn's out back right now as we speak, flexing over his workbench.' Alex stiffened. It wasn't like she'd promised she'd pop in to see Finn's studio yesterday, she'd never said, *for definite*. 'Would you like a card with these? I could get some cellophane and twine and—'

'No, that's OK, thanks. We're in a hurry,' said Alex. The racket out through the back of the shop had stopped. 'A big hurry, actually,' she lied.

'Suit yourself,' Carrie chirped. 'What was I saying? Oh yes, the old St Bertie's gang, so I've had you lot in, Finn, and Malcolm Sinclair too. He caught me last thing Monday evening, *just* caught me actually, while I was shutting up shop. Clueless as usual, didn't know what he was looking for. I tried to help but he's a typical man, panic-grabber. He bought a tonne of yellow roses in the end. I tried to tell him, yellow is for *friendship*, thinking he might want to get his wife something a bit more thoughtful but *no*. I mean, *friendship*. Show me a wife who wants *friendship* from her husband.'

Show me a wife who doesn't, thought Alex. 'Maybe they weren't for Millie?' Alex said objectively. She looked at Jem then, but Jem had turned her back again. She didn't appear to be looking at anything in particular now, only the door.

Carrie shrugged. 'Who knows? He looked a bit shifty though. Couldn't get gone quickly enough. Didn't even hang around for a card to go with them.' Carrie ducked her head a little. 'Maybe they *weren't* for Millie.'

Jem bristled. 'Maybe they were for his mother, Carrie,' she said sharply. 'Or maybe, people should just get on with their own lives and mind their own goddamned business.'

Carrie's face tensed. 'Actually, I remember now,' she said, ignoring Jem completely. Carrie began playing with another pheasant feather. 'I think they *were* for his mum. What date was Monday again?' Carrie checked her calendar. 'Yep, it was… Mum made me pencil it in when I took over.' '*Don't forget, Mayor Sinclair likes to come in on the same day, every year, for a small bouquet, Carrie.*' Carrie pursed her lips compassionately. 'Mal must've been taking the flowers for his mother, because his dad can't any more. Bless, isn't that sweet? Mal carrying on the tradition for his dad? It's so sad really. Did you know the mayor had died?'

'Here, you know my PIN. I'll wait in the truck,' Jem said, slapping down her card on the countertop.

Carrie scowled at Jem's abruptness. Alex watched Jem trounce out to the truck and try angrily to get in without the keys. Carrie was already feeding Jem's bank card into her card reader.

'That's twenty-two then for the peonies.'

Carrie turned back to her garish arrangement. Alex punched in Jem's year of birth.

PIN Incorrect.

Alex could hear movement coming from the back. *Agh.* Get a move on, Alex. Had she just typed her own PIN by mistake? She tried again…

PIN Incorrect.

Finn was whistling, he was coming through to the shop. Bugger it. What was the limit before the card was stopped? Three attempts?

Concentrate!

Alex eyed the card machine. Jem always used that number. No, hang on. She changed it to a word when she'd got all security savvy about people hacking into other people's private stuff, *what was it?* The whistling was getting closer. Alex vaguely remembered Jem's reasoning, she'd chosen something no-one would associate with her, in case she was ever mugged by someone she knew, presumably. *What was it?* Alex's mind had gone completely blank. Ahah! *Of course!* It was a colour. A colour Jem had detested since childhood, a colour that had spoiled her lunchbox and ballet

costumes, and party dresses, because *not all little girls liked
having it forced down their conformist little throats*, Jem had
argued.

Alex looked at the number pad and found the letters.
P-I-N-K.

PIN ACCEPTED.

Finn didn't see Alex when he walked through the far door.
He rubbed a few flakes of sawdust from his hair while he
spoke to Carrie. Alex saw most of them settle on the soft
rise of his chest and felt a small, silly thrill. 'I'm just going
to make a run to the timber merchant's up in Kerring. I need
a few more lengths before the framework's finished,' Finn
said.

Carrie cocked her hip, almost imperceptibly. Her shoulders fell out of skew and she repositioned herself in that subtle way waif-like beautiful film stars turned their chins to
camera. Alex fought an urge to cock her hip too, then cock
the other one and waddle as discreetly as possible from the
shop.

Carrie had left the flowers beside the card reader. Alex
gently set a hand on them and slipped them quietly towards
her. Carrie was listening intently to Finn's talk of ways to
keep costs down. 'Oh, don't worry about the money, Finn,
just do what you feel's necessary,' Carrie crooned.

Alex was going to go for it. She was going to slip out
before either of them noticed. She eased Jem's card from the
machine. That would be embarrassing, having to go back in
for it. She turned and saw Jem leaning against the bonnet

of the truck. Alex began walking softly towards the door, flowers in hand, *nearly there*. Jem looked up and watched her come, Alex sped up a little in that way she would speed up on Sports Days at St Cuthbert's when the finish line was near, *one last burst*! And then something went wrong.

The whole front glass wall of Wallflowers Florist's rattled violently in front of her. An intensely unpleasant pain seared through the front of Alex's face. She stumbled back and landed ungracefully on her backside, her mum's flowers bashed against the floor in a pink mess.

'Whoa, there! Alex!' He was darting towards her. A pair of CAT boots appeared beside Alex's legs. They had a tiny digger motif branded next to the laces.

'I'm fine! Perfectly fine!' Alex protested, tears of pain pooling in her eyeballs. Jem burst back into the shop. Two capable hands were suddenly under Alex's arms, easing her back to her feet.

Jem had taken her glasses off. Her eyes looked red and puffy. 'Alex! Oh my God, you're bleeding.'

Really? 'Really? Oh, it's fine, honestly.' *Did Jem say bleeding?* Hooray!

'Carrie? Tissues,' Finn commanded. Alex was mortified. Carrie nipped behind the counter and produced a tissue box.

'You can't have a door like that, Carrie. Where are the safety stickers?' Jem hissed.

Carrie held out the box. 'What?'

Alex grabbed a handful and pressed it to her face. She could taste the blood now.

'Are you OK?' Finn asked.

'Absolutely fine!' she trilled.

Finn's eye narrowed.

'That door! It needs something on it. Look at my sister!'

'Jem, really, I'm totally fine!' Alex's nose felt numb and tingly. It was making her voice sound numb and tingly too. Finn was watching her. He gently pulled Alex's hand away then crouched down so he could better inspect her nose.

'This isn't going to look very attractive, but trust me, it'll help the bleeding.'

Finn bunched up a tissue and gently inserted it into Alex's nostril.

'I'm so clumsy,' she mumbled. Oh for crying out loud. *This* was why only Jem had had any success with ballet. Blythe had signed Alex up for horn dancing instead.

Finn had got the second nostril plugged before Alex's embarrassment really kicked in. This was what her mother spoke about, a person's wrongs coming back to kick them in the backside. Or hit them in the face like a glass door.

'Well, it's normally open,' Carrie protested.

'Well it's not open now, is it?' Jem spat.

Carrie reared like a coiled snake. 'Don't lecture me, Jem Foster. If you were any good with doors, you wouldn't still be firmly on the inside of the clo—'

'Ladies!' Finn said with the cool efficiency of a bomb-disposal unit. 'I'll sort it, I have something back at the shop. Leave it with me, Jem.'

Jem and Carrie traded scowls but only Jem's chest was heaving with adrenalin.

'Come on, Jem.' Alex tried to say chirpily. *Before I die right here of embarrassment.* 'Mum's waiting.' She heard her voice, it sounded as if a bus had parked up each nostril. Alex gave Finn a feeble smile then set her eyes anywhere but near him. 'Thanks,' she managed feebly. She should have at least offered an excuse for yesterday's no show.

Finn looked embarrassed for her. 'No problem at all, Foster. See you around.'

Jem gathered up what flowers were still intact and took Alex by the arm. Nobody said anything else until they were back at the truck.

Alex fiddled the keys into her door. Jem was glaring over the truck roof, rage rippling from her. 'What?' Jem snapped.

Alex was already feeling sorry for herself. 'Jem! You're not fifteen any more, you can't just go blowing off at people because they tick you off! Was there any need for that?' She sounded completely ridiculous with all this tissue shoved up her nose.

'Any need for what? Defending you?'

'There was nothing to defend, Jem! It was my own stupid fault. I wasn't watching what I was doing.' The burden of being a total idiot intensified.

'Carrie's a bitch, Alex. You are allowed to say it.'

'She is? And you were polite, were you? You were in a bad mood before we even walked in, Jem.'

'Yeah well, excuse me for trying to do what you never had to.'

'Do what?'

'*Deal* with things, Alex!' Jem wasn't shouting exactly.

Alex looked about them at the rest of the people on the high street. It seemed busier now, even for a Sunday morning. No wonder the shops were all trading. 'What's that supposed to mean, Jem?

'Put it this way, Alex, if I didn't fight my battles, no-one else was there to. It's not like I had a big sister around, was it? In fact, the only person I ever remember having in my corner when I needed them was Mal Sinclair.'

It felt like slamming into another glass wall. Alex took in the emotions playing out over Jem's face. But Jem was the sibling she *hadn't* let down, wasn't she?

'What do you mean, Jem?' But Alex already knew she didn't want the answer.

'It means, Alex, you're a runner. You were always a good runner, faster than I ever was. You were running just now, in there. You didn't even bother opening the door first! Because you can't handle Finn. Because you could *never* handle Finn. Well running away from everything might have been the best thing for you, but when things were happening in *my* life, it would've been nice if you'd have stopped to look back over your shoulder.'

CHAPTER 28

Blythe was having her catheter bag changed. Alex was pretending to look for the card that had come with the enormous bouquet in front of her. She'd set her own handful of battered pink peonies next to them; they were already slouching limply in a vase too big for them. Alex let her eyes slope off to the view over the hospital car park. As if the morning hadn't become miserable enough, the sun had abandoned them to the grips of a torrential summer downpour.

'All done, Blythe. I'll see you in a little while. Buzz if you need anything.' Alex turned to see her mum giving the nurse a grateful smile, one side of her face bright and warm, the other reluctant to be affected. The nurse stopped at the hand-wash beside the door. Alex turned back to the flowers again.

You're a runner, Alex. Jem was right. But she'd only left the Falls to keep from making anything any worse, because that's what she'd heard him say they all needed, once. *Time and distance.* How could Jem think it was because she didn't care? It had *never* been because she didn't care.

Alex took a bracing breath. *You are a coward, Alex.* It was the same with the new marks she'd spotted on her mother's hospital bedclothes. Three days in a row she'd found a new stain but the staff were all so nice and she couldn't think of a way to ask how often the sheets were changed without sounding like one of *those* relatives. The nurse turned the tap off again. Well Alex was going to mention it now, have some balls for a change and not care who she offended because her mum shouldn't be sleeping under grubby sheets. That was reasonable, wasn't it?

Alex tried psyching herself up.

'They're beauties, aren't they?' The nurse smiled at Alex as she reached for the door handle and paused. 'Your mother must have a sixth sense,' she said, turning to Blythe. 'When I came in to take your obs, you were talking about flowers then, Blythe. Now look at them all.'

Alex's new assertiveness halted in its tracks. She regarded the whopping bouquet again. They really were beautiful, anyone would think Elton John was staying in Room 2. She could always mention the sheets later. 'They are really gorgeous. Did my dad bring them in this morning?'

The nurse stalled at the door. 'Oh they'd arrived before your dad, young lady. And on a Sunday too! They must've paid extra for that. You got yourself a secret admirer,

Blythe?' the nurse teased. The nurse winked playfully at Alex. 'If I were you, I'd find that card and check for yourself, make sure your mum's not giving your poor dad the run around.'

Alex smiled. It made her nose hurt. Almost as much as her pride did. 'I would, but… the card must've dropped out somewhere. Who are they from, Mum?'

Blythe turned her head slowly towards Alex. 'I don't know, darling,' she drawled. Alex kept forgetting. Every time she spoke, it was like learning her mum was ill again. Blythe blinked slowly. 'I was sleeping. I missed your father as well.' She was still trying to smile

Alex heard her mother swallow, a laborious considered swallow, the way people swallowed when their glands were swollen or they had the mother of all sore throats. 'Where's Jem?' Blythe asked slowly.

Alex began rearranging the bouquet as if she had a clue what she was doing. 'She's not very well, Mum… another headache,' Alex lied. It wasn't a complete lie, there was definitely something not well with Jem earlier. Something Alex knew nothing about, because she was a crap sister.

Alex found the little stick thing where the florist's card had been pronged into the bouquet but there was only a business card. *The Bay Tree Floral Studio, Kerring*. Not from Carrie's shop then. Jem would be pleased.

'Alex?'

'Hmm?' Alex had messed up the shape of the bouquet.

She gave up with the flowers and began pouring her mother another beaker of water.

'Is everything… all right… at home?'

Alex had overfilled the cup. It would spill all down her mum before Blythe would manage to sip from it.

'Sure. Everything's fine, Mum.'

Blythe patted the bed with the hand that hadn't abandoned her. Blythe's body might not be ready for much, but her eyes shone brown and resolute. Alex recognised a small part of herself. 'Look after… each… other, darling.'

'We are, Mum.' Alex smiled. But that was the biggest lie of all. They were surviving each other and every one of them knew it.

'Your father… he's a good man… Alex.'

Blythe was tiring. Alex spoke just to give her mum chance to rest. 'I know he is, Mum.'

'Don't leave.'

'I only just got here, Mum. Have you made your lunch selection yet? Would you like me to fill it out?' Had to be her right side, didn't it? Even filling in her own dinner card was a mountain to climb for her now.

Alex felt her mother's thumb move over her cheek like she was still a little girl about to be sent through the gates of St Bertie's for the day. '*No*. Don't leave *the Falls*… I want us all… to talk. When I come home.' Her mum's eyes were locked on her.

'Sure, Mum. Talk about what?'

Blythe smoothed a few strands of Alex's hair around her

face before resting her fingers on top of Alex's hand. 'We need, to talk… about your brother.'

*

Alex dialled Jem again, before she left the hospital car park. Jem might fancy a bottle of wine or something, maybe they could have a girls' night, do what sisters do. *Talk.* Jem was happy enough talking to everyone else at the minute, Mal Sinclair, that George from work who kept ringing day and night and who Alex had a growing suspicion was the person hanging up on her each time she got to the phone first.

Jem's mobile cut straight to answerphone again. Alex heard a bleep warning the battery on her phone was nearly dead.

She tried again. This time it rang.

'Pick up, Jem, pick up, pick up, pick up…'

'Hey.' Jem sounded resigned.

'Jem. Are you OK? Where have you been all day? I thought you'd come to the hospital, I've been calling the house—'

'I'm not at the house. I went for a walk. I wanted some fresh air.' Alex's wipers squeaked over the windscreen. She couldn't hear torrential rain in the background.

'Nice day for it,' Alex tried. Alex's phone bleeped again. Jem was still quiet. 'Jem? I'm just leaving Kerring General. When I get home… can we talk?'

Alex heard Jem take a deep breath at the other end. 'What

I said earlier, Al. I didn't mean it. Really, we don't need to talk about it. I'm sorry.'

Alex bit at her lip. She could just leave it there. No need to kick up any hornets' nests. She could pick up a bottle on the way home anyway, talk Jem into another shot at the DVD collection. But she couldn't accept that *sorry.*

'Please, don't say sorry, Jem. I'm sorry. If you say Carrie's a bitch, that should have been good enough for me.'

'Alex, it's not Carrie. I couldn't give a shit what Carrie gets up to. Not any more. And before you ask, I promise, it's not you. You're the last person I want to fall out with right now.'

Alex felt lifted by that.

'Mum's going to be OK, Jem. She's getting better every day.'

There was a long pause. The wipers schlumped across the windscreen again. Alex's phone battery bleeped.

'I know. Everything is fine.'

Jem sounded weird. She'd been weird for days.

'Jem?' Alex hesitated. 'You've had your head somewhere else since you went out with Mal the other night. Has something happened?' More silence. 'Jem. Please talk to me. You were right earlier. I should've been around for you, I should've been better than I was. Whatever's bothering you, you don't have to carry it around on your own. Just... let me in.'

Alex could hear small breathy sounds. Jem was crying.

Jem. 'What is it, Jem? What's happened? Did Mal say something to upset you?'

'Alex. There's someth—'

The line went dead. The wipers cleared the view again for a few seconds before the rain fought back.

'Jem?' Alex watched her screen go into power meltdown. *Shit.* She threw her phone across the dash and set her head back against the driver's seat. *Almost, Alex.* Jem had almost leant on her.

Across the car park, a huddled figure was trying to hold a coat over the front of a pushchair. Alex watched them make it a few steps in the downpour, then the woman stopped and beckoned behind her. Alex scanned along the path back towards the hospital entrance. A little girl was standing under the canopy, shaking her head.

'You're not thinking about walking all the way back to town in this…' Mrs Parsons skipped back and lifted her daughter onto her hip. Alex surveyed the sky above them for a promising pocket of blue. She watched them struggle over a kerb. 'You can't… you can't push a pram with one hand and hold your little—' Alex fired up the truck, cranked it into gear and cut a path across the hospital car park.

She pulled alongside them and Mrs Parsons skittered away to the other side of the path as if Alex's intention had been to mount the kerb and bundle them all into the boot like some crime lord.

'Sorry, I didn't mean to startle you. I don't think the buses run on Sundays, can I give you a lift?' Mrs Parsons looked even more slight in the rain. The little girl's dark hair was starting to stick to her forehead in wet streaks. 'Really, it's no bother. You live in the one of the terraced houses, at the top of Eilidh high street, right? It's on my way, we can throw the pram in the boot!'

Mrs Parsons looked like a rabbit caught in headlights. She looked for a pocket of blue sky too, and admitted defeat. Alex was already getting out to help. She reached up and offered to take the little girl from her mum's hip. Both looked unsure. 'Come on, we've shared a breakfast muffin already.' A slice of carrot cake too but Alex didn't like to mention it. 'Let's share a ride home.'

CHAPTER 29

Jem had been looking into the bathroom mirror for a while. There wasn't a single smear on this mirror, a minor miracle given the number of troubled souls that must have been through here in the last week alone. 'Always squeaky clean, Mum,' Jem said at her reflection. She stuck a finger against the glass just to be obnoxious.

How many hours had she spent in front of this mirror since her teens, she wondered. Agonising, trying to see a way forwards, to pluck up the courage it would require to tell them her tricky little secret. She'd come so close to going through with it once. It had been there, on her lips. *Just tell them. You're not a bad person. This doesn't make you a bad person. If they love you, it won't matter.*

They had been Mal's words, he'd cajoled them into Jem's head while she'd tried to work herself up like a beserker so she could march inside the house and just tell them all straight. But then Jem had joined them at the table and Alex had dropped her bombshell about leaving university and not coming back to live here and then Dad had gone mad about Jem sitting outside talking to Mal instead of coming in on time for dinner. There hadn't been room left for any more admissions that night.

You idiot, Jem. It was almost funny now, her wandering around like a complete arse since her teens, thinking she had something major to get off her chest all this time. It wasn't major. No-one would get *hurt* when she told them the truth about herself, disappointed maybe, resistant. But she hadn't hurt anyone. Even now, this last week, she'd been so frightened of her mum dying, of losing the chance to explain everything while she still could. Now one night out with an old friend and her mum was off limits. Because now there was a bigger, badder secret to keep, and Jem hadn't worked out yet how to look at her mother without it all coming tumbling out.

Jem braced her hands back on the bathroom sink and glared at herself. *She'll know as soon as she looks at you.*

Jem felt that unpleasant sicky feeling in her stomach again, it had been there since she'd left The Cavern last night for somewhere more private with Mal. 'Can we go somewhere we won't be disturbed?' he'd asked. And she'd gone willingly.

Jem rubbed at the dark circles starting under her eyes. They didn't look bloodshot now at least. She'd nearly buckled on the phone to Alex and then, thankfully, the phone had cut out. Jem let out another sigh of relief at that. Alex wouldn't be able to cope with *this*. Alex was trying so hard to play happy families, how could she possibly handle a home-wrecking scandal? How would their *dad* handle it?

Jem felt the upset lurch inside her again. She was still trying to make sense of what her own feelings were. The shame
of it. The humiliation it would cause her sister and parents
if anyone else were to find out. No, she couldn't do it. She
couldn't tell Alex, of course she couldn't. Sharing a secret
that could kill a marriage, drive a wedge between a father
and his son… Jem couldn't do it. She wouldn't. It had to stay
between her and Mal.

CHAPTER 30

'So the car actually fell and *crushed* his chest bone?' Alex said with something like the awe she reserved for late night episodes of *I was bitten, and survived!* Poor Mr Parsons. Even though Helen Fairbanks had him down as a monstrous wife-beater who wouldn't let Emma and the little ones have a single day off that horrendous hike to Kerring General and back.

Graham Parsons had a job over at Superfitters Tyres & Exhausts. It had given Alex a small angle from which she was attempting to forge a fleeting friendship with his wife, so that if there was a bruise or some other incriminating evidence Alex might somehow be able to verify and therefore vouch for it. Alex stole another glance at her passenger. People who wanted to hide bruises did not step out with strappy vests and cotton skirts on, did they?

'Mummy, when we get the pram out again, can I have one of the muff—'

'So your mum! You must be really looking forward to getting her home, like we are your daddy, aren't we, Poppy?' Poppy frowned while her mum changed the subject. Helping herself to those muffins was about as much proof that they were a family in crisis as a bruise would've been. Alex rolled with the subject change all the same. 'How often do you come back to the Falls to see her?'

Alex felt embarrassed about the truth. 'Oh, I'm a bit of a bad penny!' she quipped. Ha-dee-ha.

'What's a bad penny?' Poppy asked.

'A bad penny? You haven't heard that before, honey?'

Poppy shook her head in the rear view. 'Mr Mason likes pennies. He always takes my mummy and daddy's pennies.'

Emma moved subtly in the back and Poppy shrank back into the seat.

'A bad penny is like a phrase. It usually means something bad that keeps turning up again, like a person who keeps coming back, even if nobody wants them to.'

'Doesn't your mummy and daddy want you to come back? Aren't you a good penny?'

'Of course she is, sweetie. Only good pennies give you lifts in the rain.'

Alex tried not to run through the definition of a bad penny again. 'Do you like the rain, Poppy?'

'Mummy likes the rain. She says people don't always come to our house when it's raining lots. They stay away.'

Alex smiled at her rear view mirror. 'So do you go to St Cuthbert's? We used to call it St Bertie's. I went to St Bertie's. And my brother and sister did too. It's highly recommended.'

'She starts in Mrs Sinclair's class in September, don't you, sweetie? You like Mrs Sinclair, she's kind.'

'Oh, you mean Millie? She is, she's lovely. So do you know Alfie, Poppy? From pre-school? Is he a nice boy? Did you know, his daddy's a police officer?'

'He's not nice when he's putting a snail inside my welly boot,' Poppy said assertively. 'But he's nice when he shares his biscuits.'

'Snails in your boot? Sounds like something my brother would've done.'

'How old is your brother? Is he going to be in Mrs Sinclair's class?'

'Oh, no. He's…'

'Alex's brother will be grown up now, Poppy. Not little like you. The children adore Mrs Sinclair, don't you?'

'I always wear my seatbelt because Mrs Sinclair got hurt in a car when she was little like me and now she's got lines on her legs and a funny shoe that is bigger on one side and not big on the normal side. And now my daddy's been hurt by a car as well because Mr Mas—'

Emma lurched forwards in her seat. 'This is us, with the toys.'

Alex slowed in front of a tall town house with a pink scooter just inside the front gate and what looked like a homemade Wendy house at the corner of the lawn.

'I'll help you get everything to the house,' Alex offered.

'Our house looks dark, Mummy,' Poppy said quietly.

'It's OK, baby,' Emma whispered.

Alex pulled in and shut the engine off. She hadn't unclicked her belt and gotten her door open before Emma had already jumped into action, scurrying around the truck in nervous jolty movements, flicking the pram out with one hand while the baby was propped on her hip.

'Thank you so much, I really appreciate it. Come on, Poppy, let's get inside. Come on, that's it. Before the rain starts again. Bye, Alex.'

CHAPTER 31

Alex had loitered on the pavement until Emma had managed to get the children, pram and all their things to the house. Emma had babbled something about usually inviting Alex in only she hadn't had chance to tidy up and Alex had seen something like terror wash over Emma's face while she waited for Alex to say something like, *That's OK, mess doesn't bother me!*

Alex reached her driver's side and noticed something pink and plastic-looking in the small gap between the truck and the kerb. She picked the dummy up and turned it over in her hand. 'You'll be needing that though, Emma.'

She didn't want to stress Emma out. She'd just quickly run it in then make herself scarce. Alex nipped over to the Parsons' garden gate and ambled towards the front door.

Poppy was right, their house did look dark, *gloomy* seemed a better choice. It was only early evening and the rain had stopped but there was something melancholy about the place, as if houses were like faces and the strain of too many heavy thoughts on the inside could impact the general appearance of the outside. The grass was long, too long for

Poppy to ride her scooter around on. But then who would've been cutting the lawns while Mr Parsons recovered and Emma was tied up with the children? She probably had a hundred worries far higher up the list. Finn should look into garden maintenance. One more string to his bow. Alex wrinkled her nose to see if it still hurt. It did.

She pressed on the doorbell and heard it chime through the hallway the other side. Alex gave it a few seconds then tried a jovial knock. Oh, sod. Emma was that efficient, she was probably already trying to get the baby off to sleep. Should Alex just post the dummy through? The door opened a fraction.

'Oh! Ah, me again,' Alex said apologetically. 'You dropped Isla's dummy. I didn't think you'd want to get caught short at bedtime.'

Emma hadn't opened the door more than a couple of inches. Poppy was at her legs, trying to press herself as closely to her mother's legs as possible. Emma seemed even more on edge than she had been when Alex had first pulled over to her in the truck.

'Thank you.' Emma didn't even look at the dummy, and didn't take it either. She just looked at Alex. Alex saw it in Poppy then too. She was practically burying herself into her mum, so much so it was odd that Emma hadn't told her off in that warm snappy way most mothers dealt with clingy children.

'Is everything all right?' Alex asked, not at all thinking that maybe it actually wasn't. Emma was taking deep, fer-

vent breaths, her small chest beating away the only movement in an otherwise deathly still stance. Alex saw Poppy's
fingers pinch and twist at her mother's cotton skirt. Her little legs were scrambling to put her somewhere between her
mum and the half opened door. Alex spotted a small wet
patch begin to bloom down Poppy's sky blue shorts.

'Oh, Emma, I think Poppy's just...' Alex paused.
'...really, is everything OK?'

Emma's expression didn't change. 'Thank you. For helping us,' she said quietly.

Alex heard a quiet snapping sound, the same schlump
and click of a Zippo lighter she heard her dad out on the
porch with each morning, and then the sweetness of tobacco
smoke teased its way towards the front door. Alex tried to
see over Emma's shoulder into the house but the door wasn't
open enough. She looked a question at Emma.

'You're welcome,' Alex said calmly. She mouthed the
rest. *Do you need help?*

Emma's eyes widened imploringly.

'What's happening?' Alex whispered. 'Is it your husband?' It was a stupid question. Her husband was back at
Kerring General in a body brace.

Emma shook her head, she was trying not to cry. 'Bad
penny,' she whispered.

Alex looked at Isla in her mother's arms and felt her heart
thudding. What should she do? Go in? Make a scene? Where
was her phone? In the truck, with a flat battery. *Shit.* Alex
could feel her heart beating in her neck. She pressed the

dummy into Emma Parsons' hand and held on to her. 'Bye then!' she called cheerily. Then quietly under her breath, 'I'll get help.'

Alex walked calmly back down the Parsons' garden path, past the little pink scooter with the ribbons hanging sodden from its handlebars. She passed a few houses then broke into a run, something she was good at by all accounts.

All the shops on the high street had finally shut. Alex ran towards the big blue doors into her father's garage. Dan had written a paper on domestic violence as part of his study course for the food bank. He'd told Alex of terrible case studies. Of people like Emma Parsons; shy and private and in desperate need for somebody to just notice and intervene. Whoever was inside that house had scared the life out of Emma and her little girl. Oh God! Should Alex have taken the children? Pretended she was picking them up for something before coming for help? *Why didn't you think of that while you were still standing there?* thought Alex.

Alex saw the doors to Fosters' Autos were locked up. The panic bit down harder. She stopped and let her eyes travel along the high street. Where was the nearest phone box? There used to be one up the side street where the haberdasher's was. Alex burst across the road and spotted an open door into Carrie's florist, the scene of this morning's unpleasantness. Carrie would have a phone. Alex burst in. 'Carrie! I need your phone!'

'Alex?'

'Finn! Where's Carrie's phone? We need to call the police, now!'

'Alex, slow down!'

Her chest hurt with effort, there was a metallic taste at the back of her tongue. 'I think – I *know* – someone's in trouble. Emma… Mrs Parsons… Emma Parsons in the first terraced house near the footpath, I think someone's in her house, she's on her own, with a baby and a little girl… she's *scared*!'

Finn set his phone in Alex's hand and led her back out onto the pavement. 'Show me.'

Finn gave Alex just enough time to relay her door-step conversation before breaking away. Alex watched him sprint ahead to the house with the overgrown grass. A man was walking out through Emma's front door, suited and cocky and carrying a television from Emma's house.

'All right are we, boss?' Alex heard the suited man wheeze to Finn. Alex baulked. It was the man who'd intimi-dated her so easily after stepping out on the road in front of her. The guy who'd resembled a big, ominous gorilla.

'Yes, mate. That your TV, is it?' Finn's voice was still, no hint of exertion of any kind.

Alex caught up. The man had one of Alex's breakfast muffins pinched between his fat fingers. That, even more than the television in his arms, ignited a fury inside Alex. Emma squirrelling food and him taking it from her.

'What's it to do with you?' he said, squaring up to Finn.

'I've called the police,' Alex lied. She would've called them if Finn's phone hadn't been so technological. Finn moved to stand in front of the other man, blocking his way in a kind of non-threatening-but-ready-for-it stance. Alex carried on into the house. Inside Emma was rocking her daughters, doing that silent sobbing thing women seemed to learn once they became mothers.

'Emma? Are you hurt? Are the girls OK?'

There was hardly anything in the Parsons' living room, barren except for two sofas, a small area of toys and a doll's house beside the fireplace. Alex spotted a phone. 'Don't worry, Poppy. You're OK now, sweetie. Emma, who was he? I'm calling the police.'

Emma shook her head then held it against Poppy's. 'You can't, we've been cut off.'

Alex heard voices out front. She felt an old sensation then. Finn wasn't a meathead, he could get hurt. Again. Bloodied and bashed again because of her. Alex heard Finn laugh at something then, a hard laugh with none of the warmth that came so naturally to him. Like when he'd fished the bee from her hair, or tended her bloodied nose. Or when he'd stung himself raw to fish her from a patch of nettles.

Alex could still see out of the front living room window. The thug's face had turned an even red but Finn was calm, steadfast. Maybe he wasn't the laidback teenager he had been when Alex's dad had gone crazy. Finn had filled out since then. Jem's *buff* description wasn't far off. He was also a good few inches taller than the other man, plus Finn's hands weren't full of stolen television.

Alex crouched beside Poppy and put her hand on Emma's knee. 'Emma, why is he taking your television?'

Alex glanced back outside. Finn was smiling pleasantly, he had his arms folded across his chest as if he was catching up on the game or talking over his day, or stopping himself from punching the other guy's lights out. Poppy's crying was easing into a series of erratic breaths. Alex placed a hand at Poppy's back and rubbed it the way her own mother might. Blythe could make almost any upset better with just a gentle rub of the back.

'Mr Mason burnt my roof.' Poppy broke out into tears again. The noise startled the baby and she began to cry too. Alex turned to Poppy's doll's house, several cigarettes had been stubbed into the little roof terrace.

'Emma, is that man a *bailiff*? Was he *in* the house when you came back here?' said Alex softly. Weren't there laws about bailiffs and threatening behaviour? Alex knew there were, but she'd also heard enough stories at the food bank to never want to find out first-hand how staunch their work ethics were.

'Daddy will fix your doll's house, sweetheart. When he's better. And we don't need that silly old television. It's all adverts anyway, isn't it?' Emma's crying had stopped then, as if she knew she needed to keep it together for her daughter's sake. 'We can play in the garden instead. In the sunshine.'

Alex looked back outside. Finn might look reserved but the other man's lower jaw was jutting out now, tempting someone a lot braver than Alex to stick a good punch on it. Alex watched him place Emma's TV on the wet grass. He took a bite from Alex's muffin and set it down on the television. Finn was opening out his wallet. Alex watched as Finn handed over a stack of notes. Finn had always been the peacemaker. The pacifist, the talker-downer. Ted had taken it as a sure sign of his cowardice. That and the fact that Finn hadn't pulled Dill free in time. A tiny part of Alex wished her dad was here now, to deal with the man who'd thought nothing of sullying a little girl's doll's house, just because he could.

The man thumbed through his new collection of pound notes and then grinned, as if whatever this horrendous situation was, it could now be taken with a light-hearted pinch of salt. Alex felt something hot and unpleasant beginning to swell inside her. How dare he leave this woman and her two little girls terrified, and then *smile* because he had a bit of money in his hand?

Alex straightened up and stalked back outside. 'Don't pay him anything, Finn! The police can deal with him. And you're not having another bite of that, you horrible, *horrible* man.' Alex snatched the remaining muffin and sent it sailing over the Parsons' garden boundary. Perhaps the nasty piece of work didn't like that, it was hard to tell with him still smirking that Hollywood smile but suddenly there was an uninvited hand firmly gripping Alex's wrist. He held

Alex's arm aloft, like she was a naughty child caught steal-ing. Alex pulled against him and felt his strength. For an out of shape thug, he had a deceivingly good grip.

'Take your hands off her. *Now.*' Finn's voice had changed to a low ominous rumble, like a storm about to break.

Alex suddenly had a thought. Actually she had two, the unpleasant side effects of adrenalin suddenly fleeing her system perhaps. Firstly, she hadn't actually called the police yet. And secondly, she'd just put Finn in a situation even the most excitable of pacifists wouldn't really be ready to deal with. Alex was still considering this when Finn moved fluidly, gracefully. Apparently the thug's interpretation of *now* didn't meet Finn's expectations. Finn locked one hand on to the other man's crisp black shirt collar, and cracked him a solid right hook across the cheek with the other, wiping that Hollywood smile clean off his big jutting-out chin.

CHAPTER 32

'So it's my guess that Mrs Parsons has been walking herself and those little girls ragged, every day, just so she they wouldn't be at the house if the doorstep lender turned up.' Mal had managed to talk nearly the whole time he'd been at their house without making eye contact with Alex.

Doorstep lender. Calling a loan shark a doorstep lender was like calling a vandalised car a freebie customisation job.

'Poor woman. I don't know how she's been coping.' Alex chewed a little at the inside of her lip. Emma had been so distressed, after Finn had levelled the guy. Finn; the violence-doesn't-solve-anything turner of cheeks. Alex let him loop around her mind a few more times. Finn had travelled halfway around the world and had returned home an efficient bad guy-busting machine. He hadn't even hesitated. It hadn't helped Emma Parsons much though. She was petrified now about the next time the unsavoury Mr Mason visited, which would be soon, he'd promised, as he'd scurried off back to his four-by-four. He was going to add the cost of his suit to Emma's tally, the interest rate for which was currently running somewhere around the 65,000% APR mark, Mal said.

'How can they do it? To a woman with two little girls?' Alex went on.

'Alex, they actively target women with very young children, you know that's how it works. They intimidate them, threaten them, some of the bastards offer to run them out of the area so they can *work* it off if they need to. I've heard of these animals meeting kids outside schools and walking them home, just to let their mum's know that they have access to their children. They're scum.'

Access to their kids? Over loans started at £100 or so? What, in case warnings that included breaking people's sternums weren't explicit enough?

'What about her husband?'

'She won't say whether our friend Mr Mason was involved in Graham's accident or not. Why would she? She's alone with two little girls. It's not like these people work alone, is it?'

'Well, hopefully she'll get some sleep now that she's staying at the Longhouse.' Finn had insisted on taking Emma and her girls back to his mum's place. Susannah had swung into action like a triage nurse in the field. Alex had done her best to blend into the background while Susannah had shown Emma to one of the guest rooms and Finn had gotten Poppy a bowl of ice cream and sprinkles. Alex had tried to shuffle off home with minimal fuss, but then Finn had given her a book on ancient Minoan ceramics as she was leaving.

'I saw this in a galleria in Crete. I knew you'd appreciate it, Foster. I had a feeling I might get a chance to give it to you one day.' Crete had been one of Finn's stops on his way *out* of Europe. He must have carried it halfway around the word for her. 'That book has more air miles under its belt than a coconut,' Finn's mum had told her.

'It's not a long-term solution though is it? Mrs Parsons needs to do something about that debt, and Susannah's not going to be able to keep her free of charge next week when her paying guests arrive for Viking Fest.'

'I suppose not,' Alex said, remembering what that vile man had done to Poppy's doll's house. *Bastard.* 'Are you sure I can't get you a cup of tea or something, Mal? Must be a long day for you.'

'No, thanks, Alex. I've got to get back, Millie's cooked and er… Alfie's lost a tooth and won't go to sleep until I've seen how clean it is for the tooth fairy,' Mal said, rubbing a hand over the bottom of his new beard.

Despite the funky beard, Mal still had the same soft way about him he had when they'd played together on the rope swing as children. He couldn't have upset Jem the other night, could he? They'd already agreed that point, Mal Sinclair couldn't upset himself.

'Your mother-in-law's been showing off her photos of Alfie to my mum.' Alex smiled.

Mal laughed under his breath and nodded to himself. 'Helen's pretty enthusiastic.'

'She's been great with my mum,' said Alex. 'Thanks

again for what you did for her, Mal. We really appreciate you helping her like you did.' Mal smiled wearily. As if being thanked tired him in some way.

'I'd better get motoring. Actually, Alex, I was wondering… is Jem home? I just wanted to have a quick word if she's around.' Mal was garbling anxiously again. It made Alex feel a little anxious too.

Alex still had to face the Jem bullet. Something was going on with her and after the unpleasant events of the evening Alex hadn't had a chance to talk to her yet. Alex had a feeling she might be about to discover all the ways in which she'd failed Jem as a sister.

'Sure, Mal. I'll just call her down.'

The puppy immediately scrambled to her feet to follow Alex out into the hallway.

'Jem?' A few footsteps then a door opened somewhere up on the landing. Jem appeared at the top of the stairs. 'Mal's leaving now. He wanted to speak to you for a second first.'

Jem came quietly halfway down the stairs. 'Where is he?'

'Lounge. You want a cup of tea?'

Jem nodded, it was the first flicker of something with soft edges since yesterday. Alex walked into the kitchen quickly shadowed by the puppy. She filled the kettle over her mother's large butler's sink and set it to boil. The front door rattled and Alex watched Mal and Jem wander down the side path.

'Looks like we're out of tea bags, dog,' Alex mused. *Ah*

no, hang on… her mother always kept a stash in the pantry. Alex crossed the kitchen and opened the doors into her mother's walk-in. There was a window in here letting a stream of dusty evening light flood into her mother's food store. The window was small, looking out onto the east side of the house where Mal had parked his police car. It used to give an excellent vantage point during games of hide and seek, or when they'd tormented Jem with Dill's water guns.

Alex picked a handful of tea bags and glanced out of the tiny window.

'For old friends, they look miserable hey, dog?'

Jem was looking at her feet a lot. Mal was sitting back against his police car with an intense expression. Mal had just said something Jem didn't like.

'What do you reckon they're talking about, dog?' The dog was more interested in Blythe's dried herbs. Alex was going to look away, toddle off to make tea, but Jem had just pushed a hand through her fringe and was resting it now on the back of her neck. Maybe she had another migraine.

Jem started shaking her head, pointing towards the house. No, walking towards the house. *Did Mal just try to stop her?* Alex felt her heart speed up. Was she witnessing something she shouldn't?

Through the back end of the house, Alex heard their dad's pickup rumbling up the track. She grabbed at the tea bags and stumbled back out of the pantry. The puppy yipped and skittered out from beneath Alex's feet.

Alex busied herself arranging teacups and spoons and

listened to Mal's car pull off down the track. The front door opened.

'You don't have to be so frosty with him, Dad. He's a nice guy.'

'What's he hanging around here for? Didn't the two of you see enough of each other the other night?'

There was a long pause. Alex focused on the box of teabags as if her life depended on it.

'Why don't you worry about yourself, Dad? And I'll worry about me.' This was new. The yelling had always been around Alex, not Jem.

'What were you talking about out there? Why's he sniffing around?'

'Ask Alex! Mal was here to see her, not me!' Jem trounced off into the back lounge.

Alex listened to her dad follow Jem down the hallway. 'So how come I didn't see him talking to Alex then?'

'I'm not a child, Dad. I don't need you to sanction my conversations! I can talk to who I please.'

'He's married! Do you think his wife would appreciate the two of you being seen out together, gallivanting all over town? Drawing their own conclusions?' He wasn't exactly shouting. Not exactly. But even from in the kitchen Alex could hear a hint of something she didn't like, rising to the surface. A dormant volcano, rumbling.

Jem must've heard it too and seemed to switch tack then. She became light, jovial, flippant, when her mood over the last two days had been anything but. 'Dad, Mal was only asking me something *about* Millie. He wanted my opinion on a piece of jewellery he's thinking on for her, OK? That's all!'

Jem used to do that when she was little. 'Mum, I was *only* giving my dinner to Rodolfo because he's been looking a bit skinny lately, that's all,'… 'Alex, I was *only* in your room to check Dill wasn't in here, that's all.' A little bit of truth to sail a cargo of fibs. Alex hovered with the kettle over the cups. Whatever Jem and Mal were just taking about outside, it wasn't jewellery.

Alex strained to listen through the house. Their dad changed tack then too. 'It's not you I'm worried about, Jem. I know you wouldn't…'

What? What did he know she wouldn't do? Alex set the kettle back down and waited for her dad's muffled voice. 'I just don't want the wrong people hanging around you girls. No good will come of it.'

CHAPTER 33

Alex sat in her truck and listened to the last dying ticks and hums of her engine. The late afternoon sun was filtering its way through the boughs of the old birch tree where their old rope swing still hung, illuminating pockets of the garden like stage lights. Something metallic, tinfoil, was catching the light where it fell on the front porch.

I guess that means I'm not cooking tonight then, thought Alex. Just what she needed, more time to kill by herself. A pattern had begun to emerge over the last three days. Alex went to the hospital. Ted went to work. Alex went home. Ted went to the hospital. Alex offered to cook for Jem and Ted. Jem confined herself to her bedroom with a headache. Ted ate at The Cavern. Alex ate alone. All these years Alex had thought she needed to excommunicate from the Falls, when actually she could've stayed right here and kept her distance from everyone just swell.

Alex left her truck, ignored the stone path and cut straight across the lawn to the front porch. She peeled back the foil. 'Quiche. And still warm.' Her stomach growled. It was a step up from the jar of Jem's peanut butter she'd planned to attack later. There was a note with the food.

Alex,
I don't have anything else to thank you with, but thank you.
Emma.

'You didn't need to do that, Emma.' Alex imagined Emma sitting with the girls at the long table Susannah's paying guests had breakfast at, hopefully eating piles of delicious warm quiche right at that very moment while Susannah clucked around them shovelling more food onto their plates.

Alex picked up the quiche and let herself into the house, the puppy ready to accost her before she'd even got through the door. 'Hey, puppy dog. You're fast becoming my best friend around here.'

Alex should have dished a few thank-yous out today too. She'd gotten as far as looping the high street twice looking for a parking spot. She'd been just about to jump out and quickly pop into the hardware shop but then her dad had driven into the garage yard and Alex had decided that actually, she was a bit pushed for time and it probably wasn't fair taking up that parking space for just a few minutes when someone might need it for the day.

So she hadn't managed to get to speak to Finn after all.

Alex wandered into the kitchen and cut herself a sliver of Emma's quiche. She leant over the sink and ate it. *Good quiche, Emma... bloody hell, that's good.* She cut another slice and ate that too. The puppy watched every morsel as it went. Alex broke off a clump of pastry and dropped it for her.

'If it wasn't just us here all the time, we could put it to a vote, pick a name for you.' That's how it used to be done, when they were little. Blythe came up with a shortlist, and the vote swung it. If Alex knew where her mother's opera records were kept nowadays, she could have a quick look through for inspiration. They couldn't be far. When they were kids a weekend hadn't gone by where Maria Callas hadn't resonated through the floorboards into Alex's bedroom. Dill would wander in to Alex's room, groggy-faced and floppy-bodied, complaining 'the woman with the supersonic singing voice spoiled my lie in, *again*'.

Norma had been her mum's favourite.

The puppy begged for more food. Alex broke another piece of quiche for her.

'*Norma*?' Alex said it aloud to see how it fitted. 'I like it.' It was an obvious choice, really. Blythe had tried to explain the gist of the opera to them several times. Some low down dirty chap was supposed to love Norma, the mother of his children, but then decided he preferred her friend instead. Betrayal, heartbreak, children caught up in the fall-out.

'It's culture, girls,' Blythe had said.

'Sounds more like *Jerry Springer* to me,' Jem had replied. 'The same's probably happening in most households in the Falls, Mum.'

Alex wrapped the quiche up before she ate any more and took this morning's laundry upstairs, Norma following her up. In the far corner of her parents' room, a pile of her dad's overalls sat abandoned where he'd come home tired from work and hospital visits and not eating properly. Alex was trying to ignore her growing paranoia, but everyone seemed to be avoiding her, except Norma.

Alex set the laundry down on her mum's bed. Norma looked up at the doorway just before Alex heard the front door open downstairs.

'Jem?' Alex called across the landing.

'Hey.'

'Hey.' Jem had managed to avoid being alone with Alex since their near-phone conversation yesterday, before Alex's battery had cut out. 'Where have you been all day? I thought you might've come down to the hospital.' Alex tried for upbeat but she'd heard an accusation in her own voice.

Jem trudged up the stairs and appeared in their parents' bedroom doorway.

'Nowhere. Around. I think I have a swollen glands or

something, didn't want Mum to catch it.' Alex felt a tiny squeeze of suspicion in her chest.

'I think maybe Mum's got bigger concerns than a swollen gland, Jem. I'm sure she'd prefer that to not seeing you right now.' Alex felt something tighten in her stomach. They hadn't been tetchy around each other since they were children.

Jem set a hand against the doorframe and shook her fringe from her eyes. 'Don't lecture me, Alex, OK?'

She wasn't lecturing her. Jem was being unfair. Alex folded her arms around her dad's mucky blue overalls. 'I'm not lecturing you, Jem. If I was lecturing you, I might say something like, *Do you realise, Jem, that Mum's in hospital and you haven't bothered to see her for three days now.*'

Blythe hadn't even asked where Jem was today. It was as if she expected her to stay away.

'You're right, Alex. What a crap daughter. I mean, *thank God* Mum's got you to visit every,' Jem put a scornful finger to her mouth and tapped her lip, 'sorry, *how* many years do you leave between visits?'

Alex tensed. It didn't even constitute a fight, Jem had just wiped the floor with her on her first swing. Knockout punch.

Jem looked suddenly lost. As if she didn't really know how she'd landed such an effective blow either. Alex swallowed. Jem lay her head back against her doorframe. 'I'm sorry, Al. I'm just… working a few things out.'

Alex had seen that already. Through the pantry window.

'Like what, Jem. What's going on?'

Jem looked at the floor. 'Stuff. Just… stuff.'

The room fell silent for a few moments. That was Jem and their mum then now, going through *stuff* after spending time with Mal Sinclair.

Just ask, Alex. Ask what's going on with Mal. Alex took a deep breath and opened her mouth to speak.

'How's Mum, Alex? I know I should have shown my face but…'

Jem was getting dark circles beneath her eyes. Was she sick? Alex's questions about Mal disintegrated. 'I'm not sure, Jem.'

'What do you mean?'

Alex didn't know what she meant exactly.

'Nothing, really. I don't know, yesterday she just seemed… really good, but today she was just kind of quiet. Disinterested. She just needs to take it easy I guess, like Dad said.'

'Dad needs to take it easy. He has too much on his shoulders. Where is he, at the hospital I suppose?' There was something defensive in Jem's tone again.

'Think so.'

Jem tapped one heel against the toe of her other foot.

'So you've made up then. You and Dad.'

'What do you mean? We never fell out.' No, Ted had just grilled her on Mal's reasons for hanging around the farmhouse. Jem clicked. 'He's entitled to ask why there's a policeman in our house, Alex. Give him a break, would you? Dad's not the bad guy everyone makes him out to be, Alex.'

'I don't think he's the bad guy, Jem.' How could she? Fathers had disowned daughters for far less than Alex had put him through.

'I just don't think you know where he's coming from sometimes. I guess I didn't either. But I think we should cut him a bit of slack at the moment. I know he comes across hard, but he's only looking out for us, Alex. And for Mum.' Jem's voice wobbled. 'He'd be lost without her.'

Jem's shoulders began to bob up and down. She pinched her nose to hold the sounds in.

'Hey, Jem. Don't get upset.' Alex moved around the bed but Jem had straightened up, the same way she had after Robbie Rushton knocked her off her bike. She didn't need consoling. Alex stopped a few feet from her.

'They'd be lost without each other, Jem. But Mum's not going anywhere,' Alex said firmly.

Jem took a deep breath. 'There are different ways to lose a person though, Alex.'

Jem turned and disappeared through the doorway. Alex followed her onto the landing.

Lose her mum? How else was their dad going to lose Blythe? 'Mum's not losing her mind, Jem, if that's what you're worrying about?'

'Look, I'm just talking nonsense. I have a headache. I'm going to bed. I'll see you tomorrow.'

Jem's door was closing before Alex said anything else.

Alex walked back into her parents' bedroom. She shook out her dad's overalls and checked the pockets before putting them into the laundry basket. There was nothing worse than picking spun-dry tissues out of piles of damp washing. Alex dug into the zipped pocket from the front breast. She pulled what looked like a business card out and held it up in front of her. There was a picture of a potted tree on there. *The Bay Tree Floral Studio, Kerring.*

Alex turned the florist's card over in her hand.

Blythe,
What a stroke of bad luck.
I do hope Ted's taking good care of you,
like a good husband should.
Louisa

CHAPTER 34

'Alex? Your mum has a visitor. A Mrs Sinclair? Shall I let her know Blythe's sleeping?'

Alex straightened up in the green vinyl chair. Louisa Sinclair? *Here?* Alex had churned the question around and around in her head since pulling that florist's card from her dad's pocket last night. Two questions. Why was Louisa sending excessive bouquets for her mum with, frankly, very poorly chosen words of support and, more to the point, why had her dad taken the card?

The nurse was waiting wide-eyed for an answer. 'Just so you know, I think she's brought baked goods with her. In case that influences your decision.'

Louisa Sinclair? Baked goods? *And* flowers? 'No, that's OK. She can come in if she likes.'

The nurse nodded and ducked back out of Room 2. Alex found herself straightening up her vest and running her fingers through her hair, smoothing down as many wayward bits as possible before the mayor's widow deigned to enter. Good job Jem wasn't there. Again.

'Alex?' said a soft voice. Alex looked up, momentarily

dazzled by the blonde peeping around the door. 'Are you sure it's OK to come in, she's sleeping? I do come bearing cookies, though.'

Millie Fairbanks, Mrs Sinclair now, was exactly the sort of woman little Poppy Parsons would want to be welcomed by on her first day at St Cuthbert's Primary. Everything about Millie, Alex thought, from her English rose complexion to her honeyed voice was as inviting as a vanilla cupcake. Alex thought she was getting Louisa, the wicked Sinclair of the West to Millie's friendly, cookie-baking good Sinclair of the East.

'Hey, Millie. It's fine, come on in, cookies, that's so kind.'

Millie eased into the room, her hands protectively clamped around a small basket as if trying to prevent any sounds escaping from inside the wicker and disturbing Blythe. Alex gestured to the seat beside the hand basin.

'Don't thank me too quickly,' Millie whispered apologetically, 'my mum baked them with Alfie.'

'That's really kind of you, Millie. Thank Alfie for me.'

It really was very kind of them. Alex had a flashback of Jem and Mal through the pantry window, the way their body language had betrayed them. Alex shifted uneasily. She suddenly felt as if she were keeping a secret she didn't exactly understand. Like one of those people who tried to get through customs with someone else's suitcase on *Customs & Excise: Conveyor Belt to Crime.*

'You might want to keep an eye out for a policeman's

head though, sorry. I have an awful feeling there's an officer about to turn up where he shouldn't.'

Alex stiffened, *oh God*, she was here about Malcolm. She was going to ask awkward questions about her husband Alex didn't know the answers to.

Alex swallowed. 'Policeman's head?'

'Alfie thinks he lost one of his Lego bits, somewhere near the kitchen worktop we were kneading the cookie dough on. I'm really sorry, it's a policeman, looks a bit like George Michael, the 90s version.'

'Oh! Oh, OK.' Alex would be useless as a drugs mule. One hard look from an airhostess and she'd be a sweaty wreck. 'I'll nibble with care then.'

Millie sat elegantly at the edge of her chair. 'How's your mum?'

'She's OK, thanks. Getting there.' Actually, Blythe had been a bit lethargic so far today.

'Did they say how long before she can go home?'

'I don't think they're really sure themselves. Mum's lost some of the mobility down her right side. She needs to be able to get out of bed I think before we can start planning a homecoming.'

'She'll get there, Alex. You're all supporting her. My mum feels bad that she can't get here today but the Reverend's asked her to help brainstorm a tea and cake afternoon for the nursing home so the residents can watch the boat race next weekend.'

'Is Viking Fest next weekend?'

'Yes, have you been home for one? They're good fun. Mal raced last year but they had so many hassles with all the extra traffic coming through the town, he's been assigned to duty this year.'

'No, I haven't seen one. Not since it was just the lowly boat run, I mean.'

'Well whatever you do then, don't tell my mother. She has about a thousand photos from last year's and she is *not* afraid to sit you down for two hours and bore you to death with them.'

Alex smiled. 'Helen likes Vikings, does she?' Alex had a sudden mental image of Bill Fairbanks dressing up in furs and buckles behind closed doors for Mrs Fairbanks. Shudder.

'Probably.' Millie laughed. 'But they're mostly of Alfie throwing eggs at the invaders from the riverbank. He got upset when he saw people throwing their eggs at his dad though, it's probably for the best Mal's not racing this year.'

'Eggs? They pelt the invaders with eggs now?'

Millie's forehead wrinkled. She still looked serene. 'They've used eggs for years.'

'Oh. I did wonder how they were managing to let people go downriver on the floatables now with groups of spectators firing dangerous missiles at them. So they don't just send a couple of Viking targets down the Old Girl now and try and sink them?'

Millie seemed to shrink into herself. 'No. Mal's dad kind

of outlawed the whole bow and arrows thing after… didn't Jem tell you?'

Maybe she had. Alex had always been so eager to get off the phone before Jem tried to talk her into going home for any length of time. Millie was looking uncomfortable, she was doing that thing people did when they thought they'd tripped up and had starting talking about a forbidden topic.

'The mayor did that, after Dill died?' It was easier for people if you just threw Pandora's Box wide open for them.

Alex saw a flicker of relief in Millie's big brown eyes. 'Mal said Alfred didn't want any other little boys practising with bows and arrows along the riverbank after that, so now the entries are all manned and the spectators all get to take part lobbing eggs at the invaders. Little boys don't get so excited about losing eggs as they do sharp things, Alfred said. That was the reasoning, I think.' Millie smiled awkwardly.

That's why Alfred Sinclair had been mayor. The sort of person to put sanctions in place, thinking ahead for the safety of children everywhere while Alex hadn't even managed to safeguard one.

A pause was stretching out between them. 'Sorry, Alex. Do you want to talk about this?'

'Sure. It's fine. Actually, Millie, I like to hear about old faces. Life in the Falls. I haven't been here much.'

Millie nodded. 'Well Mal's dad was definitely part of life in the Falls, right to the end. It didn't surprise me that Alfred changed the river race rules. He was such a big softie,' Millie continued. 'And you should have seen how he doted on our Alfie as soon as he was born. He was a smashing grandfather. Always watching Alfie like a hawk in case he hurt himself. Mal said his dad had always been sensitive like that. I guess it wasn't unusual that Mal had seen him so affected,' Millie said cautiously, 'after what happened to Dill.'

Alex vaguely remembered the mayor coming up to the house with Mal after Dill's service. He hadn't looked like the mayor at all without all the finery around his neck or Louisa on his arm. His eyes had looked bloodshot, Alex remembered because his long sad face had reminded her of a basset hound's. He'd reminded her of Rodolfo.

'The mayor cried for my brother?' Maybe Mayor Sinclair had felt some terrible regret or responsibility for giving Dill that bow and arrow set in the first place.

'Mal said his dad was devastated about it. The death of a child is a terrible thing though, Alex. Who wouldn't have been touched by what happened to your family?'

'That was nice of him.' Alex smiled. 'I'm sorry he passed away. Jem said he was a really nice guy.'

'He really was. Mal misses him dreadfully.'

The conversation tailed away beneath the sounds of Blythe's gentle snores.

'Actually, Alex, I wanted to ask you how Jem's doing these days.' Alex felt a cool quiver down her back for some reason, as if she was about to be asked for an alibi.

'Jem? She's fine. You know Jem, bit of a closed book.' Nothing incriminating there.

'I was hoping to grab a coffee with her at some point. We used to be good friends once upon a time. It'd be really nice to catch up with her now we're all older. I was quite jealous of Mal Friday night.'

'Jealous?'

'Well it's hard getting out with Alfie. I told Mal he could've stayed home and I could've gone for a drink with Jem,' Millie laughed, 'but I guess they have more history and Mal was so keen to check on your mum and things.' Alex nodded in agreement. 'It's funny, now that I teach, I see things so differently.'

'How do you mean?'

'I used to think of Jem... this is going to sound off but I don't mean it in a bad way.'

'Go on.'

'I used to think of Jem as a bit of a tough nut. I was a bit scared to be friends with her, actually, even though we were all thrown together when our mums were practising for choir and Easter services and all that stuff.'

Alex grinned. 'It's Ok, Millie. Jem *was* a tough nut.'

'I know, I know, but she wasn't tough *bad*, she was tough *good*. I could've done with a couple of Jems in my class last year, girls are so catty and, *boy*, do they hold a grudge.'

'Even at five years old?'

'You'd be amazed how awful some of them are to each other, Alex. And they can be like pack animals too. Really mean. A girl like Jem would have levelled out that sort of unpleasantness.'

'I don't remember school being that way.' Alex had really enjoyed school as it happened. It had been the college summer holidays when it had all gone to shit.

'Honestly, Alex. Girls are mean. You know, my mum took me to a dance recital about six months after my accident, just to watch obviously. I was only six, but I can sure remember it. Carrie Logan walked straight up to me and said she was taking my spot at the bar because I couldn't dance ballet if my legs didn't match. *Cow.*'

Alex fought not to glance down at Millie's lovely long legs, to check if she could still spot the giveaway lines and dinks where Millie's surgeries had been after the front end of her mother's car had crumpled against the wagon.

'But *Jem*, wow. Jem walked straight up to Carrie and jabbed her with her finger and said that she was holding my place until I was well enough to go to ballet again and if Carrie even tried taking my spot at the bar she would give Carrie's new ballet slippers to your dog!' Millie fluttered with hushed laughter. It suddenly occurred to Alex that hers wasn't the only family suckerpunched by fate. The Fairbanks hadn't deserved their lot either.

Alex looked at her mum sleeping. Blythe believed in fate. She'd told Alex many years later that even though Finn's dad had done wrong not checking Helen's brake fluid properly, it still might not have made any difference. 'Some things are just all part of a bigger picture, darling,' her mum had said. Whether Helen had braked late or not, she'd had little chance avoiding that wagon. Take away Finn's father's hand in it even, the snow still hadn't let up all day, the construction wagon still hadn't taken the bridge cautiously enough. 'Fate, darling. Everything comes full circle in the end.'

'Jem was always fearless like that,' Millie finished.

'Sorry?' Alex had drifted away for a second.

'Jem. She's fearless. Not like me, I'm a total wimp.'

Alex puffed out her cheeks. Now that she thought about it, the confident little hell-bat Jem had been once seemed to have gotten lost along the way. 'She's not always fearless, Millie. I think it's a shield she uses.' *Only not with Carrie Logan any more.*

'Maybe. Although Jem had calmed down quite a bit by the time Carrie started to get at her. You did know that Carrie used to be awful to Jem too? In high school though, I mean.'

'I got that impression,' Alex replied. 'I was at uni but I know Jem was in and out of the school office for a while. I'm surprised Jem didn't just flatten her, back then.'

Millie's eyes widened. 'That's what I used to think. Especially as Jem had been so bolshie up until then. But Carrie, well, we all knew she had a bit of a mean streak, but I think she must have had something on Jem. Leverage. For Jem not to stand up to her. I wish I'd have been braver and stuck up for Jem but I only ever saw her on the bus, none of our classes were together.'

'She had friends though, Millie. Didn't she?' Alex couldn't bear the thought of Jem wandering the barren landscape of Eilidh High alone.

'Oh yeah, Mal was practically joined at the hip! He didn't mind putting Carrie in her place for picking on Jem,' Millie said proudly.

Alex exhaled. Good. Good for Mal. Alex reached into the basket Millie had brought in with her and helped herself to a misshapen cookie. She gave it a quick once over. No sign of George Michael on first inspection.

'Did you ever ask Mal what it was all about? With Carrie and Jem?' Alex chomped.

'I did ask Mal, but he said he couldn't remember. Honestly, I think Mal just didn't want to gossip about Jem, even to me. Mal's always had a soft spot for your sister. They were like brother and sister themselves, don't you think?'

They were like brother and sister at one point. But Mal had better not have a soft spot for her now. Alex shook the thought away. *Don't be ridiculous.*

'I guess it's nice, that they can catch up with each other, now that they're all grown up,' Alex said. Because what was wrong with two members of the opposite sex sharing a platonic evening? *Nothing!* Absolutely nothing. So they'd stayed out a bit late. It wasn't like anyone had tried to cover any tracks or anything.

Millie took a cookie too and bit into it. 'It was a shame Jem had to go home early though, Mal's a nightmare for going back to the office and staying there half the night. The paperwork he has to deal with is unreal,' Millie said daintily around her mouthful.

What? But Jem hadn't come home early that night.

A piece of cookie had stuck itself to Millie's lip. Alex focused on that crumbly fleck at the edge of Millie's mouth. Now would be a good time for George Michael's head to turn up, a cracked tooth might just save it. Steer this conversation back out of dodgy territory.

Alex gnawed down hard on her own cookie.

Millie went on, 'Sometimes I feel like we're both drowning in paperwork, Mal with his incident reports and me in lesson plans. Is Jem feeling better now, stomach upset, wasn't it?'

Alex was grappling for something to say without it smacking of a lie when the bedclothes moved beside her. Blythe woke like a child, a few seconds' disorientation then a lazy smile for her company.

Thank God.

'Mum, *hi*. Did you have a good sleep?'

Millie tucked her blonde waves behind her ears and leant in towards Blythe's bed as if about to listen to a child read.

'Mum, Millie's here to see you. She's brought cookies too.' Potentially with pieces of melted plastic in them but, 'Isn't that nice of her and Alfie?'

Alex watched her mum's face fall. Blythe looked suddenly wracked with concern. 'Alfie? Alfie who?' she drawled.

'My Alfie, Blythe. Alfie Sinclair. You've seen his photos,

probably at least a hundred of them if I know my mum,' Millie said light-heartedly.

Alex saw her mother twist the bed sheet in her left hand. 'Alfred Sinclair? Oh no, he mustn't come in here.'

'Mum?' Alex felt a small flush of embarrassment. 'Millie hasn't brought Alfie with her.'

'No. No. No. No!' Blythe was trying to speak too quickly and her slurring was worse for it.

'Mum? Are you feeling all right?'

'Should I get someone?' Millie asked, rising from her seat.

'Alfred Sinclair… is a… spineless… bastard. That's… what your… father… thinks.'

Alex felt her eyes widen more than Millie's. Millie looked horrified. 'OK, Mum. It's OK. Just rest, it's OK.' Good God, what was she talking about? She *never* swore. And little *Alfie*?

Blythe was getting more and more agitated. She looked firmly at Alex though as if she had something of burning importance to tell her.

'Sorry, darling. I'm so… sorry.'

'It's OK, Mum. Don't upset yourself, everything's going to be OK.' But Blythe was broken, tears already streaking down her pale face. Alex felt her throat close. She looked back to Millie, shell-shocked beside her chair. 'Millie? Would you mind going and calling one of the nurses, please?'

CHAPTER 35

'You could've drowned!' Alex said, mildly hysterical. Norma chewed smugly on the wayward ball she'd just retrieved. Alex grimaced at her while her heart rate levelled out. Norma had absolutely no regard for the fact that this stretch of the river could've been far deeper than it was or that she could have possibly, *maybe* just set in motion a series of cataclysmic events by launching herself in after a piece of squeaky plastic.

Alex slumped onto the grassy embankment and kicked her shoes off. The walk hadn't cleared her head as much as she'd hoped. 'Sorry, darling,' her mum had wept. Sorry for what? Alex shook her head. *How could you ever think you had anything to be sorry for, Mum?*

It wasn't fair. It was such a stupid childish sentiment to keep coming back to, but it *wasn't fair.* Alex angrily rubbed the droplets of water from her calves and ankles. She needed to get a grip. There were worse things than the cold shallows of rivers, far worse things, but these were the things she usually spent her energies worrying about. Alex looked out across this shallow stretch of the Old Girl. She wouldn't have darted in after Norma quite so heroically had her mum not been clouding her thoughts.

'You stay there, Norma… sit… no! Don't shake!' Alex manoeuvred her bum and sat awkwardly on the dog lead in a bid to anchor Norma to the spot for just a minute. Any second now the puppy was going to realise that she could still wriggle from her collar if she tried hard enough.

Alex replayed in her head the way her mother's voice had wrapped itself around the word *bastard* earlier. Jem hadn't been home after Alex had made the grim journey back from Kerring General this evening, Alex hadn't yet offloaded this particular nugget. Instead she'd gotten the dog and her lead and walked straight out of the house again before anyone could come home and hear her relay Blythe's suddenly erratic behaviour. Ted would've gone straight there from the garage a little while ago, he might be finding out for himself right about now.

Alex fumbled around at the stones by her feet. Poor Millie, the look on her face. 'Alex, your mum's not well. Really, please don't worry about it, leave that to the medical staff. Anyway, Alfie's five years old for heaven's sake, I'm pretty sure other than his feelings on green vegetables he hasn't given anyone any reason to call him a spineless bastard just yet.' Millie had put her teacher's head on and tried to be reassuring. 'Unless… You don't think Blythe meant Alfie's granddad do you, Alex? No, sorry! I'm just randomly guessing now. *Everyone* liked the mayor, didn't they?'

Alex had come up with her own explanation. Her mother was losing her mind.

Alex sent a stone sailing over the shallows towards the timber posts, each carved into their own abstract Norse design, set along the water's edge. She heard the splosh then a tug against the lead beneath her as Norma took an interest in the noise on the water. She wasn't aiming for anything specifically. She didn't know what to aim for any more. The goalposts kept shifting. Everything was in a constant state of change. Jem was leading the way, then she was hiding behind her bedroom door. Ted was infuriated, then gentle, then infuriated again. And now Blythe, yesterday eating lunch with visitors, today *swearing* at them. And Alex was just as guilty, running hot and cold all the time. Staying away from Finn, running to him for help. Not having the decency to go thank him for his help. She was out of order.

Alex let another pebble go over the water. It broke the surface somewhere near the middle of the Old Girl. Her dad used to say she had an aim that would make Eric Bristow weak at the knees. Was that the reason her mum had agreed for Alex and Finn to take Dill practising, instead of waiting for their dad to get back? Maybe if she hadn't been such a show off. Maybe it was just fate like her mum thought. '*Some things are just fated to be, darling. Everything comes back full circle*.' Fate. It wasn't a big enough word.

Alex's head began to spin. Would any one thing in isolation have made the difference? If Alex hadn't been a crack shot, would they have even bothered taking the bow and arrows? If Dill's nerves hadn't been so damaged at birth, would he have held on better in the tree? If he hadn't been fighting with Jem, if their mum hadn't wanted him out of the house for a while, if their dad hadn't gone to help that lady on the emergency call out. Even the nettles. A series of inconspicuous events. All coming together.

Something else broke the surface of the water. Alex looked briefly at the new series of ripples just a few feet from where she sat on the embankment. She looked for a fish.

'You're losing your touch, Foster.'

He was standing on the river bridge behind her, earphones hanging from either side of his head, the evening sun making its dying statement across his skin. Alex exhaled slowly before her breath could catch. He strolled down towards the grassy embankment and along the footpath towards her. Finn tripped on something but turned his stumble into a little self-conscious jog before regaining his poise. It made Alex smile. Her head was throbbing and still he'd managed to affect her that way.

'Penny for your thoughts?'

He'd been robust yesterday. Formidable. Now he was just Finn, softly spoken, clumsy. Ready to be an ear, a shoulder, a best friend.

Alex rubbed against the chill starting over her bare legs. She huddled them under her chin as if she was five years old snuggling up for story time in Millie's reception class. 'You would get a *lot* for your money, Finn.'

She hadn't wanted it to be Finn that would help untangle it all for her, her mother's wobbly recovery, her sister's secrecy, her father's mood swings. But it was always just so easy with him.

'Mind if I join you?' Finn waited politely for permission to sit in the grass with her. Norma had no doubts and was investigating his running shoes with gusto. 'Hello, beautiful,' he laughed. Finn reached down to reward Norma's affection. That laugh used to be the backdrop to their summers. Now it made the hairs rise on the back of Alex's neck like a drug. Something she'd already done cold turkey for.

'Sure.'

Alex waited for the inevitable doubt to sink home as Finn sloped into the grass beside her, but it didn't come. The anxiety of disappointing her father, the guilt for wanting to be this close to Finn for just a few innocent minutes, it didn't come. It was as if Finn kept it all away. Alex took a steady breath and let it out slow. The sunlight had found itself low enough now to touch the river, the Old Girl pretty in gilt.

'I owe you an apology, Finn.' It was something of an understatement. She should start in reverse chronological order, she might be done by Christmas. 'I'm sorry I put you in that situation yesterday. That horrible thug, he could've had a knife or...'

'A nifty karate chop?'

'Or anything,' Alex continued. 'I should've... been more considerate.'

Finn finished fussing Norma and sat her on the grass in

front of him. Norma rolled over and yielded wholeheartedly to him. Finn began rubbing the pink of her belly. 'The guy was about to eat your cupcake, Foster. I know how girls get about cupcakes.'

Alex lolled her head over her shoulder. He needed to know that she was being serious. Finn returned Alex's look with a conceding nod of the head before he turned to the water too. Something flexed over his jaw. 'No need to apologise, Alex. It's been a long time since I saw you like that. It was good.'

'Like what?'

Finn lifted his chin and breathed easy. 'Like the Alex I used to know. Before you started tripping over your own feet trying to be so… *considerate*.'

'Oh yeah, I've really nailed that one to the board.' Because picking Finn up and setting him down again when she felt like it was so considerate wasn't it? About as considerate as sitting here with Finn now would be to her father. 'You could've been hurt, Finn. Because of me.' Finn had his elbows set on his knees. He looked over his shoulder at her, eyes narrowed in thought behind hair damp from his run. 'There are different ways of being hurt, Foster. Anything that monkey had to offer yesterday could've been patched up using a cotton bud. I'm a big boy, I can take a few bumps and grazes.'

Alex knew he could take them, she'd seen him take them from a father burning with drunken, broken-hearted fury. 'Anyway. When he touched you… he shouldn't have done.

I didn't like it.' Alex felt a small rush of adrenalin, as if Finn had just said something dangerous. They should talk about something else.

'Do you think Emma and the girls will be all right?' Alex blathered. 'I don't think I'd have been able to sleep last night if your mum wasn't putting them up.'

Finn squinted at the view. It was the same heavy serious look he had when he was sketching or painting, working out the fine details of what was holding his interest.

'He was a loan shark. Loan sharks, bailiffs… all I know is, if they think you owe them, they'll keep coming back until they've decided you don't.'

Alex shuddered at the thought of that man coming back anywhere near those little girls. 'Did Emma make a statement?'

'My mum called the station. Mal came down to the Longhouse but Emma wasn't really ready for talking much about it, yet anyway.'

'Oh.' Alex had given the brief version to her dad last night in passing. Ted had said something about him considering toxic debt like that once, when the garage was struggling. Only Blythe had insisted she'd go out and get work herself. Cleaning up at the Sinclairs had been one of many jobs Alex remembered her mother leaving the house for.

Alfred Sinclair is a spineless bastard. That's what your father thinks.

Alex's head began to swim again. Maybe there had been some long forgotten argument with Mayor Sinclair back then? Something trivial and buried until Blythe's stroke had short-wired everything so she could finally blurt it all out now.

Alex realised a silence was growing between them.

'It was a breakfast muffin,' she said casually. 'Not a cup-cake.'

Finn smiled and went along with the change in tracks. 'A breakfast muffin?'

'Bacon and egg.'

'In a muffin? Little paper case and everything? Genius.'

Alex allowed herself a small stealth smile. 'I thought you'd appreciate that.'

Finn was a connoisseur of breakfasts, sort of. Back when the Longhouse was just a lowly bed and breakfast, Susannah had got up at first light and made a welcome breakfast for a party of five who never showed. Susannah didn't usually get upset, but after all that time and expense baking fresh drop scones and blueberry muffins and every item neces-sary for a B&B standard Full English breakfast, she was livid. It was all the waste that did it, she said. They'd only just had the Harvest festival down at the church and they'd been collecting for Malawi and something about seeing all that food go in the bin while children starved in the world had tipped Susannah over the edge. Alex and Finn were sup-posed to be going for a mooch around the Falls, but Finn had eaten his way through the majority of his mum's break-fast spread to cheer her up. They hadn't made it further than Godric's gorge before he'd turned a funny pink colour and his digestive system needed a long sit down. Finn thought he'd invented the all-in-one breakfast muffin then, lying on the granite shelf behind the second waterfall up the gorge, while Alex tried to think up new destinations to add to their *Great Adventure* list.

Finn jostled beside her. 'You know I thought of it first. The mighty breakfast muffin. Worth a scuffle for any day, I'd say.' Finn's smile broke first. His eyes warmed with it and for a few seconds all seriousness from his face was lost. When it returned, he was looking straight at Alex over the top of his shoulder, his body still facing the water shielding himself, not giving her too much. 'God damn.' He shook his head almost imperceptibly.

'What?' Alex asked, her back straightening just a little in case she'd done something wrong.

'I'd almost forgotten that smile.' Norma tried to waddle off. Finn cleared his throat. 'So how long before you disappear again?' His voice had reverted back to light hearted, his words heavy all the same.

'Once Mum's home,' Alex said, suddenly hit by the diminishing likelihood of that being any time soon. If they could just get her home, it just felt as if everything would click back into a bearable rhythm with Blythe back to steer them all to calmer waters. Finn didn't ask. He knew everything he needed to from his mum probably.

'How are things going up at the house?' He knew not to ask that too, but he had done anyway. Alex felt ashamed. She could lie, tell him that they were all pulling together, *smile for the camera!* But Finn knew, he'd seen the carnage himself so there really was no point.

'Jem's being off. I just have this feeling, I should be worried for her or something. It's throwing me a bit.'

'Doesn't sound like Jem.'

'I know. First she couldn't keep away from the hospital, now she won't go near the place.'

'Maybe she just wants to keep an eye on you guys at home?'

'That's the other thing. When Jem's home, she's not around much then either. She's either in her room, on the phone. Or she's nipping out for milk or bread or some other reason that takes her away for an hour or more.'

I think my sister might be in love with Mal Sinclair. There's an odd tension between them and my mother saw them kissing outside Frobisher's Tea Rooms when they were teenagers once, Alex wanted to say. But even in her head it sounded preposterous.

'How's… everyone else?' Finn. Ever the diplomat.

'He's, kind of lost.'

'Of course he is, Foster. She's his wife. Your mum is everything to him. I get that.' Finn got that. Alex's dad had only shown Finn anger and hostility but Finn still got that Ted Foster was driven just as vehemently by love. It would take a hell of a lot more than that to bridge the gap between them though.

'I don't know how to help him.'

'You're here, Foster. That's how you're helping.'

'I think my dad would find it easier if I wasn't under his feet. He's hardly home either, I feel like I'm chasing them all out. I don't know, maybe I should just go home for a few days, let him and Jem regroup or something.' Become the visiting guest again.

'It won't make a difference, Alex.'

'What won't?'

'You going anywhere. Trust me, I tried it. It just geography. Miles don't separate people. Thoughts do.'

'Thoughts?'

'Yeah. Thoughts, feelings… whatever you want to call it.' Alex wanted to look away but was held by intense green eyes. 'I stayed in the Falls for eight years thinking you'd come back, Foster. When you didn't, I thought maybe I'd try somewhere else in the world for a while.' Alex felt a sharp pain in her chest. Like she needed to breathe more deeply but couldn't. 'I tried lots of places, Alex. I was away for nearly two years trying to find somewhere. But it didn't make any difference. You were with me the whole time.'

CHAPTER 36

'Hey,' Jem said softly. Alex was propped in the doorway to Dill's room, the backs of her shoulders pink from a too-hot bath, her dark hair bundled up inside a damp towel.

'Hey,' Alex replied. She looked how Jem felt. Tired resignation in the set of her shoulders. Jem let her eyes trail off into Dill's bedroom. The door she'd chased Dill behind and kicked in anger the last time they'd been in this house together.

Jem felt a familiar ache inside. 'Do you know the last thing I ever said to Dill?'

Alex looked into Dill's room again, as if the answer might lie inside. She shook her head.

'I said that I hated him. That Mum and Dad never wanted him, he was just a mistake that came along later.' Jem chewed on the edge of her lip. 'He'd seen me trying to put your makeup on that morning, said I looked like a clown.' Jem laughed emptily. 'Not just trying on makeup though, he saw me messing around.' Jem rolled her eyes. 'Practising how to kiss... on the bathroom mirror.'

Alex smiled. Jem knew she didn't need to explain the

calibre of ammunition that would've given to their brother at the time. Jem felt that ache again.

'I got so mad at him, he said that I'd scare all the boys away and the girls would laugh at me. He just flipped my switch. So I chased him into that bedroom screaming at him like a lunatic until you and Finn came back to the house, remember? Mum talked you into taking Dill out with you guys.'

The makeup hadn't even been for the boys. Jem had only been trying it on to please the girls before the new term started back at Eilidh High. Carrie Logan, mainly, because Carrie's take on Jem's appearance had been much the same as Dill's at the time, only Carrie liked to deliver her critiques with more venom.

You aren't seriously wearing those shoes are you, Jem? They look like men's shoes.

Jem, do you ever use conditioner? Your hair is so wiry, like my horse's tail.

Jem, every girl in the school knows how to shape their eyebrows by now. Everyone except you.

Why wouldn't you kiss Jackson at the disco? He says you're frigid. You're not a fridge, are you, Jem?

Jem looked at her sister. Alex had gone quite still. Jem hesitated. There was always a sadness about Alex when anyone talked about Dill or Finn, as if she couldn't permit herself to enjoy the memories of either of them.

'That's what nine year old brothers do, Jem. Annoy big sisters,' Alex tried. 'He didn't mean any of it.'

'I know.' Of course Jem realised that. She understood the difference between silly mudslinging and real, palpable, spite. But Dill hadn't made it to adulthood. Dill didn't know that Jem hadn't really hated him like she'd said, did he? 'I never got the chance to put him right again before...' Before they'd brought Alex back to the house wrapped in blankets and their mother had fallen to her knees on the front lawn, crippled with anguish.

Jem saw Alex stiffen. 'It was just a silly thing between siblings, Jem,' Alex said.

Jem nodded. She knew that. But that Dill might've died thinking that she didn't love him had haunted her.

Alex looked pained again. Like she was in a constant state of treading on eggshells. 'Are you hungry? I didn't know where you were or anything, Jem, I haven't made anything to eat,' Alex said apologetically.

'No, that's OK. I should've let you know, I've got to go out in a while anyway.'

Alex had *again?* written all over her face.

'Work?' Jem saw the doubt flash over Alex's eyes and then something else. 'Jem, I'm so sorry! I'd forgotten about your "big unveiling". How's all that going?'

Jem fidgeted. 'Not great, actually. George has decided to push things on.' No kidding. George turning up in the Falls? Jem hadn't seen that one coming. Maybe George was right and Jem did need a push, but just thinking about it was enough to put a fine film of sweat above her lip.

'Still gently nudging you, is he?' Alex asked.

'Something like that.'

Alex nodded without giving Jem a hard time about it. Jem felt a surge of deceitfulness. She was wronging Alex. Alex was busting a gut to close the distance between everyone and here Jem was, doing her best to widen it. It was all starting to wear Alex down, Jem could see it right there in front of her. She shouldn't have snapped at Alex outside Carrie's florist yesterday.

'Al? Can we talk?'

Alex held her hands in front of herself, one rubbing over the other. 'Sure. I have something I need to speak to you about too. I was just going to get dressed. Want to come in my room?'

Jem stepped out of Alex's way and followed her across the landing into the guest room. 'Alex? Did you wear your pumps in the bath? I saw them at the bottom of the stairs, soaking.'

'Norma got a bit carried away up near the old town bridge. That collar you adjusted doesn't fit her properly.'

'Norma?'

'You said she needed a name.'

'The crazy priestess, right?' Jem had been bombarded with opera at weekends too.

'It suits her.' Alex smiled, closing the bedroom door behind Jem.

Jem wandered over to the window and checked the view outside hadn't changed. 'I like it.'

'Hopefully Mum will too when she comes home.'

Jem buried her hands into her jean pockets and turned to lean against the wall. Alex sat on the end of her bed.

'How is she?' Jem asked weakly. She shouldn't have abandoned her station at her mum's bedside, it was just, *how* could she go to the hospital? Blythe knew just by first glance when Jem was holding on to a secret. Bar the big one. Blythe had never cornered her on that one. *That's your second biggest secret, now*, Jem reminded herself.

Alex pulled the towel from her head, a wet mess of chestnut hair slumped around her delicate face.

'*Ancient Minoan Ceramics*, yours I take it?' Jem picked up the book from the chest of drawers beside her and flicked through a few of the pages. Something flittered to the floor. 'Shoot, sorry. I lost your page'

Alex stopped towelling her hair while Jem picked up the scrap of paper.

'Sorry, was this your bookmark?' She held out the little scrap of paper to Alex. 'Do you know which page you were on? Huh, look at that, it's a heart.' Jem turned over the torn shape in her hand.

'It's not a heart. It's a leaf.'

Jem saw Alex's expression falter. 'What's up, Al?'

Jem watched Alex take the paper shape as if it was a rare stamp and set it down delicately on the bedside table. 'Nothing. Just, seems like there's a headache everywhere I look at the minute.'

Jem listened as Alex relayed what had happened when their mother had woken. How Millie had mentioned Alfie, the change in their mum's awareness, her language. 'I think she must have been referring to the mayor. *Alfred Sinclair* Mum said. Millie said *Alfie*, but Mum definitely said *Alfred*. When Dad comes home, do you think I should ask him what she meant?'

'No.' Jem hadn't meant it to come out like a bullet, but there it was, hard and to the point. 'The nurses said they'd keep an eye on her, Alex. Dad doesn't need this on his plate too. I think we should let him concentrate on getting her back home. He needs her home, Alex.'

Jem had thought about her parents a lot lately. How strong their marriage had always been, how Jem had just wanted something as strong and honest and *normal* as her parents' relationship for herself one day. But things were never what they seemed, were they? She was only just getting that. And while she'd been burying her head in the sand since meeting up with Mal, her mum had been slipping towards this new delirium that had descended upon her.

Jem felt her breath get short. She'd been complacent. She'd let Malcolm throw her off course. Now she needed to get back on it. No more putting things off. She was going to deal with what she could, while she could. Before it was too late. Starting with her sister.

'Alex. About yesterday, outside Carrie's. I didn't mean— '

'It's OK, Jem.'

Jem flopped down onto Alex's bed. 'No it's not.

'Jem, really, it's OK. You were right. I wasn't around for

you when you were having a rough run. I should have asked Mum more questions, found out what was going on. Supported you. I'm glad you had Mal around. Someone to lean on.'

A silence stretched between them.

Jem ran a finger over the flowers embroidered onto her mum's bedlinen. 'Can I ask you something, Al? If you had the choice, to keep a secret to yourself in case it hurt somebody or be brutally honest, so they at least knew the truth… what would you do?'

Alex watched Jem carefully. 'Total honesty, or damage limitation?'

Jem nodded.

'With your sister, do you mean? Who will love you whatever you might say?' Alex had left it for her, an invitation hanging there in the air. Jem wanted to tell her, one of her secrets at least. The now-mediocre one that would only blow up in Jem's face, not the full-blown bundle of dynamite one that promised to obliterate their whole family. Alex was still watching her, she'd gone quite still. It was a St Cuthbert's Primary cornerstone that Alex cam back with. 'Honesty is always the best policy, Jem. I'd go total honesty.'

Jem sucked in a deep breath and felt her nerves beginning to jangle.

Alex set her hand over Jem's. 'Jem, whatever it is, it can't be as much work as keeping it all to yourself. I know what I'm talking about here, Jem. Look, what you said to me outside Carrie's yesterday, it was right. And I'm not trying to make excuses, I should have been there for you and I'm sorry that I wasn't. But I probably would only have been a naff sister if I'd have stuck around anyway. I'm crap at confrontation, I hate violence and I don't know a lot. The only thing I do know, is that it's heavy carrying something around with you that you don't think you can share with another soul in the world. It gets really heavy, Jem. Trust me on this. Whatever it is you're holding up all by yourself, if you can, go and set it down.'

The thoughts screamed through Jem's head. *I want to, Alex! I want to tell you and I want you to say that it's OK! And you won't judge me and that you'll love me for who I am whether you approve or not!*

Jem wanted to say all of these things, but she was already running behind. And Mal was expecting her on the track to the plunge pools.

CHAPTER 37

Alex wasn't looking for reasons to bump into Finn. 'No I'm not,' she said aloud, because actually saying it might make it more true, kind of like *I don't believe in ghosts* or *I'm not that far into my overdraft.* She wasn't here, sitting across the street from the Longhouse for any other reason than she wanted to check in on Emma Parsons... and say a proper hello to Susannah after making herself scarce yesterday, before Susannah had a chance to attack her with food and kindness... and give Susannah these few surplus items from her mum's pantry, chip in a little while Susannah was helping out the Parsons family.

Alex tapped her fingers across the top of her steering wheel. A cynical voice popped into her head. *Who. Are. You. Kidding.*

Alex took the small paper leaf from her jean pocket, all neatly folded like a pound note, and looked at it again. It was just a scrap of paper. Something that meant nothing... and something. Finn used to leave them lying around for her to find after one of their tutors had told him to take a leaf out of Alex's book. Little paper leaves had flittered from most of

Alex's college books after that. Little paper nudges, saying nothing and everything.

Alex turned it over in her fingers. Finn had put it inside the book for her to find, the book he'd found in a side street gallery in Crete and carried around the world for two years with him. For her. Alex took a breath and gave in to the montage of images already flipping through her head. Finn standing in the cold, snowflakes like confetti in his hair. Finn in the dim light of her room, skin slickened with sweat. The glimpse of his torso yesterday, when he'd reached under his top for a wayward earphone.

Alex's finger tapping intensified. She was being ridiculous. 'Utterly ridiculous!' she said aloud. 'Just go and knock.'

She reached to take the keys from the ignition and caught movement over at Susannah's place. Poppy darted out from behind the sheets hanging on the line across the back lawn, Finn fumbling clumsily after her into the clearing.

Poppy was aiming something at him, *a water pistol?* Only she was having trouble with her aim, gripped in a bout of laughter.

That's it, Poppy... now. Yes! You got him. Alex smiled. 'You big goon, Finn.' She watched him stagger towards Poppy as if his legs were made of wood, waving his arms around giant killer-crab fashion. Dill had taught him the killer crab. Alex watched Finn scoop Poppy up and sit her on his shoulders, her head thrown back in laughter. Something hopeful pulled inside Alex.

Susannah's white sheets flapped behind them and another killer crab Alex hadn't been expecting burst through the garden towards them. Poppy turned her water gun on her new assailant. Who was that? Finn pushed the woman away, playfully. Alex felt her centre of gravity plummet through the bottom of her truck. She watched Finn and Poppy duck and dodge the athletic brunette. Ah. Waterbombs. Brilliant. Oh, and another one. Down his t-shirt?

Alex held on to the key for a moment, her heart pattered unpleasantly, she thought she might need to wind down the window for a small gust of air but her body was already swinging into action by itself. The truck engine rumbled to life around her, her hand automatically shifting the gearstick into first. *What are you thinking, Alex? Are you losing your mind too?* She shouldn't be here.

Alex stole another glance over at them. The brunette was slipping her arms into a denim jacket. She slapped Finn softly and playfully on the back. Poppy got a high-five before the brunette skipped out of the Longhouse's entrance drive and turned out onto Eilidh high street. Alex watched her scoop the long dark hair from the neck of her jacket and set it all free down her back. And then she slipped into an Audi and zipped off.

Alex looked back to Finn and Poppy still playing.

Plan B. Alex needed a Plan B. Something useful to do. Something useful and helpful and nothing at all to do with green eyes or tiny scars on noses or meaningless little scraps of paper. Alex clumsily dug out the paper leaf and scrunched it in her palm. Finn would have put it in the ceramics book years ago. He'd probably forgotten it was even in there. She flicked it into the box of surplus tins of kidney beans and pineapple chunks she'd dug out of her mum's pantry. Plan B suddenly presented itself.

Millie. Millie could pass on the things Alex had put together, Millie knew Emma and Poppy, maybe it would help the Parsons if Millie had a reason to go over there and talk to Emma about the foul Mr Mason?

There. That was useful, helpful. A decent reason to be cruising around the Falls in the nice summer top Jem had lent her before Jem had stepped out of the house looking like a movie starlet. See! Not a pointless trip out at all, Alex would hang by Millie's place on the way home. Now, in fact. She could drive there right now.

*

Alex took the high street as far as St Cuthbert's Primary then made a left onto the grove where Helen had said Mal and Millie lived now. It wasn't hard finding it, the police car out front helped.

Alex pulled into the kerb and jumped out. Her flip-flops slapped awkwardly against the gravel running up to Millie's house. She checked her ponytail was still somewhere near the right spot on her head and pressed the doorbell. There was laughter the other side. It sounded like Millie was home.

The door opened and a jovial looking Mal stood in the doorway.

'Hi, Mal. I hope you don't mind me just calling by.'

Mal's eyes darted to the box of goods in Alex's arms then back to her. The smile turned into something more strained. Mal pulled the door closed a little and sandwiched himself in the gap, like Emma Parsons had when Alex had gone back with the dummy.

'Alex!' Mal called. The laughter in the background stopped. 'What er, what can I do for you?'

Alex felt bad for disturbing them. 'Sorry, Mal, is Millie home?'

'No,' Mal said casting a look back over his shoulder. 'Sorry, Alex. Millie goes up to her folks' with Alfie on Tuesdays. They have dinner. Can I pass on a message?'

Mal seemed restless. Alex got the distinct impression she was disturbing him. Mal would make a useless bad cop. He was too soft, one of those people who'd always worn his feelings on his shirtsleeve. Like his dad, by all accounts.

'Um, can you ask her if she wouldn't mind passing these on to Emma? It's just all sitting unused at our place and Susannah could probably use a few extra emergency supplies. I'd take them myself but I er...' *but I'm frightened of the way I feel when I'm around her son.* 'But I thought maybe Millie might like the chance to touch base with Emma, before the children start back at school.'

Mal practically grabbed the box. 'Will do. Sorry, Alex, you've caught me on the hop. I've got something burning on the stove.'

'Oh, sorry. Sure, I'll leave you to it.'

'Thanks, I'll tell Millie.' The door closed again before Alex had even left the step. She stood stunned for a few seconds. Something moved in the window. The lounge curtains were being yanked closed, Mal had gone inside and was battening down the hatches. Alex and Finn used to do the same. Close the blinds to the annexe in Susannah's garden, just so they could have some privacy, watching movies and messing around with Finn's art stuff in peace. 'My antennae are twitching!' Susannah used to say when she came over to check on them. Alex used that phrase all the time now. Mostly at work.

Alex's antennae were twitching.

She moved over to the living room window. Mal had left a crack in the curtains. Her dad was the same, it was something unique to the male of the species, an inability to leave soft furnishings in an orderly fashion. Alex glanced through.

Jem? A shot of cold adrenalin ran down Alex's spine.

Malcolm was comforting her. Was he reassuring Jem that Alex had gone? The coast clear? Alex felt giddy. Jem was holding a glass of wine. A glass of wine! In Millie's home! Oh God. Alex knew it. She bloody knew it. Jem had gone out dolled up tonight, lippy, jewellery, the works. Alex peered through the window. Jem knocked back a glug of wine; she looked concerned. *So you should, Jem! He's married! He has a child! What the hell are you doing? And in their home!* Mal rubbed Jem's arm, Jem rewarded him with a smile.

Get your hands of her, Sinclair, you cheating shit, Alex growled at the glass.

Alex heard a car roll onto the drive behind her. The lights shone on her, peeking at the window but she didn't care. The driver shut the engine off and got out. Alex couldn't see through the twilight at first, her eyes hadn't adjusted to the car lights turning off.

'Alex? Hi!'

Oh God.

'Millie! Hi.' Alex looked at the ground floor window. *Shit… SHIT!*

Millie stepped elegantly along the gravel in her flip-flops, her ballerina posture still present. 'How's Blythe now? I've been worrying about her. Sorry, what brings you over here, Alex? I should probably ask that first. Alfie? Come on, baby.'

A little pair of legs clambered from the back door of Millie's car. *No!* Not with her little boy here too. 'Me? I just wanted to drop off a few things, for er, Mrs Parsons. You know her better than I do and umm…'

Jem was about to get sprung. Alex did not condone it, but this was not what any of them needed right now. Maybe Jem was having some sort of blowout? She'd been under a lot of pressure, with work… and their mum and… Alex baulked at the thought of what an affair might do to someone as straight-laced as their mum. Someone who had championed lightning strikes and marriage and soul mates, to both of her daughters. Alex caught sight of Alfie's profile in the hazy evening light and something familiar knocked her off course for a second. It was a trick of the light. He probably shared that same look with a hundred little boys. 'Alex?'

'Sorry. Yeah, um, these things for Emma Parsons…' Alex needed a diversion, to spare that little boy from hearing his parents fall apart. 'I've given them to Mal but, ugh, I'm such a klutz, I think I dropped my car keys into the box I just gave him.'

Alex skipped over to the front door and began banging aggressively on it. She couldn't watch Millie let herself and Alfie in quietly and just walk in on them, wine in hand.

'Alex, it's OK, I have a key!' Millie said.

Alex pushed her own keys farther into her pocket. 'It's OK! Mal was just here.' She drove her finger hard into the doorbell again. And again and again.

'Alex?'

'Hello again, Malcolm!' Alex was nearly shouting. She'd recited a whole monologue this way once, when she'd won the prestigious role of a tree in one of St Bertie's summer productions. She was projecting, loud and true, just as she had so her dad could hear her at the back of the school hall. *I am a tree, as strong as can be, a tiny acorn grew into what you now see.* 'Oh look! Millie and Alfie are home! Hello Alfie!' She sounded like C-3PO, only less articulate.

Mal and Millie were both looking at her as if she'd arrived from outer space. Alex laughed loudly enough that it sounded like she'd lost her mind. She just needed Jem to hear her. *And then what was Jem going to do? Shimmy through Millie's kitchen window?*

'Alex, are you all right?' Mal winced. He was pulling the door to again, hiding what or *who* was on the other side.

'Oh, I don't believe it!' Alex said in her loud robotic tone. 'I thought I'd lost my keys. They're here! In my pocket!'

I am a lunatic. Unhinged as can be...

'Alex, would you like to come in for a glass of water or something?' Millie asked. She'd set a hand down protectively on Alfie's shoulder. Alfie had cocked his head, intrigued by the nutcase on his parents' doorstep.

'No!' Mal blurted. 'I mean, I've... just started painting that skirting you've been on at me about, Mils. The place is a *mess.*' Mal laughed awkwardly. Now *he* sounded like C-3PO. And painting? In a nice polo shirt and jeans? Alex could smell aftershave, not paint. Come to think of it, she couldn't smell what he was burning on the stove either. *Bastard.*

Alex saw them then. Jem's ankle boots, sitting in a neat little pair just inside Millie's hallway. Alex's heart was thumping. Was Mal going to try and fob his wife off from coming inside too? 'Mum?' Alfie held up a finger with something suspicious on the end of it.

'Oh, Alfie. Hang on a second.' Millie looked resignedly at Alex. 'Let me just go rinse his hands. He's not well, that's why we had to come home early, before Nana Helen's treacle sponge, isn't it? Come on, to the kitchen, Alfie.'

Millie was going to see the boots. Alex resisted the urge

to dive on the floor and grab Millie's good leg just to give Jem a few more seconds to get out of there.

Millie and Alfie disappeared into the house. All was lost.

Alex waited for it in silence. Mal was standing in the doorway doing everything to avoid eye contact. *At least move her shoes, you big shit.* Alex wanted to scowl at him but it was pointless while he wouldn't look at her.

'Malcolm is a super son-in-law,' Helen had said.

Alex's heart hurt for Millie and Alfie. And for Jem too. It would be another wedge between them all, another rock for the Fosters to break themselves upon.

'I've got to go,' Alex said croakily. 'Tell Millie… I'm sorry.'

Alex turned to walk back down the Sinclairs' garden path while Mal pulled the door closed behind him. He stood there on the doorstep, was he watching her leave? Or just avoiding going in and facing the music? Alex walked, waiting to hear Millie come tearing back to the front door demanding answers from her husband.

'Alex!' Alex turned, Millie was shuffling past Mal, still stiff in the doorway. 'Sorry, Mal's right. The place is a mess. Men and paint huh?'

Alex casually let her eyes drop to Jem's boots. They weren't there any more.

Millie looked back to Malcolm and then to Alex again. 'I was going to ask, would you like to have a cup of tea some time, Alex? Away from the hospital. I saw Jem recently and she said she thought that maybe you'd enjoy getting out somewhere other than Kerring General?'

Alex felt herself grimace, stupidly. Had Millie just moved Jem's boots? *What?* Why would she? Or was it actually *finally* happening? Alex was losing her mind.

'Um, yeah… that would be great, Millie, thanks for asking.' Sure it would. Alex could go for a drink with Millie and Jem could hotfoot it round to see Mal. Perfect.

Alex did a quick one-eighty glance across the neighbourhood, trying to pick out a frantic figure suspiciously leaving the property, but Alex was the only one.

CHAPTER 38

'You've been staring at that box of cornflakes since I've been downstairs. Thinking of sending off for a break-fast bowl?' Ted stood rigidly over the kitchen sink, one oil-blackened hand braced on the worktop, the other hold-ing another cup of coffee to his lips. Alex looked at the cold toast on her plate. She had nothing. 'I was hoping to talk to you last night about your mother, but you were sleeping,' Ted went on.

Alex hadn't been sleeping. She'd been blotting out the world with her duvet. 'I was tired. Sorry.'

Ted drained his cup and looked back at the farmed land-scape rolling away from the house. 'The nurses think your mother was running a temperature last night. They're going to be making a few checks today, just to be sure everything's as it should be.'

Alex heard the doubt in his voice. Ted was trying to reassure himself as much as her. 'I'll keep an eye on her today, Dad.' It was about all Alex could offer. Alex saw the line of her dad's profile harden. There was a period of time that might've meant something unpleasant was coming. A temper frayed. But he wasn't the same man he had been back then. The last time Alex had heard him lose it was when she'd come home from university, halfway through the first term. To tell them that she was dropping out. Finn should never have followed her to the city, turned up on a winter's night, shaking her perfectly constructed little bubble of a life like a snow globe. Nothing had settled back in its place after he'd left, after Alex had sent him away. So she'd come home.

'She can't just *drop out*, what is she going to do with herself, Blythe?' Ted had ranted. Not *you*. Not, *what are* you *going to do with yourself*, because back then he seemed to do anything to avoid talking directly to Alex.

'I'll get a job, Dad,' Alex had assured him 'I won't be dependent on you for long.'

Blythe had set her hand on Alex's. 'We don't mind if you are, darling. We just want you to be happy.'

Jem had come in late for dinner. She'd walked straight past them all at the kitchen table and upstairs. Alex remembered thinking that Jem would eventually hold it against her, the heated voices whenever Alex was back home.

'There are things I can do here, Dad,' Alex had tried. 'Maybe I could volunteer for a while at the school, see if they'll take me on as an assistant. And think of the time I'll save. It was a three year course, I could be contributing to the house instead of racking up student loans. And the distance, I won't be too far away that I can't help Mum out here, or I could help in the office at the garage maybe?' Alex had blabbered hopefully.

'Time? And *distance*? Those are your reasons for giving up a life opportunity, Alexandra? This is what you really want? Rattling around this two-bit town, *volunteering*?'

'Ted, dinner's getting cold.' her mum had tried. But Ted was finally addressing Alex and she wouldn't let it go.

'You used to say this town was built on community spirit, Dad. Mum volunteers at the church. That's what people in this town do, they follow their parents. The mayor has lots of volunteers at the town hall, Jem could ask Mal—'

'You're not volunteering for the goddamned Mayor!' he'd blazed.

Blythe had stopped fussing over the dinner table then. 'Edward, let's just calm down a minute. I don't want her giving her degree up either. But she just wants… to help.'

Jem had appeared in the kitchen doorway, she'd looked pale and mildly panicked. Alex had wondered if she'd just witnessed a terrible accident. 'Everyone. I have something important to tell you,' Jem had blurted. Jem's face had glistened, like she'd either been sweating or had just splashed cold water over it.

'Just a second, Jem,' Blythe had said, but their dad was already too far gone.

'*Help? Help? Not everything can be damned-well helped! Sometimes, all you can hope for is time, and if you're goddamned lucky… distance! I want her down there, in that university. And that's final!*' He'd brought his hand down so hard onto the table that the small clay dish Dill had made in preschool had bounced from the table-top and exploded against the floor tiles.

Jem had known not to say another word.

Their mum had left the table trying to pretend she wasn't crying and had spent the rest of the night trying to hold Dill's dish back together while the glue took. It was an apt metaphor for their family.

*

Ted reloaded another cup from the coffee pot and set it down on the table in front of Alex. 'I didn't catch your sister last night either. You happen to know if she's planning on visiting your mother today?'

Alex swallowed. It had been Mal who had dropped Jem off home the day Dill's dish got smashed at dinner. Had Mal Sinclair been the 'something important' she had to tell them? Had they always been fated to be together?

Alex sipped her dad's coffee. It tasted the way he used to make it for her on cold afternoons at Foster & Son's. 'I think she's coming in with me. Once she's up.'

Ted scratched a finger against the side of his mouth. Alex heard his bristles give beneath his nail. 'Good. Your sister's been spending time with a few old friends while she's back home.' Was it a question? Alex sipped again. Only one old friend, as far as Alex knew. An old friend who was married now, with a child… 'It's not a good idea,' Ted stated coolly.

Were they talking, privately? They hadn't held a private

conversation together since, well, in as long as Alex could think back to. 'What's not a good idea, Dad?'

'Jem won't listen to me, Alexandra. She's hot-headed, like I am I suppose. But she'll listen to you.'

No she wouldn't. 'About what?' Alex asked shakily. She felt her heart rate increasing slightly while Ted found his words.

'I want you to tell her to keep her distance from the mayor's boy.'

Alex felt a tightening in her stomach. 'Why?' she croaked.

Ted's lips had formed a hard straight line. He looked unsure about what it was he wanted to say. He looked into the bottom of his empty coffee cup. 'No good will come of it, Alexandra. Some people just bring trouble with them. Even if they don't mean to, the pain they cause doesn't hurt any less.'

Her dad's eyes felt sharp on her then, ice blue and bottomless. Alex shifted uncomfortably, her dad broke off and looked solemnly at his boots instead. 'I know you girls think that you have *friends* in this town, but there are some people who are just no good for you. People it would be best not to bring back from the past.'

Who was he even talking about now, Jem or Alex? Alex felt obliged to look straight at her father then. To take a direct hit, hear what it was he finally had to say after years of dodging the topic.

'I know that people make mistakes, Alexandra. God

knows I've made enough. It doesn't make a person bad, necessarily... or maybe it does, I don't know.' He hadn't used to sound unsure on that point.

'What are you trying to say, Dad?' Alex was taking shallow quiet breaths.

'What I'm trying to say is, if the mistakes we made can't be put right, and all we've got is an opportunity to never repeat the things we did wrong... the things that helped cause those mistakes to happen in the first place... then I think that any person, any *good* person who loves their family, would do things differently the second time around. Wouldn't they, Alexandra?'

Alex clenched a hand around her mug. 'That's the thing about mistakes though, Dad. Nobody ever means to make them.' She could feel it coming, the first real opportunity to say it to him. That one little word that had always seemed so insubstantial. *Tell him, Alex. Just let it out... I'm sorry.*

'But they still happen though don't they, Alexandra? People still get hurt.' Alex's heart was thudding now. 'All we can do is learn from our mistakes. That's the responsibility that comes with hindsight. Once the landscape's changed, it has to be trodden differently. I'm worried you girls don't understand that.'

Alex swallowed. 'I understand that, Dad.' No making the same mistakes. Finn had never been the mistake though.

'Good. Let's hope your sister sees it that way too.'

CHAPTER 39

There was a Mexican standoff at the hospital. Alex, Jem and Dill used to play Mexican standoff at the dinner table with the peppercorns their mother had kept in Dill's clay dish, before it became glued back into the Frankenstein version of its former self. They would each take a single peppercorn, set it on the palm of one hand in front of poised finger and thumb and bide their time, because whoever flicked first might miss and would then be open to a two-pronged attack with no more ammo left to defend themselves. It was stupid really, there were no prizes, just the accolade of not being the first one to get shot with a peppercorn.

Alex ran a finger back and forth along her lips. Jem twisted her silver bracelet around her wrist. The morning had been a cool exchange of one or two and occasionally three-word answers.

'Drink, Alex?'

'I'm fine thanks.'

'How long before the doctor comes?'

'Soon. Hopefully.'

All just a warm up while Alex had waited for Jem to fire the first big hit. Brutal honesty, Jem had agreed after Alex's oh-so-informed counsel. Brutal honesty had sounded better before Mal had hidden Jem in his home. *Mum, Alex! I have something to share with you. Mal and I are in love, and we can't help it.* Alex had been waiting nervously for Jem to spit it out, but then before Jem had got there, Blythe had suddenly flicked a peppercorn of her own. Blythe had looked at the wall clock and innocently asked in her new unsteady monotone, 'Has Rodolfo been fed yet?'

Rodolfo? *Rodolfo?* Rodolfo had lived a long and happy life, but he'd died while Jem was still in high school. Blythe's shooting skills had just put her firmly in play. One shot, and she had felled both of her daughters. This new heavy silence had been welcome after that.

'I'm just going to go see if I can find the doctor,' Alex said, rising from the vinyl chair. Her skin squeaked as her thighs pulled free from the seat. Jem had deftly slipped out of the room earlier as soon as Rodolfo's name had come up. The staff knew. They were on it, that's what Jem had whispered when she'd come back. Now Alex wanted to know if Dr Okafor was on it.

Jem nodded and Alex briefly reconsidered if she should leave them alone at all. 'No undue stress,' The nurse had said earlier. *No revelations about home-wrecking, Jem.*

Dr Okafor was scribbling notes when Alex stepped out onto the ward.

'Ah, Miss Foster. I wanted to talk to your father, is he—'

'You can talk to me, Doctor. My father won't be here until this evening and I'd like to know what's going on inside my mother's head, if you don't mind?' She sounded curt. She hadn't meant to but, good. Maybe it was about time she found her voice.

Dr Okafor nodded and clicked at his pen. 'It is not uncommon for there to be some memory loss and—'

'She hasn't lost her memory, Dr Okafor. This morning she woke up, had her breakfast, talked about current events in the newspaper and then forgot that our family pet had been dead for nearly eight years.'

'Miss Foster, I was going to say, memory loss *and* disorientation can be relatively common. Please, we are keeping a very watchful eye over your mother. As I mentioned when Mrs Foster was first admitted, it can be quite a disorientating experience, not to alarm you but I must reiterate, recovery can take months or years, even after discharge. Your mother is not unduly worrying us just yet, Miss Foster. But we are watching very closely.'

'Well that's what we're here for, isn't it, Alfie?' Helen Fairbanks blustered up the ward behind Alex and Dr Okafor, rosy cheeks beneath her spectacles and printed silk scarf hanging lopsided from her neck. 'Don't worry, Doctor. My grandson here has 20/20 vision, don't you, Alfie? He'll spot anything untoward with my good friend Blythe, won't you, my little love?'

Alfie nodded obediently at his grandmother as Helen took

Alex firmly by the elbow. Alex looked down at Millie's little boy and felt weighted with betrayal.

'Aren't you going to say hello, Alfie? This is Alex, your mummy and daddy both used to play over at Alex's house when they were all little. Isn't that funny?'

Alfie leant in to his grandmother. 'That's the lady I was telling you about,' he whispered, 'the one who was being a weirdy at our house last night.'

Helen's face brightened at her grandson, then she gave Alex one of those *Kids! Aren't they just the funniest?* looks.

Alex smiled sheepishly at him. *Damn it, Jem.*

Helen bustled Alex back from Dr Okafor, who had already returned to his notes, and steered Alex along the corridor to Blythe's room.

'Now then, Alexandra. Millie told me about yesterday, how your mum's not feeling herself. Well I'm here to help. When the Reverend's wife had her stroke, the doctor told the Reverend how familiarity can help, friendly faces and whatnot. So I'd like to come down every day, if that's all right with you and your father? And Jem too, of course?'

'That's very kind, Helen. Mum wouldn't want to put on anyone.'

'Nonsense. She'd do the same. Now then, I hope you didn't mind me bringing Alfie with me, it wasn't my intention—' Helen held on to the door before they went in '—only Millie needed a bit of time with Malcolm, he doesn't get many mornings off and Millie had booked them an appointment with the, ooh I really shouldn't say but...'

Marriage counsellor? Divorce lawyer?

Blythe dropped to a whisper. 'Can you keep a secret, Alex?'

Wrong sister, Helen! Alex could say. *Jem's your gal for that!* Or the alternative, *No thanks! Don't want it!* 'Yes, of course, Helen.'

Helen squeezed on Alex's elbow as her eyes glazed over with delight. 'Millie's expecting! I'm going to be a grand-mother again!'

Alex felt her automatic smile kick in. *Oh. Fuck.* 'That's wonderful news, Helen.'

Helen winked and tapped her nose. Alex nodded agree-ably as her cheeks started to burn.

Helen pushed through the door leaving it for Alex to hold open while Alfie trundled through beneath her arm, spiky blond locks escaping beneath his red cap.

'Blythe, my darling. You look ravishing.' Alex hadn't thought about her mother's friendship with Helen, whether she could forgive Millie's being hurt through the Fosters again, albeit emotionally this time. Blythe was trying to smile at Helen. Alex could feel a light sweat starting over her back.

'Hi, Helen. Hello again, Alfie!' How could Jem be so relaxed? Poker-faced? Alex watched her move to free up the chair for Helen, not one iota of unease around Millie's mother and son. 'I like your hat, Alfie.' Jem smiled. Alex's guts twisted.

Alex looked over at her mum. Alfie's name had been

enough to trip her off yesterday, agitated her. Alex watched for any signs of a replay but Blythe was upright, alert.

'Oh, Alfie darling, take your hat off so Blythe can see your lovely face again. She hasn't seen you for weeks,' Helen cooed, straightening Alfie's shirt over his shorts.

Alfie waited to be tidied up before ruining Helen's efforts and wriggling onto her lap. Helen swept the baseball cap from his head and ran a mother's hand through his blond tufts. 'There, all better. Now then, aren't you going to say hello to Blythe?'

'Hello,' Alfie said with a small shrug.

Alex watched her mum's expression fill with warmth. Most of Blythe's face was giving in to a smile that was all for Alfie. And then just as quickly, it drained from her face. Alex saw the desperation washing over her features. Jem saw it too. Blythe opened her mouth.

'Dillon? My baby boy? *Oh*, where have you *been*?'

CHAPTER 40

'What are you doing?' Alex had been so invested in emptying the under-stairs cupboard, she hadn't heard Jem coming.

'Looking for Mum's opera records. I'm going to take them into the hospital.' Alex set another armful of LPs in another dusty pile on the hall floor. Norma had lost interest and was sleeping beside the tower of board games Alex had found in there, along with the unused sewing machine Granny Ros had bought in a last ditch effort to convert one of them into a seamstress, and twenty-four empty jars ready for an orgy of big-batch jam making.

'You can't take all those to the hospital,' said Jem.

'Yes I can.' See, Alex was getting the hang of this being straighter to the point lark.

'OK, so can I ask why? Or are you going to snap at that too?'

'I'm not snapping,' Alex snapped.

Jem set a hand on her hip. 'You've hardly spoken to me over the last couple of days, Alex.'

Me hardly spoken to her? 'I thought it would be nice. For Mum. Maybe if she had something more familiar around her, she wouldn't get… confused again.' Alex was clutching at straws and she knew it.

Jem blew her fringe from her eyes. She hadn't bothered meticulously styling it today. Yesterday had rocked her; it had rocked them all. Alex had left it to Jem to pile the worry on their dad. Alex still hadn't even asked Jem how she'd approached that particular chestnut. There was no easy way to tell their dad that, thanks to the intricacies of the human brain, Dill had followed Rodolfo all the way down Blythe's confused memory.

'What's this?' Jem said, turning the uppermost board game so that she could better read the box.'

'They're the games that were in here.'

'No, this isn't a game. *Back To Your Roots.* Oh, I remember these,' Jem said warmly. 'This is one of those box set thingies they had at the town hall library, when Mum was working there. Remember?'

Alex glanced at the box in Jem's hand. Blythe had convinced her bosses to buy them in when genealogy-fever had set in the Falls, as a way to bring in some revenue to the library and hopefully more interest in local ancestry.

'This one must be the tree Mum did for Dad. Fancy a quick look? You could have a break,' Jem said hopefully, 'I'll make the tea?' Why was Jem so keen to spend time together all of a sudden?

'You go ahead.' Alex said. 'I'm going to sort these records.'

'Alex,' Jem sighed, 'even if you do take them all down to Mum, what are you going to play them on?'

'The record player. It has a headphone socket, I've checked. I just need a plug to wire back onto the cable.'

'Well keep away from my hair-straighteners. I need that plug where it is.' Jem was trying to be upbeat. Alex might've smiled but she thought how sleek Jem's hair had been when she'd been standing in Millie's lounge.

'Any ideas where Dad keeps his small screwdrivers?' Alex said nonchalantly.

'In the workshop. He has about a million. You might even find a plug in there. He always keeps stuff like that. Just don't let him catch you in there.'

'Why?'

'I don't know, he said there are dangerous bits of machinery in there. I think he thinks we're still little girls, sometimes.'

Jem wiped the dust from her *Back To Your Roots* box pack. 'It's a shame these didn't catch on.' There had been a surplus at the library. Eventually everyone had been gifted one of Blythe's *Back To Your Roots* sets. The girls had been thoroughly relieved when this set had turned up in their dad's Christmas pile and not one of theirs.

'So what if local families are linked up way back down the line? Who cares? It'll just mean more Christmas cards to write,' Jem had said.

Perhaps there was a crossover somewhere back along the line. Alex saw her mother again, reaching for Alfie to go sit with her, not realising why he'd looked so terrified.

'My mum's hallucinating!' Jem had sputtered at the nurses. Only she wasn't hallucinating. There *was* something of Dillon in Alfie Sinclair, Alex had seen it too. The way Alfie's cowlick threw his hair up at the front? Serious eyes, too old for such a little boy? It wasn't that easy to name it, but it was there.

A crossover, Alex thought again. Everyone knew, the Sinclairs and the Fosters were the two oldest family names in the Falls. It wasn't impossible that Dill and Alfie had both dipped a toe in the same gene pool, was it?

'I'll leave you to it then, shall I?' Jem said impatiently.

'Sorry. I was just… thinking.'

Jem softened. 'How long do you think you'll be? I thought we could go into Kerring together today? Maybe grab some lunch on the way through town? I've been thinking about what you said, actually. About carrying things around, setting them down…'

About brutal honesty, Alex remembered. Alex snapped again. 'Mum doesn't need anything else on her plate right now, Jem. Maybe you should keep it to yourself for a while?' Her voice sounded harsh. She tried to sound softer. 'You can't drop any bombs on her now, Jem. I know what I said before about total honesty but, you can't now.'

Jem looked down at herself and then repositioned the family tree in her arms. Alex had pulled the rug out from under her; she'd stolen back her sisterly encouragement. Jem nodded. 'You're right. It can wait.'

Alex felt like a bitch. But she was protecting them, her mum and Jem. This was tough love. 'And I think we need to be more of a family unit for her too, cut out all the other distractions. Spend more time together here. The three of us.' Mal was not invited. She waited to see how that one sank in but Jem didn't argue.

'You're right. But Dad's a hard one to nail down, Al. You know how he deals with things, he works, or plays back-gammon down at The Cavern. That's how he copes.'

'I know. But Mum's *really* not well, now. Jem, she's seeing *Dill*. You did tell Dad that, didn't you? So he knows how serious this is?'

Jem looked away for a second. 'I did.'

'And?'

'He changed the subject.' Jem's face crumpled. 'Can't we just leave him to do what he needs to get through it?'

'He can't change the subject! Jem, she thinks that Alfie Sinclair is Dill! Did you see how heartbroken she was when Alfie didn't want to sit with her? When Helen bundled him out of the room?' Alex felt a sudden warm rush from her eyes.

'Al, it's OK—'

'Its not OK, Jem!' Alex wiped her face in defiance but it was useless. The warm spilled down her face onto the dusty LP in her lap. Blythe had sobbed when Helen had taken Alfie out of the room. She'd called for him. Shouted his name again and again. And then she'd wailed with the same crushing despair when he wouldn't come back.

Alex had heard her mum like that before, on the front lawn, when Alex had been taken home from the Old Girl wrapped in blankets and disbelief. That awful guttural sobbing.

'Dad needs to face it, Jem, how ill she is. I think we should eat together tonight, the three of us. We're never all in the house at the same time and we *need* to work together on this. We need to be solid for her. She needs us,' Alex said quietly. But Alex didn't have the best track record for standing and fighting for anyone.

CHAPTER 41

Alex picked her way amongst the tools in her dad's work shed. He'd customised an inflatable dinghy in here once, back when he'd still thought of the Falls' preoccupation with all things Viking as a bit of harmless fun and the river race included normal water-craft instead of dubious rafts fashioned from empty plastic bottles and optimism.

Alex scanned the workbenches for any sort of labelling system but it all looked like a headache, pots and trays of bolts and metal things she couldn't identify. Her mother's record player probably didn't need a whole new plug, she'd decided. Working at the food bank had taught her to be frugal with everything. 'We live in a throwaway society!' Dan had declared. 'Someone's toaster stops working and what do they do? Head to Argos!' Alex's toaster had in fact stopped working shortly after Dan had made that very point. Alex had experienced some minor thrill at having success-fully diagnosed a dodgy fuse and fixed it all by herself.

She scanned the walls of tools and boxes. *Fuse… If I were a fuse, where would I be?* Something small and yellow shot into the gloom of the workshop and startled her.

'Norma, I left the house for *one minute*. You're like my bloody shadow.'

Alex began rummaging through a run of pull out trays looking for a screwdriver. She'd put a joint in the oven to slow roast while she tried fixing up the record player. Jem had gone on to the hospital without her. Alex bristled as the same questions surged back into her head like a rogue wave. How could Millie have not seen Jem the other night? Jem must've passed Millie to grab her boots from the hallway, mustn't she? Or had *Millie* moved Jem's boots? But why would Millie move Jem's boots and then pretend that Jem wasn't in her house? What possible reason did she have? Millie would only have been duping *Alex*.

None of it made sense. Maybe they could talk it all out later over the family dinner Alex had bullied them into. They could talk about Blythe's delirium over the main course and then move onto the Jem–Malcolm–Millie saga over dessert. Brilliant.

Alex moved along the workshop further into the gloom and crunched on something. *Ugh, please don't be a snail…* Dill had pinched Jem's roller blades once and returned them with a nice even layer of snail guts and shell from the path outside. Jem had gone mental, eventually. The Reverend had been over at the time and Jem had had to hold it in. Alex couldn't look at a roller blade now without thinking about entrails.

Alex tentatively took a look at what was under her feet.

There was enough light in here to bounce off the broken glass strewn across the workshop floor.

'Norma. Come here, girl.' Alex scooped her up from the floor. Amongst the glass, a splintered wooden frame sat abandoned. Alex picked it up carefully and held it up to the light. More glass tumbled to the floor. Norma struggled under Alex's arm and she straightened up to hold her better. Alex examined the damaged photograph left clinging to the remnants of the picture frame. She knew this picture. By heart. A perfect day, committed to memory. Along with the other perfect stuff. This was one of the pictures Granny Ros had taken and given to Alex's mum to hang in the hallway, probably because it featured the mayor and his wife.

Alex blew any sharp fragments from the image. 'Jem's seventh birthday and the pink dress debacle.' Alex knew it was Jem's seventh on account of the big blue number seven sitting centre point on the cake Granny Ros had frosted in lilac, a halfway compromise between Jem's blue and Granny Ros's pink preference. Alex remembered Louisa Sinclair bringing that dress over for Jem in case she didn't have something pretty to wear for her own party. Their mum had made her wear it for politeness' sake. Despite Jem's grimace and Louisa Sinclair skulking in the background looking utterly out of place in a non-mayoral home, this picture had been one of Alex's favourites. Not only did Jem look hilarious in her puffy pink sleeves and puffier pinker eyes, but they'd all been on there, in happy coexistence. Before the big one hit.

Alex frowned. *Why would you leave this on the floor like that, Dad? And not pick it up for safekeeping?* Alex followed the faces on the photograph to her father, Ted causing gleeful havoc with two young hysterical boys thrown over his shoulders because, if Alex's memory served, Malcolm and Finn had taken the last two bowls of jelly. Alex smiled sadly at their faces. At Dill, pudgy in their mum's arms while Blythe looked fraught with the stresses of house guests.

Alex did a double take at Mal. He'd been much fairer then, his hair a sandy blond. Alex squinted. It was uncanny. She hadn't ever thought about it before now. Mal's hair had darkened significantly by the time Dill was running around annoying everyone so they hadn't looked much like each other at all, not on the face of it. Plus Mal rarely came up to the house by then anyway, not like Finn. *Finn.* Alex looked back to Finn. He looked goofy then in his Superman t-shirt and neat haircut. Back when he was still allowed to come up to the house and Ted didn't yet blame him for the mistakes Martin Finn had made at the garage. For the mistake Alex made following him into the bushes.

'I wish we could all go back,' she said into the dusty gloom. But they couldn't. All they could do was clutch at the memories of what they all used to be. Memories like broken glass, to be handled with care. Tightly enough that they didn't fall away, gently enough that they didn't cut too deeply.

CHAPTER 42

'Food smells nice.'

Jem was fiddling with her bracelet again. She'd painted her fingernails a pastel colour and was running one around the contours of the fine silver leaf skeletons wrapped around her wrist. There was a time Jem had thought of nail polish as an aberration. Another mark for the cheerleading brigade with their fake tans and lip-liners. Alex had barely remembered to put a brush through her hair this week but Jem was all camera ready for a meal they'd both been stood up for.

'Smelled even better when it was hot.' Alex glanced at the clock. Nine, they'd agreed. So Ted could spend some time at the hospital first.

'It still smells great, Al. Maybe he just lost track.' He hadn't lost track. Visiting hours finished at 8.30 p.m. He wasn't coming.

'It's been on the table for nearly an hour.'

Jem took another sip from her wine glass. Alex didn't want wine, it wasn't fair when their dad had cut it out completely to go wafting it around but then what did Alex know?

Jem knew what the limits were, Alex was just a house guest who occasionally spent two hours preparing a family meal no one would end up eating.

'Just, cut him some slack, Alex. He's trying his best.'

'So am I!' The tears were coming. They made Alex speak too quickly, trying to outrun them. 'I asked him what time to eat, I… I… I cooked *this* because it was on Mum's recipe list under Ted's *bloody* favourites…'

'It's not you, Alex,' Jem said solemnly.

'What? It's not me it's him? Ha! He can't stand to be around me for more than ten minutes, Jem, unless he's reminding me to keep away from Finn. He *hates* me.'

'He does not hate you, Alex!'

'Then where is he, Jem? Why isn't he here, so we can at least *pretend* to be putting on a united front for Mum?'

Jem looked like she had tears in the pipeline too. 'He loves you, Alex. You know he does.'

'Maybe he does. But he'll never get over what I did. He'll never get past the thought that I was at it with Finn when we were only looking for a stupid dock leaf.' Alex shook her head as the disbelief washed over her again. 'A dock leaf! I was worrying about a nettle rash while Dill was drowning.' Alex clamped a hand over her mouth. Jem was already on her feet.

'Alex, that's not why he's not here.'

Alex pulled out the photograph she'd found in the workshop from her back pocket and set it on the table. 'No? Then why can't he even bear to see us all on the same photograph together, Jem?'

Jem looked long and hard at the image until tears began sliding down her cheeks. 'Where did you get this?' she asked quietly.

'In his shed. It looked like it had been stamped on, Jem. *Stamped* on.'

Jem wiped her face. 'You don't understand, Alex.'

'I think I do. He can't bear to look at this photo because Finn's in on it with us. And it wasn't even Finn's fault! Finn tried to get him out, but he couldn't. And now Dad can't even have this in the house.'

Alex rose from her chair.

'Where are you going?'

'To do what I've been too much of a coward to for the last ten years. I'm going to tell Dad that I'm *sorry*. And then I'm going to get out of his hair so you two can at least eat together and have *one* conversation about our mother losing her mind.' Alex rubbed at the tears steadily streaming from her face.

'Alex, don't go looking for Dad, please.'

'Why not?'

'Because… there are things you don't know about.'

CHAPTER 43

Alex looked at the empty gazes of the two sculpted Valkyries flanking what was to be the boat race's finish line on riverbank. Alex had dressed up as a Valkyrie once in college to go collecting for the Air Ambulance. *Wings* had been the theme. Finn had waddled around town shaking his bucket in a creepy *Wizard of Oz* style winged-monkey suit. But the Vikings held that the Valkyries, with their swan feathers and swords, were otherworldly, steadfast, unyielding beings. The deciders of those who would live or die in battle. Alex had rather fancied the idea of shaking her bucket as an otherworldly, decisive being.

Alex slowed automatically on the approach to the bend outside The Cavern as Ted had always insisted she do, just to be safe. She cleared her throat and ignored the Valkyries. *Decisive. Steadfast.* Had she been having a laugh? She couldn't even keep her emotions in check. It was like she had no control of herself when she was back here. Seventeen again, incompetent again, floundering in the current.

Alex pulled into The Cavern car park a bit too sharply, the speed-bump that hadn't used to be there sending her bouncing around violently in her truck. Alex's heart was instantly thumping. She slapped a hand against her steering wheel and let out an embittered sound. *Sorry. SORRY!* It was such a small word she'd never been able to present it to her dad. It would be like offering one of the families at the food bank a vol-au-vent and expecting it to fill them up. So she'd just always let it sit there, stuck in her throat instead, a weak little sound she was too ashamed to make in front of him.

Valkyrie. Ha! What the hell had Finn ever seen in a wimp like her? Finn didn't shy away from anything. But Alex? Oh *yes*, with Alex there were *always* conditions she now realised. Apologise? Sure, if she knew her dad would accept it. Talk to Finn? No problem, so long as it wasn't out in the open where people could see it and question it and hold it up as proof that she wasn't *that* sorry for what had happened at the Old Girl.

Alex looked past the uneven white walls of the pub to the welcoming glow of light spilling from inside. She realised now that nothing she did would ever be enough to change anything between them. And that was fine, because she understood. She did a terrible thing, and she was sorry for it. She'd been sorry for it every day for the last ten years. But whether he accepted it or not, whether he wanted to even *hear* it or not, she was finally going to say it to his face. Right now. Inside this pub.

Alex slammed her door and stormed past her father's recovery truck across to The Cavern's rear entrance.

The sweet aroma of ale and people hit as soon as she

walked into the commotion of the bar. Hamish was laughing heartily behind the draught pumps, a plait had appeared in his long red beard. She looked away before he could spot her and call a hello. The pub was thick with people. Alex might've recognised many of their faces if she'd bothered to look at them, but she was only looking at the far stairs leading up to where the old boys still held backgammon and poker nights. The same poker night Finn's dad had been in such a rush to get to when he'd hurriedly signed off Helen Fairbanks' car.

Alex felt the resolve slipping from her heart so she skipped up the stairs two at a time before there was no resolve left at all. She barged through the doors into the upstairs bar and glanced across the cosy space, gentle laughter and male conversation giving the gloom a tavern-like ambience. Alex spotted him, sitting beneath a gallery of the pictures chronicling past boat races, elbows on the table as he sat nursing a stack of counters. She weaved her way amongst a couple of bar tables, older men in twos and threes sitting hunched over chess and chequers.

The man sitting next to Ted looked up at Alex then jabbed her dad with an elbow. He nodded over to her as she stalked towards them. Alex saw him push the glass away across the table towards the man opposite him. Was he *drinking*? Was coming home such a push that she'd driven him to *drink*?

He wouldn't look at her, he was the only one at his table who wasn't looking at her. 'Go home, Alexandra. I'll be along shortly.'

He still wouldn't look at her. Alex felt her lip tremble like a little girl's. 'You said nine o'clock. I cooked,' she managed.

One of the men at the table was trying to be funny. 'Uh-oh, Edward. I do believe you're in trouble, old lad.'

Another piped up from beneath his flat cap. 'Run along, Ted. Your dinner's ready.' A ripple of harmless laughter broke out amongst them. Harmless and jagged all at once. Something hardened inside her. Alex watched her father, saw his mouth hitch up with an unsure smile, like he was the child trying to save face in front of his friends.

'We need to talk.' She heard the tremble in her own voice.

'I said I'll be along shortly.' He looked at her then, a father's warning. It might have carried enough weight too, but then he picked up the dice and sent them tumbling across the red felt of the backgammon board. One flick of the wrist and he'd dismissed her, given her all the reason she needed to scuttle back off like the coward she'd always been.

Mum needs us, Alex Foster. You will not run away from this.

She reached between the shoulders of the two strangers sitting in front of her and, without thinking, flipped the edge of the backgammon board violently into the air. Ted caught the board awkwardly but the counters had all gone tumbling to the floor, a couple of pint glasses with them.

The sounds of men erupted around her but her own biting hurt had her in a tighter grip than anything they could muster.

'You won't come home until late every night, Dad. That's fine! You don't want the muffins I bake and bring down to the garage for you because you've seen me talking to Finn in the street, *that's* OK too! I understand! But I've spent *two* hours cooking you a meal tonight that you said you'd be home for and you don't even show up for it.' They were all staring at her now. They saw her now. She could feel angry tears, damn it, they probably all thought they were for a piece of slow-roasted beef. She wiped a sleeve rattily across her cheek. 'I'm sorry, Dad. I'm sorry for what I did, for letting you down. For letting my brother down. And I'm sorry I left him on his own for just a few stupid, stupid minutes. I'm sorry that you can't come home and talk about Mum now because that means talking about Dill too. I'm sorry. I'm so sorry, Dad.' She was losing it. *You're losing it, Alex.* She sucked in another broken breath. 'And it's all right that you hate me… I hate me too. For what I did. And I don't expect you to feel any different towards me now, but I just wanted you to know that…' Ted was looking straight at her, cold fox like eyes carrying as much despair as Alex was. She could feel it all about to drown her out. 'I'm *sorry*, Dad. But I lost Dill too.'

CHAPTER 44

'Come on in.' Susannah Finn had a calmness that reminded Alex of her mum. Good in a crisis, slow to judge despite everything her son had put up with as a result of a teenage romance with the wrong girl.

Susannah had just been locking up the front doors when Alex turned up wielding nothing but a bank card and an apology for disturbing any Longhouse guests so late.

'I'd say I'll put the coffee on but I've just had Finn put me in a new drinks bar,' Susannah said proudly waving her hands at the extension she was leading Alex into. Alex hadn't had chance for a full tour when Finn had talked her into helping him coax Emma to stay.

Alex hadn't thought about the logistics of turning up here with Finn around. Hearing Susannah talking about him already, maybe it was best if she found somewhere else tomorrow. There were other places she could go, only whether or not they were taking bookings this close to Viking Fest was another thing altogether.

'And you can put that bank card away.' Susannah patted one of the stools and nodded at the smoothed section of tree trunk Finn had fashioned into a long rustic bar. Alex sat dutifully where she was told while Susannah took down two cocktail glasses from the shelf behind her. Susannah chuckled as she put them down on the wooden bar top, they had little Viking horns poking out either side. 'For the tourists.' She smiled, pushing her dressing-gown sleeves up her arms. 'Now I'm not a big drinker, you ask your mother, so what shall we have?' Susannah clasped her fingers together like an emphatic science teacher about to concoct something in a test tube. Alex looked over the timber frame extension Finn had built onto the back of Susannah's lounge. She could just see a light on in the summerhouse across the lawn where Finn was now living.

'Ooh, we'll have a drop of that, and a nip of that one... There you go. Try that, young lady.'

Alex took a sip. '*Wowsers*. That's... unusual,' she sputtered.

'Mmm, I like it!' Susannah declared. 'Tastes a bit like my fabric softener. Yummy.' Susannah squinted her eye and poked her tongue out. 'Maybe I'll just put a pot of coffee on. Before I kill one of us.'

Alex tried another sip out of politeness. It was harder to swallow now her stomach knew what to expect. Susannah took it off her. 'For Heaven's sake, stop worrying about offending people. It's a ruddy cocktail.'

'Sorry, Susannah. I don't really drink.'

'And I'll bet you never drink cocktails when you do. You never were a girl for all the glitzy nonsense, Alexandra.

Not like the others who'd come calling for my Finn, not that he ever took any notice.' Susannah pulled at one of her dangly earrings. 'It's one of the reasons I always liked you so much, Alex. And your sister, actually. None of that shiny polished business all these girls chase around after these days. I always preferred to see little girls with mud on their knees and grass in their hair anyway.'

'Like Poppy?' Alex smiled. 'I saw her playing with Finn. She was holding her own.'

Susannah smiled. 'Yes, like Poppy. I think Finn's got another fan in that one. She's going to be terribly disappointed when she clicks.'

'Clicks?'

'That Finn only has eyes for another girl.'

'Oh,' Alex said. The athletic brunette. Alex might need that drink after all.

'He might have had his flings but you're the one, you know, Alex. He hasn't found another one since you left. I told him he might be in for a rough ride, the last thing I wanted for him was a repeat of the trifle incident, as I call it. But, as it turned out, Finn didn't want to go upsetting your father about it anyway.'

'Upsetting my dad?' Alex heard the inanity in her voice. She had a ringing in her ears. She felt that dazed and confused feeling she remembered experiencing after emerging at 3 a.m. from the university nightclub a handful of times.

'Well, actually that's not wholly true. I don't think Finn minded upsetting your father as such, it was just, well he knew that the last thing *you* wanted was for your father to be upset. So, Finn… well I suppose he was waiting to follow your lead. Leave it to you to take the next step forwards.'

Only, Alex had never taken the lead. She'd cut Finn loose. Because her dad couldn't handle the thought of them, even on a photograph together at Jem's seventh birthday party apparently.

Susannah was watching the thoughts play out across Alex's face. 'You know, I'd always hoped you might come home for good, Alex. See where your paths led you both, now that you're both a bit older, and wiser.'

Alex wasn't wiser. She was just as clueless now as she was back then. Alex tried to hold it down but Susannah had already spotting it coming. 'Now, then! There there, Alex, don't let it all get you down. I wasn't thinking of forcing you into marriage while you're here!'

Alex tried to smile. 'It's not that.'

'Well then, my coffee's better than my cocktails, I promise.'

'I'm sorry, Susannah.'

Susannah patted the top of Alex's hand. 'You've got *nothing* to be sorry about, Alex,' she said firmly.

'Yes I do.' She'd never seen her dad not know how to react to a situation. He'd stood up, the backgammon board held awkwardly in his hands as the rest of The Cavern's loft had fallen into silence. She'd apologised to them too. Maybe if she dished out enough apologies, one might stick somewhere.

'Oh Alexandra. You used to be such a spritely girl. When you left here the other night, I said to Finn, *That girl looks like she's carrying the weight of the world on her shoulders and not just for her mother's illness.* Even now, all these years on, Alex. It's not right.'

Alex forced a smile, but it *was* right. And it was right that she didn't go bothering Ted any more back at the house. That was his domain; he couldn't relax with Alex there. She could get her things tomorrow, while he was safely at the garage.

Susannah began fussing at the coffee machine behind her. Alex got a hit of fresh coffee beans. 'You were well suited you know, the two of you. Finn's a worrier too.'

'Finn's a worrier?' Finn had always been so laidback, half the time Alex found herself glancing over at him to check he was still there, in the art block at college, on the riverbank through the summer.

'He's a terrible worrier! He just keeps it to himself, and very effectively too. He had a terrible time after his father left, as you know.'

Finn had never said much about his dad. Not like Alex, she'd talked Finn's ears off about hers. There was really only ever the one occasion Finn had openly spoken of his dad, and that conversation had nosedived into a confused, upsetting experience not helped by the fact he and Alex had both been naked at the time.

Alex remembered Finn's body as he'd shook with

frustration. She felt a crazed sort of regret. 'He didn't really ever talk about his dad.' Her voice came out scratchy.

'Well why would he have? There wasn't much nice to say about Martin. This is such a small town, Finn felt the burden of his father's actions in more ways than was fair to the poor boy. Some of the children teased him at school, you know, about Martin caring more about his gambling than he did about his own son. How Finn's father was the reason Helen's daughter had to have all those terrible operations on her little legs and that Finn's dad was going to be thrown in jail when the police caught up with him. I had to hear that from his class teacher, mind. Finn wouldn't tell me what they were all saying. Didn't want to upset me.'

'Kids can be cruel,' Alex agreed. Only it wasn't just kids. After Dill's accident, her dad had thrown everything he could at Finn, as if all the evils in the world had started with that one dodgy service on Helen Fairbanks' car and with Martin Finn long gone it was only right that his son shoulder the blame for it all.

'People, Alex. *People* can be cruel. I know human beings go bonkers for their own offspring and I suppose I'm guilty of that too but really, my son's a good person. He always has been, even when he was little, Finn was such a brave little boy. It used to break my heart seeing him wait for his father to return. Christmas morning, birthdays, I lost count of how many times he'd be looking out the front window for him.' Susannah's shoulders dropped. 'Martin didn't deserve our son.'

Finn had told Alex how he'd had to love his father in secret. She wondered it Susannah realised just how much of a burden Finn had been shouldering.

'Did Martin ever get in touch, after he'd left?'

Susannah's eyebrows rose as she sighed. 'He sent a letter once, when Finn was about fifteen. Said he was sorry for what he'd done. That he was trying to sort his habits out. But that we were better off without him. He knew he had a problem with the betting and he didn't want it rubbing off on Finn. Shame his considerations didn't run a bit deeper and him put aside some of his gambling money for his only child.'

'Didn't Martin pay maintenance?'

'You can't collect maintenance from someone who disappears off the radar!' Susannah scoffed. 'He'd promised Finn a little black puppy, the last of a litter up at the Rowland's farm. Finn was so excited, Martin said he was going to collect it on his way back home the night Helen had her accident with that wagon, but Martin… never came back. Finn broke his heart for his father, and for that little puppy. I couldn't afford to take it on. After Martin left, money was very tight. I got behind with the bills, and then the bailiffs started to come by. I'd hide with Finn in the back cupboard, pretend we were playing hide and seek until the knocking stopped. Then one day, he just seemed to click. Maybe I hadn't laughed enough, or I hadn't made it into enough of a game, but Finn refused to hide. He knew we were hiding from the men knocking on the door and he didn't want to hide any more. So he marched right up to that front door and threw it open, demanding to know their business.' Susannah smiled with something pride-like and melancholy. 'There were two of them. They told him they needed the bills paying. While I was pleading with them, Finn had gone to raid his penny jar.'

Alex thought of Finn, calm and clinical in Emma Parsons' front garden, emptying his wallet. Finn wasn't a helpless little boy any more. Alex glanced again to the lit window at the end of Susannah's lawns.

'Of course, they took most of what we had that day. But I've always wondered, had they not have taken the television, would Finn have spent so much time playing with his pencils? Would he be as good as he is now, if he'd have been sat watching hour after hour of brain-sucking kids' shows instead of tinkering with his art things? Of course, it'd have been nice if they'd have left the sofa, mind.'

Susannah fixed the coffees and thrust one in front of Alex. 'Milk and two sugars wasn't it?'

'You remember.'

'I remember everything, Alex.'

Susannah was so like Blythe, just a few words in place of hundreds. Alex blew over her mug. Unlike back home, she'd only felt like a guest here for as long as it had taken Susannah to walk her through to the drinks bar. Now she was just Alex again, sitting across from someone who knew her well enough to be frank. 'How's your mother?'

Alex reached up to sooth the sharp pain she'd felt suddenly in her head. 'Not great. She thought she saw Dill yesterday.'

'What?'

'Helen brought her grandson in.'

'Alfie?'

'He does kinda look a little like Dill did.'

'Yes. Yes he does.' Susannah breathed in deeply. 'I take it your father's not doing too great either then?'

Alex shook her head. 'You can stay here as long as you wish, Alexandra. I'll find room. I'll not have you thinking you need to go back and put up with Ted Foster's mood swings because he thinks he's the only person who's ever been affected by a bad situation.'

'It's not that clear cut though, Susannah.' Her dad wasn't a bad person. Finn might've had a rough ride but Alex remembered a different time when her dad was different too.

'Nothing is ever as clear cut at people like to convince themselves, Alex. Sometimes I wonder if that's not why your father was so desperate for you kids to keep your distance from one another,' Susannah said sourly.

'What do you mean?' Alex felt a small edge of betrayal. Susannah was not a fan. One blowout with her dad and Alex was open to hearing what Susannah thought of him. Alex was already wishing she hadn't asked. Susannah looked off through the black glass towards the annexe. The lights were off now. Finn had gone to bed and so wouldn't come over here to the barn. Alex eased down a little.

Susannah opened her mouth to say something and then

thought better of it, Alex could tell. Susannah had a second shot. 'I just think your father was desperate to blame somebody for what happened at the river. And Finn fit the bill. I'll never forget that day, when Finn came home. Eighteen years old and he cried himself to sleep that night like a little boy.'

Alex set her mug down and stared into it. 'Finn didn't deserve to be treated the way he was. I tried to explain to my dad, Susannah. But he saw us both covered in nettle rash, he thought—'

'I know what he thought, Alex. And he was wrong. He was wrong to throw those sorts of accusations at the two of you.' Susannah's expression was deadly serious. 'I wanted your father strung up for what he did to my son on your front lawn, but it was Finn who wouldn't press charges.'

That didn't surprise Alex one bit.

'Your father had no idea what an effect Dillon's accident had on Finn. Your mother did but then Blythe is a calmer, gentler soul. She knew about Finn's nightmares. I used to find him wet with sweat some nights. We'd go for months and then another would hit.'

'I'm sorry, Susannah. I didn't know.' Finn had never told her. Jem had suffered nightmares afterwards too. Their mum had taken her off to a psychologist because of her sleep problems. Alex felt a searing pain in her chest. The ripples of that summer afternoon were endless. 'I'm sorry, Susannah,' she said again.

Susannah was watching her intently across the counter

top. 'I know you are, Alex. Everyone in this town knows you are, sweetheart. You could go and get yourself one of those golden flags with the dragons' heads off Eilidh high street wave it in the air, and shout how sorry you are, and it wouldn't be any more obvious than it already is just looking at you. But you've got to let it go now, my darling girl. Before there's nothing left of you except for how sorry you are.'

Alex glared at the coffee mug in her hands. Susannah put her hands over Alex's.

'Your mother should have told you this, Alex, and I told her so too. But I think she was always worrying too much about bringing it all up, in case it upset your bloody dad.' Susannah breathed in deeply and lifted her chin. 'I know you don't want to hear this, Alex, and Finn won't thank me for saying it. But someone who should be one hell of a lot sorrier for their part in all this is your father.'

CHAPTER 45

Alex had spent the night in one of Susannah's simply furnished guest rooms overlooking the driveway into the Longhouse and the beginnings of Eilidh high street. Not, thankfully, the rear of the property and Finn's bolthole. The sun was just climbing over the hills behind Godric's gorge. Alex had already got dressed and had been planning on keeping up her surveillance of the road outside, waiting for her dad's blue recovery truck to roll past so she could go collect her things from the house, but Susannah had knocked with a breakfast call.

Alex did the best she could with her hair and opened her room door. She needed her toothbrush before she sat down there with anyone. She checked her breath and made a grab for the second complimentary mint next to the bed, popping into her mouth as she left the room.

Alex turned and thudded into a passing guest. 'Oh! Excuse me!' Her voice was silvery and polite. Alex stepped back and saw the killer dark hair first. *Knockout cheekbones* flashed into her head. Alex started to apologise but something was making its way down her throat.

Don't panic. Alex breathed in through her nose and felt the mint tug in her windpipe. She thumped her chest.

'Oh my God, are you OK?'

Oh my God, I'm choking! But the woman with the cheek-bones was already beside Alex banging the hell out of her back. The mint imperial shot from Alex's mouth and spun across the polished landing floor to a pair of little naked feet. Poppy had stopped brushing her teeth in the door-way of her room to watch the trajectory of Alex's breath freshener.

Alex's heart was thudding.

'Are you all right?' the brunette asked, her worried expression peeping out from behind the long flawless layers of an obviously high-end haircut. High-end haircut and a decent killer-crab impression. Fate smiled down more on some than others.

Alex wiped the saliva from her chin. *Classy, Alex. Real classy.* 'I'm fine… thank you.' She winced.

'I've never nearly killed someone before, are you sure you're OK?'

'Totally fine, really.' She was so attractive it was flustering Alex. Alex was beginning to feel more concerned about whether or not her breath smelled OK to this girl than not being able to breathe in the first place.

'Are you… a guest here?' the woman asked. She seemed genuinely perplexed to see Alex.

'Um, kinda.' She was looking at Alex like she was wait-ing for her to catch on to something conversation-worthy.

'You?' Alex asked. *You know she's a guest here, you plank.* 'Here for the Viking Festival, I mean?'

'Ah, yes. I am. But, ah… I don't really know what it's all about. I could do with a tour guide or something.' She laughed huskily.

'I think I saw a booklet on the reception desk downstairs. There's probably a map or something—'

'Oh, that's OK. The landlady's son said he'll give me a quick tour of the town if I want. But thanks.' She had a high-end smile too. It made Alex wish she'd held on better to that mint imperial.

Poppy was still watching from her room doorway, her cheeks full with toothpaste froth. The brunette was still smiling. No wonder her cheekbones were so perky. Alex smiled back. Neither of them seemed to know what to offer the conversation next. In fact, it was getting more awkward by the second and Alex was having to battle growing feelings of self-consciousness just from standing this close to someone so stunning in running Lycra.

'Thanks for the Heimlich.' She smiled weakly.

'No problem. Glad to be of help.' The brunette shot a hand out. It was an odd, uncertain movement, like offering to shake the hand of somebody interviewing her for a job.

'I'm… Gina.'

Alex took her hand. 'Alex.' Alex followed the long honed arm to the silver bracelet on Gina's wrist. Alex would've admired it, out of politeness, but Gina pulled her hand away and set it behind her back before Alex got a proper look.

'Anyway, guess I'll see you at breakfast then.'

Alex seized the opportunity. 'See you.' Alex watched Gina walk lithely down the stairs before she turned to collect the minty missile before it got stuck to Poppy's foot.

'Mummy says you shouldn't eat sweeties while you're walking,' Poppy said as Alex approached.

Alex put her thumb up. 'Your mummy's very right.' She smiled. 'Are you and Mummy all right now, sweetie?'

Poppy nodded.

'I'm glad you're feeling better,' Alex said. She heard the door go downstairs and peered over the banister into the lobby. Alex recognised the greying blond hair against blue work clothes immediately. Alex froze while Ted cleared his throat below her. She stepped back against the landing wall as Poppy disappeared back into her mother's room. Alex hadn't thought about the aftermath of her outburst at The Cavern, she didn't have a plan in place that went much beyond collecting her things this morning.

'Ted?' Alex heard Susannah's voice below the stairs. 'Gotten lost, have we?'

Alex waited to be called down like a naughty girl hoping to be let off a punishment.

'Is my daughter here?'

'You've seen her truck in the yard, Ted. You know damn well she is. Not that you care much.' Susannah's tone took Alex aback.

'Don't tell me what I care about, Susannah. I love my daughter more than you'll ever know,' he hissed.

Ted's words took Alex aback even more. Alex felt a surge of adrenalin.

'How is Blythe? Does she know you're chasing her daughter away?' Susannah said under her breath.

Alex heard one of her father's deep breaths and held on to her own. 'The hospital called this morning. Blythe has an infection. Something in the urinary tract or something. I just wanted to let Alexandra know, her mother's been saying some strange things lately.'

'Yes, I heard. Quite the resemblance between your Dillon and Louisa's grandson.'

Alex heard an accusation in Susannah's voice she didn't understand.

Ted fell silent at first, then ploughed on. 'Blythe's confused. They think this infection might be the cause. I thought Alex would feel better if she knew they were treating her for it now.'

'I'm sure she will, Ted. That girl could do with some good news.' Alex heard her dad moved towards the door and it snap closed again. 'What are you playing at, Ted? Don't you realise, you're not the only one suffering?'

'Don't preach to me, Susannah. Now let me through.'

'I will preach to you. That girl turned up here last night in a right old state. What are you trying to do? *Punish her*?'

'Don't be so goddamn ridiculous, Susannah. I love her. She knows that.'

'Does she? Don't you think you might be wise to let *her* know that then? Instead of letting her remain this invisible non-person who's so frightened to rock the boat, she won't even save herself from drifting out to sea! You're going to lose her, Ted. I am warning you now. And you are an old fool if you let that girl go.'

'Thank you for your advice, Susannah, but I think I can manage my own relationships. Why don't you concentrate on that angelic son of yours and leave my daughters to me?'

Susannah's voice changed. 'Finn's no angel, Ted Foster. But he deserves better than you ever gave him.'

'I let him into my home! Despite that good-for-nothing husband of yours. And how did he repay me?'

Their voices were sharpening off, gritted angst stifled by tight lips.

'Don't you dare. I won't have it. Not in my house.'

'If he hadn't have been messing—'

'Don't. You. Dare. You're forgetting! You're not whiter than white, Ted Foster.'

Alex's heart was thumping now. 'You blame everyone else for what happened down at the Old Girl, but where were you that day, Ted Foster? We both know the answer to that. I'll never forget walking past Frobisher's. You looked like a ghost when you saw me looking in, and her there, draping herself all over you like a piece of tacky jewellery.'

Alex swallowed.

'You don't know as much as you think, Susannah,' Ted said quietly. Alex could feel something jumping in her throat. She felt dizzy with it. 'I know you weren't supposed to be where you were when those three kids were down by the river. So don't you dare put any more on my boy than you already have. Because I will not stand for it.'

A name! A name, who were they talking about? Alex needed a name.

'You think what you like, Susannah.'

Alex held her breath.

'I think you're an old fool, and I'd have told Blythe had she not have been heartbroken already for your little boy. But you were a damned fool for having a wife like Blythe at home and having your head turned by a woman like Louisa Sinclair. And if you keep letting that poor girl of yours go on punishing herself, if you push her away for good, then you're a damned fool still.'

CHAPTER 46

Morning breath had toppled a place in the rankings of things Alex was currently concerned about. She'd managed to sit through breakfast with Susannah trying to feed her up, Emma Parsons battling to feed her baby and the statuesque Gina repeatedly looking at Alex over the rim of her tea-cup. Another guest had joined them. He'd hardly joined the conversation either, sitting quietly instead over a boiled egg with a napkin tucked into his crisply ironed shirt.

Alex had robotically risen to help tidy the things away when Susannah caught her staring out onto the lawn. 'He's not working today. He's just tidying his tools up at the florist's this morning. He'll be finishing off his entry for the river race if you wanted something to do later, after you've been to see your mum.'

Alex winced. She didn't want Gina to overhear. Not see-ing as she was getting along so swimmingly with Finn. Alex smiled a reply to Susannah. She didn't tell her that she couldn't face Blythe like Susannah had managed to all these years, pretending she didn't know that her father had been having an affair with the mayor's wife. Alex had gone back to her room briefly, to let her breathing regulate itself, but fresh air was the best tonic for nausea so she'd found herself out here in the garden, pushing Poppy on the swing instead.

Dad. And Louisa Sinclair.

Alex remembered her mother the morning of Dillon's accident. 'Oh Alex, please? The kids are driving me insane, Jem's about ready to kill your brother. He's not going to make it to his ninth birthday at this rate. Just take Dill for a while, would you, darling? Your father said he won't be long.'

Alex pushed Poppy mechanically. Ted had told them he was going on a call out. Not to Frobisher's Tea Rooms tucked away on one of Eilidh's back streets.

'Do you want to see something special?'

Alex's trail of thought broke. Poppy's big brown eyes were shining up at her, a few strands of wayward hair falling in front of them. Alex swept them behind Poppy's ear. 'What, sweetie?'

Poppy jumped up and took Alex by the hand. She had warm hands, still pudgy from toddlerhood. Poppy led them across the grass towards the side door of the annexe.

'Oh, no, sweetie. I don't think we should go in there.'

Poppy pulled. 'But look. Finn's making it for me.'

Alex peeped inside Finn's studio doors, Poppy was yanking surprisingly hard on her hand.

Finn had several canvasses all on the go at once. Alex scanned them for something more expected, like one of the vistas from the hills behind the plunge pools, but they were all animals, dogs mainly. *I don't remember you being that much of a fan, Finn.* Poppy went and proudly stood beside the only workbench and Alex realised why she'd been so keen.

Alex stepped inside the studio and followed her to the doll's house on the side. Even in its early stages Poppy was going to end up with something more spectacular than the dollhouse sitting back at her family home, probably still with a cigarette butt melded into the top of its roof terrace.

'My mummy says that Finn is a really kind man.'

Alex rested her hand on Poppy's head. 'Your mummy is right about that too.'

A chirpy morning voice came from the doorway behind them. 'Morning, ladies. So who's going to help get my river raft onto the back of my truck?'

*

Alex had taken Finn up on his offer of a free, still-in-its-packaging toothbrush from his mother's secret cache while Poppy had looked on with something disdainful in her expression. Alex knew how she felt. She'd felt pretty disdainful when she'd had a close up of Gina.

Alex thought about her dad and Louisa Sinclair. An image of them in a secret tryst at Frobisher's circling Alex's mind like a shark, disappearing from view for a few minutes and the *bang!* Slamming in for another bite.

Finn had hammered a peg into the bank and tethered one end of his raft to it before pushing the raft out over the water. So far, it was floating. Alex watched him skipping around on the embankment. She twirled a length of cottongrass between her fingers. Why shouldn't Alex have come here with him? Why shouldn't she do what the hell she damned well pleased? Everyone else did.

'I didn't drag you up here for nothing.' Finn nodded at the water, a broad smile reaching across his face.

'I'm not getting on that thing,' Alex laughed nervously. He should've brought Gina up here for that. Gina was clearly diehard, she'd brought her running Lycra on a weekend away sightseeing.

'Come on, Foster. You're faster than me too. If it starts to go, just… run for it.'

'I can't run on water, Finn. Anyway, you're the captain.' Alex waved her hand out towards the water, daring him to test his skills.

'You know, if this thing sinks, it's not going to do much for my marketing campaign.'

'Marketing campaign?'

'Yeah, for my business.' Finn sat his hands on his hips, looked wistfully off to the hills and pushed his chest out.

Alex tried to focus on the handyman logo on his t-shirt rather than the outline of his body underneath it. Alex tried not to laugh like a teenaged girl. 'Nice.'

Finn exhaled, pretending the effort to look physically impressive had cost him. 'Well, I have faith. I reckon it'll

float.' Finn reached down and began taking his trainers off.
Then a sock.

Alex stopped twirling the cottongrass. 'What are you
doing?'

He yanked at his other sock. 'Call it, a leap of faith.'

Alex watched as he loosened the rope from the peg. Finn
took the keys and phone from his pocket, then his wallet and
put them all into Alex's hands.

'Finn, your float… it's floating off.'

But Finn was walking in the opposite direction, away
from the bank. He made it several yards away, turned and
broke into a sudden run. Alex watched him thunder past her.
She sat wide-mouthed as Finn lunged from the embankment
and sailed, somewhat gracefully, through the air before
landing much less gracefully onto the surface of his raft. The
plastic tried to bounce away out from beneath him but Finn
sprawled himself over it like a pond skater.

'Are you mad?' Alex called.

'You never doubted me, did you? Go on, you can admit
it!'

Alex laughed while Finn scrambled to fish the three bottles that had come free of their bindings and were bobbing
away from the rest of his vessel. It felt good. Not a polite
laugh, a real laugh, one that made her chest feel great for it.

'I need a first mate!' Finn called. He slipped off the side
of the raft and stiffened as the water came up to his waist.
Alex shook her head and looked to the floor. Her pumps
hadn't fully recovered since the last time she'd got them

wet. Although her nerves had done surprisingly well. 'I'll pass, thanks.'

'Come on in! The water's... bloody *freezing*! Can you believe we used to swim in this?'

Alex felt the first twinge of something uncomfortable. She didn't want to reminisce. In fact, after hearing her dad and Finn's mum going over old times this morning, Alex didn't want to think about anything older than half an hour ago.

Finn waded back to the edge of the plunge pool and offered Alex a hand. She could see the tiny goosebumps beneath the wet on his skin. 'I promise, Foster, if you fall in, I'll rescue you.'

It was such an innocuous statement. Not at all something that would normally wind a person, but it knocked all the breath out of her. She couldn't just gallivant around because her dad had once and Alex had only just found out about it. That didn't give her the right to act like it was all fun and games again, larking around by the river.

'Sorry.' She swallowed. 'I need to go. I forgot, I'm meant to be somewhere else.'

'Alex, I didn't mean—'

'No, honestly! I forgot... to do something. Honestly, everything's fine!' Alex saw heavy recognition behind his eyes.

Finn stepped from the water and reached for her arm. 'Alex, please... Stop running.'

'I'm not running.' She laughed. She was *not* running.

'Aren't you? Look, I'm an idiot, I should have chosen my words better.'

'You don't need to do anything, say anything better than you do, Finn. OK? Don't keep… jumping through hoops. You don't need to.' There was no point.

'Then don't keep making me.'

Alex went rigid. Finn didn't look cold any more, he looked hard, as though the cold wouldn't touch him. Alex turned and began to walk. This was a mistake. Coming here, together.

'Dill would've been on that raft before I'd have finishing asking him,' Finn called after her. Alex stopped dead, her back still to Finn. 'He thought you were awesome, Alex. Eight year old lads, they're not supposed to look up to their sisters, it's not cool for boys to think that way. But he did. He wanted to run like you, Foster. Pitch balls like you. Skim rocks, just like you. Always you.' Alex closed her eyes while a gaping hole yawned inside her. 'But I don't think he'd have looked up to the person you are now.'

Alex breathed. She looked up at the blue above her, marshmallow clouds hanging jovially in the air. 'What kind of person am I, Finn?'

'Afraid. I think you're afraid.'

She faced him then. 'Afraid? What on earth do you think I'm afraid of?' She tried to laugh it away, but there was a bitterness in her mouth.

'I think you're afraid of ever having another ounce of joy in your life, Alex. Because you're not entitled to it.'

'What I'm not entitled to, Finn, is to swan around like I don't care.'

'Do you honestly think anyone thinks that you don't care, Alex? Don't confuse *swanning around* with celebrating the fact that you have a life to live.'

'How can I celebrate that, Finn? When Dill can't?'

'You start by celebrating his life, Alex. Enjoy the things that would bring him pleasure. Laugh at the things he'd find funny. I know you're still in there, Foster. I saw the girl I know stand up to a meathead in the Parsons' front garden. I miss that girl. And I know Dill would've looked up to that girl too.'

Alex carried on walking. Finn had all the answers. He always did. Black and white. Right and wrong. He didn't bother with all the grey there was to wade through.

Alex kicked through the grass. She didn't even know where she was going, the track home was downhill, not up. The earth began to get wetter the closer to the first waterfall she got. Dill wouldn't look up to her. There was nothing left to look up to. They would have all just been one disappointment after another for him, Alex, her dad, even Jem creeping around with Mal. Blythe was the only good one amongst them.

A hand reached firmly around hers and snared her from behind. 'Alex?'

She would not cry. 'Don't follow me, Finn. When are you going to get it? None of us are good for you.'

Alex could feel the cold from the water cascading down

the rocks beside her, a film of wet forming over her shoulders. Finn hadn't let go of her hand. His face was serious, resolute. Wet hair plastered haphazardly across his forehead. 'That's my mistake to make. Let me make it.' His fingers were finding their way between hers. They fit as if they'd been made to.

Alex looked at their hands intertwined. 'Finn, I can't.' It hurt her to look at him, the wounds she could see in guarded green eyes, the tension through his shoulders.

'Can't what?' he whispered. His voice was almost lost to the sounds of water washing away behind them. Finn brought his other hand up and nestled it against her neck. Alex felt the cold press of his wet clothes against her. Her skin was alive, a million sensors relaying to her brain all at once that something wonderful and dangerous and beautiful was happening. Like lightning.

Alex closed her eyes and felt his breath over her mouth. His lips pressed over hers and she was falling again, down, down, down into her bottomless heart. She tasted him. Sweet and earthy and she knew then that she wouldn't find her way back to the surface again. Finn's mouth moved tenderly over Alex's while the water fell around them. She was breathing him in, inhaling great sweet lungfuls of him after all this time holding her breath, all these empty years convincing herself it didn't matter. That she didn't ache for him. That she hadn't been suffocating without him.

Alex felt Finn's hands drop to her waist. His fingers skimmed the edge of her hip. Goosebumps rose all over her body. He lifted her from the ground, her body instinctively wrapping around his, holding him against her with everything she could before she had to give him up again.

Finn pressed her gently against the cool rock face. He laid a kiss over her mouth, her cheeks, her eyes, nuzzling into her like a forgotten song. He'd missed her too. She was his. She'd always been his.

'You're shivering,' he said quietly against her ear.

I know, she wanted to say, but her body wasn't her own.

Finn pulled back, just enough that she could feel his words against her lips. Alex swallowed. She didn't want him to say anything. She just wanted to be here like this. Enveloped in him. Hidden behind a curtain of water, where the world wouldn't find them again.

Finn laid his forehead gently against hers and whispered, 'I used to wonder how it might have been different for us, Alex. If I'd have got to him in time. If your dad would have asked me to dinner… or to help him at the garage… or let me take you out. If he'd have been grateful, every day, that I was in love with his daughter, instead of hating me for it.'

Alex felt a heaviness pulling her way again. Finn sensed the change, his hands loosened. Alex let herself slide back to the rock beneath her. The lightning was burning out, that's what lighting did. It disappeared leaving only the damage in its wake as any sign that it ever even existed.

Alex swallowed. They weren't kids any more. There were consequences. They couldn't play at this like it was all a bit of fun to be dabbled with when they felt like it. She'd felt this way before. She'd taken her eye off the ball *because* she'd felt this way before.

Finn's stance shifted. The water roared behind him. He was waiting for it. Waiting for her to throw him away again.

'I'm sorry...' she started to say. *I have to go.* She could say it. So long as she didn't feel his skin against hers again, she could say it. 'We're not kids any more, Finn—' she rasped.

'I know.' Finn took a step closer. He was breathing heavily, waiting for her to choose the next step. He was giving her the choice. It was always her choice. Alex stepped towards him, as if she could, as if it wouldn't matter. Her heart ramped up. Finn leant in to her and Alex felt their hands together again, unsure who'd reached for who. 'Please, Foster. Don't go back out there. Stay with me.'

CHAPTER 47

Jem's black coupe was sat alongside their dad's workshop when Alex walked up the track to the house.

There wasn't really anything stopping her from going home now, Susannah had said it, Ted wasn't whiter than white. No whiter than Alex anyway. Who knew, now that they were on a level playing field, maybe they'd finally be able to speak naturally to one another.

Alex felt a pleasant ache through her body; her back still wet where he'd pressed her against the rock shelter. She blinked against the afternoon sun and saw him again, eyes wild and startling, his body solid and gentle and sweetly frenzied. Alex's heart reacted to the memory, a breath catching in her throat. Finn had offered to drive her back to the Longhouse but the lines had been blurred. She was going to walk back, and then she'd found herself walking in the direction of the farmhouse instead. *Susannah will need the room back for the weekend check-in anyway*, Alex had told herself. She could think about getting her truck later on at some point.

Sheep bleated in the near distance as the crop fields

started to break into green pasturelands. Alex pulled at a piece of field grass and slowed her pace. Blythe used to let them walk down this lane into town to the sweetshop when they were younger. Blythe always knew when Alex had bought too many sweets because she would drag her heels getting home, so she had chance to eat them all before anyone could see. Alex was dragging her heels now. Finn had been her secret indulgence. She could still feel the evidence all over her. Finn was still in her hair, on her skin. She could still taste him on her mouth.

Alex checked her pockets for the keys. She felt the photograph she'd shown Jem last night. Maybe her mum had smashed the photo, maybe she knew that Ted had been sneaking off with Louisa and couldn't bear to look at Louisa's husband-stealing face.

Alex suddenly stopped dead on the lane. *Did Mal know?* Jem said that their dad had gone off at Mal at the hospital when he'd taken Blythe there, accused Mal of upsetting her in some way. Did Mal know about the affair? Could he have told their mum in the churchyard? Is that what had made Blythe ill?

Alex's heart was flittering when she made it to the gatepost of her parents' farmhouse. She glanced across the lawns.

'Speak of the devil.'

Mal Sinclair's police car came into view around the side of the house. Alex carried on walking while the front door opened and Mal stepped out onto the porch. He'd shaved for the occasion. His beard, all gone. He looked ten years younger for it too. Jem leaned in for a goodbye hug and Alex seethed a little. *Nice touch, Officer. Even in broad daylight.* He was as bad as his mother.

Alex followed the path up to the house. Norma padded out next to Jem's legs then saw Alex from the porch and shot out across the lawn. Alex felt bad then for having not thought about her, Norma had been the most honest relationship she'd managed have while she was here.

Norma bounded across the grass and scrambled at Alex's legs. Alex fussed her automatically. 'Hey, girl.' Norma wanted to play but there was a storm building in Alex's heart.

'Alex.' Mal smiled politely. 'I was just checking in on your mum.'

'I'll just bet you were, Mal. Maybe go check in on your wife and child instead?'

Mal looked at Jem. Jem's mouth dropped open. '*Alex?*'

Alex noticed a sore patch of pink developing around Jem's mouth. Blythe had gotten a similar rash once too, when Alex's father had grown a beard so he looked like Kris Kristofferson in *A Star Is Born*. Aside from a burning anger beginning in the pit of her stomach, Alex was unfazed by Jem's tone.

'Where's Dad?'

'Work, I suppose. I don't know, why? I haven't seen him since you went charging down to The Cavern last night. What did you say to him, Alex? He nearly knocked the door off when he got in. And why did you stay at the Longhouse all night? And why are you soaking wet?'

'How do you know I stayed at the Longhouse? If you haven't seen Dad this morning?'

Jem glanced sheepishly at Mal. 'Lucky guess.' Jem was shacked up with the local law enforcement, she probably knew every bugger in the town's movements now.

Alex turned and faced Jem squarely. She felt her nails biting into her palm. 'You know when Granny Ros was trying to teach us poker? Do you know how we always used to know when you were bluffing, Jem? Your lip twitched.' Jem almost reached up to feel the evidence, or maybe it was her rash from Mal's beard. Alex hoped it bloody hurt.

'I think I better be going,' Mal said shiftily.

'You do that, Mal. And say hi to your family when you see them.' Alex could taste the words like bile in her mouth. Goddamn Sinclairs.

Alex got a good look at Mal's new look as he stepped down on the front porch towards her and her blood turned cold. A small dimple appeared on one of Mal's cheeks when he smiled. She couldn't see it before he'd shaved. A single indentation, as if the other dimple had gotten lost somewhere.

Alex felt a spur of sudden, dizzying nausea. Dill's dimple had been the other side. They could've had the pair between them, Dill and Mal. The photograph in Alex's back pocket felt heavy as she remembered the likeness between a younger, blonder Mal and her brother.

Oh God. Oh God. Her dad had been sleeping with Louisa Sinclair. *Had he…* the thought stabbed at her mind… *had their dad fathered Malcolm?* But… that would make Malcolm their half-brother. Alex looked at her sister and saw the puzzlement in Jem's face. *But… but Jem, and Mal… Shit.*

Alex rushed up the three timber steps to the door but didn't even get inside before it erupted all over the seat where Ted liked to take his morning coffee.

'Alex! What's wrong?'

'Is she—'

'Just go, Mal. I can handle this,' Jem said firmly.

No you can't! Alex thought, the horror of her realisation brought on another violent cramping in her stomach. Alex wretched again. *Oh God, Jem… you've been sleeping with our half-brother.*

CHAPTER 48

'It's just not acceptable. We understand it's delicate, but if everyone's husbands started hiding out at the end of visiting time, we'd be overrun with them. And he really can't keep lying on the bed with her in those overalls. Oil is a terrible nuisance to get out of the sheets.' The nurse hadn't wanted to embarrass Ted so she'd collared Alex as soon as she'd walked onto the ward instead. Alex had gotten one sweaty palm on her mother's door before she'd been intercepted.

Alex nodded apologetically. The nurse kept tapping her clipboard against her chest. 'How often has he been doing this?'

Ted had been lying next to Blythe when the nurses thought everyone had gone home. So much for hospital security. So much for the behavioural patterns of a typical philandering husband. Sneaking around so he could lie next to her mother each night? Before slipping away again for a nightcap at The Cavern? Alex wondered if her father's dedication had been born from love, or guilt.

Alex remembered what she now realised had been Louisa Sinclair's Aston Martin rolling out of Foster & Son's the day she'd thrown milkshake all over Finn. Was it still going on? 'Dad's never been very receptive towards Mal,' Jem had told her.

Alex fixed on the movements of the clipboard. Had he known that Malcolm was his child all along? Was that why Ted hadn't wanted Mal around Jem? Not because Alex had conditioned him to distrust his daughters' boyfriends but because he couldn't face his own illegitimate child? The potential for something unnatural to blossom between them?

Alex put a hand over her stomach. She was still experiencing sporadic bursts of nausea. Some father he'd been to Mal. He'd been distraught for Dill, but his *other* son? Ted had treated him like he treated his other vices, he had a preferred brand of tobacco, preferred brand of whiskey... Mal was just the wrong brand of son.

'And he wasn't here last night because we were already on to him. But put it this way, nearly every morning your mother's bed sheets have had oil on them, and every day they've been changed again for her.'

Alex nodded briefly, relieved she'd been too much of a wuss to moan about the grubby sheets. 'I'll speak to him.' It would be a breeze compared to the conversation she needed to have with Jem. *Sorry, Jem! You can't keep having an affair with Malcolm, I'm afraid. He's our half-brother. Shall I get you the peanut butter?*

The nurse cocked her head and looked warmly at Alex. 'I don't want to be a killjoy. It's actually rather romantic, really, your dad still needing to cuddle up to your mum at their age. How long have they been married?'

Alex rubbed a circle over her stomach. She felt drained. 'About thirty years.'

'My goodness. They must love each other dearly. That's rare these days. We live in such a throwaway society, don't you think? Toasters, marriages… nobody makes do and mends any more. Anyway, I'll leave you to it. Go on in, she's feeling much better now for those antibiotics.'

Alex tried to shake some of the tension from her shoulders. She stepped into her mother's room. Blythe turned her head slowly from the light streaming through the window. She looked serene, her silken red hair all about her against the pillow as if she were a mermaid suspended underwater.

'Morning, my dar-ling.'

Alex felt her mood buckle. She could cry for her mother's voice. Did Ted feel that too when he was here? Did it make him feel better to clamber up next to her? Alex wanted to bundle up onto her mother's bed and cuddle with her until she felt better too. *Hurry up and get better, Mum!* She wanted to say. *You're the key! We all need you, you're the only one who can fix us.*

'Hey, Mum. How are you feeling?'

Blythe managed a smile. She looked tired, but that desperate glassiness in her eyes had gone. She was Blythe again. How could he have betrayed her?

'I'm good, my darling. Come… sit by me.' Alex did gratefully. Blythe's left hand was occupied with an IV but she pressed it weakly over Alex's as if she was trying to anchor her there. 'I love you, Alex,' she said clumsily.

Alex's felt a pain in her heart. 'I know, Mum. I love you too.'

'I want you to…' She seemed to lose energy. Like a toy in need of winding up in between sentences.

'It's OK, Mum. Take your time. Would you like some water?'

Alex looked around for her mother's cup but Blythe increased the pressure between her hand and her daughter's. Alex gave her mum her full attention.

'I want you… to tell your father… that I love him too.'

'He knows, Mum. You tell him all the time.' Alex felt the shame of knowing something hideous her mother might not.

'Promise me… you'll remind him.'

'Of course I will, Mum. You can remind him yourself.'

'I love you both… so much.'

Alex smiled weakly. 'We know, Mum.'

'And Jem… and Dillon.'

Alex looked up at the new bag of chemicals filtering into her mother's hand. They weren't working, she was delirious again. 'I miss him so much… I miss you too… I miss the family we were.'

Alex watched a few escaped tears begin steadily from her mother's eyes.

'It's all right, Mum. Don't get upset. We'll all be all right.' But it was an empty promise; Emma Parsons had probably made similar empty promises to little Poppy every time that monster had left their house with all their money.

'Be patient… with your father. He needs you.'

Her mother always knew how to shift the earth with just a few small motions. 'If I'm ill… another stroke… all I want… from you… is to be close to… your father again.'

She wasn't delirious. She was asking for the impossible, but not from delirium.

'Promise me, Alex.'

Alex could see the effort it was taking for her mother just to squeeze Alex's hand. How the hell was she going to pull that one out of the bag? Blythe increased the pressure slightly.

'All right, Mum. I promise.'

CHAPTER 49

Jem was frenziedly chopping salad; her shoulder blades rising and falling in uncomfortable jerky movements. Alex took another long drink of the tea Jem had ready for her when she'd got back from the hospital. It was odd, seeing the shoe on the other foot, Jem nervously toiling away while Alex sat here at the kitchen table, Norma on her lap, in a mist of calm understanding.

Alex knew what she had to do now. For the first time since she'd been home her role was clear. She had to stop this. This thing between Jem and Mal. And she had to do whatever was necessary to get along with her father. It was the only thing her mother had asked of her and she was going to damn well do it. Somehow.

Norma flopped back down to the floor and padded off.

'Will Dad be joining us?' asked Alex.

Jem glanced over her shoulder. 'Yep. So can you guys try to get along? *Please?*'

Alex bit resentfully into a breadstick. 'Don't worry, Jem. I think I'm done blowing his hair back for a while.' Alex thought about that statement. Only if her secrets stayed nicely tucked away beneath the waterfall. She'd left Finn standing behind the wall of water, half dressed, knowing that she'd cemented the pattern between them. She'd flitted back in to Finn's reach for another taste, and then had hotfooted it out of there again when her nerve had left her. Before any uncomfortable conversations could start.

Jem stopped chopping. She began scraping a carrot Alex had watched her peel already. 'Well maybe it's my turn to blow his hair back. There are too many secrets in this family anyway,' Alex heard her mutter.

'What do you mean, blow his hair back?'

Jem turned around and leant back against the sink. Veggie scraper in one hand, pencil-thin carrot in the other. 'I have something I need to talk to you both about.'

The hairs stood up on Alex's neck. She hadn't managed to come up with a way of telling Jem about Mal yet. Half-brother. *Half*-brother. Nope. The half didn't make *any* difference, you couldn't have a half-incestuous relationship any more than you could be half in love, or half pregnant. Jem was not going to be half horrified now was she?

'About what?' Alex asked shakily.

Jem set the carrot down on the side. She flexed her fingers, then picked it up again. Nervous wasn't Jem's usual style.

'I was putting it off, like you said. I wanted to talk to Mum first, but you were right, she's not up to it but you're going to find out eventually and I don't want you hearing it from someone else and people talk and—'

Norma began barking in the back lounge seconds before Alex heard her father's recovery truck growling up the track. Alex's heart was beating as quickly as the words were crashing out of Jem's mouth. Jem was looking towards the hallway and Norma's warning, the rash around Jem's lips had gotten worse today, Alex noticed, despite Mal's de-bearding. Maybe she was allergic to him. Maybe it was Mother Nature's way of telling oblivious human beings, *Stop! You can't snog him! Your face will break out first and if that's not enough I'll give your offspring gills!* Alex couldn't stop looking at that rash as Jem was chewing on her lip. Alex shuddered. They must be snogging like teenagers.

'You need to stay away from Malcolm Sinclair,' Alex blurted. It had just come out. Exploded from her mouth like a crackerbomb.

Jem stopped chewing at her lip. 'What?'

Alex's chest was thudding. Ted's truck had just rolled past the kitchen window towards his spot next to the workshop and Alex had just loosed a conversational monster for him to walk in on. 'He's no good for you, Jem.'

'What? Mal's a good friend, Alex. You sound just like Dad, you know that?'

'Maybe Dad has good reason, Jem.'

Jem straightened. 'For not liking *Mal*? No, he hasn't actually, Alex. I know Dad's going through the mill, but Mal's a good guy. He hasn't done anything to make anyone have any reason to take a shot at him. And if anyone's going to try and criticise him to me, they'd better have their facts straight.'

Jem tensed her jaw. Alex had expected some resistance but she hadn't expected a full on defence from the outset. Alex felt a flicker of something angry and unpleasant. Jem wasn't even *trying* to hide how she felt about him. About Millie's husband.

'He's *married*.' Alex slapped a hand on the table.

Jem grimaced. 'And?'

'Nice, Jem. Really nice work.'

Jem slapped the carrot peeler onto the draining board. 'What the hell do you mean by that?'

'I like Millie. And what about Alfie? Doesn't it bother you?' Alex was hoping to appeal to Jem's sense of honour, get a result before she had to bring out the big guns and be brutally, mortifyingly honest. But Jem wasn't playing ball.

'I like Millie too. And Alfie's a great kid.'

'You've been sneaking around with him, Jem!'

'What?' Jem looked busted. 'How do you know that?'

'Oh, come on, Jem! I saw you, in Mal's front room. You were pretty cosy in there, giggling and sipping wine while Millie wasn't home, and Mal never said a word! Your own sister turns up and he doesn't even say a word about you being inside the house! I know you've been seeing him, Jem. That's why he never speaks when I answer the phone, isn't it? Because the two of you have been meeting up in secret and I might recognise his voice!' That still didn't explain Millie's part in covering for Jem but Alex was already set in motion. She could suss out the loose ends later.

Jem looked stunned. 'You're right, Miss Marple. We have. But you're mental if you think I've been seeing *seeing* Mal. Are you nuts? *Mal*?'

Jem looked genuinely shocked at the prospect. Well she could look as shocked and stunned as she liked. Alex wasn't falling for it. She wasn't falling for anyone's face value ever again thanks to Susannah Finn's revelations about their dad's extra-marital activities.

'What's the big news then, Jem? What's the big deal Mum's not up to hearing, if not that you've been knocking off your old boyfriend?'

Jem laughed. 'Mal was never my boyfriend!'

'Mum saw you both! Snogging once outside Frobisher's!' There, definitive proof.

OK, so that evidence was a bit shaky but Alex had still knocked her sister off course, she could see that. Jem wasn't nervously clinging to the carrot any more, she was squinting, trying to piece something together in her head. Boots were coming up the path. Alex glanced towards the hallway.

'Mal was never my boyfriend, Alex. Believe it or don't, that's up to you. But it's good to know that if you disapproved of my choice in partner, you'd go right on ahead and tell me so.'

'Stop waving that carrot at me. So you're saying, you haven't been holding out for Mal all these years? That he isn't your sodding lightning bolt?' Alex's skin wanted to crawl off and run away every time she suggested it.

'I haven't been holding out for Mal,' Jem said coldly.

'So why haven't you ever brought anyone home to meet Mum and Dad?'

'Why haven't *you*, Alex! Oh yes, that's right, because you're *not really* crazy about Finn are you Al? And you're *not really* too much of a wimp to do something about it.'

Norma toddled along the hallway to the front door. Alex heard her dad making sounds of encouragement as he shuffled into the hallway past her. Jem turned back to the sink. Alex rattily lifted her teacup back to her face. They would always break a fight before their dad got a chance to wade in. It was easier for sisters to keep a dispute going if no one tried to moderate it.

Ted moved across the hallway into the kitchen doorway. 'Evening.' He gave Alex a glance, the first since she'd flipped out in the middle of his backgammon game, but Alex couldn't match it without picturing Mal's mother and him so she looked at the breadsticks instead. 'I'm just going to go get washed up.'

Jem turned and watched him go up the stairs from the sink. Some of the annoyed colour Alex had put in her cheeks had faded to a pale, sickly pallor. Jem didn't look so confident all of a sudden, like all the fight had just leaked out of her. She rubbed at the pink skin on her face.

'You'll make it worse. You should ask Mum what she used when *she* had beard rash,' Alex said sourly.

Jem looked at Alex. 'Beard rash? It's my eczema, Alex. It always flares up when I get stressed.'

Eczema? 'So what are you stressed about, Jem?' Alex asked accusingly.

Jem looked back to the stairs. She pushed both hands through her hair and braced herself against the sink behind her. Jem took in a breath like one of these free-divers Alex couldn't fathom. 'It's not Mal who's been hanging up on you, Alex. It's my boss.'

Alex felt herself grimace. 'Your boss? Why would your boss hang up on me?'

'Not just you, Dad a few times too. I know, it's hardly a great start, but... well, I told George not to call the house in case you answered but the phone reception up here is totally shit so—'

'You're having an affair, with your *boss*?' The relief flooded Alex's veins like one of those lovely warm sedatives they gave you at the dentist.

'What's with all the affairs, Alex? Jesus Christ. Not an affair,' Jem hissed in exasperation. 'We're in a *serious*, MONOGAMOUS, relationship, OK?'

'But not with Mal?' Alex established with mirthful relief.

'Yuck, no. I think Mal's really great, I do. But that would be like... I don't know, I imagine a lot like going out with my own *brother*.' Jem grimaced. Alex wanted to jump on her and lock her in a grateful embrace. A whole horizon of damage limitation was opening out before her, Jem might not even have to know about their dad's and Louisa Sinclair,

Alex could spare her from it, save her the hurt. And then another thought made its return.

'But, you were over at Mal's, Jem. I saw you in there. And you've been out, nearly every night, Jem.'

Jem came to the table and slipped into the chair beside Alex's. She clasped her hands together and tapped them to her mouth like they used to when they were supposed to be praying in assembly. 'Mal and Millie have been letting me and George relax over at their place. George turned up here in the Falls last week. It wasn't the plan but George wanted to support me while Mum's so poorly and by the time I knew anything about it…'

'George is here?' What an old romantic. 'So where is he? Where's he staying?'

Jem breathed steady. 'Over at the Longhouse.'

Alex ran through all the guests she'd seen there. Someone old enough to head up a big jewellery designer. Someone stylish and attractive, staying at the Longhouse alone. Alex frowned. Boiled egg man? Alex tried to picture Jem eating a boiled egg across the table from the guy who'd tucked his napkin into his shirt. Who even wore a shirt on a weekend away? No matter. Boiled egg man was a stratospheric step up from Malcolm. Even if he did hang up on people.

'So when do we get to meet the elusive George?'

'Soon. I hope. Only… did Dad look wiped out to you? Just now? I don't think tonight's the night to go into this.'

A diversion was probably what they all needed. 'Jem? You're talking yourself out of it. Why?' Alex heard an unimpressed voice through her head. *Why did* you *talk yourself out of staying with Finn yesterday, Alex?*

Jem swallowed and rubbed at her raw skin again. Alex felt a sudden pang of guilt. Was Finn a diversion too? Was Alex going to keep him a secret until she broke out in a nervous skin condition?

Jem put her hands in her pockets so she wouldn't rub her face any more. 'I'm not sure that George is going to be everyone's cup of tea.'

CHAPTER 50

Alex pulled around the Longhouse and parked up next to several more cars that hadn't been here before the bank holiday weekend. 'Goddamn tourists are already descending like one of the great plagues. That's the traffic shot to shit,' her dad had complained before Alex had made her excuses and gone to bed early last night.

It was an odd feeling, being the angry one. It didn't make honouring her promise to her mother any more straightforward though. Odder still was that her dad seemed to be making an effort again. Was it possible that she'd actually shamed him the other night at The Cavern? Last night, before the complaining about the tourists had started, he'd actually stretched to a couple of conversations about the weekend's festivities in the town – who was odds on favourite to win the boat race, how much Hamish would charge for his authentic mead – as Jem had shovelled salad onto their plates with the same ashen expression she'd had when their dad had first walked in through the door. This George of hers had to be a big deal. Jem hadn't stopped fidgeting the whole time in case Alex brought it up, she could tell. Jem's eyes had darted towards Alex, nervous and birdlike, on the few occasions Alex had bothered to speak.

'Morning, Alex.'

Emma Parsons was stepping across the lawn from the back of the Longhouse, a basket of laundry under her arm closely followed by Poppy and a peg bag.

'Hi.' Alex climbed out of her truck. 'How are you?'

Emma set the basket down. 'Good, thanks.'

'Where's the baby?'

'Susannah's spoiling her with cuddles.' Emma looked down and set a hand on Poppy's head. 'It was all a bit hectic at breakfast Friday, I still haven't had a chance to thank you, Alex.'

Alex batted it away. 'The quiche was amazing, Emma.'

'I meant, in person. Properly.'

Alex looked at Poppy's big wide eyes and hoped again that she hadn't brought any more trouble to the Parsons' door. 'I didn't do anything, Emma. Finn was the only one of any use.'

Emma smiled crookedly. She looked like Poppy when she smiled, the same way Jem looked like Dad when she laughed. 'Finn and Susannah, they've both been really great to us.'

'They are really great,' Alex agreed. Was it wrong that she felt more at ease here than back at the farmhouse? Was that still her fault? Her dad having an affair didn't cancel out all the hurt Alex had caused their family.

Gina, leggy and lithe, skipped down the lawns from the

barn and walked around the Longhouse up towards the high street. Long dark hair flowed behind her and Alex remembered how shocked she'd been when Finn had made the first move behind the waterfall. He could have anyone he wanted and Alex was awkward and complicated, not at all like Gina. Gina threw a wave over to Alex and Emma while simultaneously slipping a slender arm through her backpack.

'I used to have a bum like that.' Emma smiled. 'Before children.'

Alex got another look at Gina's toned legs, an even brown beneath a little khaki skirt.

'You still have, Emma. Must be all that walking to the hospital. How's your husband?'

Emma smiled fiercely at Poppy who was crouched between her knees scouring the lawn for daisies to put in her peg bag. 'He won't be home for a while yet.'

'What about you, will you be going home for a while yet?'

Emma folded her arms around herself protectively. 'Our *friend* will be back at some point,' she said, carefully watching that Poppy didn't catch on. 'And when he does come, what happened last week, it's going to be expensive. One way or another it will.'

'Emma, tell Malcolm everything, he'll be able to help. Our family have known him a long time, he's a good guy.' Alex's confidence in Malcolm wasn't completely restored but she sounded convincing for Emma's benefit. Jem had offered up this *George* character as her only supporting argument that there wasn't anything untoward going on with Mal. And it should have been enough, Alex knew that. But her dad's infidelity had thrown her. Until this George materialised, in the flesh, Alex was holding off a fraction.

Emma was looking intently at Poppy. She caught Alex watching her and smiled. 'People, *problems*, like that don't go away, Alex. Not without either a lot of money, or some sort of divine intervention. And we don't have either.'

Alex chewed at the inside of her cheek. 'Officer Sinclair might be able to help, Emma,' Alex tried.

Emma sighed deeply. Her eyes had turned glassy. 'Why is it, there is so much tragedy in this world, children being hurt, good people suffering, and yet bullies like Mr Mason get to roam the earth completely unchallenged? Terrible things happen to people every day. Why don't people like *him* ever get hit by a... by a...' Emma waved her hand around looking for the words, '...a bolt of lightning?'

Alex had thought the same thing a thousand times. Where was the balance her mum believed in?

'I don't know, Emma. But how are you going to be able to go home again?'

Emma looked like so many of the mothers Alex had seen at the food bank. Unsure of the next move, unready to think that far ahead, just grateful for a momentary reprieve and some small semblance of kindness from strangers.

'Susannah said we can stay for as long as we need. I'm trying to do a few jobs around the place to help out. She has got a lot on with the festival tomorrow. Hopefully she's glad I'm here.'

'I'm sure she is.'

The doors off the back extension went again and the hard-boiled egg man stepped out. Was this George? Jem's George? Everyone else Alex had noticed here was paired or grouped up. Hard-boiled egg man was the only lone ranger. If Alex was honest about it, part of her reason for coming this morning was to get a good look at him. Alex watched him quickly scurry to catch up with Gina. Emma was watching him too.

'Some city type. He's been sniffing around that woman since he arrived.' *Ah, another ladies' man*, thought Alex. *T'riffic*. She hoped Jem hadn't chosen a bad egg.

Alex cocked her head. 'I didn't catch his name at breakfast Friday. George, is it?' She was probing. Well she was allowed, it was what sisters did, wasn't it?

'No, it's Craig.'

'Craig?'

'Definitely Craig. I remember because it's my brother-in-law's name.'

Alex did another mental recap of Susannah's house guests for an eligible bachelor she might've missed.

'Oh, I was sure I heard Susannah mention George in the breakfast room.' Alex was a rubbish liar.

Emma gave it a second or two's thought, probably out of politeness. 'No, don't think so. I helped her with the booking diary this morning. She needed everyone's car registrations inputting under their room numbers. Definitely no Georges.'

'A *puppy*!' Poppy squealed, peering in through Alex's truck window. Norma began scrambling at the open window. 'Can she come out so I can stroke her, please?'

Poppy had been miffed when Alex had helped Finn with his raft Friday. Her little heart had been bruised each time Finn had laughed for Alex. A bundle of fur and all was forgiven.

Alex walked back towards her truck. 'Sure you can. I'm sure Susannah won't mind. Let's put her on her lead though.' Alex fished Norma out through the window and tethered her to the gateposts running alongside the parking area. Poppy dove to her knees, dropping the pegs and daisies like discarded thoughts for someone else to worry about.

Emma laughed at her. 'So what brings you here this morning?' she asked Alex.

Alex had stayed awake half the night with it, thinking it all over and over again. Thinking of her excuse to come over here. Alex could answer Emma with *I've finally brought Susannah's casserole dish back,* or *I've come to suss out my sister's boyfriend.* But the truth, the real truth, seemed more important. 'Actually, I've come to see Finn.'

There. Not so hard was it? The sun hadn't clouded over, the integrity police weren't here to cart anybody off.

Emma smiled knowingly 'Good for you, Alex.' Alex wasn't the only one Susannah had been sharing cocktails and conversation with then. Alex tensed. Susannah wouldn't know about yesterday though, would she? Finn wouldn't have... no, of course he wouldn't.

'Oh, no, puppy! Don't do that, you'll hurt your neck, silly.' Poppy yelped just as Norma teased her head from the last grip of her collar.

Alex groaned. 'That dog is a flipping escapologist.'

Norma was onto something, excitedly sniffing the ground. Alex watched her scramble over towards Finn's studio space.

'She can smell the other dogs. Finn paints dogs in there,' Poppy informed them with a spindly, outstretched arm.

'I'd better go get her back then. Before she spoils any of Finn's work. Bye, Emma, bye, Poppy.' Alex smiled at Poppy but her heart was bruised again. *Sorry, Poppy. But if my dad can't guilt me out of this, I'm afraid you've got no chance.*

Alex made it to the doors into the studio and knocked nervously. She'd been trying not to think about her dad meeting Louisa the morning Dill drowned, trying not to dissect how his actions might also have played some small part in the events leading up to the accident. She'd promised her mother that she'd get along with her dad. And she had every intention of achieving that goal somehow. But whatever lay ahead for them now, whatever they were going to work towards, it had to be honest. It had to be unconditional. It had to include Finn.

'Hello?' Alex inhaled the familiar scent of oil paints and turpentine on old rags and jam jars.

Finn had his radio on. He used to paint to the radio back in college. Kerrang mostly, but sometimes, when he thought no one was listening, Smooth FM. Alex didn't recognise the song playing, something melodic over an acoustic guitar, not enough to drown out the new tempo beating in her chest.

Norma trundled over to the figure sitting with his back to Alex and made her own introduction to Finn's ankle.

His upper body bunched like a teenager's as he twisted and peered down at her. 'We meet again.'

It suddenly occurred to Alex that Finn probably didn't want to be included in her plans to move forwards. He'd called her last night. She hadn't answered. She'd been thinking it all out. He hadn't called her again.

Finn glanced over his shoulder and offered Alex a perfectly polite smile, rooting her doubts firmly through the floor.

'Another canine subject,' Alex tried, nodding at his canvas. 'Millie Fairbanks used to have a dog like that. She used to tie it to her wheelchair on the way to school. Do you remember?' It was an ice-breaker at least.

Finn put a last shadow to the black Labrador's snout and set his brush down. He twisted a cloth through his hands, the backs of his arms flexed against his pale red shirt. Alex thought of those capable arms, the way they'd held her somehow despite the slipperiness of the damp air and their impatience to tug and grasp at each other before anyone might stumble across them. Her pulse hitched up a little.

'I remember.' He smiled. 'Saw it every day. Rowlands

gave it to her, to lift her spirits after she came out of hospital.' Finn's tone was off. Alex felt a tension.

'Rowlands?'

'The farmer. Millie's puppy was supposed to go to another kid, only his dad did a runner before he'd paid for it so...' Finn shrugged. 'Deal was off.'

Finn scooped Norma up and ran his fingers through the ruff of her neck. Alex had already put her foot in it. She imagined a young Finn then, a little boy having to watch someone else love the puppy he'd been promised.

'It looks great, Finn. You've obviously got the pet portraiture down,' she tried.

Finn laughed a half-hearted laugh. He was laughing at her, for trying this ridiculous chit-chat. *She* was like one of those horrible teenage boys her mum had warned her about. 'Watch out for those awful little testosteroids. They take advantage of nice young girls and then the next day, don't even acknowledge them!' Alex was a horrible little testosteroid.

'It's not exactly the National Gallery stuff,' Finn answered.

'But it brings a bit of extra income in,' she pressed. 'You've done so many...' Alex gabbled, looking about the studio. 'Is this one for anyone local?'

Finn's eyes looked tired. 'No. First time someone's emailed in and just asked for a portrait, actually.'

'Don't they have to come and sit or something? Have photographs taken?'

'Usually. Not with this one though, just a few emails and an order paid in full. I should've finished it by now, the guy's coming to collect it tomorrow but Carrie kept on adding to the job over at the florist's. Then I got roped into entering the raft race, so…'

The raft! It had floated off by the time they'd emerged from the waterfall. Finn had rubbed the back of his wet head and glanced downstream for a second before quietly watching Alex gather up her things.

A silence stretched out between them. He was starting to look as uncomfortable as Alex felt. Would she go and watch him in the boat race? she wondered. Would she go and cheer him on, because she wanted him to be hers and it shouldn't matter to her who knew because he could undo her with just a look – *just a look!* – so God *only* knew what could happen if she saw him bare-chested in a Viking helmet?

'Must love black Labradors then, I guess.' She was struggling for conversation.

Finn raised his eyebrows and was boyish and rugged again. 'People pay hundreds for a picture of their dog, and I've never had one commission for someone's child. Weird, huh?'

'Weird,' she agreed. 'Maybe you're better off painting dogs. Humans can be tricky creatures.'

Finn's features were hardening off again. 'Hard to work out, you mean? Temperamental? Indecisive? Hot and cold?' He looked at her briefly then ran a hand over his head knocking the hair from his eyes. And then like that, the seriousness abated. When had he gotten so good at that? At shutting down any glimpse that he might be hurting in some way.

Alex cleared her throat. 'I was thinking… *complicated*.'

Finn picked through the brushes on his worktop and started putting them into various jars. His jaw tensed. 'You're right, Foster. Animals are a *lot* less complicated than people. They're more honest too. Not afraid to love you out loud.' He began gesticulating with one of his brushes. 'A dog sees his family and… that's it, no holds barred, it wants to go crazy for them and protect them and enjoy them and not care about anything else in the world. Dogs are *faithful*, Alex,' he said, whipping his head around to look at her. 'They're *loyal*. They don't love you secretly and then expect it to be enough.'

Alex quietly pulled in breath. He was right. On all counts. She buried her hands into her back pockets and tried to think of something useful to say. Finn had brought his arms across his chest, the underside of his inside-out plaid shirt in paler shades of red. There was a fleck of paint sitting in the stubble on his cheek where he'd been holding his brushes in his mouth. Alex wanted to reach out and wipe it away for him, or maybe she just wanted the excuse to cross the few feet to him and touch him again. Pretend they were still back up at the gorge. Something inside her clunked into place. She looked at Finn then, this great guy who'd been such a big part of her life, and felt suddenly exhausted. She was tired. Tired of trying to bury the adolescence they'd spent together, tired of trying to make sense of a terrible twist of fate. She was tired of pretending how she felt about things all the time but mostly, she was tired of being a wimp. This awful, wimpy echo of the girl she was once.

'Would you like to come out for a drink with me, Finn?'

She saw the surprise dart across his face. It made her feel both ashamed and exhilarated all at once. Norma wriggled to reach his neck better, her head bobbed beneath his chin like a nuzzling fawn.

'You and me? Out, out? As in, where other people are?'

She was a terrible person. Finn was a good guy, honest, loyal, and since the sun had worked its magic over the ends of his hair, billboard-beautiful, Alex thought, if you liked your men a little rough around the edges, which she probably wouldn't have done had Finn not fitted so snuggly into that bracket now.

'How about The Cavern? I'll buy you a Valhalla burger?' Something warmed in his expression. Alex smiled with him, she'd seen the Valhalla burgers on Hamish's menu board on her way through the pub.

Finn's face sobered. He understood. Alex's dad would most likely be in The Cavern or, at least, Ted's friends. Alex hated that it made a difference, that a simple offering to go out and spend an evening together like grownups was some kind of momentous testament to how she felt about him. How she'd always felt. It wasn't testament enough.

'Popular place, The Cavern,' he said.

Alex nodded. 'It is.'

'Might we, er… bump into your—'

'You're right. We might. How about you come pick me up and we'll go to The Cavern from there?'

No mights. They were highly likely to bump into her father now.

Finn cocked his head and frowned. 'From your place?'

It would all end in tears, of course. But then didn't it always? It was about time people started crying for the gains and not just the losses.

'My dad's place,' Alex confirmed. 'I mean, if that's OK with you of course. You don't have to, I mean—'

'Your place will be fine, Alex.' He smiled. 'I'll borrow Brünnhilde's body armour from the high street, but your place will be just fine.'

CHAPTER 51

'Jem, I need to borrow something to wear.' Jem was sat in the middle of the lounge floor, a sea of documents and photocopies strewn around her like she were some kind of insect plonked at the centre of a large paper flower. She reached over the papers to the hearth and set her wine glass down. 'What are you doing?' asked Alex.

'Thought I'd go *back to our roots*,' said Jem, fishing out the box lid and wafting it so Alex could see the family tree set their mum had started. 'I've gotten as far as great-great grandma Alice. That's her in the hallway, isn't it? The miserable looking one?'

Alex looked nervously at her wristwatch. He was coming at eight. She still had an hour yet. She'd showered already, had a go at taming her hair into something deliberate, she'd even sneaked into Jem's room for another rifle through her makeup.

'You'd look miserable, Jem, if you'd raised a lovechild out of duty because the man you'd married had been at it with the locals.' Alex felt a twinge of anger at her father again. At least he hadn't rocked up one day with a baby

Malcolm under his arm and said, *Here you go, Blythe, don't say I never bring you anything!*

'What?'

Alex snapped away from thoughts of Mayor Sinclair being the poor bugger who'd raised a cuckoo in his nest. Seeing as Jem still had a good relationship with Ted, she didn't need to find out about all that, Alex had decided.

Alex sighed. She wished she hadn't got into this either. 'You remember, Mum told us. Great great granddad William was a bit of a git. Had a soft spot for some blonde, she died in childbirth and he brought the baby back for Alice to take care of.' Extra marital affairs obviously ran in the Fosters' bloodline.

Jem rifled through a pile of notes. She held up a pad where she'd been scribbling her own. 'I remember. So, our great granddad Benjamin, wasn't actually great-great-grandmother Alice's son?'

Alex squinted while she did the maths.

'*No*,' she said, half-sure.

'Benjamin was biologically another woman's son…'

'So Mum said.'

'So we're probably related to another family from around here?'

Eugh. Whose idea had it been to start trawling through this lot? 'If William's mystery blonde was from the Falls, I suppose so.' Alex shrugged. 'So, can I borrow a pair of jeans or something? I've only got what I came up here with.' As much as Alex still loved her Jaws t-shirt, it wasn't really first-date-in-yonks apparel. Oh God. Did this count as a first date in yonks?

Jem scratched her head with a pencil. 'There's a pile of clean washing on my bed. Help yourself. Might need ironing though.' Jem slipped the pencil into her mouth and tapped at her teeth with it. 'Your hair looks good down, Al. Really good. Where are you off to?'

Alex lifted a self-conscious hand to her hair and swallowed. It was more of a gulp, which was silly, this was her idea after all. To be up front and open and honest.

'Alex, are you all right? You've gone a funny colour.'

Alex could feel her hands had gone clammy. She blurted out a stream of information for Jem to chew on. 'Finn's coming to pick me up. We're going to The Cavern. I'm going to buy him a burger and we're going to have a few drinks and catch up.' And laugh, hopefully, laugh and smile and talk and zone out the rest of the world for a few precious hours. 'Finn's coming *here*?' Jem's eyes grew rounder. 'You know Dad's not going to the hospital tonight, right? I think he's been at The Cavern this afternoon so he's probably going to be home soon. There's only so much backgammon even he can play.'

Alex tried to ignore the dull thrum of agitation beginning to niggle away at her.

She tried to shrug nonchalantly. 'Why would he have been at The Cavern this afternoon? He always goes in the evenings.'

'They're running a bet on the river race tomorrow, he said

he was going for a flutter. But then he also said he was going to meet me for a sandwich at Frobisher's at lunch time. Anyway, he stood me up. I take it he had to go on a callout first or something. He probably called me but this crappy reception up here.'

Alex shrugged. Well he definitely hadn't been at the hospital this afternoon. Alex had left Finn's studio, dropped Norma back at the house and gone straight to Kerring General while Jem had gone to spend some time probably trying to convince this *George* to return to London and come back to meet the family at some other, less fraught, time.

'So, jeans are in your washing pile?'

Jem nodded.

'Don't suppose you have a top in there too?'

Jem swished her pencil in the air like she was conducting an orchestra. 'Knock yourself out. But you have bigger feet than me, so no stretching out my shoes.'

'Thanks, Jem.' The tension was easing between them, finally. All Alex needed now was to check this George chap out and they were good. On the same page again. Sisters playing for the same team.

'Al? I fixed the record player. We'll give it a whirl when you're all glammed up. Then we can take it in for Mum, give her something better to listen to than the drivel they keep putting on the TV for her."

'Thanks, Jem. I think she'll really like that.'

CHAPTER 52

Fifty minutes later, Maria Callas was soaring through the house, released like a bird from her dusty album sleeve.

'Why doesn't Mum listen to her records around the house anymore?' Alex asked, trying to form her words through a mouth awkwardly held open.

'Sh, stop talking, you'll make me smudge.' Jem had gotten fed up already with the complications of genealogy and children born out of wedlock and was perfecting Alex's lipstick instead. Alex looked at the concentration in Jem's cool blue eyes. This is what they'd skipped. While Alex had been off setting up home alone and Jem had been trying to survive school.

Jem met Alex's eyes and saw the question still there.

'I don't know, Alex. Maybe she didn't think she should.' But Alex didn't notice Jem's odd choice of words.

I do, Alex thought. Blythe had stopped singing in the choir. Then she'd stopped listening to music altogether. Maybe their mum had changed in more ways than they saw after Dill died, maybe Ted thought so too and had sought solace in Louisa's arms for that very reason. 'There, bloody gorgeous.' Jem twisted Alex by the hips to look in her dresser mirror. Maria was just climbing to a crescendo when the front door rattled open noisily. Alex checked her watch.

'Relax, it's only ten to.' Jem smiled. 'It'll be Dad.' Because *that* was a relaxing thought, minutes before Finn was due.

Downstairs the door slammed closed. Alex saw the same question flash across Jem's face too.

'*Go on*, dog! Don't bother me.' Jem frowned at Alex then walked over towards the landing. Alex followed.

'Ah, there you are. Not out gallivanting then?' Alex stood beside Jem and looked down the stairs. Ted was slumped up against the wall, Norma studying him from a few feet back. Jem threw Alex a look. He'd been drinking. All afternoon by the looks of him.

'I didn't think you'd be back here...' he slurred. 'Not when you could be...' Alex watched her dad wave his hand at the front door behind him, '... out there... running around with your little friend.' Did he know she was going out with Finn? How did he know that already?

'Calm down, Dad,' Jem said quietly. 'I haven't been running around with anyone.'

Alex looked at her. 'I don't think he's talking to you—'

'I saw you!' Ted exploded. 'I stopped at the churchyard today, on the way to the Tea Rooms, to see my daughter.

Hand in hand you were, so don't tell me you haven't been running around!'

Alex tried to make sense of the agitation ingrained in the lines around his eyes. He wasn't looking at Alex. He was looking burning fury at Jem.

'What's does he mean, Jem?' It was hanging in the air, a heavy, colourless, tasteless toxic thing, competing with Callas for airspace. Alex could feel it, dread-like in her mouth.

'He's drunk. He's misunderstood,' Jem said in a level voice. 'Dad, let's get you a coffee.'

'What does he *mean*, Jem? What did he see?' Alex's neck was pulsing.

'We were comforting each other, Alex,' Jem said, tears beginning in the corners of her eyes. Alex felt too nauseous to cry.

'Who?' Alex swallowed. 'Who were you comforting?'

Ted bellowed upstairs. 'I don't want a goddamn coffee! I want you to stay the hell away from the Sinclair boy!'

Alex's heart began to beat too fast. Hand in hand, he'd just said. Jem and Mal… holding hands.

'You said you were seeing your boss. You promised.' Because a promise was a rock-like thing, immovable, unbreakable. Alex felt the colour drain from her face. There hadn't been a *George* staying at the Longhouse.

Jem wiped her cheek defiantly and stalked downstairs. 'I am not justifying myself. Dad, you need a coffee. Then we'll talk.'

Alex felt dizzy. She had to tell Jem. What Malcolm was to them now. That she couldn't have a relationship with Malcolm. She *couldn't*!

Ted tried to stand up straighter and staggered into the console table sending the phone tumbling against the floorboards. Jem turned to watch him while Alex scrambled down the stairs.

'I don't want to talk about it, Jem. I don't ever want to hear a word of it again.' Alex watched her dad stop mid-sentence. He seemed to choke on his words for a few seconds. Alex recognised the sound of him clearing his throat, fighting the raw emotion trying to claw its way up into his voice.

Jem looked like a little girl standing up to him. 'I know how you feel about the Sinclairs, Dad. But Mal's different. I'm not a child, Dad. I can see him if I choose, he's my *friend*,' Jem said shakily.

'I don't want to hear of it!' Ted snarled. 'And I don't want you to have anything more to do with that boy. Goddamn it, why can't they just stay away from us?'

Ted was borderline, that knife's edge between molten anger and soul-crushing desperation. Jem was only just holding it together too, Alex could see it in her face. 'Dad?' Alex tried. She set a hand gently on his shoulder blade.

'Who's been in your mother's things?' he said, lifting his ear to the final bars of 'Casta Diva' resonating through the air around them. Alex pulled her hand away again as if he'd

been hot to the touch. She hadn't heard Finn's truck outside.
Only Norma fixated at the side window onto the porch had
given her any warning.

'I have,' Alex said calmly. She heard defiance in her
voice. Probably not enough to filter past whatever it was
he'd been drinking, but it was still there.

Her dad looked glassy drunken eyes at her. She was lost
to him.

'I know, Dad. You don't want me in Mum's music. Just
like you don't want me in Dill's room, touching his things
either. Why don't we just be honest for a change and call
it like it is? You don't want me here full stop. Well I'm
sorry, Dad, but I've promised Mum that we'd try our best.
So I'll let you decide how that's going to work out.' She
hadn't wanted it to, but the hurt was there too, jostling with
her new-found bravery. She'd wanted to ride on the back of
her anger for his betrayal but the fight had gone right out of
her.

Alex could feel the first warmth of despondent tears coming. Jem's were already falling. Something inside her ached
for Jem then. Alex couldn't go out and leave her with this.
Jem didn't need to hear it from Ted while he was drunk. That
he'd desecrated their family for a fling with Louisa. When
Jem realised what that meant for her and Mal, it was going
to be horrific enough without hearing it while he was in this
state.

Alex saw the shadow moving across the lawn through
the window. She had almost made it. She'd almost gone out

with Finn despite her dad, and now she was about to cry off before even reaching the garden gate.

Alex turned for the door and moved to intercept Finn before he made it up to the house. He knew what a car wreck Alex's family was, he didn't need to take the tour again. Alex opened the door and stepped outside, the wooden porch creaking beneath the battered pumps she'd had to team with Jem's skinny trousers and gypsy vest. She didn't care how she looked now, and neither would Finn. She just needed to get him off Dodge while the going was good.

Alex pulled the door closed behind her and stepped down onto the lawn. Finn was halfway up the path when she reached him.

He'd shaved. He'd done something to his hair, too. Styled, but not. He looked so nice, it pinched just to look at him.

'Hi,' Alex offered first. She was trying uselessly to take some sort of control.

'Hey.'

Alex was already looking at her feet. Finn put his hands deep into his jean pockets. When Alex managed to steal another look, he looked eighteen again. Only less unsure. 'You look beautiful, Alex. I hope you're hungry because I am star—'

'Finn, I'm really sorry—'

The door swung open behind her. 'What the hell are you doing on my land?'

Ted was stumbling less now. Gravity seemed to help him navigate his way clumsily down the steps to the garden path. Finn looked over Alex's head and assessed the situation the same way Alex watched him assess a landscape he was about to draw. The way he would size up the angles of a hillside or the turbulence of a river, before deciding how best to confine it to canvas.

'I'm sorry, Finn. Something's come up,' she said hurriedly. Finn let his eyes rest back on Alex momentarily, just long enough to try to reassure her before his face seemed to set into something harder, more statuesque. She didn't know why she did it, to break his concentration from her dad maybe, but Alex reached out a hand and pressed it gently to his chest. 'Please, Finn. I'll call you tomorrow. We'll do something. Anything you like.'

'I said, what the hell are you doing on my land?'

'Finn's just leaving, Dad.' Finn had already turned his body away slightly, he understood it made no sense to stay.

'You're damn right he is.'

Alex had put a hand out behind her, a silly subconscious gesture of protection. For the man at her back standing nearly a foot taller than she did.

'Ted,' Finn said. And it was like a touch-paper had been lit.

'Your good for nothing old man didn't need telling twice,' Ted snarled, 'what are you waiting for?'

Alex felt it behind her, that subtle hostility men could do

when a switch had been flipped. She looked at Finn. He looked like a statue of himself. *Just go*, she wanted to say. But something had seized inside her too.

Jem stepped out from the house. Finn stood firm across the grass. 'You got something to say to me, son?' Alex had never heard her father use that one tiny word to such devastating effect. *Son* was the last thing Ted thought of Finn as. *Son* was the last word in the world he would sully without good enough reason.

'I do actually, Ted.'

Alex felt the panic rising. Finn gently moved Alex a few feet towards Jem.

'I love your daughter, Ted. I'm sorry you find that difficult, but it's the truth. And there's no getting away from the truth.' Alex felt giddy. Finn didn't look relaxed exactly, just certain. Calm in his certainty.

'What did you just say to me?' Alex pictured Susannah here, telling Finn to go back to the car before the trifle, and his nose, was destroyed.

'I said… I love your daughter.' Alex moved to stand between Finn and her dad again but Jem caught her arm. Finn didn't even break his concentration. It might as well just have been him and Ted standing on the lawn while the sun gave up the day. Then it all happened so quickly. Ted, a man the wrong side of a drinking session and the wrong side of sixty, moved with a focused poise. Alex hadn't even seen his arm draw back before her father's fist made dull heavy contact with Finn's mouth.

'Dad! No!' Alex screamed. But it was too late, he'd already done it. Finn staggered, he doubled over but he didn't go down. Alex pulled free, she reached Finn and took clumsy hold of his face so she could see what he'd done.

'Oh my God, Finn. Why did you say that!' A steady flow of crimson was flowing from his lips. Finn pushed Alex back towards Jem and straightened himself. There was something dangerous in his eyes. Alex had seen it before, in Emma Parsons' garden. For the first time in her life, something told Alex to fear for her dad instead.

'Say it again,' Ted snarled.

Finn's fists balled for a second, ready, and then released. 'I said, I love your daughter.'

Ted's fist thudded back into Finn's waiting jaw, a sickening thud of knuckles against teeth. Jem gasped. Alex felt herself shut down into some strange suspended state. Like she was watching them all from underwater.

Jem began crying, soft small whimpers that didn't belong to her.

'You think you're good enough for my daughter, *Finn*? I know men like you. Men who think they can take what they want while better people pay the price for it. Your father, he took what he wanted from us. That poor little girl, mangled in a car that bastard had serviced. Destroying my business so my wife had to go skivvying for more no-good bastards!' Ted turned viciously to Alex, hunkered like an animal. 'And you *still* like this boy, Alexandra?'

'I'm not my father,' Finn said firmly.

'Apples don't fall far from the tree.' Ted looked away absently. He swayed on his feet. 'If his father hadn't rushed that car job for Helen… If I could have trusted someone to work for me again… working all those long hours all the time, neglecting Blythe…'

Finn was holding his sleeve to his bleeding mouth, he was the only one who didn't look to be trying to make sense of what Ted was saying.

'I should never have been with *her* that day, listening to her poison. I should've been with my boy. MY boy! While you two were fooling around together!' he snarled. 'But I let it happen. Let it start, because I wasn't watching. And then I lost her. I let him get his hooks into her, because I was saving a business your no good father ruined.'

Ted's voice had sharpened off again, acrid little words like blades. He stepped towards Finn, rippling with rage.

'Now you tell me again, *Finn*.'

Finn looked at Alex again then, silently imploring him not to say any more. She wasn't ashamed for it this time though. She didn't want Finn to say it. She didn't want that lovely face of his to be hurt any more. Alex looked at him. *Don't say it, Finn, please.*

Finn smiled, he understood. And then he turned back to face her dad again.

'I love your daughter.'

Ted made an unearthly guttural sound, the sound of a man

who could punch all night long before his fury finally died out. Finn stood ready to let him.

'No!' Alex darted between them. 'No more, Dad. Please, no more.' Her voice was shaking in her chest. There was nothing of her dad left in those fox-like eyes, nothing she recognised. 'Please, Dad. No more.'

It took a few moments, and then Ted Foster found his way back, a flicker behind the eyes and then he turned and staggered back to the house. Alex's lungs were trying to match the rhythm pumped out by her heart. Jem was regaining control, asking Finn in broken monologue if he was all right. From inside the house, 'Casta Diva' began playing again from the start, the volume turned up to its highest.

'I think he's gone mad,' Jem said shakily.

Alex was trembling. Did it matter? Did it matter what anyone had done, if this was the destination they'd all arrived at? The home waiting for her mum?

'Jem? Go back with Finn to Susannah's. Make sure she looks at his mouth. He might need to have it seen to.'

Finn looked up. 'Alex? Come back with me.'

'I can't.'

'Alex, don't do this,' he said.

'It's not your fault, Finn. It was never your fault. But we can't live like this. It's not fair on anyone. Jem, go with him. I'll look after Dad. Please.'

'Alex. Please, come back with me.'

Finn had wiped most of the red away, but his teeth were

stained with it, his face already swelling from the latest wounds she'd caused him. She couldn't keep hurting him like this. She looked away.

'Alex, *please*.' Finn looked wounded, desperate. 'Don't make me love you in secret, Alex.'

She was wronging him. Either way, she was wronging him. She should have never come back here, she realised as she turned shakily for the house. Alex swallowed down the shakiness in her voice. 'I'm sorry, Finn. For everything.'

CHAPTER 53

The Old Girl looked calm beneath a summer moon. It hadn't been a conscious thing, coming down here, Alex's feet had just led her, through the copse of trees and along the footpath cutting across the meadow. She hadn't used this route since she and her father had run down here, unaware that they'd already lost the race. Alex re-crossed her legs and felt the cool earth through Jem's cotton trousers. The fear had gone. How could she be afraid of anything any more when the worst had already happened? Alex watched the moonlight catching on the water and thought back to the moment she'd found her dad sitting in his truck in the layby. The way he'd looked before she'd got to him. Had he been on his way home from high tea with Louisa? She'd suspected but did she really know? For sure? It didn't matter any more. She couldn't bring herself to hate him, how could she? He'd still lost his son.

Alex had wanted to take care of him tonight, she'd turned the opera down from the deafening setting he'd cranked it up to in hopes of soothing him off to sleep, but then he'd found Jem's bottle of red and had taken into the lounge, throwing Jem's family tree papers across the room as he went.

Somewhere over Alex's head, the evening breeze disturbed the leaves of the alder tree Dill had fallen from. She'd thought Dill was in St Cuthbert's, but he wasn't. He was still here. By the Old Girl.

You're driving yourself mad, Alex.

Alex kicked off a shoe. Then the other. The water looked so calm. The Old Girl's mood wistful, benign. Alex rolled up Jem's trousers and stood quietly for a few moments in the peacefulness of the night. She took a few steps towards the bank and felt the first bite of nettles at her feet. She stood there for a few seconds, until the stingers had done their worst and the sensations died away to a meaningless nothingness. And then she stepped into the cold embrace of the water.

The water came up to her calves, accepting her without fuss. She hadn't rolled her trousers up nearly far enough but no matter. Alex moved out into the cold bite of the water. The Old Girl was calm, still. Almost as if she were sleeping.

Wake up, you bitch.

There was no logic behind it, no distant plan, but Alex kept going. The water was rising, tightening that feeling in her lungs as it climbed past her knees, her thighs, her hips. Her breathing became sharp and shallow, and then she gave herself to it, a committal lunge forwards and she was pressing through the cold black water. The Old Girl put up no fight, no currents, no tree roots to snag her feet on. A matter of a few surreal seconds and she was at the opposite side, huddled breathless to the bank.

Alex's breathing felt giddied and laboured, she could hear the protestation in her heart, as her body screamed at her, *Are you MAD?*

She hadn't stopped for the sensations of nettles or cold on her skin. But something had got inside, something that stung and ached and was making her convulse in vicious shivers. And then it all rose up. A swell of hurt and anguish and shame and regret. Alex's head bowed as it all came tumbling out in a flurry of pathetic sobs. She cried that way, for Dill, for them all, shivering and wet until a broken drunken melody found its way through the darkness.

Alex scanned the bank opposite. She could see the clearing near the alder tree, where she'd left her pumps. Was her body going into spasm? She tried to hold herself still as the singing, if it could be called that, made its way closer through from the meadows. The moonlight picked out only his face and silvered hair, the rest of him invisible in the camouflage of dark overalls.

Ted staggered through the darkness, drunk and emotional. He'd never known the words to any of Blythe's arias, they used to giggle at him when he tried to roar along to them in pidgin Italian.

Ted stopped singing. Alex heard him groan and then glass breaking somewhere over by the trees.

'God damn you!' he shouted.

Alex shivered as she listened over the water lapping gently against her waist.

'God damn you for taking him from me!' Alex heard his anger break into a free-fall of weeping. 'You old bitch!' he tried, but the tears had him in a tighter grip than his anger.

Ted staggered closer to the water, Alex could see him better now in the clearing. Here the river would only come up to his chest, but Alex still felt a flutter of concern, building and building like a tide. He shouldn't stand so close after drinking so much, the Old Girl knew how to seize upon a weakness.

'He was my boy. *Mine*! Dillon Edward Foster! He was *my* son!' Alex's anguish was making a U-turn, and then something caught her dad's interest. Ted bent down and picked something up. He seemed to sober, instantly.

'Alexandra? *Alexandra!*'

Alex twitched at her name. Her shoes fell from his hands and bounced against the earth. Ted started pacing along the riverbank just like Norma paced behind the door before Alex let her out.

'*Alexandra!* No… not my girl, NOT MY BABY GIRL!'

His voice was thick with panic. Ted jumped down clumsily into the water. He hadn't even taken his boots off.

He can't swim in those boots! And his overalls! Alex had felt the weight in those overalls when she'd tried pegging them out on the line! *No, no, no! You'll be anchored to the riverbed, Dad!*

'Dad, it's OK!' she called.

'Alexandra? Where are you, baby? I'm coming!'

'Dad! Wait! Don't come in any further—' But talking and swimming was a stretch too far. Alex shut her mouth, fear finding its way back to her where a short while ago it hadn't even dared to try. She was vulnerable again. Someone she loved was in the water too. Again.

'Alex? I can't see you!' Alex heard the desperation in his voice, high rasps of panic escaping from a man too drunk and too distraught to save anyone. A heavy splash and she knew he'd stumbled.

'Dad!' Alex took a mouthful of water. 'Dad!' she spluttered. That one mouthful had filled her up, choking the bravery right out of her.

She could hear thrashing, was he under? *Please*, don't let him be under! Alex dug deep, ignoring the cold in her arms and legs. She wouldn't run this time, she would swim. She would be efficient. She would be not be useless.

Alex half thrashed, half staggered across the last stretch of water where it petered away against the riverbed. 'Dad?' she gasped. She grabbed at his head, pulling it free of the water where he'd stumbled under the weight of his sodden clothes.

'Dad, are you all right? Dad, talk to me! *Please!*'

Ted ruptured into heavy sobs. 'Alex, my girl. My baby girl. I thought…' He pulled Alex into him, clamping huge able arms around her small frame. He held her firm and close to him, like she was a little girl again. *His* little girl again. 'I thought I'd lost you, girl. I thought I'd chased you away.' He pressed a kiss firmly against Alex's head and held it there, gripping her for dear life.

Alex started shaking. Violent spasms of relief, or maybe it was just the cold. 'No, Dad. You didn't lose me.'

She could feel his fingers, clamping her firmly in his embrace and felt something ease, a tightly wound coil that had kept her too tight to function properly all this time. 'I'm so sorry, Alex. I'm so sorry. Please, can you forgive me?'

CHAPTER 54

Alex stirred. She lifted her head from the gentle rise and fall of a body asleep beside her and surveyed her surroundings. Norma's ear twitched, she opened her eyes briefly then went back to sleep on the rug. Alex squinted at the clock on the mantelpiece. It was nearly five in the morning. She stood and wrapped the blankets around her shoulders. Norma watched her lean forwards to stoke the fire she'd made in the front room. *A fire, in August?* her mother would have said. But then a fire had been a far easier option than getting a grown man out of wet overalls. Besides, they'd both been exhausted from the walk back. It had done wonders for purging the alcohol from her dad's system, a good thing because they'd still had a lot to talk about on reaching the farmhouse.

Alex leant over her dad. He was sleeping against one arm of the small sofa they'd pulled up to the hearth. She pulled his blankets higher up his chest again. He was like an old grey sleeping bear.

No-one else would know about what had happened

between them tonight. How they'd both finally managed to put enough of the noise aside to just talk.

Alex had finally told him. How Rodolfo had barked. How the water had been too quick for her. How hard Finn had tried. She told him how Rodolfo had tripped her into the nettle patch, and how Finn's shirt was only on inside out because he'd been painting that morning and had called for Alex to go and look at his work. How they'd taken Dill out because he'd been teasing Jem about her attempts to look more like her girlfriends. Alex hadn't felt on trial, or in danger of tripping over something that might reignite the fires again. She'd just felt that she was setting down a heavy load while her father quietly let her. The only thing she hadn't told him, was that she'd been struck by lightning once, and had loved Finn every day since.

Alex opened out her blanket and stood in front of the embers, warming herself like a moth at a lantern. Her hair had matted into damp clumps over the ruined vest Jem was going to kill her for. Or maybe she wouldn't. Jem had bigger monsters coming her way.

Alex stared into the glow.

'Susannah Finn give you any pearls of wisdom while you were staying over at the Longhouse?' Ted had asked her. 'You and her boy… Are you as close as he wants? The way he says he feels?'

Alex knew what Ted was really getting at. *Did she know.* Had Susannah or Finn ever told Alex that her dad been caught huddled up in the corner of Frobisher's with the

Mayor's wife all over him. Did Alex realise that Dillon and Malcolm shared too much of a likeness not to share at least some of the same blood. Had Alex pieced it all together.

'No, Dad.' Alex had answered him. It wasn't the truthful answer but it was the answer he most needed to hear.

'Don't you think you should tell him then? Put him out of his misery? He seemed… genuine.' There had been something regretful in her dad's voice, the first possibility that he might have done wrong by Finn? Maybe that was a wish too far. It was too late now anyway.

'I've done some things, Alexandra, that I wish I hadn't,' her father had said. 'Not told you enough how much I love you, for one. Not been quick enough to bring you back home to us where you belong, for another. What you said in The Cavern the other night, it was right. I wasn't the only one who lost your brother, but I couldn't see past that for a long, long time. There were other things happening back then, before Dillon's accident. Things that clouded my mind.' Alex had watched the firelight play over her dad's worn features. 'I was so angry, at the world,' he'd gone on, 'I thought you were best out of it all, away from anything that might make your life any harder than it already was up here after your brother died. And then before I knew it, you were out of sight, in every way, and I didn't know how to bring you back.'

Alex watched the dying firelight clinging on to the coals. *It's not about who's done what any more*, it was about saving their family, giving her mother the husband and daughters she needed to come home to. The only way Alex could do that now, to head off any more skeletons from rattling out of any closets, was to put some real time and distance between the people they now were, and the people they had all once been. And maybe one day, when he found someone with less baggage to spend his love on, Finn might even forgive her for it.

Alex wrapped herself again and sat back against her dad's solid body on the settee. Something had changed between them. There had been truths left unspoken, but for the things they had shared, hopefully forgiveness. Or at least under-standing.

Still there were other things bothering Alex when she finally drifted off to sleep again against the rise and fall of her father's chest. The look in Finn's eyes when she'd sent him away again rejected. The truth that was about to come crashing down on her sister.

Jem.

A tension spiked in Alex's chest. Jem still didn't know. And Alex had sent her away with Finn, without first tel-ling her that Malcolm Sinclair was almost certainly their half-brother.

What if Jem hadn't stayed at the Longhouse like Alex had asked her to? What if she'd just seen to Finn's split lip and then disappeared somewhere? She hadn't come back here yet.

Alex gave the clock on the mantel another tentative look and listened to the sound of her father's heart beating its steady rhythm while he slept. She closed her eyes tightly and sent a small prayer up to the powers that be.

Wherever my sister ended up last night, please, let it not have been with Malcolm.

CHAPTER 55

Jem looked like a fifteen-year-old as she walked up the track to the house. Alex had watched her head bobbing steadily over the hedgerow. Norma pulled again at the corner of Alex's blanket where it touched the dusty floor of the front porch.

Even their dad's gentle metronomic snores hadn't lulled Alex back off to sleep for long. A fresh pot of coffee and an hour on the front porch watching the climb of the sun and Ted still hadn't moved from his spot through the lounge window.

Jem rounded the gatepost in the same skinny jeans and baggy white tee she'd been wearing last night. Her hair falling messily over her shoulder in a loose chunky braid, her fringe poking into tired eyes.

'You look like Mum,' Jem said softly as she crossed the lawn towards Alex.

Alex squinted into the morning sun, her thumb busy over a little sharpness on her mug. 'So do you.'

Jem slowed as she approached the porch steps. 'How is he?' she asked, holding back where their mother's flowerbeds ran up to the timber deck. Blythe's poppies were in full bloom. A bright red warning against a backdrop of mint and sage.

'Sleeping it off. How are you?' Alex asked tentatively. Jem had a deep reddish brown on her sleeve. Alex might've thought it was paint if she didn't know better.

'I'm not the one who's had to babysit a grown man all night.' Jem looked over the house as if it had just landed from Kansas. 'I didn't mean to leave you with him all night, Alex. I was coming back, but…'

'Jem? Can we talk?' Alex blurted. Jem scratched her top lip. Her skin was as raw as ever. 'We need to talk.'

Alex lifted the cooling coffee pot from her dad's smoking table and poured the cup she'd had ready for when he woke. Jem stepped lethargically up onto the porch and slumped tired limbs into the other chair.

Alex passed her a cup of lukewarm black coffee and poured one for herself.

'Where did you stay last night?'

Jem sipped from her mug and grimaced. 'I stayed at the B&B.'

'The Longhouse?' Alex asked. A cynical voice was already trying to whisper to her, *Not with anyone called* George *she didn't!*, but Alex stamped it down and kicked it from her head before it had a chance.

'I don't know any other B&Bs in the Falls.' Jem was being defensive.

'You don't look as though you've slept much.'

'Neither do you.'

No, Jem, I haven't. And after what I've got to tell you, you probably won't sleep easy ever again.

'I need to tell you something, Jem. Something you're not going to want to hear. But you need to know,' Alex said flatly.

Jem stopped sipping her coffee. Alex started with a deep breath.

'It's about Mal…' Alex ventured, 'and Dill. And what Mum said when she saw Alfie at the hospital.' Alex's heart was already in her throat.

Jem sat back into her chair and looked out across the lawns. 'It's all right, Alex. I already know.'

Alex felt herself rigidify. 'You *do*?' she was incredulous, relief and surprise all in one hit. 'But…'

Alex couldn't find her words. Hang on, they'd been holding hands… Ah, but wait! They were at Dill's grave when Ted had passed them on the way to the Tea Rooms, they were comforting each other, like Jem said! Maybe because they'd realised that Dill belonged to them *both*!

Alex let out the breath she'd been holding. *Thank you, Universe.* 'But… why didn't you tell me, Jem?'

'Why didn't *you* tell *me*?' Jem said wide-eyed. 'Because it *hurts*, Al. Just like you said. I've been thinking about it constantly for the last ten days. I can't get my head around it.'

'Me neither,' Alex agreed glumly.

'I mean, *Mum*… having it off behind Dad's back with the mayor. How could she do that to Dad?'

Alex felt the coffee catch in the back of her oesophagus. For a split second she thought it would be all right with a steady swallow, but then it scratched and she spluttered it all over her mother's poppies.

She'd survived the Old Girl, twice, only to drown in coffee on her parents' front porch.

'What did you just say?' she wheezed, her chest trying to suck in air while her lungs were trying to expel everything moist inside them.

Jem's had gone quite still. 'You said you knew!'

Alex carried on spluttering. Jem had got it wrong. So wrong. 'But how… why do you…'

Jem ran her fingers through her hair and held on to a clump at the top of her head. Alex held the last few coughing spasms down in her torso. 'Mal's dad… he left Mal a letter. For when he died,' Jem said, startled.

'Saying *what*?' Her *mum*? Her *mum* had the *affair*? Alex saw Jem's chest rise with an extra big breath as if she was about to go free-diving. 'Jem? Saying what?'

Jem gave herself a few seconds and then focused on something inside her cup. 'The mayor didn't want Mal to hear it from Louisa. He didn't want Mal to hear it from himself either, the spineless git, so he left Mal a letter in with his will. So the good old Mayor Sinclair wouldn't have to answer any difficult questions,' Jem said quietly.

'Go on,' Alex said. She was listening carefully now. This had legs, this tale Jem was surely mistaken about, it had supporting evidence… *Paperwork!*

'Do you remember when Mum and Dad were still friendly with the Sinclairs? Before Dill was born?' Alex felt the hairs stand on her neck.

'Vaguely. I remember Dad moaning that Louisa had been a stuck up wretch at one of the parties Mum had made them go to.'

'Do you remember Mum cleaning for them?'

'Yes.'

'The mayor wrote in his letter that he missed speaking to Mum when she got more hours working in the family records office and stopped cleaning for them. So he took up an interest in tracing his ancestors. Mum had given Louisa one of those family tree sets or something. So Alfred took it to the Town Hall, for Mum to help him with.' Jem shrugged and shook her head to herself. 'That's where it started.'

'What started, exactly?' Alex said soberly. She'd was just getting to grips with her dad's infidelity, now she had to start the process all over again.

'It was just the one time, or so it says in Malcolm's letter,' Jem said carefully. 'But once is all it takes.'

Alex felt a jumping in the side of her neck. 'All *what* takes, Jem?'

Jem didn't need to say it. Alex had already seen it in all the similarities that still rung true between Malcolm and Dill. Alex had just got her facts in the wrong places. Malcolm wasn't the child born from an affair. Dillon was. Dillon was Blythe and Mayor Sinclair's son. A catastrophic error on Alex's part, resulting in the same consequence all the same. Alex looked out across the lawns where they'd all played together, growing up. 'Dill and Mal are half-brothers, aren't they?'

Jem clenched her teeth. Her eyes were becoming more bloodshot. 'The mayor seemed to think so.' Enough to give Dill a very shiny bow and arrow set a couple of weeks before his ninth birthday anyway. Alex's heart plummeted like a pebble through water. She hadn't imagined there being anything much worse than her dad fathering another child beyond their family, of *gaining* a son. But she'd been wrong. Ted had never gained a son, he'd lost one. He'd lost Dill. In every way possible.

Alex felt a tremor inside her. For the man snoring on a settee in the lounge, oblivious to the hurtful secrets steadily being unpicked out here on the porch on a glorious bank holiday Monday morning.

'He loved her, Alex. The mayor was in love with Mum. He told Mal that he'd asked her to leave Dad, but she wouldn't. She didn't feel the same way, it had been a terrible mistake. Can you believe he would say that in a *letter*? No wonder he didn't want Mal hearing it from Louisa. It was hardly going to be a better version from her, was it?'

'Louisa knows?' Alex managed. 'How?'

Jem laughed, a harsh, pitiless sound. 'Louisa had been snooping through the mayor's papers once, probably checking how much she was in line for. Bet she wasn't expecting to find Dill named in the mayor's will.' Alex shot a look at her sister. Jem shrugged softly. 'The mayor wanted Dill and Mal to share everything he left them, straight down the middle.'

Alex was trying to absorb it all. 'But when? When did Louisa find out? Why didn't she confront Mum?'

'And let the world know that she'd been elbowed over for her old cleaner, Alex? Can you imagine Louisa Sinclair shrugging that one off?'

'But *when*? When did Louisa read the mayor's will? How long has everyone know about this?'

'*Everyone* doesn't know about this, Al. Mal found out about six months ago, when his dad passed away, I've known since Mal and I went out for that drink last week.'

'And Louisa?'

'Mal isn't sure. He thinks it must have been the year Louisa sent him to his grandparents' and he had to miss the boat race. The same summer Dill died. Mal remembers his mum and dad arguing before he was sent away for the week, and when he came back he was just told… about what had happened at the river… and that his mother didn't want to talk about it again. I guess the mayor changed his will after that anyway so Louisa didn't have to worry about her or Mal losing out any more.'

It was starting to seep in. The times they'd all played together, the birthday parties. Blythe keeping busy in the kitchen while their dad got stuck in horsing around with the kids. Her head was throbbing. 'Does Dad know, Jem?'

'If he does, he's gone a very long time pretending not to.

I want to say that I don't think he knows, but I'm not sure I believe that, Al. Helen Fairbanks had a quiet word with me last week. The groundsman at St Cuthbert's thought he saw Dad the morning after Mum went into hospital, tearing flowers apart at Dill's grave. Helen asked me if he was coping alright.'

Alex thought back to the yellow petals fluttering over the ground when she'd gone to visit Dill. Jem looked at the house, checking for signs of life before she continued.

'The mayor sent flowers for Dill every birthday. I think those were the flowers the groundsman saw Dad destroying.'

'But… the mayor died… months ago?' Alex was trying to squeeze pieces together that wouldn't fit.

'I know. But he asked Mal to carry on taking flowers for Dill, every birthday, Alex, in the evening when us lot had all finished paying our respects. The mayor didn't want Dill's memory lost to the Sinclairs. That's why Mal was at St Cuthbert's, when Mum got ill. He was leaving flowers… for his half-brother. *Our* half-brother.'

Tears began sliding down one of Jem's cheeks. Jem looked even more like their mum when she cried.

Alex leant over the armrests and huddled against her sister. *Mum.* Alex hadn't even thought about her in the hospital since Jem had started to talk. So Mal had upset Blythe then. Her dad had been right. Because he knew what Mal and Blythe would have been talking about when Mal had turned up with the evening flowers.

'Dad knows, Jem.' The flowers had confirmed it. It was all starting to fall into place. *Like a ghost*, Susannah had said. Ted had looked like a ghost, sitting in Frobisher's Tea Rooms with the mayor's wife.

Jem wiped at her face. 'We don't know for sure though do we, Alex?'

'No. We don't. But I think Louisa told him. Dad wasn't on a callout the day Dill fell in the river, Jem. He with Louisa in Frobisher's Tea Rooms. Susannah Finn saw them. Deep in conversation. Can you think of anything else they'd have been in deep conversation about?'

Jem shook her head, Alex felt the guilt at having thought her dad had been sleeping with Louisa. For jumping to the same conclusion Susannah had when all along, it had been her dad who'd been betrayed.

Alex let her mind trail off. She closed her eyes and heard her father's voice through her head. *He was my boy. Mine! Dillon Edward Foster! He was my son!* And then last night, when Ted had been broken hearted as the drink had gotten the best of him. *I should never have been with her that day, listening to her poison. I should've been with my boy.*

'Alex?' Jem called softly. 'You're spilling your coffee.'

Alex righted her cup. 'Louisa told him he'd been raising another man's son.'

The words twisted in Alex's throat on their way out but they hung heavy with truth when she heard them. Alex remembered stumbling from the copse of trees across her dad in the layby, sitting there ghostlike in his cab. Hands braced on the wheel.

'No wonder he'd thought the worst of me and Finn. If Mum could behave like that…' Alex trailed off.

'We can't tell Dad that we know. It would kill him,' Alex finally said.

'What do you mean?' Jem asked.

'He'd already lost Dill, Jem. Don't you see? Before Dill had even fallen into the water, Dad had already lost him. And then Dill died. And even Louisa decided to let it be. That's what Dad has been afraid of, Jem, seeing you with Malcolm… he didn't want you to find out. We can't bring it all up again now, Jem. For Dad's sake. As soon as this is spoken out loud and people learn the truth, Dad will lose Dill all over again.'

'But Malcolm has already spoken to Mum about it, Alex!'

'But Mum doesn't know that *we* know, does she?'

'No. I mean, *I* haven't said anything.'

'And do you think that Mal would be discreet? If we asked him?'

'On whose behalf, Alex? Mum's? The woman who nearly stole his dad away? Who gave birth to his half-brother and never said a word in all the time I was friends with him? Or do you mean on Dad's behalf, who's bust Mal's balls at every opportunity in a bid to scare him off? Mal hasn't got any loyalties to either of our parents, Alex. We can't expect him to have.'

Jem put her head in her hands. Alex exhaled slowly. It

occurred to her then, they'd been forgetting someone in all this. 'What about loyalty to Dill? I don't love Dill any less for being my half-brother. Do you?'

'Of course not, Al.'

'Well Dill was as much Mal's brother as he was, *is*, ours, Jem. I don't want to pick through the ashes for salvageable fragments of our family if this all blows up again, I don't want Dill's memory dragged through all that. Would Mal want that for Dill?'

Jem exhaled and set her hand over the sore patch near her mouth. 'I'll speak to Mal. He won't say anything. And neither will Millie.'

'And Mayor Sinclair is dead. That just leaves Louisa and our parents.'

'What are you saying, Al?'

'I'm saying, we should just leave it to them, Jem. Dill's gone. If he was alive, it would be different. But he's not. There's nothing to gain from opening up an old wound like this. Mum isn't well enough to deal with it for a start.'

Alex sat back into her chair and leant her head back against the wood. One of her mum's wind-chimes dangled above her from the porch overhang. She watched the small metal shapes try to rotate in the breezeless air. A cloud, sun, several stars and a lightning bolt, all twinkling in the light.

Alex listened to Jem's steady breathing and the sounds of Norma's claws pattering over the porch decking.

'That wasn't what you were going to talk about, Al,' Jem murmured after a while. 'I cut in about Mum, you were

going to say something else. About Dill and Mal, but obviously not the same revelation I had to bring to the table…
What was it?'

Alex closed her eyes. 'Nothing. Secrets. Crossed wires.'
She tried to formulate something more substantial. 'So you
must have stayed with George last night then?' George the
invisible house guest Alex still had a few questions about.

'Who else would I have been with?' Jem had a strange
expression on her face. Alex didn't have an answer. 'I was
upset when I got there last night. Finn disappeared before
his mum saw him and George wouldn't let me leave until I'd
calmed down. I fell asleep up in the room.'

'Oh?' Alex's nose for scandal had been proven unreliable
on an almighty scale. She wasn't exactly qualified to doubt
Jem, not after getting it so wrong about her parents. It was
just, where was this George? Alex felt suspicious every time
Jem mentioned him, and she didn't have a reason for it.

Jem gently rubbed her fingertips over her eczema.
'George wants to meet you. Today, actually. I thought we
could all meet here at lunch, maybe go to the boat race
together. If you guys hit it off, I mean. We don't have to all
go, you're not under any obligation or anything.'

Jem rubbed at her eczema again.

'No, Jem. Actually that sounds *great*.' Jem was just full of
surprises this morning. 'What's with the change of heart?'

Jem shrugged. 'Finn.'

'Finn?'

'Last night, he could've floored Dad, Al. Finn's a fit

healthy guy, he could've danced around him and put Dad straight on his arse. But he didn't. He just… stood there. I don't know why he didn't fight back. Maybe he didn't want to detract from the point he was making. All I know is that Finn made me feel like a coward last night.'

Jem was not alone on that score. Alex always felt like a coward next to Finn.

'You're not a coward, Jem. You made Robbie Rushton cry with your fractured wrist.'

Jem's face warmed, ready for a smile that didn't quite arrive. 'Thanks. But you're wrong, Alex. I have been a coward. Finn will take a beating for you… a beating for loving you. Well, it just so happens that…' Jem hesitated, 'I'm in love with somebody too. I am. And it's about time I came out and said how I feel about George. Because it's special, isn't it? To feel that way?'

Alex saw the blood dried into the arm of Jem's t-shirt. 'It's special, Jem. Of course it is. It's just not always straightforward.'

'But it is, Alex. If it's real, it *is* straightforward. I've only just got that. And if you love Finn the way he loves you, Al, you need to hurry up and get it too.'

CHAPTER 56

'Breakfast! Come and get it!' Ted boomed up through the house.

Jem moved across the landing and threw Alex a shrug at the bedroom doorway before heading downstairs. Alex set the paper leaf Finn had left for her to find back inside the top drawer next to her bed and followed her sister. A power shower and some fresh clothes and, despite the night's events, she was feeling fairly human.

Alex pattered after Jem into the kitchen. Norma was chewing on their dad's's slipper while he stood hovering over a frying pan. 'Omelette a la... everything.' He said, running a fish slice through something vaguely omelette-like, sliding each half onto a separate plate. 'Don't tell your mother I'm eating bacon, she's obsessed with my choles-terol.'

Ted waved the fish slice at the table already set with coffee and juice and Blythe's special occasion crockery they were forbidden to touch unless the Reverend came around.

'Now don't keel over in shock, I know I'm a little out of practice,' he said carrying the plates of burned omelette over, 'but I used to cook a mean omelette for you girls and it's about time you got to taste one of your dad's old specialities again.'

Ted set Jem's plate down first and pecked her on the head. Alex watched him move around the table to set hers down in front of her. Alex felt her dad put his hands on her shoulders and press a kiss to her head. He gave her a gentle squeeze before letting go of her again.

'I was thinking, seeing as you girls have dug all your mother's dreadful records out, I might take that record player down to the hospital with me today, see if we can't get a bit more life into that room of hers. What do you think?'

The cordless in the hall rang. 'I've got it, you girls get stuck in.'

Jem looked across the table at Alex and raised her eyebrows. 'What did you do to him last night? Lobotomy?'

'More of a baptism,' Alex said.

Jem looked puzzled but Alex wasn't giving her any more on that. She shrugged and looked at her plate. '*Speciality?*' Jem whispered. 'Is that a… *marrowfat pea*?'

Alex grinned. 'Pretty sure I just saw your jar of peanut butter out by the hob too.'

'Blythe!' Ted exclaimed into the phone. 'How have you got to the payphone?' he said walking into the kitchen. 'It's all right, love, take your time. I've got all the time in the world.' Ted put the phone on loud-speak and set it down between Alex and Jem's glasses of orange juice. 'You're on

the speaker, love. The girls are here. We're just having…
muesli.'

'Hello, girls.'

Alex and Jem exchanged looks. 'Hey, Mum.'

'Hi, Mum. How are you?'

'I'm really, really, good. They brought… a phone on… a trolley.'

'That's great, love,' Ted said softly. 'I'm coming down to see you, in about half an hour. The girls are going off to watch the boat race, aren't you, girls? I'll have to be at the garage this afternoon though or the buggers will start parking in the yard, bloody tourists.'

'We're going to come see you this evening, Mum. When the traffic's eased through the Falls, OK?' Jem said.

'OK, darling. I was just… calling… to say that the doctor… is pleased. I'm meeting… a phys… phys…' Alex watched her dad wince at the phone and held her breath, '…physio… therapist… tomorrow,' Blythe managed.

'That's *great*, Mum!' Alex smiled. 'That's the next step to getting you back here, with us.'

'He said my heart… is behaving itself.'

'I already told the docs that my wife has a strong heart,' Ted said, clicking the phone back to normal. He nodded towards their steaming breakfast plates before wandering off into the front room, taking Blythe back all to himself.

Jem picked up one end of her omelette. 'I didn't know charcoal was an *ingredient*.' She smiled. 'Quick, bin it while he's not looking!'

'Way ahead of you, Jem.' Alex smiled, passing Norma another finger-ful under the table.

Jim skipped over to the bin. Alex crept after her to the sink to wash her hands. Right now a burnt omelette was the biggest crisis they had. Which was pretty marvellous. Alex reached over the sink for the tap but there was something soaking in there. 'Woah, wait a sec,' Jem said. 'Let me just get that out of the way.' A faint tinge of yellow was still ingrained into the fabric of Jem's white t-shirt.

Jem inspected it. 'Sod. Why is blood such a bugger to get out?' Alex felt her morning pop like an air bubble. Jem must've felt it too. 'Hey? What's up?'

Alex shook it off. 'I'm fine. Great, in fact. Mum's feeling better, Dad's happier. Everything's great,' she lied.

Jem gave her a hard look. 'Some things leave their mark though, don't they, Al?'

CHAPTER 57

'Jem, you've been up and down at that window more times than Norma!'

Jem flashed a nervous smile and began pacing past the clock on the mantelpiece again. Jem had done a U-turn. They weren't going to have lunch when George arrived. That might be weird, she'd decided. So George was just coming up for a good old-fashioned cup of tea. In three minutes, so said the mantelpiece clock.

'Jem, calm down. I'm starting to wonder if he's got three eyes or something.'

Dark features. Portuguese somewhere down the line. Ambitious. Hard-working. That was all Jem had given up before snapping that if Alex didn't stop asking questions she was going to *call George right now and cancel!*

Jem began twisting the silver bangle around her wrist. She'd let her hair down and had used expertly applied makeup to disguise the excema that had still hadn't seemed to have calmed down any. Alex was seriously considering having a word with this George about the pressure Jem was under at work. This big unveiling thing she had going on was stressing her out, big time. Alex had tried to talk about it twice since their dad had headed off to the hospital and both times Jem had practically recoiled.

The sun glinted on a car pulling through the gateposts and Alex felt an unexpected thrill of excitement. Jem had never brought a boy home. Alex had found herself second guessing what he looked like, what his interests were going to be, all the things that had drawn Jem to a guy she'd been secretly dating for two years now (two years!) without breathing a word.

'Nice car!' Alex trilled, walking through to the hallway. Jem sank onto one of the lounge settees and carried on twisting her bangle.

Alex laughed to herself and walked through to the kitchen, peering through the window over the sink. She honestly didn't know what Jem was so agitated about, 'It's not like I'm going to sock him one on the garden path, Ted-style,' Alex had tried to joke. Only it wasn't that funny at all.

Alex went on tiptoes to get a better look at the driver of the silver Audi pulling up to the house. She couldn't see that well because of the shades but…

'It's all right, Jem. False alarm. Unless George is rocking a ponytail,' Alex said light-heartedly. Jem sat down on the sofa. Then was up on her feet again. Alex shook her head and moved to open the front door and assist their visitor. Her dad said they always had tourists up here now, calling in to ask for directions.

Alex watched the car door schlump open in that way

expensive car doors did. A familiar face looked around at Alex, the same awkward look Alex had seen when they'd first bumped into one another on Susannah's landing. Jem appeared next to Alex on the doorstep.

'Oh, hey!' Alex said warmly. 'What are you doing up here? Are you lost?'

Gina looked to Jem then back to Alex. She scratched at her shoulder with the arm of her sunglasses then hooked them over her figure-hugging black vest. Alex thought of Lara Croft Tombraider and tried to stand up a bit straighter.

'No, I think I've come to the right place,' said Gina.

'Al?' Jem said shakily. 'I think you must have already met. This is George.'

*

'So, what about when you were at St Cuthbert's Primary?'

'Well, I wasn't thinking about it then, Alex. I'm not a raving sex-pest.'

Alex rolled her eyes. 'But at high school?'

'*Definitely* at high school.'

'You knew then? All that time ago?'

'All that time ago.'

Alex had listened while three cups of tea had gone cold so far, and each time George had engaged with Alex, all she'd been able to think was how many boxes George ticked on the list of things Alex would hope for Jem to find in a partner. Witty, check. Smart, check. Gracious enough to let Jem explain things at her own pace, patient enough to listen to Alex's less intellectual questions. Check and check. And not forgetting kind (and sufficiently knowledgeable in first aid) enough to perform the Heimlich on strangers in B&B corridors.

'But what about Mal? The snog outside Frobisher's.'

'How do you even know about that?' Jem blurted. Red rising in her cheeks.

'You and *Mal*? You never told me that,' George gasped theatrically, she had only been *Gina* for the purposes of subterfuge. 'Does Millie know? I think I should tell her.' George broke a grin and Alex felt a bit like a high-school sprog in awe of one of the older, funkier girls. Alex needed to make more effort with her appearance. Especially with exotic creatures like George roaming the earth. Drop dead gorgeous. That was another box George ticked. But then she hadn't brought anything to the table yet that Jem hadn't.

'I told you, Mum saw you,' Alex informed her.

'Ah. Well, that was my idea in fairness to Mal,' Jem admitted. 'Kind of an acid test.'

'You kissed Mal Sinclair… to check if you were gay?'

'It seemed like a good idea at the time.'

'Well I can't blame you for that, Jem.' George smiled. 'Mal's a true gent. He deserves a life full of kisses from adoring friends, I think.' George gave Jem a knowing look and for the first time since George had walked in, Alex felt like a gooseberry.

'Shoot,' George exclaimed. 'Do you mind if I just nip out

and make a call? I've asked my cousin if she wanted to come and see the Vikings with her friends and their kids. They might be wandering the town waiting for me to get in touch.'

'You can use the house phone? The reception's a bit sketchy up here,' Alex offered.

'That's OK, really. Phillipa can *really* talk, and my car seems to be like some kind of signal booster anyway. Let me give it a whirl first, give you guys some time to digest.' George got up from the table, leant down and kissed Jem chastely on the cheek. Alex watched George let herself out then saw the uncertainty in Jem's face.

'I love her,' Alex blurted.

Jem exhaled. 'Really?'

'Really, Jem. I think she's *great*.'

Jem broke into a relieved smile. 'I love her too. And I don't want her to be a secret.'

'So you and Mal, you really weren't ever getting it on with him then?'

'Nope.'

'He knows, doesn't he? That you're…'

Jem tapped a finger against the milk jug on the table. 'You can say it, Alex. That I'm gay.'

OK…

'Mal knows you're gay?'

'Yes. Mal knows. Carrie told him. Carrie told *everyone*.'

'*Carrie?* Carrie Logan? How… *When?*'

'Year ten at Eilidh High. About a year after you left for uni and didn't come back.' Alex looked at Jem, there was nothing in her expression that said she'd meant for that to come as sharp as it did.

'What happened, Jem? With all that? I know you hated school but Mum never really went into it all that much. Other than the shrink part.'

Jem tapped the milk again. 'I did not need a shrink.'

Alex had needed a shrink. Although Jem had matched her on the sleepless nights and had gone one further with a very drastic hair cutting incident. 'What *did* you need, Jem?' Alex didn't want anything else coming out of the woodwork and biting any of them later on. She'd heard enough secrets to last a lifetime in the last week but she'd rather get any last stragglers out of the way now.

'Just a better group of friends, Alex. That was all. Carrie and her circle, we'd been friends up until that summer. I think she had a thing for Mal though, wanted to be the next Louisa Sinclair probably. Anyway, she didn't like me hanging around with Mal. Of course, I didn't realise it then, why she was always making little digs, about my clothes, my favourite music, anything really… to knock me down a few pegs. But I was an idiot. Instead of just telling her to shove it up her arse, I tried to fit in. Be part of the gang.'

'That's what all fourteen-year-olds do, Jem. Try to fit in.'

Jem laughed. 'I was never going to fit in with Carrie. You know, once, I'd borrowed a scrunchy off her, do you remember those? Anyway, I'd borrowed it, probably trying to look more like perfect Carrie, anyway after I gave it back to her she accused me of ripping it, and then sewing it back together. She showed me the stitching and everything. *Exhibit A!* It was the dumbest thing. She'd obviously done it herself, but it was more important for her to be spiteful than to just… be cool. Be friends.'

'She sounds like a sociopath.'

'Nah. She's just a cow. But a really big one.'

'I take it you don't hate her because of *Scrunchygate*, though?'

Jem sobered. 'No. I hate her because I let her convince me she was my friend.'

Jem read Alex's expression. 'I was fourteen, remember. Like I said already, an idiot.'

'So what did our sociopathic friend do?'

Jem repositioned the silver bangle at her wrist. 'Nothing. Just kids' stuff. Stupid kids' stuff. There was a sleepover, at one of the other girls' houses. I hadn't been invited before because I was always hanging out with Mal. Carrie got them all to pretend that they… y'know, practised kissing… like on each other… before the school disco came round. The stupid thing is, I didn't agree to it because I was *gay*. Or because I *wanted* to do it. I just didn't want to be the only one who *wouldn't* do it.'

'So you kissed Carrie Logan?'

'Eugh, God no. I just *agreed* to. That was all it took, then total ostracism and a year of hell.'

Alex hated Carrie Logan. She actually *hated* her with a violent white-hot fury.

'But Mal… He was great. Always looking out for me, on

the bus and stuff.' Jem shuddered at the recollection. 'And then it really turned sour when Mal had a go at her at the river race. We'd been having a good day, minding our own business. The mayor had brought in the new egg rules and Mal had egged every one of the targets on the river, I'd hit about half. Then Carrie and her lot started shouting things from the bridge. Apparently I was a "typical lesbo who even threw like a man".' Jem smiled to herself. 'They'd obviously never seen your aim, Al.'

Alex felt a new flavour of rage building in her body. Carrie Cowbag Logan and her craptastic neon shop had had twenty quid out of Jem's account because of Alex.

'Forget Carrie, Jem. The important thing, is you're happy. And I'm happy for you.' Alex grabbed Jem's hand and held it fiercely.

Jem pressed her head unexpectedly against Alex. Alex squeezed into her. Jem smelled like strawberry lip-gloss. 'Thanks, Al. Really, you don't know what that means to me.'

What, to love a person and have the blessing of your family to carry on loving that person with happy abandon? Alex knew exactly what that meant.

'So what about Mum and Dad?'

Jem sucked in a huge juddery breath as if she'd been crying. 'You know what I said about love being straight-forward? Yeah, well… some love's a bit less straightforward than others.' Jem was fiddling again. 'I don't think I'm there yet, Alex.'

Alex set her hand over Jem's where she was bothering at her bangle. 'Jem, I've hidden under a rock for years. All it does is make you more frightened of being out in the open. Just tell them.'

'But what if they can't handle it? What if they don't want anything to do with me?'

'Reject you? You're their daughter, Jem. How could they ever reject you? It might take them a while, to get their heads around it, but they love you, Jem. We all do. Unconditionally.'

Alex watched the thoughts playing out over Jem's face. 'So when are you going to tell Dad straight about Finn then, Alex? Because it's no different. Not really.'

Alex narrowed her eyes. Had Jem deliberately led her here?

'Dad can't handle that right now, Jem. What if—'

'What if he rejects you? You're their daughter, Alex,' Jem parroted. 'How could they ever reject you? It might take them a while, to get their heads around it, but they love you, Alex. We all do. Unconditionally.'

CHAPTER 58

Jem pulled her Ray-Bans down her nose. 'I'm so glad we walked down, look at them all... we've been invaded! Again!' she trilled. It had been building all weekend, Eilidh Falls in the grip of her own growing tension finally peaking today with the arrival of hordes of day-trippers – most wearing something in faux fur – arriving en masse to witness what was steadily becoming a cult festival, according to George's Twitter feed.

'Pick her up, Jem. Before someone steps on her. I don't trust that collar either,' Alex said.

Jem bent down to pick Norma up off the pavement as another family in plastic horned helmets barged past them for a photo with the new town Mayor, fully kitted out like Odin himself, standing on something that made him look very prominent and imposing at the top of the river bridge. Alex glanced at the throngs of people scurrying like ants up and down the bridge, traffic stopping and starting erratically as pedestrians cut impatiently across the road without looking.

Hamish was standing out front of The Cavern, looking

twice as authentic as the mayor, huge arms crossed while he shook his head disapprovingly at the chaos. Alex carried on weaving them a path between the re-enactment tents, trying to find a good spot closer to the water. Jem was scanning the crowds. George had gone from the farmhouse back to The Cavern to find her cousin, they were supposed to be meeting Alex and Jem by the Valkyries at the finish line. Millie was going to bring Alfie along to watch the fun too seeing as they'd already had the chance to build the beginnings of a good friendship with George.

'Do you see them anywhere?' Alex asked, trying to pick out familiar faces between the fluttering red and gold banners flanking the high street. 'The place is rammed. I keep looking but—'

'Hey! Jem! Alex! Sorry we're running a bit late.' Alex and Jem both turned. 'Blimey, this place is *crazy*! I hope we get a good spot near the water. I want to see which maidens the victors offer their banners to!' Millie beamed.

'Me too, maybe Finn won't take no for an answer, Al,' Jem muttered before giving Millie a hug.

'Hi, Millie.' Alex wanted to hug her too. For the aggro Millie must've been dealing with each time Mal had needed to let off steam about the whole mess with his dad. For letting Jem and George have somewhere to take a time out so Jem didn't implode with it all. But Millie was like her mum, Helen didn't wait for praise either. 'Hi, Poppy.' Alex smiled. Poppy Parsons was holding on to one of Millie's hands.

'Poppy wanted to come see the invaders, didn't you,

Poppy? While Mummy helps Susannah at the Longhouse. We're going to be doing a project on the Vikings when you start at St Cuthbert's with Alfie, aren't we, sweetie?'

Millie turned and spoke quietly. 'I have a plan. Get the kids to play together and maybe we'll be able to keep a better eye on poor Emma. Help them out.'

Her mum was right about her balance theories. People like Millie existed in the world to balance out people like Carrie Logan.

'Emma should've come to watch the race too, let her hair down,' said Alex.

Millie leant in closely and whispered again, 'She wouldn't. I asked. Emma's too frightened that man they owe all that money to might be in the Falls.'

Alex wished Finn had thumped him harder.

'Where's my buddy Alfie?' Jem asked.

'There he is!' Poppy pointed towards one of the stalls selling eggs. *Loki's Yolkies* read the sign stuck to the front of the table. Mal had Alfie on his shoulders and was teetering towards them, a large tray of mucky eggs in his hands. Another car horn sounded aggressively up on the road by The Cavern and Malcolm squinted in that direction.

'Someone's dropped a clanger. That bridge was supposed to be controlled traffic but the new guy was too busy getting dressed up to give the OK. Take these, Mils, I'm going to have to get something sorted up there, before someone's flattened.'

Millie took the eggs while Alfie reluctantly dismounted

his father's head. Alfie grimaced. He looked so much like Dill now it was hard for Alex to take her eyes off him. Alex felt Jem squeeze her arm.

'Hello again, Alfie,' Alex said. 'Hi, Mal.' Jem set Norma back down on the grass for Alfie and Poppy to fuss.

'Hey, Alex.' Mal gave half a smile and Alex caught a glimpse of that dimple again.

Would this have been how Dill would've looked now? His darker genes kicked in, like Mal? Alex held a hand out. She wasn't sure why, but a hug seemed the wrong choice. By Alex's miscalculations, Mal had been her half-brother for a few days. She'd got it wrong. But at the very least, they still shared one in Dill.

Mal took Alex's hand and, in a handshake, everything that needed to be said and unsaid – about their parents, their brother – was there in their hands.

'Can we take her for a walk *pleeaase*?' Alfie asked, big dark eyes chasing Dill from his features. Alex straightened his little red baseball cap.

'I'm not sure, kiddo. Norma's a big naughty, if she sees someone she likes she might try to make a run for it.'

The Tannoy boomed and the crowds turned like parishioners to face the new Mayor, but the sound system wasn't working properly so no-one could hear him.

Disgruntled voices rippled out across the crowd. Alex watched Mal concentrating on the successor to his father's throne. Whatever discoveries had been made about Mayor Sinclair, he was still Mal's dad. 'The new mayor doesn't have nearly as much charisma as his predecessor, Mal,' Alex offered.

'Thank you, Alex. I appreciate that.' Mal nodded. 'Right, I'll catch you all in a while.' Mal planted kisses on Millie and Alfie. 'Keep those ruffians away from your mother, Alfred,' he said, setting an egg firmly in Alfie's eager hand. Alfie nodded his head seriously.

A klaxon fired and the crowds began to cheer, waiting for the first signs of homemade rafts to come floating down the Old Girl.

'There you are! Come on, gang, we're all set up!' George said, appearing beside Millie. 'We're sat on a blanket and everything. Phil doesn't *do* damp bottoms,' George said theatrically.

'Who's Phil?' Millie asked, ushering the children after George who'd picked Norma up and was already striding gracefully into the crowd.

'Philippa,' she called over her shoulder. My cousin. She's here with her chap, Carter, and their friends. They've just adopted two brothers.'

'Who, your cousin?'

'God no,' George called back over her shoulder. 'Carter can't tie his own shoelaces. Their friends, Amy and Rohan.'

Alex and Jem followed George to a large picnic blanket where a group of adults and three kids were waving flags in anticipation of the first raft to come down river. Alex hung back leaving Jem to do most of the meeting and greeting, they were George's people, and now they were Jem's too.

One of their group, a man with crazy curly hair, was asking what the eggs were for. Millie was explaining in her school teacher voice.

'So the idea is, we're the Saxons, and we've got to pelt the invaders before they get to conquer our lands. Or in this case, the plastic finish line over there being held by the women from the WI.'

'Ah, man! We're going to need some of those then!' the guy with the hair yipped.

'I'll get them,' Alex volunteered. 'I was going for more eggs anyway.' She smiled. She wasn't in the chatting mood, not since Jem had mentioned Finn. 'Back in a sec.'

Alex disappeared into the mass of bodies, yelling now as the first couple of rafts were getting bombarded with eggy missiles by the spectators lining the bank. The first raft was being manned by a *Viking* with a skinhead. The second by a chap at least a foot shorter than Finn. Alex went back to the task at hand.

'Just a dozen, thanks.'

Next to the egg stall, Eilidh's nursing home had cordoned off an area for the residents to watch the festivities. Alex smiled at the row of people, their little white heads like a formation of cotton balls, wafting in the fresh air.

Alex pulled a note from her bag and paid Loki for his yolkies. The Tannoy crackled and Alex joined the crowd in turning to face the voice. Alex experienced a small surge of adrenalin. Carrie Logan had appeared on the bridge, all shiny and sleek for the occasion, a couple of less shiny, less sleek friends flanking her like two slices of stodgy bread around a piece of cheap ham.

'Like a man in furs, do you?' George had appeared at Alex's side. She was looking to the mayor, rabbiting into his mic.

'Maybe.' Alex smiled. 'Actually, I was just thinking what an arse Carrie looks with her cronies up there. Fighting to be centre of attention. She used to go to school with my sister,' Alex explained. Jem was worth a hundred of Carrie.

'Carrie? Carrie Logan?' George said. Her smile had evaporated leaving George locked on to the row of faces over the bridge.

'Excuse me, Alex, I'm having a word with that spiteful cow.'

Alex caught George's arm and nearly dropped her eggs. 'George? It was a long time ago. Just leave it.'

'They pinned her down in a classroom and cut all her hair off, Alex. It's going to take a long time for Jem to forget that.'

Alex tightened her grip on George's arm. 'What? But, Jem said…'

George's head furrowed. 'What? That she'd cut her own hair off? Because humiliating yourself at school is *such* fun. You know that she had to sit and lay herself bare to a shrink, because your mum thought that Jem was having some kind of mental breakdown after Dill? Because she couldn't tell anyone what had really happened to her? Because Carrie might out her if she did?'

Alex's mouth had gone dry. Jem had worn a hat for most of the year that followed, when necessity demanded she left the sanctity of her bedroom. Up on the bridge, Carrie was laughing at something the mayor was saying to her. Alex felt her neck aflame. She wasn't used to the taste of anger in her mouth, she was starting to quite like it.

Jem pushed through the crowd to George and Alex and the egg stall. 'Rohan and Amy's little boy is frightened of dogs. Even daft ones like Norma here,' Jem said waving one of Norma's paws. 'Do you two want to go up onto the bridge, get a better view? Ooh, yay… more eggs.'

Alex was ready for a word with Carrie. She'd just imagined dangling Carrie straight off the bridge by her perfectly sleeked ponytail. George looked from Alex to Jem. 'Let's just stay on the bank, Jem,' George said calmly. 'There are too many cars up there for the puppy.'

'OK,' Jem breezed. She got back to watching the rafts run the gauntlet. One in particular had caught her interest. 'Don't look now, Al.'

Alex did look. Finn was riding the river on his dubious looking float with all the finesse of a washing machine tumbling down a hill. He'd tied shards of fabric to the back of his raft so they drifted behind him on the water. She felt a little flip in her stomach at the thought of the last time she'd seen his wet hair plastered across his face like that. Of that rock shelf behind the waterfall, how it had felt pleasantly cool beneath her.

'Actually, I'm going to go. Here, you guys have these,' Alex said, passing the tray of eggs to Jem.

'Alex? Come on, throw an egg at Finn.'

Alex's head suddenly hurt. He'd said that he loved her. He'd stood there and let her dad hurt him again and again. But he wouldn't not say it.

'Dad'll be back at the garage now, Jem. I'm just going to go see Mum,' she tried to say cheerily 'I'll catch you guys later, have fun.'

'Alex. Stop *running*.' Jem looked serious. 'Just talk to him. Isn't he worth at least that?'

Alex shook her head. Finn was worth so much more than that. 'Do you ever think that maybe it's for *his* benefit, Jem? That I just stay away? He's the one who always ends up bleeding. Do you know what it's like to see him that way? Knocked down, over and over, and know it's my fault?'

'It's not your fault that he keeps getting back up for more, Alex! That's his choice and you're trying to stop him from making it! Finn wants to stand his ground. Isn't that what you do for the people you love? Fight for them?' George was looking at her boots, trying to blend into the rest of the world.

Alex could feel her chest heaving with angry uncertainty. 'Because someone always gets hurt, Jem! When I'm with him, someone *always* gets hurt!'

Norma whimpered. Alex was vaguely aware that several spectators were now tuning in to the Jem and Alex show.

Jem put her hands on Alex's arms. 'What the hell do you need, Alex. Before you'll get it? A sodding *sign*?'

Alex wasn't angry at Jem, she was angry at herself, and Mayor Sinclair, and the Old Girl, and Carrie Logan and her asshole mates. But Jem was the one doing the prodding. Alex snatched her arms back with a fierce shrug.

'You know what, Jem? That's *exactly* what I'm waiting for. A sodding *sign*.' Alex heard herself laugh wildly. 'I want a bolt of *sodding* lightning to find me out, right now in this crowd, an apology from the god damned universe for *all* the crap it's thrown in our path. A bloody good omen, just so I know for *sure* that, ACTUALLY! This is all just spot on because I'm *meant* to be still out of my mind crazy bad for Joseph Finn!' she hissed flamboyantly.

Jem straightened. Alex had run out of breath. George looked decidedly awkward. Well, she might as well know now what she was getting into with Jem's lot.

It had gone quiet in their little circle by the egg stall. The new Mayor was asking Carrie and her friends over the microphone to tell the crowd which Viking they were backing. Carrie tittered like a schoolgirl through the speaker system. 'Well, Mayor Jones, we at *Wallflowers Weddings and Floral Design* like to remain impartial...'

That's it, Carrie. Get your advertising in.

Finn was just navigating himself under the river bridge, he'd been hit by as many eggs as the rest of them. 'You want to see me fight for someone I love, Jem?'

Alex picked up a few eggs and turned her body towards

the river. She twisted herself and sized up her target. Alex snapped her arm, releasing the first egg hard enough that she felt an unpleasant yank in her shoulder socket. She missed. She didn't care, it had helped her adjust her aim. She made sure the second two eggs were better. The mayor was a necessary casualty. But Carry had taken most of the overshoot. The third egg found her out nicely, clipping the top of the river bridge, throwing Carrie up a faceful of karma.

Alex was breathing heavily through her nostrils. A few audible gasps in various pockets of the crowd began rippling into light-hearted sniggers. Jem and George wore similar expressions on their faces, wordless mouths hung open in surprise.

'What the… THIS IS *HUGO BOSS*!' Carrie protested over the mic. Alex cupped a hand to her mouth and yelled over the tourists. 'Sorry, Carrie Logan, of *Wallflower Weddings and crappy Floral Design*! I should've got my sister to aim. *I* throw like a *girl!*' she shouted coldly.

George grinned.

'Alex? What the hell are you doing?'

'Humiliating her, hopefully.' If only a little bit.

The mayor made a joke about no-one liking shameless advertising and a rubbishy quip about egg on his face. Carrie was already slithering off into the crowd. Alex felt strangely exhilarated. Then the next invader made it to the finish line.

Finn was paddling his way over to where the river shelved. He jumped into the last few feet of water and waded to the embankment, spectators and a few frisky WI members slapping his back while he began untying his banners.

'You can start a turf war with an egg, but you can't just go and talk to him, Al?' Jem looked at her hopefully but Alex could feel the fight evaporating from her bloodstream.

Finn didn't look like he had any fight left in him either. He looked exhausted. Alex tried not to watch him, stepping through the spectators towards them. Water was streaking down his cheeks, just like it had up at the gorge. If Alex hadn't known to look at his lip, she might not have noticed the swelling her father had put there. Jem was deliberately silent when he reached them.

'Well done,' Alex croaked. 'For making the whole run.'

'Thanks.' Finn smiled self-consciously at George and Jem. A silence began to grow amongst their odd quartet. Norma whined again.

Say something, Alex. Just say something. She could see the cut in his lip now.

'I need to go get cleaned up.' Finn said. He nodded a *bye* and moved past Alex without further comment.

Jem nudged her.

'Finn, wait!' Alex called. Finn took a few more steps then turned lethargically. He was worn down. She had worn him down. 'Do you… want to throw some eggs with us?' she said clumsily. *Throw some eggs? Do you want to throw some eggs?*

Jem bit her lip and looked away. Finn exhaled deeply. 'No. Alex. I don't want to throw some eggs with you. But thank you for the grand offer.'

Her face felt tingly and uncomfortable. 'Finn? Or we could grab something for—'

'No. Thank you.' His mouth had tensed, his skin was breaking out in goosebumps while Alex kept him here with her bumbling nonsense. 'I don't want to throw eggs, Alex. I don't want to grab anything to eat. I didn't want a drink at The Cavern or a Valhalla burger last night if I'm honest with you, *which* by the way I have been at every opportunity.' Alex felt herself shrink. That tingling in her face was getting hotter. 'I just wanted to hang out with you, Alex. That's it. That's all. Anywhere you wanted, I'd have gone.'

Alex stood numbed to the spot. Finn shook his head like he was annoyed at himself, then turned to walk away. He stopped. Alex watched him turn back again. His tanned face was turning an annoyed pink blush. 'You know what, Alex? I really hope your mum gets better soon, and then you can hurry back to your little safety zone, and you won't have to worry about getting your feet wet, or little bees in your hair or anyone embarrassing you by telling your dad how much they feel about you.'

'You didn't embarrass me,' she said. But her voice sounded small and feeble.

'No? You sure about that? Because when I sat down and thought about it last night, it finally occurred to me that that's *exactly* what I do to you, Alex. I embarrass you.'

George shifted uncomfortably beside her. One of the spectators listening in made a little sound of disapproval.

'You don't embarrass me, Finn.' How could he think that? How had she let him think that?

Finn shook his head and strode back over the grass towards her, water dripping off his hair in great wet ribbons along his face. 'So it would be OK then, would it? If I give you my banner? Tied it around you and claimed you as my own, Alex?' He laughed. There was a hard edge to his voice that made Alex want to look away from him. He stepped towards her, one of the coloured flags from his boat hanging limp from his hand. 'Can I claim you as my own, or would you be too ashamed to go home and tell your daddy?'

He was being hurtful. Deliberately hurtful. He'd never done that before. Finn's eyes were burning. Alex felt her bottom lip fighting not to wobble.

'I'm not ashamed of you, Finn. You could never embarrass me.' Although he was coming a little bit close to it right now.

Finn smiled. He didn't say a word. She saw him reach towards her, soaking wet and taut with the things he wanted to get off his chest, and, for a foolish moment, Alex thought he was going to throw her in the Old Girl. His arms moved easily around her waist, the backs of her legs, and he lifted her as effortlessly as he'd lifted her behind the waterfall. The crowd throbbed with a collective cheer, they thought this was all part of the festivities.

Alex felt him scoop her up, the wet from his clothes

seeping into hers, an old lady clapped excitedly from the old people's home area. Then he threw her over his shoulder to the delight of the watching tourists.

'Put me down, Finn.'

'Go on! That's how you show 'em,' one spectator shouted.

'Get her home in front of that sink!' cheered another.

'Did Vikings have sinks?' a woman nearby asked.

Finn was turning around for the crowd, presenting Alex backside-first for them all to see.

'Finn, put me down!' She thought he was about to, he'd moved his hands to another position, but he slipped her back into his arms like he was about to carry her over some invisible threshold.

'Go on, then, invader! Stop flirting and give her your banners!'

Alex looked up at him and felt her eyes burn as angrily as Finn's were. And then he leant down and heatedly pressed a kiss to her mouth.

The tourists around them erupted, Alex heard several giggles and claps and camera phones going off and a quiet 'holy shit' from Jem. But Finn didn't stop kissing her until he thought he'd made his point.

Alex tried to keep a hold of her anger, but it wasn't enough. She could feel herself starting to slip into the abyss, tumbling down to reach feelings that had only ever risen in her for him. For Finn. And then like that, he set her back down again on the grass.

'That was definitely worth the drive up here,' someone

said. 'Do all the invaders do that? When's the next one coming downriver?'

'Ooh, wait, he'll give her his banner now! It's so romantic!'

Finn was staring at her, oblivious to the crowd he'd drawn. Then he turned and walked away. Alex swallowed. She watched Finn give his banner to one of the delighted old ladies from the nursing home. She rewarded Finn with a peck on the cheek and a quick squeeze of his bicep. Alex wished he'd just thrown her in the river.

'Alex, are you OK?' Jem said quietly.

'Yo, George! Where did you get this t-shirt for me from? Did they have them in any other colours?' The guy with the bushy hair had walked right into them. 'Helluva shot, by the way.' he said turning to Alex. 'That aim was *mental*!' He hadn't seen the second show Alex had put on then. 'So, George? Where can I get me a few more of these tees, dude?'

Jem came quietly over her shoulder. 'You said you wanted a sign, Al.' Jem nodded at the guy with the bushy hair.

Alex felt dazed. She looked at George's lively friend. He was wearing a piece of merchandise some enterprising local had knocked up with just a simple slogan and a couple of iconic symbols, synonymous with the god of thunder. 'Simply *Thor*geous' his t-shirt read, alongside the image of a mallet, and because thunder was tricky to convey pictorially, a huge golden bolt of lightning.

CHAPTER 59

Alex found her dad sleeping in the office at the back of Foster's Autos. Apparently he couldn't burn the candle at both ends. An all-day bender followed by a dip in the river, a heart-to-heart with his daughter, an omelette challenge and a morning visit to Blythe was ever so slightly too much for a man in his sixties.

Alex leant against the doorframe watching him, a strange calmness in her body.

He was almost completely grey now. His face was softening with age, the hands that had thrown them all as children effortlessly into the air above the water at the plunge pools now worn and gnarled. She would love her father until the end of her days. That had never changed.

Ted's eyes opened. Love was unconditional, wasn't it?

'Hi, Dad. Can we talk?'

Ted pretended not to startle, rubbing at the tiredness in his greying face.

'Alex, hell, I must've dozed off,' he said, as if it was the first time in his life that he'd caught forty winks back here. 'What is it? Has the hospital called?'

Alex shook her head. 'No, Dad. Everything is OK.'

She'd had to tell him once that she'd hit a stone with her tennis racket and somehow it had pinged off and cracked a pane in next door's greenhouse. Her dad had seen the whole thing but had still waited for Alex to pluck up the courage to tell him. He'd said Alex had looked guilty before the stone had even hit the glass.

'Alexandra? What is it?'

'I don't want to upset you, Dad. I love you.'

Ted shifted in his chair. 'And I love you. Always the same. Never changes.'

Alex locked her dad's words into her mind, squirrelling them away in case they were the last ones she was going to get to keep, and then she let it come. 'But you don't know who I am, Dad.'

'You're my little girl. That's all I need to know.'

But that wasn't all he needed to know. Alex didn't want to be loved because she did a smashing job of hiding how she felt for Finn, any more than Jem wanted to be loved because she'd never told them she was in love with George. That wasn't love. Love was warts and all.

'I love him, Dad.'

Ted looked awake now, ice blue eyes giving the only colour to his face.

Alex breathed slow and steady. 'I'm not asking you to approve of it, Dad. But I am asking you to acknowledge it. I love Finn. I believe that I always will. And when I leave here, I'm going to tell him.'

Not because she was expecting anything from him. She wasn't. She'd burned that bridge one too many times. 'I think he deserves to know the way he makes me feel. He deserves to know that I'm not ashamed to say it now, not even to you.'

Ted cleared his throat. He wasn't going to see it. He couldn't bring himself to see the man Finn was. 'I didn't come here to disappoint you, Dad. Or to let you down in any way. But this is something I should have told you, something I should've stood up for, before I first left the Falls. And when Mum's better and I've gone back to work and I don't see Finn again for another decade or more, at least he'd have heard me say it out loud. Instead of me loving him in secret.'

Ted's fingers were resting over his moustache. His eyes hadn't left Alex's once. She felt her chin tremble and tried to clear her throat the way her dad did. He looked as dumfounded as Alex had been with Finn on the riverbank just now. 'I'll leave you to it then, Dad.' Alex turned and stepped out through the office door into the cool dark of the garage. A voice followed her into the gloom.

'I almost lost your mother once.'

Alex stood still. Ted's voice sounded thin and tight behind her. 'Almost lost the love of my life, because I'd been distracted. Stopped telling her how I felt about her.'

Alex's heart began to thump gently. This hadn't been in her plan, she hadn't wanted to hear any truths in return. He'd been too drunk to remember the things he'd let slip about her mum's affair and Jem and Alex were happy for him to still think he'd held on to his secret. Alex looked over her shoulder. He was standing in the doorway behind her.

'Dad—'

'Let me finish Alex. Your mother's not perfect, but she's a damned sight closer than most. And I'll never love another woman the way I love Blythe, not if I lived my life a hundred times over. But there was a time I didn't tell your mother enough just how much I love her. And then I made the same mistake again, and I didn't tell you enough either.'

Alex was holding her breath, she felt a bit queasy.

'I love you, Alexandra. And that boy Finn is right to love you too. And if you love him like you say you do, you'd better go tell him.'

CHAPTER 60

Alex walked out the yard entrance to the growing sounds of panicky folk music and made a left onto the high street in a daze. The boat race must be drawing to end, the road looked clearer of people down towards the Cavern end of town, everyone seemed to be migrating up here towards the terrace where hog-roasts and mountains of root vegetables had been staged for a rustic banquet. Alex read the banner that had been stretched between two of the trees peppering the terrace. *Feast With The Victorious Vikings!*

Alex's mobile vibrated in her shorts pocket. Jem had insisted they all keep their phones on today in case anyone got lost in the crowd. Like they couldn't just walk back to the house or something. Alex flipped open her message.

Manic Monday! Dishwasher's kaput! Having a mental breakdown! When are you coming baaaaack?

Alex smiled and tapped out a reply.

Hey buster. Should know more after hosp. this afternoon but Mum on mend, responding well to treatment, thnk gdnss.

Will be back before you know it. Just tying up a few ends. A x'

The loose end in question was just stepping out of his hardware shop. Alex slipped her phone back into her pocket and waited for a chance to cross.

Finn was locking the door when she reached him, a roll of brown paper sandwiched under his arm. She'd been home for a fortnight and not once had she seen the inside of his shop.

Alex waited for him to turn around. He'd changed his clothes, a grey long sleeved t-shirt over cargo pants.

Finn turned. He stood there silently

'Hi. Do you have a minute?'

Finn's mouth drew into a hardened line. 'I have to get back. I have someone coming to collect his commission. I just came back for something to wrap it in,' he said, nodding at his roll of paper.

'It won't take a minute. I just have something I need to say to you, Finn, and then I'll leave you in peace.'

He still looked serious, his eyes narrow and guarded where they used to be full of frivolous laughter She'd put that look there just as she'd put that cut on his lip.

Finn puffed his cheeks like a teenager. 'Alex. Let's just…'

'I'm sorry, Finn. For not speaking up last night. For never speaking up. You've always deserved so much better than people gave you. Better than I ever gave you.'

He looked caught off guard. Unsure. A group of teenage

girls walked past them on the kerb and giggled at Alex's pal-
try street performance.

'Do you want to go somewhere quieter?' Finn asked. The
high street was thick with people, Alex did a sweep and
recognised many of the faces she'd grown up with, the Reverend toddling alongside a cavalcade of wheelchairs users
from the care home, Hamish shaking his head at a car going
too fast, Millie waiting to cross the road with the children.

'Alex?' Finn pressed. 'Do you want to talk in private?'

Alex composed herself. 'No. What I have to say, I can
say here.' Anywhere, in fact. Alex went to continue but Finn
had spotted something over her shoulder. Alex looked back
to where Millie and the children were waiting. Had Jem left
the dog with them? Norma was trying to wriggle out of her
collar.

'Hang on, Alex. I think Millie's struggling, the pup's tan-
gled herself around Millie's leg, look,' Finn observed.

Millie was trying to free herself without loosening her
hold on either Alfie or Poppy's hands while Alfie desperately held on to Norma's lead.

'Hang on, Millie!' Alex called over. 'I'll give you a hand.'
But she hadn't thought until it was too late. Norma looked
up with Millie, saw Alex standing across the street and
determinedly yanked her head from her collar. Alex didn't
hear the vehicle coming down through the bend, and she
didn't see little Alfie Sinclair drop his mother's hand. She
only had time to stare, uselessly as Norma, and then at a lit-

tle boy in a danger-red baseball cap, darted out into the traffic.

*

Ted had only been listening to Hamish reel off the results of the river race for a minute or two before he thought he'd seen a ghost. Ted couldn't see much of the child under that red cap, but there was something in his profile, the way his mouth was set in concentration. Ted saw Helen Fairbanks' girl and realised whose child, whose grandchild, he'd been looking at.

'Here comes another one, flying into town,' Hamish said behind him, but Ted had already started to break away. He'd seen it unfurling before the child's mother had spotted the danger. Ted broke into a run just as the dog made a run into the road. He heard a young woman's voice cry out but the little boy with the familiar face was already stepping off the kerb.

He launched himself across the first lane but Ted had raised enough children to know that kids could be just like puppies, too quick to catch. He hadn't checked what might've been coming behind him. He'd simply run for him, charging out after the late mayor's grandson, grabbing out clumsily, desperately, until he could feel the boy's soft little body change trajectory with the force of his own. A flash of burgundy squealed in front of them, something slammed hard into Ted's side.

Then just the cold stark sounds of metal and glass.

CHAPTER 61

'It's all right, Dad. Let us just take a look at him, OK?' Alex could hear the shake in her voice.

'Did you see that? Did you see it? How did they not get hit? *Two* cars! The old fella dodged *two* cars!' someone said.

She was looking for red, but all Alex could find was one superficial graze on Alfie's elbow that must've already been there because it had scabbed already. The only blood belonged to her father, and Finn, and the grazes they'd shared between them.

Alex hadn't seen Finn move from where they'd been standing. Just a blur beside her, and then the next thing the blue car had been there in front of her, nearly on the pavement, and Finn had disappeared the other side of it.

They'd just been lying there in a heap when Alex's legs had figured out how to function again and she'd scrambled over all that glass to get to them. Two grown men, and a little boy somewhere between them.

Millie was standing in shock, white and still. Poppy was crying, big rounded sobs, her hand still clamped in Millie's because that was the rule when you were charged with the care of another person's child – you made sure they got home in one piece.

'Ted? Shall we let his mum take over?' Finn said gently.

Finn was sitting on his backside, inspecting the knuckles he'd lost all the skin from but Alex's father still hadn't loosened his grip on Alfie. Alex remembered her dad taking her to watch *A Christmas Carol* at the theatre. The ghost of Christmas Present had lifted his robe and an ashen-faced child had peeped out from underneath. Alex thought of that as she looked at her father now, holding Alfie in his arms.

'Dad?'

Alex watched Finn pat Ted's hand before carefully unpeeling his fingers from Alfie. 'He needs to be checked,' Ted said to Finn, 'the boy's got a butterfly heart.'

A crowd had formed a circle around them in the middle of the high street. Someone had hold of Norma.

'We'll get him checked, Ted,' Finn reassured him. 'Are you hurt?'

Ted shook his head although he'd lost about the same amount of skin from his right cheek as Finn had from his hands. The first car had swerved to miss Norma. Alex had seen that much. But she hadn't seen how her dad had gotten to Alfie from the other side before the car coming in the opposite direction had been hit by the first. It was as if those two cars had cancelled each other out, balanced the equation, and at the centre of it all, in the eye of the storm, Finn and her father had kept Alfie Sinclair safe.

Finn got slowly to his feet. 'Alex? Take Millie and the

children inside the shop. So they can't see.' Because Finn knew how haunting that could be.

Finn was looking at what was still discernible of the burgundy car. Another circle of onlookers had formed over where the event paramedic had thought his capabilities were more needed. Alex could just see where the windscreen had been punched through from the inside. The driver of the blue car had already been helped into Brünnhilde's Baps for an icepack.

Finn touched her elbow and moved his thumb over her skin. 'Go on. I'll keep an eye on your dad.'

Alex nodded and began rustling Millie and the children towards Finn's shop. Someone with pretend blonde braids hanging either side of his ears was standing on top of the pavement litter bin to see what was happening in the other circle. 'Not looking good. The guy who was doing the CPR, he's just pulled one of the flags down from the lamppost and put it over the big guy. That's dude's dead.'

CHAPTER 62

'I thought I recognised the car,' Finn said as the nurse finished off bandaging his hands. 'I saw it on Emma Parsons' driveway, the day we helped her with her unwanted guest.' Mal was leaning back against the stainless steel hand basin. He still looked as grey-faced as he had when he'd arrived on the scene and Millie had burst into tears.

'I know. I checked the registration. It's Emma's husband's car. Same car he had dropped on his chest in the *accident* Emma was trying to convince me of.'

'But he's still in hospital,' Alex said. 'Emma's husband is still in hospital.'

'So who was driving his car then?' Finn asked.

'Driver's license says a *Mr Eric Mason*. Big fella. Looks like the Parsons' unwanted guest came back to collect his money.'

'The loan shark? He helped himself to their car instead?' asked Alex.

'Only the Parson's car wasn't roadworthy. Emma said her husband had been checking a brake fluid leak when Mr Mason had last been *speaking* to her husband. And, of course, Mr Parsons didn't finish the job on account of the jack somehow giving way on him. Emma wouldn't have had to walk all this way to the hospital every day with her girls, otherwise,' Mal said.

'Is he dead?' Alex asked. Definitely, dead.

Mal looked at the nurse, they exchanged a look professionals gave fellow professionals. 'I'm afraid I really can't say, until next of kin have been informed.'

The nurse rolled his eyes. 'I'll leave you to it,' he said, excusing himself from the room.

Mal glanced over at Alex. 'I just need to get a statement from your dad, now.'

'He's in the end cubicle, with Jem. She made him get checked out.'

Jem had nearly had a meltdown when she'd reached all the flashing lights and saw Ted being ordered into the back of one of the ambulances. Alex had heard her saying to George something about 'no more waiting'.

Finn eased himself up off the gurney. 'Thanks, chief,' he called after the nurse. 'That's my painting sideline... *sidelined.*'

'You'll heal,' Alex offered. Finn always did.

Alex saw something ping into Finn's head. 'I need to get to a phone, I've got a Mr McQueen coming out to pick up a portrait of a black lab puppy.'

'Not Leonard McQueen?' Mal asked

Finn winced. 'That's right.'

'What are the chances, huh? He's just getting his head

stitched. He was our man in the blue Ford, with all the blood pouring down his face. Those head wounds, they bleed like a bugger. Of course, Mr McQueen might not have had that head injury if he hadn't have worked so hard to miss my son.' Mal took a huge breath. 'One of my colleagues is just waiting to talk to him now, so don't go rushing back to meet him.'

'Are you all right, Mal?' Alex asked.

Mal's face was fighting something back. 'Thanks again, Finn. For getting to Alfie... I don't know what might've—'

Finn held two bandaged hands up. 'Mal, forget it. To be honest, I'm not as quick on the old feet as I used to be,' Finn winced, 'Ted Foster got to him first.'

Mal nodded sombrely. 'Ted's my next stop.' Mal opened the door and waited for Alex and Finn to walk through it.

'Mal? Do you mind if I just have a minute with Finn, please?' Alex asked.

Mal disappeared onto the A&E corridor. Alex felt her nerves jangle.

'I told you to get a better collar,' Finn said.

'What are you saying, I'm responsible?' The thought had crossed Alex's mind already.

Finn came to stand in front of her. His bandaged hand like a boxing glove as he used it to lift Alex's chin. He tried with the other bandaged hand to move the hair from out of her eyes but after a couple of attempts he just started laughing. Alex grinned at him then, she couldn't help it.

Finn grimaced. Alex saw the cut on his lip had opened again. He dabbed it with the back of his bandage. 'I don't think you're responsible, Alex,' he said more seriously. 'That stuff just happens. Unless you engineered it all to get out of finishing what it was you were trying to say to me, before all hell broke loose?'

Finn went to smile again and stopped himself before his lip pulled. Over the subtle aromas of antiseptic and cotton swabs, Alex could smell him. The sweetness she knew she'd find at his neck if ever she found herself back there again. She felt even more self-conscious about it now, it had seemed easier somehow to say it with hundreds of people milling around them.

Finn was hanging back, waiting for Alex to come good. Waiting to see if she would. 'I just wanted to tell you, Finn... That I—'

Finn stepped into her and slid his arms behind her then pressed his mouth over hers. Alex fell into their kiss. She could taste him, the saltiness of effort left on his skin after jumping to Alfie's aid, the sweetness of the cut her father had put there when this gentle delicious mouth had spoken the words she still hadn't spoken back. She fell into that kiss and never wanted to come up for air again.

'Sorry to interrupt, guys, but we need this room back. Ingrowing toenail, pretty sure you don't want to hang around for that.' Finn held Alex where she was, lips still pressed together and cocked an eye at the nurse, smiling in the doorway. Across the corridor, Alex saw Jem and her dad sitting on a hospital bed, hugging one another. She broke from Finn. 'Hold that thought, would you?'

Alex stepped out of the treatment room. Jem was walking away from the cubicle Ted was in. 'Is everything all right? Did they say if he's suffering from shock?' Alex asked.

Jem set her hands on her hips and twisted herself to have another look at him. He was already pulling the dressing from his scuffed cheek. 'Actually… no. He isn't.'

'Are you OK, Jem?'

Jem nodded animatedly. Their mother did that too, when Blythe cried at her operas and someone asked her if she was all right, because you had to be mildly insane to cry at a piece of music the way Blythe did.

'Oh my God, you've told him.'

Jem's eyes were welling up. She started to laugh. 'I thought the hospital was as good a place as any to tell him about George, in case he keeled over. Or I did.'

'And?' Alex was feeling a little shocky.

Jem looked spun out. 'He said that Mum told him years ago, before I went to uni.'

'But… you said you hadn't told her.'

'I didn't. Not a soul apart from Mal. Mum just… knew. A bit of an anti-climax, really. George said it would be. Best anti-climax *ever.*' Jem moved into Alex for a hug. Alex took in another hit of strawberry lip-gloss. 'Where's George now, Jem?'

'She took Norma and Poppy back to the B&B.' Jem was looking over Alex's shoulder. 'Look at the two of them,

Al. How did they come out that battered when the doctors couldn't find a single scratch on Alfie?'

Alex turned. Ted had just got to his feet, Finn standing casually beside him. 'Because nothing was getting through them that was going to hurt that little boy.'

Ted offered his hand to Finn. Finn offered him his own hand but wrapped in so much dressing, it looked more like a giant earbud. Ted shook it anyway. Jem bobbed her hip into Alex's.

'Thank you. For what you did.'

'No need, Mr Foster. I didn't realise you were going for him too.'

'I'm not talking about what happened today…' Alex saw her dad breathe deeply and take stock. 'I never thanked you for what you did. For my son. And I'm sorry it's took me so long to say it.'

Finn's shoulders dropped. 'I did everything I could, Ted. I swear I did.'

'I know you did, son. And I'm grateful.'

Ted looked up but Alex couldn't stop staring. He looked at her for a few moments, then he turned back to Finn. 'I'm not much of a cook… unless we're talking omelettes. But how about when my wife's back home, you think about coming on up to the house for dinner. Maybe we could put our heads together and come up with a way of getting my daughter back home? Hmm?'

Finn didn't look at Alex, he stayed perfectly set on her dad instead. 'I think that sounds like a plan, Mr Foster.'

'Ted. Call me Ted. Now, if you'll excuse me, before young Officer Sinclair starts interrogating me, I have to go tell my wife that I love her.'

*

'Don't even *think* of climbing on that bed again, Mr Foster,' the nurse warned. 'I know Blythe here is a killer redhead but no more sneaking into bed with her in those overalls, all right? If the Sister catches you, you'll have more than a grazed cheekbone to worry about!'

'What have… you been do-ing?' Blythe asked.

'Dad's a hero, Mum. The *Eilidh Gazette* are after him, aren't they, Dad?' Jem teased.

'I know he is.' Blythe smiled. 'Always was my hero.'

'You're looking really well, Mum.'

'You should see how well she's eating! You keep this up Blythe, and you'll be back to washing oil off your own bed sheets in no time!' the nurse said bustling out.

Blythe looked at each of them, something fretful washed over her. 'I'm glad… you're all here. I've been waiting… to speak to… all of you.'

Alex felt the tension coming off Jem. They'd agreed. No more talk of anything that would sully the memories they all had of Dill. No more hurdles for their family.

'You know what, Mum? Sorry, but it's going to have to wait. We're all talked out, aren't we, Jem?' Jem nodded. 'Dad's already had his ears talked off, so how about we just do the talking hey? While you rest.'

'You look... different.' Blythe frowned. 'All of you... Has something... happened?'

Jem looked at Alex then Ted. Alex patted her mum's hand. 'Nothing's happened, Mum. We're just all ready for you to come home to us. Before Dad kills someone with *omelette a la everything*.'

Blythe's eyes glazed over. 'Mum? What is it?' Jem asked. Ted came to the bottom of the bed and laid a hand on one of Blythe's feet.

'It's just... so wonderful... having you all... together.' She smiled.

Alex laid a kiss on her mother's perfect porcelain skin. 'I'm afraid you're going to have to get used to that, Mum. Because there's going to be a lot more of that from now on.'

CHAPTER 63

2 weeks later

'Never in all my born days have I cried at a piece of music. I shall never be able to hear that, what was it called again?'

'"Casta Diva".' Alex smiled.

'I shall never listen to it again without a box of tissues, I just know it.' Helen's chin was already wobbling again.

'It is a beautiful piece, Helen.' Alex smiled. She'd cried too, but so had Jem, and their dad, and it wasn't Maria Callas who'd taken them all there.

Jem was across the other side of the garden making sure the Reverend was fully refreshed. Blythe would never forgive them if they let the Reverend's glass run low. Alex thought Jem looked pale against her pretty black tailored dress, but George was keeping a close eye on her. Most of their male guests were keeping a closer eye on George.

Helen dabbed her nose again. 'Hearts are funny things, Alexandra darling. Funny things. Oh, Alfie, no you mustn't feed the dog from your plate. I'm not sure bringing him over was the best thing,' Helen whispered, 'but Millie's been so sick again this morning and Malcolm wanted to be here so badly. Go on now, Alfie, go and have a look at the tractors from the end of the garden.'

'No, Helen. I'm glad Alfie's here. He's lifting the mood.' Alex squeezed Helen's elbow and carried on doing the rounds, buy her dad some more time alone over by the tree-swing where he was sneakily sucking on a roll up, watching the tractors collecting in the bales. Alex ran a hand over the poppies while she walked around the perimeter of the porch, smiling politely at their guests. She breathed in the new lavender bushes she'd planted for her mum's home-coming and let it out slow. Helen was right. Hearts were funny things. The funniest of things. *But you didn't die of a broken heart, did you, Mum?*

Finn stepped out of the house doing his best to look comfortable in a suit and a part of the sadness inside Alex lifted.

'Hey.'

Finn set a hand on Alex's hip and kissed her head. 'Hey yourself.'

'Still feel like a penguin?'

'These slacks are still biting into my bits if that's what you mean, Foster?'

Finn gave her a lopsided smile. Alex loved his normal messy ruggedness, but she could get used to this tempo-rary, sleeker version just fine if she had to. 'I had a root around under the stairs but no tennis racquet I'm afraid.' He was going to play lawn tennis with Alfie. Help Mal occupy him while the adults did the adult thing. 'Is there a ball or anything here he can play with? What about Norma's stash?'

Alex held her to him for a few seconds and closed her eyes. Over the lavender, her mum's garden smelled of honey and butter, just as it always had. 'Finn? Do you think a person can die of a mended heart?' Blythe's heart had just stopped beating. Everything had been as it should, she'd come home to a house full of warmth and people and laughter. She'd gone to sleep contentedly next to her husband while Alex and Jem had stayed up embarrassing each other, sharing stories of childhood with George and Finn.

Finn rested his chin on top of Alex's head, she felt the warmth in her hair as he breathed against her. 'Let's hope not, Foster. Or some of us might be toast.' Alex felt the rhythm of his breathing for a few moments. 'Alex?'

'Hmm?'

'There's something I wanted to tell you, the day after the boat race.' There was an uncertainness in Finn's voice. 'But I didn't want to rock the boat. And then your mum came home and—'

'What is it, Finn?'

Finn swallowed and looked down across the lawns to Ted, observing the tractors Alfie was pointing out to him.

'Leonard McQueen.'

'Who?'

Finn squeezed her and exhaled deeply. 'When Alfie ran

into the road. The guy. In the other car. With the blood. I didn't recognise him, I *couldn't*. You saw how covered he was.'

'Finn, you're not making any sense.'

'He was my customer. He was the guy I was supposed to be meeting with the painting, of the black Lab.'

Alex watched something strain in Finn's features. 'I remember. The painting that looked like the Lab puppy you wanted when you were little. Finn, what's worrying you so much?'

'I don't want to mess things up with your dad, Alex.'

'You won't,' Alex said certainly. She wasn't going to let them fall apart ever again. 'Finn, tell me… what is it?'

'I went back to the hospital, Al. To check my customer was OK. They'd cleaned him up, but it still took me a few seconds to recognise him.' Finn dipped his head. 'It had been a long time, Foster. A long time hoping he might come by one day, just to see how I'm doing. He'd given me a false name, in case I wouldn't give him any time.'

'Who, Finn? Who is he?'

Finn chewed agitatedly at his top lip. 'He's my father, Alex. My dad came back.'

Alex watched a few red petals begin to flitter across the lawns where the poppies were bowing to the next season. She was stunned. The only thing left of Martin Finn in the Falls was a bad legacy and a scare-story for would-be gambling addicts.

'Be careful, Finn.'

'I know.'

'Is he still in the Falls?'

'No. He didn't want to put any pressure on me. I haven't even said anything to my mum.'

'And what will you say?'

'I don't know yet. He's sorted himself out. He has a decent job, lives a decent life. But he has a lot of ground to cover, Foster. A lot of time to make up.'

Alex watched her dad across the gardens talking Alfie through the mechanics of the tree-swing. Wasn't that what they were all doing? Making up for lost time?

'He's your dad, Finn. We all deserve to be happy so try not to worry too much about anyone else. Just do what you feel's the right thing. Life's too short not to.'

Finn's hand moved to the back of Alex's head. He kissed her slowly and softly, then laid a chaste kiss on her nose. 'I love you, Foster.'

'I love you too.'

An Aston Martin was just cautiously navigating its way up to the house past all of the cars parked along the track. Finn's head turned to follow it. Alex stiffened. Her dad was still talking to Alfie down by the tree-swing. He finished setting Alfie up for a push and spotted Louisa pulling up outside the garden fencing. Louisa was getting out of her car. Jem was already walking purposefully over towards the gate from where she'd been topping up the Reverend's glass again, but Malcolm had beaten her there.

Alex dropped Finn's hand and walked quickly across the lawn to where Louisa was standing gesticulating at Malcolm.

'Mother, just go home and have a cup of sweet tea. I'll be up to the house later. I'll bring Alfie.'

'I don't want my grandson *here*!' she rasped. 'It's bad enough that *you've* come. You *know* how I feel about these people!'

'Yes, Mother. I know how you feel. Now please try to understand how *I* feel.'

'She was an ungodly woman, Malcolm.' Louisa's face contorted beneath her expensive makeup and Alex felt something like pity for her.

Ted was walking up the lawn looking just as uncomfortable in his black trousers and freshly starched shirt as Finn, but Alfie was clinging to his neck and seemed to make Ted look blissfully at ease at the same time.

Alex felt her heart patter. From here, it was just like looking at her dad carrying Dill up the lawn. Maybe Ted's fondness for the little boy lay somewhere therein; Alfie and Dill were blood, after all.

Louisa watched Alex's dad carry Alfie, her face closing down like she were made of something mechanical. 'Malcolm, you take my grandson off that man's shoulders and get him away from this… this… *family*.'

'Now hold on right there, Louisa. Finn? Would you mind taking young Alfie here up to my son's bedroom? Let him choose something to play with. Anything he likes.'

'Sure thing.' Finn said, sitting Alfie onto his shoulders. 'Come on, little bud.'

Ted waited for Alfie to leave while the flush crept higher up Louisa's neck.

'Malcolm?' Louisa implored.

'This family are mine and Millie's friends, Mother. And Helen's. And Alfie's too.'

'You are *not* paying any more *respects* to this woman,' Louisa snarled under her breath. Alex saw her dad stiffen. Louisa was about to blow it. She was about to publicly wipe Ted's nose in it, in front of his own children.

Ted's shoulders relaxed. He straightened and gave the sky, then the gardens and all the visitors milling around in them a long, easy look. He looked at Mal, then Jem and Alex and finally, Louisa. 'There's no more damage to be done here Louisa. Let it go.'

'Let it *go*? I will not—'

'By all means, stay, join us for a cocktail sausage. But I won't have you badmouth the mother of my children. My beautiful wife, Blythe.'

Alex's heart was thumping. They'd worked so hard not to let this spill out where it would hurt Ted any more. Alex, Jem and Mal had all agreed, Ted would never have to suffer the indignity of knowing that they all knew. Dillon wasn't his biological son, but it didn't matter. They could *pretend*. They could all pretend, and Mal would keep his new brother quietly and safely in his heart, that was the only way forwards for them all and now Louisa was going to ruin it.

'She was an ungodly woman,' Louisa repeated slowly. Louisa was going to blow it all out in the open whatever they did.

Ted shook his head at the lawn. 'Louisa, you'd better get your stuck up ass back in that car of yours and go on your way, before you get hurt.'

'Ted,' Mal interjected.

'You're going to assault me then, Ted Foster? In front of all of these people?'

Ted shook his head again and laughed quietly to himself. 'No, Louisa. I'm going to tell you how much I loved that woman. How *easy* it was to love her, how lucky I was to share my life with somebody who was the absolute opposite of a woman like you. How easy it was for the *mayor* to love her too, and how I can't blame your husband one bit for doing so.'

Louisa's mouth hung open as if she were about to regurgitate something nasty. Her own sword had been used against her. Jem looked ashen. Alex could feel a tightness in her chest. But Ted, Ted was as calm as the Old Girl on a lazy morning.

Malcolm looked away over the fence. Jem squeezed his arm. 'Go home, Mum. It's time we all learned to move on.'

'I'm sorry, son,' Ted said to Malcolm. 'It wasn't my intention to bring any of this up in front of you kids.'

Mal nodded. 'It wasn't my intention to cause my mother to turn up here, Mr Foster. I'm sorry.'

'Sorry?' Louisa spat. 'Malcolm, how can you choose

these people?' Jem moved towards Louisa but Alex shot out
a hand to stop her.

Mal shook his head. He moved to Louisa and held her
softly by the arms. 'I choose them, Mum, because they take
their knocks and they stick together. They fight against the
current to be who they are.' Ted squinted and nodded at his
shoes. 'Go home, Mum.' Mal said. 'Go and sit in the garden
and enjoy this beautiful afternoon.'

Louisa seemed dazed as she hobbled back to the car.
But she hobbled back nonetheless. Even Jem's hostility
had morphed into something more compassionate as Louisa
rolled away.

Ted kissed Jem and put a reassuring hand on Alex's back,
patting her like he had at the Tower House Theatre when she
was little. 'Mal?'

'Yeah, Ted?' Mal said quietly.

'See if you can catch up with your boy. There's a fine set
of bow and arrows in Dillon's bedroom that could do with
a fine young lad to try them out, if you're happy for him
to? I could set him up a target right down there next to the
tree-swing. Do you think he'd like that?'

*

Alex watched her mother's wake fall into something else,
something warmer than just the saying of goodbyes. The
September sun bathed the last dwindling numbers of them
in evening warmth while the stories they shared grew long
like the shadows.

Jem had just seen the last cousins on Blythe's side into their car when she came skipping back.

'Hey, what have you got there?' Alex asked, looking at the case in Jem's hands.

'I don't know, Aunty Carol said she'd found it at Granny Ros's house, after they cleared it all out years back. It was in that pink kiddy music recorder we used to play with at her house, remember the one with the big plastic purple micro-phone and the fruit pastille stuck in the battery bit?'

Alex looked at the CD in Jem's hands. 'Bloody hell, Jem, can you imagine what's on there?'

'Celine Dion!' they said in unison.

Jem giggled. 'That was a big number, Gran said we'd killed *Titanic* for her, do you remember?'

'Let's have a listen,' Alex said.

Jem smiled and turned towards the porch where Ted was playing another game of backgammon with Finn. 'Whip Dad's Phil Collins out of that CD player, Finn. We've got something here that'll really make your ears bleed.'

Alex could already feel the squeamishness kicking in. Finn was about to taste the Jem and Alex experience, circa 1998 when their recording careers were going full bore thanks to the marvels of a Fisher Price karaoke recorder with playback function.

Alex sat next to Jem on the porch steps and cringed while the CD whizzed to start.

It hadn't even occurred to them, Aunty Carol had given no warning.

The recording started. Her voice was like cut glass. Pure, strong, arresting to ears that could recognise it anywhere. Blythe's effortless melody rang out from that stereo while they all sat, unmoving, Blythe's faultless voice filling the air around them. They listened as Jem's seven-year-old voice interrupted her mother's.

'Can you sing something else, Mummy? Me and Alex like the *Titanic* song.'

'That was really good, Mum. I think you can even sing better than Celine can,' Alex heard herself say earnestly.

Another voice cut in over Alex's. 'Mummy, Mummy, Mummy!' Alex watched her dad take a sharp intake of breath. Jem began softly crying beside her on the steps.

'Uh-oh,' Alex heard her mum say, 'I think someone's baby brother wants to have a turn, what would you like to sing, Dill?'

Alex felt a few tears fall over her cheek and flicked them away. Finn was watching her. She tried to smile at him and more spilled over her eyes.

'I don't want to sing, Mummy.' Dill's words sounded rounded and pudgy, like his little body had been back then.

'You don't?' Blythe said disappointedly. 'Well, do you think you could maybe say something instead? Into the microphone look, Dill. Then we can play it to Daddy when he comes to pick us up from Grandma's.' Heavy breathing crackled from the speakers.

'Not so close, Dill!'

'*Muuum*, he's getting dribble on my microphone!' Jem whined.

'Go on, Dill. Say something good,' Alex encouraged. 'What's your name?'

'Dillon... Edward... Foster,' Dill managed, self-consciously. 'Edward like my daddy's name.'

'How old are you?' Jem asked.

'I'm free!'

Jem cackled. 'You're *three* silly. Not *free*.'

'What else?' their mother encouraged. 'What do you like, darling?'

'I like my daddy's truck.'

'You do?'

'Yes, I love my daddy's truck and... and... I love my daddy too.'

'I love Dad too,' Alex added.

'And me! I love my *whole* family!' declared Jem.

'That's so nice, guys,' Blythe said. 'We all love each other, don't we? And it doesn't matter where we are, or what we're doing... or how long we might be apart from each other, does it? Because we all, always, know that, don't we?'

Ted was crying silently behind them where he sat.

'Mummy?'

'Yes, Jem?'

'*Please* can we sing the *Titanic* song now?' Jem burst into song anyway. 'Every night in my dreams... I see you, I feeeeeel youuuuu...'

They all listened, captivated as Jem and Alex's crooning pulled them back from sadder thoughts to tears of embarrassed hysterics as, verse by verse, Alex and Jem tried to out-Celine each other.

*

It was a good day. Dill was everywhere now. Not just at the river, but here, in the home they'd shared. He was in the creak of the garden swing, Norma's mischief, Alfie's tiredness as he fell asleep on Ted's shoulder, exhausted from all the discoveries he'd made in another little boy's bedroom. Dill was in the way Ted had watched over them all, not just Alfie but Jem, Alex, Mal and Finn too, while they'd played with his arrows on the lawns as the night crept in around them. And when Alex caught the tail end of another story Jem was telling about their brother, at last nobody remembered to feel sadness or regret for things left unsaid. They were too busy laughing.

EPILOGUE

Mayor Alfred Sinclair had a habit of jumping to conclusions.

That he might be the descendant of a great and noble Viking. That the searing pain behind his eyes was his wife's incessant nagging rather than the tumour that would unexpectedly kill him. That the little boy who looked so much like his boy Malcolm, and whose mother he had loved so intensely, must surely be his son too.

Had Louisa Sinclair have taken more of an interest in her husband's genealogical hobby, or just have been gracious enough to have accepted Blythe Foster's gift and embarked on a climb up through her own family tree, Louisa might have *not only* helped her husband to discover that he probably wasn't descended from King Cnut as he'd hoped, but that several generations back there had been a crossover between two of the oldest families in Eilidh Falls that would go on to strike like a lightning bolt in the same place twice.

Perhaps if the mayor had ventured far enough through the boughs of his family tree, he might have learned of the fate of his great-great grandmother's sister, Elizabeth Sinclair who, after a dalliance with a blue-eyed William Foster, died bringing their illegitimate son into the world.

If William Foster hadn't taken the child back for his wife Alice to raise alongside their other *legitimate* children, the Sinclair dimple might not have found its way silently through the bloodlines of *two* families in the Falls, eventually arriving like a band of marauding Vikings at the cheeks of both Dillon Foster, and his distant cousin, Malcolm Sinclair.

Had Dillon lived to reach his teens, his mother Blythe would've seen that while her son did indeed resemble the younger, blonder, Malcolm Sinclair who had once come to play over with her daughters and whose father she had so briefly shared herself, unlike Malcolm, Dillon's blond hair would not have darkened through his youth.

It would have remained as light and fair as his father's.

Ted Foster.

* * * * *

Acknowledgements

Blimey, book number three in the can… madness!

As ever, I couldn't have done it without my favourite hood-lums, Jim, Rad and Loch, the gruesome dream team. Thanks for putting up with me, fellas. And for getting on with it without so much as a batted eyelid while I disappeared into my room for months on end to write. You all put such brave faces on, the back-to-back football and WWE must have been horrendous for you. I'm going to reward you all with Downton Abbey and decent bedtimes aplenty.

A huge thanks going out to Sammia Hamer, my long-suffering, deadline-flexing editor. Never work with children or animals? Got to be easier than hormonal pregnant women, right? Sammia, thank you for letting me go at my own pace, mostly on hideously swollen ankles. Your encouragement and support was invaluable. Thanks also to Donna 'The Don' Hillyer. Always good to have you in the wings, missus. I'm going to miss yoouuu!

A hefty thanks to my mum, The Baby Whisperer. Hooray for newly retired grandmothers, Gertie! Couldn't have got this novel to the finish line without all you've done for Jesse Boy, who I should also thank for being such a chilled out, supercool kid while I was doing crazy hours at my laptop. (Would've been nice if you'd have eased up on the night-feeds though, son.)

And finally, as always, to the team at Harlequin for giving me the opportunity to be an actual, real life writer (!), and to my agent Madeleine Milburn for knowing so much more about this wonderful arena than I do, thank you!

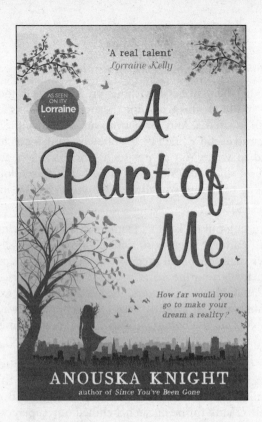